Voices Beyond the Stream

VOICES BEYOND THE STREAM

❦

A Novel

Christopher Todd Palmer

iUniverse, Inc.
New York Lincoln Shanghai

Voices Beyond the Stream

Copyright © 2007 by Christopher Todd Palmer

All rights reserved. No part of this book may be used or reproduced by any means, graphic, electronic, or mechanical, including photocopying, recording, taping or by any information storage retrieval system without the written permission of the publisher except in the case of brief quotations embodied in critical articles and reviews.

iUniverse books may be ordered through booksellers or by contacting:

iUniverse
2021 Pine Lake Road, Suite 100
Lincoln, NE 68512
www.iuniverse.com
1-800-Authors (1-800-288-4677)

Because of the dynamic nature of the Internet, any Web addresses or links contained in this book may have changed since publication and may no longer be valid.

This is a work of fiction. All of the characters, names, incidents, organizations, and dialogue in this novel are either the products of the author's imagination or are used fictitiously.

ISBN: 978-0-595-46107-3 (pbk)
ISBN: 978-0-595-69926-1 (cloth)
ISBN: 978-0-595-90407-5 (ebk)

Printed in the United States of America

For Melissa

and

For those brave people who dare to understand

All things truly wicked start from an innocence.

—**Ernest Hemingway**

Acknowledgements

❦

Many thanks to Marleen
for invaluable insight

Preface

❦

Even before I knew him as my husband, I knew him as a manic-depressive. I also knew, as our relationship progressed, that he was gradually becoming troubled by something that lived beyond his depression, a rare kind of desire, a yearning, I did not fully comprehend. When, a short time after we were married, he finally revealed to me that he was intending to write a novel, I understood that I had discovered the true source of his uneasiness.

After I inquired as to the subject matter, Chris responded openly. He told me that he was going to tell the story of three characters suffering from depression, manic depression, an illness he would eventually refer to as "the ultimate antagonist." That he was going to pursue such an undertaking did not surprise me in any way. If anyone was capable of creating such a story it was Chris. After all, he had maintained from the moment he first confided in me his love that he was a survivor and that he had lived a lifetime of depression. And I believed him.

The fictional account that follows is a part of Chris, a very large and special part indeed. For many, many years, I witnessed him conduct his research and pour himself into his literary work until, at long last, he had created the vital ingredients of the "narrative" contained herein. While highly emotional, the following pages are eloquently written and are certainly deserving of the attention of anyone searching for a novel about manic depression.

Melissa Palmer
Lincoln, Nebraska

Author's Notes

❦

This novel is not about suicide. I know very little about suicide and would never endeavor to write a book on the subject. Please understand that it is not my intention to advocate for suicide in this book. In no way do I mean to imply or suggest that suicide is an option or a solution.

—**C.T.P.**

Manic

Confusion unforeseen,
Sweeping currents of power
And the uncoordinated pain
Of tripping through the highs and lows
And coming home
Too suddenly.

Sleeplessness,
Red curtains in front of my eyes,
And a predisposition for
Contemplating the meaning of the universe,
While snacking on a lithium sandwich
Hours after midnight.

Waiting, waiting and waiting
Anxiously for nothing,
And with excitement,
So I'll be ready
For the mental void and the cognitive swimming
In the swirling tides of mental illness.

—**Hunter Kraven**
Lakeshore General Hospital
November 1994

PART I

THE DELIVERANCE

CHAPTER 1

❦

Some nights I could hear them calling out from the deepest cellars of their dreams. The frantic cries of the tragically neglected and pathetically misunderstood, the very people society had misread and labeled outcasts and had all but forgotten, echoed in unsettling tones throughout the mazes of poorly lit corridors. They often sounded very much the same, those dispirited people, as if they were all despondent members of a secret brotherhood or a miserable alliance, united eternally by the pure agony of living. Their sporadic screams shattered the nighttime stillness, the nocturnal monotony, and I was innately aware of the fact that they were suffering. After all, I shared with them their pain.

There were also the dreaded nights I listened to screams of my own resound inside my throbbing head as I lie alone in a room at the far end of one of those shadowy corridors waiting to die from the aftereffects of an intentional drug overdose. Those nights were the same nights I prayed I would pass away long before the sun appeared on the horizon. Only after I was dead would I be able to listen to peaceful, everlasting silence and escape the damnation of my depression for all time. I was a believer that death and only death would put an absolute end to all of the awful screaming and, even more important, erase my melancholy, the one thing author Robert Burton appropriately deemed "a hell upon earth."

So many nights I wended my way along the razor-edged pathways of my overworked mind as I strived to bring into harmony alternating stages of disabling mania and depression. I moved aimlessly through states of reciprocating euphoria and treaded recklessly through infernal regions of sadness that were governed by me and only me. Those changes in mood, the moodswings, dominated my life at unexpected intervals. And as I trudged through the passages of my depressed and private underworld night after night after night, I hoped that my fractured heart would explode or just stop beating altogether. So many times I wished that my shattered soul would drift beyond the swirling, violent tides of my diminished sleep. So many times I yearned for my broken self to float far away from the shores of reality, as if it were lost in a nightmare, and never return to my body in time to live another day. So very many times I petitioned God that my anima might wither and expire.

Unfortunately for me, God did not respond to my many pleas for unending quiet. God left me alone to suffer. God left me alone in the darkest hollows of my depressive mind to agonize over my splintered thoughts and to reflect on what I had done to myself or, rather, what I had attempted to do to myself. God left me alone no matter how loudly I shouted at Him and so, for what would turn out to be three of the most eye-opening weeks of my life, I subsisted on an occasional smile, a fleeting, joyful memory, an infrequent kind word from a stranger, a small measure of optimism and that is all.

Yes, I had managed to "get by" the three excruciating weeks I was held against my will on a psychiatric ward and in doing so had maintained a relatively decent outlook, especially when considering the certainty that something had changed for the worse inside of me. Nevertheless, life, as you probably already know, can be unfair and I understood that I had to move forward in spite of my burgeoning depression and my terrifying emptiness. Therefore, I chose to carry on without a single hint to anyone that I was still aching both physically and emotionally and that I was still suicidal.

The first nurse to violate the space I was occupying I ignored. I had been delivered with haste from the emergency room onto the psychiatric ward only a few minutes before she made her initial appearance and, irregardless of the sobering and bothersome truth that I was already undergoing treatment to save my injured liver from the toxic aftershock of an acetaminophen overdose, I was convinced that I did not require her attention or her care. I was satisfied that there was nothing wrong with me other than an insignificant dose of sadness, a random case of the blues.

The anguish I had endured day in and day out, year after year, was typical of me. That anguish was a basic element of my identity, an integral ingredient of the man I had always been, and I was very positive that the bouts of sorrow from which I suffered so regularly were all I had in common with the night screamers, the mental defectives who populated the psychiatric ward at Lakeshore General Hospital. Yes, that is where the similarity between us began and, more important, ended. In no way was I an affiliate of the deplorable order of the mentally ill as my incarceration inferred. No, I was not one of them. Compared to them, I was normal, very, very normal. Unlike them, I was leaving soon, very soon in fact. I was going home in the morning and I was never coming back.

I was in the wrong place. Despite my physical and emotional pain, I did not belong on a psychiatric ward. I did not even belong in a hospital. Of that I was certain. Everything had been a mistake, a mix-up, a misunderstanding. The day I would resign myself to the verity of my situation was still unknown to me and until that day arrived—and I doubted that it ever would—and became a reality I could no longer overlook, I was going to live my life my way. Therefore, I dismissed the first nurse with a nod and a wink.

A second nurse marched into the room shortly after the first nurse exited. I was reminded instantly of Louise Fletcher's depiction of the unyielding Nurse Mildred Ratched in the movie "One Flew over the Cuckoo's Nest." I sensed immediately that this nurse was not to be ignored.

"Take this," "Nurse Ratched" commanded in a tone I had never heard before, in a tone I suspected I would never hear again. Methodically, she dispensed a small bluish pill onto my bloodstained palm. The pill had a hollow center. The pill had the appearance of a tiny blue doughnut.

"No." A single, wounded syllable fell from my mouth. "What is it?" I labored to whisper. I noticed that what was left of my voice was not my own.

"It's a medication called Haloperidol. There is no need for you to worry yourself." Almost instantly, a pleated white paper cup was pushed in front of my face. Water was what I craved more than anything in the world. Evidently, swallowing a medication called Haloperidol was the price I would have to pay for such a luxury.

"Halo-*what*?"

"Halo-per-i-dol. Haloperidol."

"What in the hell is Haloperidol?" Disgust for the nurse and the medication I was now holding onto marked the worn inflection of my speech. With my free hand, I grabbed the nurse by the forearm and shoved her away from me.

"It's just a medication, an antipsychotic. Haloperidol is the generic name for Haldol," she responded with shocking calm, regaining her balance and stepping toward me once again. "This is a very small dose I am giving you, Hunter. It will help to calm you. It will help you relax."

"An antipsychotic?" I nearly shouted, surprising both Ratched and myself.

"Yes, an antipsychotic. Now put it in your mouth and drink." The pleated white paper cup was pushed in front of my face a second time. Without further inquiry, I acquiesced. I dropped the pill onto my tongue and chased it down. The tiny blue "doughnut" was washed away. I was still thirsty.

"Now what happens to me? When do I get to go home? When do I get out of here? That's what I want to know, you idiot. I want out of this place now!" My voice was suddenly resurrected, but I sounded very tense, frustrated and angry. I sounded bitter.

"The psychiatrist will be in to see you in the morning, Hunter. It's already quite late and he will be here first thing, so you need to rest right now. Try to get some sleep." Having said that, the domineering nurse spun away from me and left the room without speaking another word. Then, without warning, the overhead light was extinguished. Except for the iridescence of a single streetlight that stood tall near the hospital lawn's perimeter, and the faintest glow from a saffron bulb and a neon exit sign in the corridor, the room was black, an abyss.

I was not going to see a psychiatrist. No, I was not. That was the one promise, the one pledge, I made that night. I decided that I was going to slip away unchecked as soon as possible, just as soon as the sun came up, just as soon as the two nurses turned their collective backs on me. I was going to liberate myself from the psychiatric ward and the hospital and from my depressive, suicidal feelings on my own. Of that I was also certain.

I was stunned to hear that Ratched had actually prescribed sleep. Did she honestly believe that I was going to close my eyes, count a few sheep, and drift away just like that? You know, I think she did. Apparently she did not comprehend that there was no way I was ever going to sleep while being held prisoner in an institution so cold and unfamiliar to me it caused me to shudder with trepidation. I asked myself how I would ever sleep among all of the lunatics and pariahs, the mental rejects, while the rest of society went about its business without me. Random questions such as these raced through my tension-riddled head repeatedly. Sensible answers were not forthcoming.

Given my fragile position, sleeping was not an alternative. I understood that sleep was at a high premium that night. I knew that I was incapable of sleeping with the lights turned off, while cloaked in the unforgiving semi-darkness, while being subjected to the periodic observation and unremitting scrutiny of the two nurses. I understood all too well that I would never be able to sleep with the burning ache that pulsated from the upper right side of my abdomen where my injured liver was working overtime to offset and conquer the poisonous side effects of an intentional overdose of Tylenol, a popular over-the-counter analgesic remedy sometimes used in suicide attempts because of its potential to promote acute liver failure. What's more, I could not, would not sleep covered in my own blood. Simply put, sleep would not come easily for me that particular night because it never had before.

Sleep had evaded me always. For as long as I could remember, I had walked in the shadows. To put it another way, I had simply reached a point in my life where I recognized the chilling face of darkness better than I recognized the reassuring countenance of light. There was no doubt about it; sleeping was not a possibility. Sleeping was not an option.

CHAPTER 2

❀

From the very beginning, the very first time it permeated my thinking, I referred to it as The Image. Initially, The Image was somewhat fuzzy, a little blurry. Actually, The Image looked like a vague optical illusion of some sort. But eventually, The Image would become more distinct. Over time, The Image would flutter across the seat of my consciousness as if it were a real and separate part of something unfamiliar to me, as if it were its own being, operating from somewhere outside of my control, from somewhere beyond my reach. Still, each time The Image would oscillate through the currents of my mind, I would see the same facsimile as before. Although the clarity of The Image became more and more evident each time I witnessed its inevitable passing, The Image itself never ever changed.

    The Image is not at all complex. And even though I had my doubts back then as to whether The Image was a segment of reality, The Image is easy to understand. Truth be told, The Image is of me. I am secured to a stretcher in a frigid compartment in the emergency room at Lakeshore General. A nurse has just administered a tetanus shot. The needle hasn't even fazed me. From out of nowhere, a deputy sheriff wanders in and looks at me. From five feet away, he just stands and stares at me with his hands hanging onto his broad hips. The deputy sheriff doesn't even blink. He doesn't blink a single fucking time. Instead, he stares right through my bloody self, through my being, to the exact point where my life joins my body. I try to stare back at him, to meet his eyes with mine, but I cannot. I am much too ashamed. I look away from the goddamn deputy sheriff and his piercing eyes thoroughly embarrassed for myself.

    It occurs to me then, at the very moment I turn my eyes away from that ass-of-a-man and fix my gaze on my troubled past what it must feel like to be a circus sideshow attraction. I recall the bearded lady I saw once when I was still a boy. She pales by comparison. When I look up only seconds later, the deputy sheriff is gone. He has finally vanished. I never see him again, but his penetrating stare haunts me. That is The Image as I remember it.

I know I sound rather trite when I say this, but I distinctly remember reassuring myself that The Image was false, a fake. I told myself that The Image, no matter how lucid it became, was a strange unsolicited dream, or a misshapen carbon copy from a nightmare, and not a physical picture from my life's scrapbook. I made up my mind that the emergency room, the tetanus shot, and the staring deputy sheriff had all been an invention of my sleepless imagination, if you will. I decided that the figure I had envisioned strapped to a stretcher was not me, but an odd hallucination of another man in pain and nothing more.

I bluffed repeatedly, time after time, tricking myself into maintaining that the dense fog that shrouded both my memory and The Image would soon dissipate. As commonplace as it sounds, I promised myself that heaven would inevitably let the light shine down, the same unfiltered light that would reveal the truth, and set my enervated mind free. I admit that I reassured myself that the light of a new day would ultimately expose The Image as a phony. However, when I looked at my bandaged wrists, I knew that something was amiss. I knew that some things just did not jibe.

Although life was not making any sense to me then, I told myself not to worry. I told myself that I was innocent of any and all charges because no crimes had been committed in the first place. Despite the bandages and my searing stomach and The Image that was tormenting me, I was naïve enough to believe that I would be running away from the madhouse in the morning—just as soon as heaven's radiant light severed the shadows of midnight, and long, long before I would meet with any goddamn psychiatrist. I vowed that I would be the same man I had always been, depressed to a point, treading manic waters so that I might continue to live, barely breathing and barely out of reach of the all-knowing psychiatric nurses and the raging riptide of my depressive emotions, but alive and living freely just the same.

"Living freely" had never been all that easy for me. Steady feelings of depression had seen to that and, truthfully, there were those times when living freely had been next to impossible. Sure, I was alive most days, but I was also dead on occasion. I was dead on the inside during various grim periods of my tortured life. I was living a dead existence nearly half of the time I was swimming for my survival. I cannot explain the pure distress I was feeling almost daily any other way.

That distress was with me the extended night the two nurses—I tagged them "Big Nurse" (Ratched) and "Little Nurse"—took turns looking in on me. Every fifteen minutes or so, they pleaded with me to sleep. They pled with tremendous patience. And then, after so much pleading, the two nurses ordered me to crawl between the sheets, to close my eyes and to clear my mind, but I paid no attention to either one of them. I simply opted to ignore them. I knew that any attempt to sleep was futile. I was in too much pain to sleep. I was much too nervous to sleep and there was not a single time in my life when I had felt more restless or more alone. I was mindful that from that point forward, it was going to be me against the know-it-all nurses, me against the wretched world.

"I am going to close these blinds now, Hunter," Big Nurse said with an authoritative tone, "and I am going to ask one last time that you go to sleep."

"I don't want to sleep."

"But you have to. You can't spend the night staring out the window at nothing."

"That's life happening out there, you know."

"Right now, Hunter, your life is happening in this hospital. Your life is happening on this ward, in this room."

"What's left of my life."

"You have lots to live for. I want you to think about that."

With the blinds closed, the streetlight was stolen away from me, concealed from view. I realized then, at the very moment that I was robbed of the gleam from that single streetlight, that it was the warmth of untainted, unveiled light that I always missed the most. Whenever I found myself alone, which was really quite often those days, I missed clear, unaltered light more than I missed people, more than I missed my family. While I had been existing in the darkness of my psyche for years and years, radiant light had always been my best companion and my truest confidant. Light had always made me feel safe when nothing else had, and I knew inherently that I needed to redefine that very basic part of my life because, without a light to accompany me through the night, I had nothing to shield and protect me from the absolute blackness that was destined to find its way into my worthless body like an avenging ghost.

So there I was, left alone in the darkness of a room on a psychiatric ward in Lakeshore General Hospital, my hellish thoughts drifting on a stream of intense and manic emotions of despair. I felt as if I were lost within a furious storm that raged inside my head, a storm as violent as a hurricane perhaps, a storm seemingly too violent to endure. I wondered if the Haldol would ever relax me, as Big nurse had assured me it would, and in an effort to liberate myself from the emotional storm that was ravaging my brain, the emotional storm that was tearing at my self from deep within, I pissed away the long pre-dawn hours cheating at game after game of mental solitaire with a deck that certainly was not full and lost time after time. I played mental chess against a faceless opponent on a board that was aslant, a board where the rank and file were in disarray and the pieces were headless, and lost more than once.

I was on the verge of accepting my life's defeats, and the unwavering feelings of rejection that came with those losses, when the small world in front of my eyes slowed down and stopped spinning in dizzying circles long enough to allow me the necessary focus to sort through stacks of timeless, fading, cognitive snap-shots of all of the people I had ever known. So many, many pictures flashed into view and not a single one of those faces from my past life seemed trustworthy and so I developed a new mental snap-shot, a mental snap-shot of my own guardian angel, the angel I would bring to life, the one angel who would light the night and become my new best companion, my new truest confidant. That angel would be the one angel who would illuminate the way for me, the same angel who would carry with her the pure white light of patience and understanding.

You are probably thinking that my angel was a premonition of some kind, but she was not. No, she wasn't a premonition at all. And she wasn't a hallucination either. I had created her intentionally, by plan, out of sheer desire to have a friend in such a friendless place. From the moment she was born from my mind's eye, I understood that she was the very angel for whom I had been searching for years. I also understood that she would soon put an end to my loneliness and comfort me through the night. My nameless angel would stick by me when no one else would because she held no grudges. My angel trusted me, as I trusted her. She did not judge me. To my angel, the mistakes I had made in the past were mistakes and nothing more. And because of her forgiving disposition, I believed in my angel more than I believed in the nurses or anyone else I had ever known. Believing in my angel really was that easy.

Minutes slipped away in endless succession, and still my mind and body would not sleep. I was as awake as I had ever been when I heard the first person, a woman, cry out shortly after my passage onto the ward, which was shortly after I had conjured my protective angel. The screams from the woman whose face I could not see terrified me. I had never heard such strangled pleas before. I prayed I never would again but, in the coming weeks, night screams of the semi-forgotten people who were locked away on the ward would travel to my ears more than once.

It occurred to me then, at the moment I heard the woman scream, that I needed an auditory distraction of some sort, anything that might inhibit the woman's shrill outcry. That is when I heard the sound of my angel's beating wings and the sound of her soft whispering voice from somewhere nearby, from somewhere in the room I now shared with her.

"Deep peace of the of the quiet earth to you," my angel said in the most comforting undertone imaginable. "Deep peace to you."

I recognized those words. They were from a Gaelic blessing my mom had said to me nightly when I was still a child, before she put me to bed. Those familiar words intercepted the harsh sounds of the woman who called out over the darkest edge of night from somewhere down the corridor. The unseen woman's screaming soon ceased to be. My angel had reinforced in me the prospect that the woman would soon be okay and that I too would survive my first and last night on the psychiatric ward at Lakeshore General and return to my depressed and private life in the morning.

It was not long before I came to the realization that I should be careful not to take my angel for granted because I needed her friendship badly. I needed her friendship more than I needed Haldol or water or nurses. I was all alone on that fucking ward and I understood that the fragile form, the body I could never really touch, the mind I would never really caress, was an intrinsic part of me, a part of me that was doing more for me than simply blocking out the unseen woman's screams and the drone of the ward's night sounds. My angel was diffusing the darkness. My angel was keeping me company when no one else was. More important, my angel was rescuing me from my desolation.

"You need to sleep, Hunter." This time it wasn't my angel speaking, but Big Nurse instead. "And you need to pull that sheet away from your face so that I can see you. Okay?"

"Okay." I jerked the top sheet away from my face and, just as soon as I was certain that Big Nurse had returned to her station, I stood and yanked the vinyl blinds away from the window and threw the tangled mess to the tiled floor. I sat on the edge of the bed like a distorted human statue, holding my legs against my chest like a disgruntled toddler.

I glanced out at the dim illumination from the streetlight that warmed me in much the same way my angel did. Then I gazed beyond the streetlight, out into the unrestrained darkness of the night. The darkness beyond the streetlight scared me. That much is true. I noticed that there was no moon. I noticed that the stars were hidden in the raven-colored sky. I noticed that I could not see the stream or the lake. And yet I still suspected that there is always a small amount of hope even when the moon and stars are lost beyond a person's sightline long after twilight has expired.

Along the street below, life was moving steadily past me. The nightclubs were closing now and happy voices of late-night pedestrians drifted through my person and beyond. Those high-spirited voices punctuated my loneliness. Those raucous, drunken voices tested my fight and my resolve. Those voices resounded through my being to a place I had not visited in years, a serene place that had been out of reach for far too long. That particular place was a very special place in my head, a place where I could think and act rationally, a safe place I had not set foot since I was a child, since the last time I had been at peace with myself.

Then, from the very same corner of the ward, I heard a sound of another kind. The sound was the unmistakable sound of a woman crying, the distinct echo of a woman sobbing into the shadows. It occurred to me that she might be the same woman I had heard calling out earlier. The tearful voices of those who were trying to console her also ricocheted to my ears. I heard a man speaking in a low, soothing tone. "Time heals all wounds," he said matter-of-factly. The woman did not answer him.

Instantly, I recalled that I had heard those words spoken before. I asked myself if it was true, if the anonymous man was indeed correct. I had no way to be certain, but I considered the amount of time it might take for my own wounds to heal. In light of my mangled wrists, my flaming stomach, and my brain that was slightly "out of order," I decided that it could not possibly take too long for my injuries to mend.

Many thoughts occurred to me while I watched life turning passed me on the street outside the window that night. There were the questions I asked myself. Mainly, I wondered where I was going and what I intended to do once I got there—if I ever got there. I was, to a degree, cognizant that I was not doing anything for myself and I wondered why. For years, I had only survived, existed. I had spent a lot of time "going through the motions," merely posing, like a depressed mime of some sort. But for what purpose was I going through such motions? And for whom was I posing? And at what cost to my future and my self?

I thought that maybe I had simply made many poor decisions. I thought that maybe it was poor decision making that had left me where I was in life, which was abandoned on a psychiatric ward. Then again, there had to be something else, something besides that poor decision making that was causing me to idle, that was hindering my forward movement, my ability to "get it in gear." There had to be something more than poor decision making that was enabling The Image to live inside of me. There just had to be something more.

CHAPTER 3

❀

The Image was marching across my brain's landscape again when I observed a police cruiser turn slowly onto Center Street. I asked myself if a crime had been perpetrated recently. I asked myself if I was a suspect or, even worse, a wanted man. Then The Image raced through my veins like a perverted alien presence, a fearsome entity, turning my body ice cold. I shivered as the vision of that damn deputy sheriff mocking me with his eyes sent chills down my burned out spine before it came to rest in the caverns that were my sleepless eyes and, in a heartbeat, The Image itself became less hazy, much clearer. In a heartbeat, my view of my life had changed.

For the first time since I had been delivered to the hospital, I began to acknowledge my denial. For the very first time since The Image had infected me, I tried to get the facts straight. I endeavored to put things in order. I frisked my memory for answers and hunted for truths. I realized that I might need to take responsibility for all of the misguided actions I had carried out over the course my misguided existence. For the first time since my deliverance into the emergency room at Lakeshore General, and for the first time I could remember, I had an inclination that I might want to face those elusive truths, the very truths I had been secretly tracking off and on for years.

I tuned out the voices of the night as best I could. I listened to my angel breathing. I looked away from the streetlight. I looked at the stark white bandages that attired my sore wrists. Without a second's consideration, I tore at those bandages. I tore at so many layers of tape and gauze and jerked them all away in a single heated motion. I threw the disarranged layers to the floor just as I had done with the blinds only minutes before. I studied my newest wounds, the wounds I figured would never completely heal. I considered ripping out the stitches, but what good would that do? Like it or not, I was now forever scarred.

As the drawn out November night elapsed, and as a new day approached, and the nightwalkers slipped away to take on their lives again, the two nurses looked in on me less often. They stopped trying to coerce me to sleep. You might say that the two nurses had given up on me. As a result, I was left alone with my stinging stomach and my itching, exposed wrists and my confused thoughts and my sleeping angel and, yes, The Image that would not leave me alone no matter how hard I tried evicting it from my conscious.

The fray between night and day had been, quite honestly, the least impressive I had ever witnessed. I had watched with deadened emotion as the sun slowly rose and immediately positioned itself behind a gray wall of clouds, obscuring itself from view. As a result, the antemeridian sky was dyed several dismal hues of charcoal and the upper atmosphere was tarnished. It was readily apparent that no bright light would shine on me that winter day, as I had originally thought it would. It was obvious to me that composite misgivings would rule my perspective and my view of my own dismal life for some time to come.

It was not just another day in November, but the first day of the rest of my life. As predicted, I had been unable to sleep the night before. Instead of sleeping, I had squandered away the majority of the nighttime hours watching the traffic on Main Street pass by me. It goes without saying that it was the most awkward and difficult night I have ever experienced, let alone survived.

I did try my best to escape my apprehensions that night. I tried like hell to evade both the past and the present, but running seemed entirely pointless under the circumstances. I felt utterly defeated, so much so that contemplating my future was not possible. I tried to think of a new tomorrow, but I could not. The Image and pictures of the recent past, the pictures of all of the awful things I'd done only yesterday and in the days prior and in the weeks, months and years before that were still with me, still plaguing me, pinning me in the present. Those damn photographs hung on me like deranged silhouettes and, no matter how hard I tried, I could not shake them. They simply would not go away. For me, a new tomorrow was eons and eons away.

"So did you even try to sleep, Hunter?" Big Nurse's inquiry seemed to come out of nowhere and derailed my reckless thinking.

"No." A single, wounded syllable had fallen from my mouth again.

"And why didn't you?"

"I couldn't."

"You never even tried, did you?"

"No, I did not."

"Did you swallow the Haldol I gave you, Hunter?"

"Yes."

"Okay then. The phlebotomist will be in soon to draw some blood, so please cooperate with him." Big Nurse scooped up the blinds and the tape and the gauze and hugged the debris to her breast.

"Why wouldn't I?"

"Just cooperate, okay?"

"Yes, I will cooperate with him."

"Do you happen to know what day of the week it is, Hunter?" If there was one thing I did know for certain it was that I did not know what day of the week it was. I did not even know what time it was. All I did know for certain is that it was sometime after dawn on an overcast November day.

"No, I don't ... Tuesday maybe? Or is it Thursday? Maybe it's Friday. Hell, I don't know. I really don't think I care to know."

"Today is Saturday. That's okay, Hunter." At that moment, the phlebotomist arrived with Little Nurse in tow. He lugged the tools of his trade in a small caddy that was a dirty shade of white.

"Which arm?" The phlebotomist asked in a tremendous whisper. Like the two nurses, he was all business.

"It doesn't matter. I don't care. Pick one." It was true that it did not matter. No, it did not matter one way or the other. I did not give a damn. The phlebotomist could have stabbed me in the chest with a wooden stake and I would not have cared. Seconds after arriving, he placed a cotton ball on my newest wound and stretched a small adhesive bandage over it.

"Put a little pressure on that," he said. I did as I was told, mindful that I had been instructed to cooperate.

"My blood for a cotton ball and a Band-Aid, huh?"

"Yep. How's that for a fair trade?

"I'm not sure that it is one."

"Well, Hunter, that's how things work around here. You do your part and we'll do ours. Not too complicated really."

"So I see."

Count Dracula strode out of the room with a vial of my blood packed neatly away in his small dirty-white caddy. My arm stung where the needle had punctured the skin. Reality was beginning to wear on me now and I noticed that I could not hear my angel breathing. I realized then that my invented angel was no longer with me. I was aware that she had betrayed me, having served her dubious purpose, which was to guide me through the night. I was also aware that she had left me stranded in a hospital bed on a psychiatric ward just as soon as the sun had risen behind the wall of clouds. I knew that my angel was gone forever because there is simply no room for pretend angels on a real psychiatric ward. I understood that I had no choice but to embrace the isolation I felt. And so I came to embrace my solitude, my solitary confinement.

"Well done, Hunter. You did very well just then. Thank you for cooperating," Big Nurse said as she started for the door.

"Can't you please stay? I need to talk to someone. It's been a very long night." Those words tumbled off my tongue before I could stop them. Those goddamn words were out there now, orbiting in the room's antiseptic-scented air, and I could not take them back. I was instantly self-conscious. I felt naked, exposed even.

"I know all too well that you need to talk, Hunter. I know that there are many things you'd like to talk about, but we have other patients to check on. We have more blood to draw and more vital signs to take. Plus, to be honest, this ward is at maximum occupancy right now." Big Nurse was standing firm again, holding her ground and flaunting her authority just as she had done when she had forced me to swallow the Haldol, just as she had done when she had closed the blinds and blocked out the light. Behind her, I saw Little Nurse, framed in the doorway, nodding in agreement.

"What is this place anyway? Is this some kind of a fucked-up hotel?" I still sounded bitter, very bitter.

"No, it's not a hotel, Hunter. This is a very serious place. And we are here to help you *and* every other patient on this ward."

"So you won't stay and help *me*? Not even for a little while?" I forged ahead, pleading with this stranger, my newfound irritant, to sit beside me and to talk to me about how I had tried to kill myself only hours earlier. I sounded like a child begging his mother for a piece of candy before supper. My life was on the line and nothing was making any sense to me.

"No, Hunter, not even for a little while. But we will be back to see how you are doing in about an hour or so, maybe even sooner. Is that all right with you?"

"That's all right," I told Big Nurse. "I will see you soon then, maybe in about an hour." At that very moment, one of the many voices inside of my head told me that I would never see Big Nurse or Little Nurse again. Something inside of me also told me that suicide, the ultimate sign of depression, is a lonely, lonely undertaking because my intuition was correct. I never did see either one of those goddamn nurses again.

CHAPTER 4

❀

As I recall, I was only three years old when I experienced my first depressive episode. The screen of my memory is dominated by a phrenic movie of an incident that occurred soon after I had been punished for refusing to eat my supper. It was during that particular episode that I tried to imagine what it must be like to be dead. It was also the first time I had even the vaguest idea that something with my thinking was out of place or out of alignment. I guess you could say that I had some idea that I was not mentally healthy, that I was "flawed" in some unfortunate manner. My youthful insight told me that something might just be "shamefully wrong" with me, even though I could not pinpoint what it was at the time.

For reasons I have never fathomed, I determined that I was not going to eat my supper, and that was that. Therefore, in timely fashion, I shoved my roast beef and mashed potatoes aside and sat at the dining room table in reticent protest, my skinny arms folded in front of my skinny chest. Today, I know that it was not the menu that turned my stomach, mind you, but something else, something that was unknown to me at the time.

Because of my defiance, I was sent to my room without dessert. My mom did not hesitate. With a simple wave of her hand, she banished me. What happened next, namely the offbeat manner in which I reacted to my sentencing, was the first depressive event I ever experienced and I remember it quite well.

With the door to my bedroom closed tightly, I knelt at the edge of my miniature bed and cried. I cried and cried. And then I cried some more. I cried until it seemed no more tears would come. And as I wept, I had my suspicions that I was not crying over spilt milk, as the saying goes. I knew then, as I know now, that I was not crying because I had missed out on roast beef and mashed potatoes or because I had forfeited my chocolate cake. No, something else, something I could not put a finger on, something other than my punishment, was causing my sobbing, the kind of tears Voltaire named "the silent language of grief."

Even then, as young and inexperienced as I was, I had strong feelings that something with my thinking was in terrible disrepair. I theorized that I must be defective, that my brain must be broken, because I longed to be dead. There I was, three years old and hopeless, alone in my unlit bedroom, kneeling at the end of my bed, wishing that I was resting in peace.

You might say that as I knelt there I was praying for salvation from such a troubled mindset. I may never really know. What I do know is that I knelt at the end of my bed for hours, my face buried in my pillow, drowning in my tears, my brain searching for answers that would elude me for many, many years to come.

While I searched for leads as to what was bothering me, what was disturbing me so severely, and what was causing my insatiable desire to be dead, I called to mind the picture book "Where the Wild Things Are" by Maurice Sendak. I remembered Max, the main character, a rambunctious little boy who had sassed his mother and, because of his rebelliousness, had been exiled to his room without any supper. When I thought of Max, I thought of myself. Max and I had our loneliness and despair in common.

As the story goes, Max soon fell asleep and dreamt of an out-of-the-way island where monsters lived with abandon. In time, Max conquered the fantasized monsters that inhabited his fantasized island and promptly appointed himself king of all of the wild things. And after a brief reign as king, Max awoke from his dream to find his supper waiting for him.

The episodes of my own punishment were slightly different than the course of fictional events Max had faced. Yes, as I have already stated, Max and I had our loneliness and despair in common but, unlike Max, when I was sent to my room, I surrendered my supper altogether. More important, I did not conjure up a distant corner of the world where unruly beasts lived as young Max had done. I did not need to create any monsters like the ones Max had conceived because I was already fighting my own monsters, the anonymous, unseen demons of a mental illness commonly referred to as bipolar affective disorder, a mental illness fittingly dubbed manic depression.

At the time, I was unsuspecting that bipolar disorder, or manic depression as I prefer to call it, was the cause of my tears. While I was certain that something was stirring deep inside me, I had no idea what it was that was causing my nagging inner conflict. How could I have known the true source of my gloom? As I have already pointed out, I was only three years old. My official diagnosis was light years away.

I have suspected for a very long time now that a three-year-old boy suffering from manic depression has a tendency to view his life in the most basic terms, in pathetic shades of black and white and only in black and white. I know I did. Perhaps that is why I envisioned my wilted body lying on an unyielding mattress in a quiet room on a psychiatric ward somewhere not so far away or in a hospital for the criminally insane. Maybe that is why I envisioned nurses and doctors huddled close to my limp body, working feverishly to release me from my saddened state, laboring with haste to extricate me from my woeful existence.

I was a lost little three year old certain that something about the way I perceived the world in which I lived was unsound. There was simply too much black and not enough color in my life. I definitely understood that something was not right with my perception. At the young age of three, I was all alone and highly disturbed. I was riding my own private roller coaster. Very often, I found myself ruminating about death, my death. I did not know it then, but I was manic and depressed. I was bipolar. There is not a dessert or a punishment anywhere on the planet that could have staved off the inner turmoil caused by such radical and deadly—yes deadly—emotions.

The first glaring sign that something was wrong with me to present itself was my inability to sleep on a "regular schedule." From the onset of my mood-swings, I failed to acknowledge the very conspicuous relationship between a lack of sleep and depression. You might say that I failed to "connect the dots." I simply did not detect that insomnia is very often a symptom of depression rather than a separate affliction and, of course, neither did my parents. That said, it really is not at all astonishing that my parents began calling me "Night Owl" at a fairly young age.

I have always felt that Night Owl was as inaccurate as it was inconsiderate. I often think that if my parents had only been more aware of my ill-fated dilemma and of the illness that was beginning to rage inside of me, the depression that was gradually becoming more pronounced, they would have better comprehended the pure sadness I was experiencing day after day and night after night. Maybe then my parents would have better understood my fragile mental state and been less critical of me in general. Maybe then they would have shown me some sympathy and, yes, some compassion, and maybe, just maybe, they would have refrained from calling me Night Owl in the first place. And maybe then they would have found me some much-needed help.

I want you to know that I have never let the actuality that my parents were blind as to the full magnitude of my overwhelming depression bother or upset me. While I was at times a person I hardly recognized, I have pardoned my parents for not identifying my menacing illness until it was almost too late to save me, until I was almost dead. I feel that they should be given the benefit of the doubt because, from an early age, I had contended that it is often when a person needs help the most that the people in position to assist that person the most are the least likely to notice. I was a very young man in dire need of help. My parents did not notice.

I really should not be disappointed or surprised in any way that my parents did not identify the telltale symptoms of the vile illness that was festering inside of me because no one did. For example, teachers and coaches all missed the early signs that something was very, very wrong with me. Because those people probably had no real frame of reference when it came to dealing with depression, they probably did not notice that I was dangerously sad, dangerously unhappy. Even I did not detect the full extent of my unhappiness until it was almost too late. And by the time I was able to fully accept that something was more than a little "out of kilter," or a little "out of whack" with my self and shove aside all of my suspicions and get some professional help, I had already survived two suicide attempts.

In retrospect, I can see quite clearly that the majority of people with whom I associated most often thought that I was a typical child or, later, a typical teenager, immature and rebellious to a tee, passing through what I often refer to as "typical developmental stages." I see today that those same people saw me as a young man testing both myself and society's legal limits repeatedly. Today, it is difficult to believe that not a single damn one of those people realized, or appeared to realize, that the problematic behaviors I was acting out regularly reached much deeper than simple child's play, or much deeper than cycling periods of considerable elation, depression, anger and withdrawal. What those people failed to realize is that I was mentally ill first and immature and rebellious second. Combined, my immaturity and rebelliousness masked the very illness that was the basis for my many odd ways of behaving. One could say that because of the ignorance and naivety of others, my drastic mood swings went virtually unnoticed and, therefore, I was misjudged and, yes, misunderstood.

In addition to the intervals of odd behavior I was exhibiting, the only facet of my illness my acquaintances ever admitted observing firsthand was my difficulty sleeping. I should mention that both my friends and my parents viewed my inability to sleep as "normal" people do as "a minor setback." The way my friends and parents saw it, my strange sleep habits were nothing to worry about, "simple stumbling blocks," or even "mere obstacles." What my friends and parents were oblivious to is the manner in which I was often awake for days and nights on end, operating in an extremely frenzied, panicked state, suicidal ambition presiding over me like a diseased and demented god at the very same time mania and depression controlled my every thought, at the very same time my mind and my body danced out of rhythm and out of grace with the difficult world in which I was faltering.

There were those rare periods of desperation when I wished that my parents would have stepped in and rescued me from my deadly emotions. Those were probably the lowest times of all, the times when I should have asked my parents for help but did not. The main problem for me was the fact that I did not always know that I needed help. You see, my depression had become an inherent part of my life's overall pattern, woven into the torn fabric of my daily life. Even during those painful times I happened to conclude that I might need some help, I did not know how to ask anyone for that help. I did not know what to say to anyone. Also, I did not want my parents or friends to see me cry or bleed. I did not want them to think of me as being imperfect. And I definitely did not want my parents to blame themselves for whatever it was that was wrong with me, for something I strongly suspected was not their fault.

Sometimes I ask myself what I would have said to my parents had I found the courage and the words necessary to articulate to them what it was I was feeling on the inside. I wonder what I would have said to them then. Would I have shouted, "I cannot sleep!" at the very top of my lungs? No, probably not. Those words are not nearly specific enough. Besides, my parents already knew that. Maybe I could have casually remarked, "I'm hurting over here," which is, undoubtedly, more to the point, but perplexing as well. What would the outcome have been had I revealed to my parents that I had finally reached a dangerous crossroads, a frightening place in time and space where I could no longer measure the consequences of my actions? What if I had shared with them the fact that I was already dead on the inside and that I was finished living on the outside and that I wanted to commit suicide? I often wonder what my parents would have said to me then. Surely they would have known then that a lack of sleep was not my only problem. Surely they would have known that my problems were far-reaching and complicated.

I do not believe that there is a single parent out there who would be able to readily accept the notion that their child is suicidal. Had my parents known that I was intent on killing myself, I am positive that they would have been more than devastated. I am also positive that they would have been enraged and, because of their furor, I am positive that they would have called me "ungrateful," or something much, much worse because wasn't it true that they had always given me everything I had ever wanted, everything I had ever needed? Of course they had. So, with that in mind, I am confidant that both my disbelieving mother and my disbelieving father would have responded to any plea for help by telling me in an incensed tone to simply "shape up," or to "get it together." Suffice it to say, I generally understood my despondency and my parents better than they understood themselves. I also understood that I needed to keep my desire to commit suicide a secret from *everyone* I knew no matter how badly I hurt.

CHAPTER 5

❀

My neck was sore from sitting upright all night. I propped a couple of pillows against the headboard and leaned into them with as much force as my weakened body could muster. It was then, as I stretched away some of the deadness that lingered inside of me, that I met Jocelyn Layne.

"Are you up to having a guest right now?" I watched in silence as a mysterious young woman silently sneaked into the room without proper clearance from any of the day nurses. She sauntered right in without my own permission, interfering with my plans for an early escape. I thought it a very gutsy move and I liked it a lot.

"Tell me, miss, have you always been so brave, so forward?" I asked the female stranger who was now seeking my company. I noted that my voice sounded much more animated and much less bitter than it had sounded after I had swallowed the Haldol.

"Yes, I have been very 'brave,' as you say, throughout my life. I am a brave one for sure. I am a daddy's girl, and a tomboy, too. I have two older brothers, both of them terrific athletes, so I grew up kind of rough and tough. I had no choice but to be assertive. By the way, my name is Jocelyn, Jocelyn Layne." She quickly slid into a tacky turquoise chair that was probably best suited for a 1960's airport lounge than a psychiatric ward and slung her slender legs over one side as if she had sat there many times before.

"Oh I see," I said.

"And your name is?" Jocelyn's eyes were bottomless blue and penetrating, like the searching eyes of a wolf. They glimmered when she spoke.

"Hunter. My name is Hunter."

"No last name?"

"No. I don't have one. Not for now anyway."

"So you're shy and stubborn, huh? I like that in a man, Hunter." Jocelyn laughed. "I like that very much."

"I think that is the first time I have ever been called stubborn." I informed her.

"But not shy?" She tugged on her sandy braid. Her hair was beautiful. I admired the way her dark-blond bangs cascaded over her flaxen eyebrows and the way her abbreviated tresses barely touched her small, feminine ears.

"I have been called shy plenty of times," I admitted. "But never stubborn."

"So what the hell happened to your wrists, Hunter?" Damn! I had forgotten about my wounded wrists! I had forgotten that I had torn off the bandages only hours earlier. I had forgotten that my self-inflicted wounds were now out in the open, exposed to anyone and everyone, especially Jocelyn Layne.

"What in the hell do you think happened to them?" I was unexpectedly on the defensive, keenly aware that my inquiry was strictly rhetorical. I have never known why, but in the same instant I responded I glanced at Jocelyn's wrists. I saw that they were severely scarred. I knew the scar tissue there could mean only one thing. "So what happened to *your* wrists?" I asked her point blank.

"What do you think happened to them?" she fired back, catching me entirely off guard, seeming to challenge me.

"Well, if nothing else, we have our scars in common," I said just as soon I had managed to recover my frangible composure. Suddenly, I was relieved. I was relieved to know I was not as alone as I had originally thought. I felt that I might just be in extremely good company.

"So, you cut yourself, too, huh, Hunter?" Jocelyn's question seemed pointless, redundant and, yes, even rhetorical.

"I did," I admitted. "I also overdosed," I blurted, trying like hell to avoid discussing my lacerated wrists any further, trying like hell to divert Jocelyn's intrusive gaze.

"Was it acetaminophen?"

"How did you know that?"

"Overdosing on acetaminophen is really not that uncommon. It's a stupid thing to do, but, sadly, not uncommon. Would you believe that I once swallowed enough acetaminophen to snuff out an infinite number of headaches? So have several other people I know. Some of those people are on this very ward this very minute, suffering from a dangerous kind of toxicity, their livers and even their kidneys poisoned through and through."

"I know of no one who has ever overdosed—on anything," I stated.

"So tell me then, what made you do it?" Jocelyn's wolfish eyes shone like pellucid crystals. There was simply no escaping her shimmering stare.

"No real reason. It was time to go. That's all I can say."

"All you *can* say or all you *want* to say?"

"Both."

"Wow, Hunter, are you ever full of shit!" she quipped with a grin on her face that seemed to both taunt and pity me at the same time. "Everyone has reasons. I can understand that you might not be able to identify those particular reasons right now, so soon after you tried to kill yourself, but I know that you had several defining reasons for attempting to take your own life." Her steel blue eyes bore down on me. I felt naked and vulnerable. I reached for the top sheet and pulled it over my defenseless body, taking extra care to conceal my wrists. With the white sheet pulled up to my chin, I felt that I must resemble a strange kind of corpse, a living corpse.

"The nurses asked me the same thing, why I did it I mean."

"That's because it's a standard question."

"I didn't know."

"Just wait until you see the psychiatrist. He'll really want to know why in the hell you did it, what the reasons behind your intentions were. Work with the psychiatrist. Be honest with him. Things will progress much more smoothly if you are truthful. You can trust me on that one. It's the best advice I can give you right now."

"Please save your advice. Keep it. I am definitely not going to talk to any psychiatrist—not ever. And that is the truth." I was tempted to tell Jocelyn that I was considering an escape, but I changed my mind. Some information is not meant to be shared—with anyone.

"Oh, but you have to meet with a psychiatrist. It is, to cite an abused cliché, 'standard operating procedure.' That is how the stupid 'system' works here and, well, everywhere else I think."

"Are you sure? Are you really sure?" I was trying to avoid the likelihood that I would soon be visited by a fucking psychiatrist.

"Yes."

"So tell me more about this 'system' of yours, Jocelyn."

"The system is not mine. The system is the system. And, as far as I can tell, there is no changing it."

"If that's true, then what happens to me next? Where do I go from here?" More than anything, I wanted her to tell me that I was going home.

"First, a psychiatrist will evaluate you. Second, he'll prescribe something for you, an anti-depressant or a mood stabilizer or maybe even both, and, third, get you the hell out of here."

"Really?"

"Of course. Evaluate, medicate, vacate. That is the system in its most simplest of terms," she intoned as she rolled the loose-fitting sleeves of her sky blue robe up to her elbows.

"So when are you leaving?"

"Soon, kiddo. I think so anyway. I suspect I will be out of this place soon."

"So you have seen a psychiatrist already then?"

"I have. I have seen several psychiatrists several times now. Meeting with the psychiatrists is a rule, protocol. If you think that you are going to escape this place and step back into society without seeing at least one psychiatrist first, Hunter, then you have misinformed yourself."

"No, I have not."

"Well, I think that maybe you have."

"So do you think, Jocelyn, that you could stay with me when the psychiatrist gets here?" For the second time, I was asking a stranger to keep me company. Life still wasn't making any sense.

"Why would you want that?"

"Simple: I'm scared of being alone with a psychiatrist," I admitted.

"Hunter, I know that he won't allow that."

"How do you know?"

"Well, I have been rotting away on this god-awful ward since the middle of October already. And this is my second time here. Plus, I know that the psychiatrist, whichever one you get initially, will want to talk to you alone, one on one." Jocelyn swung her slippered feet to the floor and sat up straight in the outdated turquoise chair. She smiled a grand smile, a smile that appeared to be all-knowing. "Just think, Hunter, you are now a suicide survivor." Her smile disappeared.

"Yeah ... I guess I am."

"There is no guessing about it. Do not fret, though, my dear. You are not alone."

"Yeah, I suppose that's true, too. So I am not alone ..." Although Jocelyn was now an associate of mine, the mere thought of the suicidal fraternity of which I was now a member filled me with dread.

"So tell me, Hunter, what exactly was going through your mind at the time you did it? What were you thinking? And please be truthful."

"Maybe the truth is none of your goddamn business, Jocelyn, or hasn't that occurred to you yet?" There I was, on the defensive again, still afraid to share the truth with her. Hell, I was afraid to share the truth with myself.

"Look, if you don't want to tell me anything, you don't have to. Just don't try to feed me any of that 'I had no reason' crap."

"Who in the hell are you, Jocelyn Layne? Are you Nancy Drew? Oprah Winfrey? Which is it? You sound like a female Phil Donahue, asking way too many questions, prying into my life, examining me."

"Is the caller there?"

"Aren't you the smart one?"

"Look, maybe I should just leave," Jocelyn hissed. But instead of making her way to the door, she gripped the arms of the turquoise chair so tightly that her knuckles glowed white. Almost instantly, I sensed that Jocelyn really did want to stay with me in that horrible room and that she really did want to know more about what my horrible thought processes were before I had tried to end my horrible life. I also sensed that Jocelyn, while a veritable scrapper on the outside, was equally as timid on the inside. Instinct told me that Jocelyn did want to help me, if that was at all possible. Jocelyn definitely meant well. I was sure of that.

"No, stay with me. I will tell you what it is you want to know. It's not a problem. Really. Please stay with me, Jocelyn. I really don't want to be alone right now." Just like that, my fear and nervousness of sharing the truth with her and my shy and stubborn self had vanished altogether.

"Well, tell me what you were thinking at the time you attempted only if you want to." Jocelyn's voice sounded somewhat disheartened.

"Don't worry, I think that I want to tell you or tell someone anyway. Besides, and even though I sound rather clichéd saying it, I realize that I really could use a friend right now. I can't bear the solitude any longer. Plus, talking about what I was thinking as I started to lose consciousness, as I started to die, might actually be good for me, therapeutic even. Who the hell knows? Am I right?"

"Yeah, maybe it will do you some good," she said with an enthusiastic nod. "And, Hunter, you are right; who the hell knows?" The zestful tone that had characterized Jocelyn's voice when she had made her unexpected entrance had returned. Jocelyn no longer sounded disheartened or defeated but upbeat and triumphant instead.

"But then you have to tell me what you were thinking when you attempted, too, Jocelyn. And, even more important, you have to tell me what your so-called reasons for attempting suicide were. Is that a deal?"

"Okay, it is. Yes, let us call it a deal then. Of course I will share with you all of the crushing details. Fair is fair I believe." Jocelyn leaned forward in the turquoise chair. The sleeves of her robe slid down her girlish arms, concealing her scars completely. "So tell me, Hunter."

"Tell you what?"

"Quit playing dumb. Playing dumb does not seem to befit you. I suspect that you are smarter than that. And please don't stall. Just tell me … tell me what were you thinking about in the moments before your life turned from gray to black. What crossed your suicidal mind at the exact moment death rushed in to meet you?"

"Simon didn't say."

"Well, at least your sense of humor is in tact."

"Maybe."

"So don't tell me then."

"I guess I was consumed."

"Consumed? Consumed by what?"

"Consumed mainly by thoughts, by thoughts. I was consumed by the kind of thoughts that made me think that I might at long last die a free man, even if dieing a free man meant that I might live on in pain in another time and place."

"A free man? Free from what?"

"Free from the chokehold my depressive emotions had on me and, well, free from the police."

"Free from the police, Hunter?" Jocelyn was tugging on her sandy braid again.

"Yes, the police. You see, I believed that my impending death meant that I would be able to evade the goddamn police for good. I was also thinking that the skirmish with the depressed beast that had been living within the borders of my tired mind and body was finally over, and I felt victorious because of it. I felt as if I'd finally won the battle of all battles against the depressed suicidal monster I had been losing to for so many, many years. That is what I was thinking, Jocelyn, before my world turned from 'gray to black,' as you put it."

"You were running from the police, Hunter?"

"Yes, I was running from the police, but that can only be a story for another time, another day."

"Ha! So you did have your reasons then."

"No, I don't think I did. The fact that I was running from the law and depression are not reasons. In no way are they reasons, Jocelyn." I tossed the top sheet aside.

"The hell they aren't," Jocelyn quipped, as she stood and dragged the turquoise chair in my direction, closer to the bed where I was now perched like a human gargoyle, and sat down again. She had repositioned herself so close to me that I could smell her breath. Her breath had a medicinal odor. "Those may not be your only reasons for attempting suicide, but they are still two reasons worth noting."

"You know, Jocelyn, having more than one reason is not a prerequisite for attempting suicide."

"What do you mean?" She tilted her small head to one side. "How can you possibly believe that?"

"It's not that difficult to understand, especially when you accept the fact that depression is its own reason. Depression is reason enough for a person to want to just 'end it.' Depression is sufficient as a motive and no other reasons are warranted. Depression really is quite capable of operating alone, on its own accord. Depression is ample reason for a man to want to kill himself. And, yes, I did say the word 'fact,' Jocelyn."

"So now it's a fact, huh?"

"Yes."

"What makes you so sure?"

"Well, I was really very, very depressed when I tried to kill myself. That is what makes me so damn sure."

"Everyone who attempts suicide is depressed, Hunter," Jocelyn countered with the slightest hint of concern in her voice, a voice that sounded as fearless as it was forthright. "That is nothing new, being that depressed. Millions of people are. I can tell you that without any reluctance whatsoever. However, for you and for everyone else who has ever considered suicide an option or a solution, it was significantly more than depression acting alone. You did have more than one reason for behaving the way you did. You said so yourself. You said that you were trying to evade the depressed 'beast' that was living inside of you as well as the police."

"Well, I was."

"So there you go then. Your depression was already there, living inside of you, but something else, another reason, or many more reasons you haven't mentioned yet, spurred you, pushed you over the brink."

"You can't possibly mean over the edge."

"Of course I mean over the edge. I have no doubt that it was your existing depression, depression brought on by any number of painful events, combined with the actuality that you were running from the police, that motivated you to attempt suicide."

"And, Jocelyn, what makes you so sure?"

"I know from experience. That is what makes *me* so sure. Please realize that I have 'been there' several times now."

"So you've had to run from the police, too? Is that what you're telling me?"

"No, I haven't had to run from the police. Me running from the police? Not very likely."

"So what is it you are trying to tell me then? Get to the point. What have you had to run from?"

"Depression. I've had to run from depression. What I am telling you is that while I've never had to run from the police as you have, I've had to run from depression countless times, and, in doing so, I have learned that depression is ugly and dangerous, but not its own reason for a person to attempt suicide."

"Well, even I know that depression is ugly and dangerous. So what is your point? You're losing me."

"My point?"

"Yeah, what's your point?"

"My point is this: It is when depression is combined with another reason or many reasons, dangerous motivators, such as your having to run from the police, that it is not only ugly and dangerous, but deadly as well. Dangerous *and* deadly, Hunter."

"I have had to run from depression, too, you know."

"Of course you have. I'm not saying that you haven't. What I am saying is that while depression is ugly on its own, it is when depression combines forces with an outside incentive, a few bona fide reasons, that it is as ugly as ugly can be. Depression, Hunter, needs accomplices to carry out its dirtiest of deeds, namely suicide. Again, you will just have to trust me here. Plus … Oh, I think this one is here for me." Jocelyn nodded in the direction of the room's only doorway.

"Jocelyn?" A nurse I had not seen before, and would not see again, peeked her head inside the room and interrupted Jocelyn's diatribe.

"It's time for me to take my morning meds, Hunter. I will be back soon enough. You can count on that." Jocelyn exited the colorless room as quickly as she had entered it.

I had just enough time to consider what Jocelyn had said to me so far, before she returned to sit across from me in the turquoise chair. I agreed with her held principle that depression is always ugly, always dangerous. However, I did not agree with her viewpoint that depression needs outside incentives or "defining reasons" to lead a person to suicide.

Jocelyn had refused to compromise, though, and I admired her for having demonstrated such determination. I had known Jocelyn for mere minutes and I already admired her more than I admired anyone I had met since being admitted to Lakeshore General. And while I disagreed with Jocelyn for the most part, I still respected her opinion more than I respected the opinions of the trained psychiatric nurses and much more than I trusted the opinions of my departed angel.

"I'm back!"

"Well, that was fast."

"I didn't want to leave you without first giving you the chance to finish your woeful tale." Jocelyn settled into the turquoise chair again and exhaled.

"Oh, I see."

"See what, Hunter?"

"See nothing.

"Come on, what do you see? Tell me."

"I see, Jocelyn, that you really are interested in what it is I am saying to you."

"Of course I am."

"Thanks."

"So anyway, we have now established possible *motives* as to why you attempted suicide, Hunter, but you still haven't revealed what was going on inside your jaded mind at the time you tried to take your own life."

"I told you that I was laughing.

"And why were you laughing?"

"I was laughing because I had evaded the police and my own ugly, grotesque depression as well or so I thought."

"Yeah, but what else? What were you thinking?"

"Nothing. Nothing. Nothing. Not a goddamn thing. Nothing was going through *my* head at the time *I* attempted suicide, Jocelyn. Except for what I have already told you about finally having won my freedom from the law and ending the battle with the depressed beast living inside of me, not a fucking thing was going through my head. Nothing! I simply laughed. Yes, I laughed. I laughed more than once as I patiently waited with the clearest conscious for my life to come to an end."

"I trust that is true, Hunter."
"Yes, it's true. That is the truth and nothing but the truth, so help me God."
"Okay, I trust you then. I trust you."
"Do you really?"
"Yes."
"I think that maybe I trust you, too, Jocelyn. I do not agree with you completely, but I think that I can trust you," I said as I leaned back against the pillows again, mindful that I had made a friend with a real living person for the first time in far too many years.

CHAPTER 6

❀

"You do make a solid point or two, Jocelyn. You really do," I stated, aware that I was now controlling the tempo of our conversation, aware that I was now standing, or sitting for that matter, in the limelight.

"Such as?"

"Well, as I've already told you, I feel that you were accurate when you claimed that depression has many different faces. What's more, I believe that you were also accurate when you asserted that the many faces that comprise depression are ugly because it is true that there is nothing alluring about depression in the least."

"Well, we are in agreement on that then."

"However, Jocelyn, you were inaccurate, or dead wrong I should say, when you stated that depression needs 'outside incentives,' or 'accomplices,' or what you referred to as 'defining reasons' to drive a person to suicide."

"You really do believe that, don't you?"

"Yes, I do. I have contemplated suicide on numerous occasions and have attempted to take my own life twice now, and I feel strongly that I did not have any outside incentives or accomplices or reasons other than real live depression making unsolicited decisions for me. Depression was motivation enough for me to want to take my own life. I think that you need to abandon the 'defining reasons theory' and accept the stance that depression is its own provocation."

"No, I don't, Hunter. No, I do not. You need to accept what it is I am saying to you." Jocelyn pulled hard on her sandy braid and let it fall a third time.

"To a degree, I already have."

"To what degree, Hunter? I would like to know to what degree."

"Well, as I already told you, I think that you were correct when you declared that depression is ugly because depression is the gawdy visage of gloom, the mask that represents all that is not well with a person, all that is not accordant with the universe in which the rest of the population lives and breathes. Even I understand that depression is an evil culprit, a scheming practical joker. Depression is a frightening foreign essence that plays constant tricks on a person. Depression ducks in and out of the blackness like a lamentable clown, laughing at you when you are crying, crying when you are making every effort to laugh. Depression is an adversary, a nemesis, and, Jocelyn, I have recently discovered that depression is the ultimate antagonist."

"An antagonist, you think?"

"Yes, an antagonist."

"I don't think I can argue with that. No, I don't think I can."

"Also, when a person is depressed, I have discovered that it's really very arduous for that person to differentiate between past, present and future because depression strips away a person's point of view. It's difficult for the depressed person to differentiate between yesterday, today and tomorrow."

"What do you mean?"

"I mean that a depressed person loses all track of time. A depressed person loses his way. Life is moving steadily passed us right now, Jocelyn, and here we sit, lagging behind, unsure of exactly how much time we've lost."

"And not really caring that we have lost time, huh?"

"Right."

"My parents don't see it that way. Would you believe they think that I'm just being immature when I waste away the daytime hours staring at the walls of my room, accomplishing very little—if anything—while life progresses without me? Just think, I am basically screaming for someone to save me from my fucked-up state of mind, and my parents just fucking think that I am being fucking immature. I don't get it, Hunter."

"You know, there are times my dad tells my mom that I am simply 'keeping pace with a different drummer.' Yeah, he quotes Thoreau. He tells my mom to leave me alone. He tells her that I am fine. I know that can't be the correct answer, though."

"Unfortunate for you and unfortunate for them as well. Besides, I don't think that Thoreau was referring to depression when he said that."

"Yeah, I doubt it. It's a sad situation, being so misunderstood I mean."

"Yes, it really is, Hunter. It really is. You know, I have often noticed that the negativity that resides within the pained outlook of a depressed person is unwavering. I see static negativity in the actions of all of the depressed people I meet. I tend to think that the negativity I see in those people is steady, unchanging. I also think that the same negativity could be to blame for the manner in which a depressed person loses the ability to focus on life's positives. Hunter, I am speaking from experience here."

"I believe that you are."

"That damn negativity is so unchanging that the few positives that are actually present in a depressed person's life are suddenly discounted as being impertinent. Does that make any sense to you?"

"Yes, it does make sense to me, a lot of sense. I thought about that angle all night, you know, so it should make some sense to me. Depression forges truth with lies and reality with make-believe. As a result, a depressed person's overall prospect for a brighter future is unduly compromised, clouded over. Depression does make it extremely difficult for a person to accentuate the positives in life, something that is, I believe, essential for living well, something that is essential for day-to-day survival. And finally, depression makes it difficult to know whether a person is doing okay or not."

"Nice, Hunter. So tell me, do you think you were doing all right, doing 'okay' I mean?" she asked me at the same time another nurse I would never see again silently peeked her head inside the room with a nod that could best be described as "approving" and vanished.

"You know, Jocelyn, I assumed I was doing okay. I figured I was 'in control.' I really did. In spite of my nightly bursts of mania and the unsolicited periods of elation and the increased activity and the steady feelings of depression and the intervals of decreased activity and my suicidal impulses, I sincerely believed that every facet of my life was copasetic. I actually believed that I was truly normal even though I was sometimes aware that I did not always think normal thoughts or do things normally."

"What wasn't normal for you?"

"The manner in which I thought about suicide so often is one. Thinking about suicide is anything but normal."

"Yeah, thinking suicidal thoughts is as far from the boundaries of 'normal' a person can get."

"I see that now. Outside of actually attempting suicide, thinking about suicide is the most conclusive sign there is that depression is wreaking havoc on a person's mind and life. Thinking about suicide is a threatening process, a deadly venture, Jocelyn. Of this there can be no doubt. That particular point is not subject to debate."

"I am no longer debating anything with you, Hunter. However, I do wonder how it is you know so much about depression. It is apparent that you've given depression a lot of thought."

"Yes, I have. I really have. I have definitely given depression a lot of thought. It's likely that I've given depression a lifetime of thought. Also, I see now, as I sit here listening to you, that I have lived depression. Yes, I have lived depression. I have lived it."

"Well, you probably have. Just remember: there is absolutely no turning back from a suicide attempt, Hunter. When it comes to suicide, what's done is done. The scars on your wrists will stay with you forever. You are branded now."

"So I see."

"Hunter, I have lived a lifetime of depression, too. And so far, I've survived it the same as you. Keep in mind that you have not beaten depression just yet. And neither have I."

"Yeah, but, Jocelyn, maybe you will."

"Maybe. And maybe you will, too."

"I don't think so."

"Makes suicide and depression seem so commonplace when we speak of them so casually, doesn't it?

"Yeah, it does. You know, for reasons I still cannot identify, I am still holding onto the belief, my belief, that I am still just as normal as the next guy and that my suicidal behavior is typical of everyone. The way I see it, everybody I rub elbows with has trouble sleeping and coping to such an extent that they wish that they were dead the same way I wish I was dead. To me, that is normal thinking."

"But, Hunter, that may very well be the most obvious definition of abnormal thinking there is. Can't you see that?"

"I'm not sure that I can. To be honest, I'm not sure that I want to see that side of things, the view that thinking about suicide is abnormal. I have felt so strongly for so long now that people have depressive days and manic nights and think about death and suicide as often, or as regularly, as I do I don't think that I will ever see things any other way."

"But you can. You really can. Just give it some time and I think that you will see things differently."

"Look, I have believed for a very long time now that everyone lives a life so incredibly unbearable they secretly aspire to commit suicide the same as me. I don't believe I can reprogram myself to think otherwise. I have almost always believed that such feelings of sadness and helplessness are a standard component of everyday living for everyone, and not just for me. The way I see it, death by suicide should be an accepted option, a solution."

"I used to think that way. But suicide is not an option or a solution, Hunter. Although we speak of it rather casually, suicide is not as commonplace as you may think."

"It must be more commonplace than you are willing to admit or I wouldn't be here. And neither would you or anyone else for that matter. This ward wouldn't even exist."

"I think you may soon see things in a new light, after you have been properly diagnosed and medicated and counseled that is. Regardless, I am sure you are capable of being helped."

"Well, I'm not."

"You know, mister, you may see someday that your depression is nothing that can't be treated. Have a little faith in the system and in yourself. Give yourself a chance. I think you are slightly disillusioned right now. Try and be a little more optimistic."

"Jocelyn, you don't seem to be all that optimistic. And so what if I am disillusioned? Being disillusioned does not change the fact that depression and suicide are generally considered dirty words and are rarely discussed openly in the 'real, tangible world,' as you refer to it. Even among the closest of friends, the subjects are essentially considered taboo."

"Yes, they are, Hunter. And that is disturbing to you and to many other people, I know." Another nurse stopped in the doorway, jotted something onto a small notepad and disappeared. I heard my voice shift into a whisper.

"I have tried to discuss candidly more than once both depression and suicide with friends, the people I trust the most, but the topic of discussion always changed to something else, to something more ordinary, long before I had the opportunity to make my point that death by suicide is a sad reality in a sad, sad life."

"You must have sounded more than a little unbalanced, wanting to talk about depression, and especially suicide, in such a direct manner, don't you think? I tend to think that some things are better left unsaid. Wouldn't you agree with that, Hunter?"

"No, I would not. I wish that depression and suicide were discussed more honestly and up-front. I can't talk about the emotional and physical pain I am feeling or about my suicide attempts, but other people can talk openly about their diabetes, their heart disease and their hemorrhoids without any apparent reservations whatsoever."

"Yeah, that's true."

"There are those times when I assume that people want to kill themselves, but conveniently opt to keep their suicidal aspirations to themselves. I believe people are determined to keep such suicidal aspirations private, classified."

"There are probably some people who do just that, Hunter."

"You know, my own suicidal dementia operates behind the drabbest panels of secrecy in much the same way I presume everyone else's does. And while my neurotic state enables me to be introspective from time to time, it certainly does not allow for objectivity the way I think it should."

"Well, I think it's difficult to be objective when you are suicidal."

"That might be true. I do think that I could have established some level of objectivity had I not been so fucking depressed, so fucking suicidal. The depressed cognitive state in which I was imprisoned prevented me from being able to see and think clearly."

"Well, Hunter, that should give you an even better idea of what it is like to exist within the contours of a depressed person's mind. And you should also see, in due time I think, that you had more than one bona fide reason for attempting to take your own life. You will see what it is I am saying to you in due time."

"In 'due time,' Jocelyn?" I asked. I was instantly reminded of my seemingly-doomed liver and the likelihood that I might be as good as dead in due time whether I liked it or not. "I really do not believe that I have much time left."

"Why not? What makes you say that?"

"Because no one will tell me how I'm doing exactly. Plus, I can feel the pain of my liver and my body gradually shutting down. I can feel my body dieing."

"You are not dieing, Hunter. The physical pain you are experiencing right now will pass. I know it will. Believe me. That pain will pass. Try focusing on the mental pain you are feeling. Ultimately, it is the mental pain you will have to extinguish if you are to live well, if you are ever going to live a life that is worthy of you. Extinguish the pain in your head first, Hunter. Extinguish the pain in your head."

CHAPTER 7

❧

"So now it's your turn to tell me. What led you to do it? And what were you thinking as you prepared to die," I asked Jocelyn, trying like hell to hide my physical pain and stay strong for the sake of finally hearing her answer. I had to know what her reason, or reasons, had been. I had to know what she had been thinking as her life began to end. What's more, I now possessed a right to know. We had made a deal, a verbal trade. Jocelyn had to tell me why she did it and what she was thinking at the time she did it. As far as I was concerned, she did not have a choice.

"Yes, I'll tell you. This time, though. Okay?"

"Yeah, this time then. For now anyway."

"Well, Hunter, most people ask me if it was over a guy, but it wasn't. It hardly ever is, you know. So many times I wanted to be dead and my wanting to be dead had nothing to do with boys or men. I am sure of that. As I have already stated, I believe that suicide attempts are brought on by a culmination of unfortunate events and not just by any one thing or by any one reason. But still, people try to guess every which way like a bunch of novice sleuths in a pitiful race with one another to crack their first pathetic case."

"A culmination of unfortunate events, huh?"

"Yes."

"So what were the events that led to your second attempt then? If you weren't running from the police, and if it wasn't over a guy, then why'd you do it? What were your *reasons?*"

"Hunter, would you please slow down?"

"Sorry."

"Why I did what I did is difficult to explain, very difficult. I can't just list off the events that preceded my attempt as if I were reading a grocery list to you."

"Well, I think that it should be easy for you," I said, sounding like the persistent know-it-all nurses. The thought that I might be behaving like those fucking nurses bothered me very much. I shut my mouth and held my breath as best I could.

"Well, it's not easy. Although I can say that I suppose my *reasons* for attempting suicide were conceived when the real, tangible world I was living in ceased to be. Maybe my reasons for attempting suicide were born when my own real, tangible world was no longer a physical place I inhabited, but a place inside my troubled mind. Understand that there were a few moments of lucidity, those precious moments when I realized that I did in fact exist as a member of the real live human community, but the realization itself always came too late. By the time that particular realization would hit me, I would have already stepped beyond the realm of so-called reality and into another dimension, a suicidal dimension."

"What is a suicidal dimension," I asked, my voice marked by noticeable curiosity.

"I suspect that on one mental level or another you already know what a suicidal dimension is, Hunter. Anyway, a suicidal dimension is, as I define it, a state of mind, and not a physical place. It is a secret, secluded site found only in the most remote hollows of the suicidal mind. A suicidal dimension is a place only a person with intentions of attempting suicide can enter."

"I don't quite follow you. Then again, I think that maybe I do. God, I really do sound like a hypocrite when I say it that way."

"It's like another place in time, a suicidal dimension. For the person on the verge of attempting suicide, a suicidal dimension is a separate, inescapable location, a distant location unknown to any person of sound mental health."

"It all seems pretty complex to me, yet vaguely, vaguely familiar."

"I am not trying to sound complex. And I certainly do not mean to sound profound or anything like that. I just want you to know that in the days and hours and minutes and seconds before each one of my suicide attempts I had entered another universe, a translucent universe in which everything I saw and touched was very, very surrealistic."

"In what way?"

"Well, everything about my life was perfect at first glance or so it seemed. But after I looked a second time, nothing was perfect at all or so it seemed. It was as if everything that was closest to me was out of place or out of the ordinary. Suddenly, everything in my life had an unconventional dream-like quality."

"It's possible that I've been to the suicidal dimension you speak of," I stated. "Well, maybe anyway. Maybe."

"Just 'maybe,' Hunter? Think about what it is I am saying to you right now. If you are willing to pry open the door to those rooms in your mind where depression flourishes, I think you would see that you understand more about suicide than you are willing to admit."

"I understand a lot more than I let on."

"I don't doubt it, especially since you have attempted suicide once already."

"It's twice now. Remember?"

"Right. Twice."

"So in what way were things perfect in the beginning? And what changed?"

"Things were perfect in the beginning because I was an honor student, president of several clubs and liked by almost everyone I knew. I was really quite popular. I was appreciated. More important, I was not suicidal at all. But then, while I was at the top of my game, so to speak, everything changed. My grades slipped, I stopped taking part in club activities and I began to alienate the very people I had once gotten along with so well. I even pissed off my closest friends. I was suddenly incapable of relating to the people around me, let alone myself. I had hit an all-time low. I was suicidal as hell, Hunter, and I did not fully comprehend at the time what was happening to me. I was living a very disconcerting reality."

"You figured out that something was wrong later on, after it was already too late, *after* the damage had already been done, didn't you?"

"How did you know that?"

"Like I already told you, I think that I have 'been there.' I think that we have traveled similar roads to get where we are right now."

"True, kiddo. I'm honestly thinking that you have been there. And, yes, I think that the roads we've traveled to get to Seven Southwest are probably similar, very similar."

"So that is your reason for attempting suicide this time, your fall from grace?"

"Not completely. As I've already told you, there is always more than a single reason acting alone where suicide is concerned. There is more to this particular tale of mine."

"Like what else?"

"Well, the real clincher came when my mom died of a heart attack a little more than a month ago. My mom's death 'sealed the deal.' I had been sinking gradually for years. Reasons for my wanting to attempt suicide again were 'piling up.' And suddenly, I had my last reason. Suddenly, I had all of my motives, all of my causes, all of my incentives to kill myself. And there you have it."

"I am so sorry about your mom, Jocelyn. I truly am."

"That's nice of you to say."

"Jocelyn, what happened to you when you heard that your mom had died? What was your reaction?" I asked, overlooking the fact that asking her what her reaction to her mom's death had been was a very stupid question indeed.

"I went into shock of course. Then my world as I knew it came crashing down all around me. I don't think that I've been the same ever since. I know that I am not the same person I was before my mom died. Actually, I am a shell of the person I once was."

"How do you mean?"

"Well, I'm even more depressed and suicidal lately. I didn't think that was possible. Also, I'm edgy most of the time. I'm pissed off all the time. I often feel as if I am on the verge of doing something bad."

"You could have fooled me."

"But it's true."

"So what did you do when your mom died? Tell me, how did you *react*?"

"Like I already told you, I went into shock. Looking back, I can see that I snapped. Yeah, that's what I did; I snapped. Something inside of me just shattered, exploded. Then, late one night, while the entire town slept, I boarded a bus bound for anywhere or bound for, well, nowhere in particular. That is how I *reacted* to my mom's passing."

"You're telling me that you ran away?"

"I am. I ran away in the middle of the fucking night. To me, my situation was that dire. Can you believe that I ran away, Hunter?"

"I believe you. I don't want to believe you, but I do."

"Why don't you want to believe me?"

"I don't want to believe that you are capable of running away for any reason under any circumstance. Jocelyn, I want to believe that you are capable of standing your ground."

"Hmm … I'll take that as a compliment, Mr. Hunter."

"But didn't it occur to you that your pain and your sadness were originating from somewhere inside of you and that you could not run away from that pain and sadness no matter how hard you tried to escape them?"

"No, it didn't. The thought never crossed my mind. Not then anyway. I probably still don't know. Actually, I'm still unsure."

"That's strange, you know. After two suicide attempts, I think that you would have figured that out by now. I know I have."

"That's good for you. And I really do mean that. As for myself, I may accept that stance soon enough. Who knows? What I do know, though, is that I never planned to do it, run away like that I mean. For me, running away was like being lost in another woman's dream. I was lost in the dream of a stranger. There I was, lost in a stranger's dream, witnessing somebody else running away from her past, present and future. I hope that makes some sense to you."

"It does. Had you ever run away before?"

"No. No, I never had. I had never even thought of doing something like that—not ever."

"So where did you go?"

"It doesn't really matter."

"Why not?"

"I don't remember."

"Jocelyn, you really can't remember where you ran away to? I don't buy that."

"Well, you'd better."

"But I won't."

"Okay, Hunter, I admit that I do remember. It's just that I'm doing my best to forget. Besides, I don't think that my destination is important right now. It isn't relevant. It doesn't matter where I ran to now that I am here."

"I suspect that it does matter and I wish that you would tell me."

"Well, I'm not saying. You need to move on already."

"I'm not going to give up that easily."

"You *aren't* going to drop it, are you?"

"No, I'm not."

"I went to see my mom."

"See your mom?"

"I went to see my mom one last time. I rode a bus to the city where she was raised, to the streets where she played as a child. I went to see her grave."

"I would consider visiting your mom's grave 'one last time' relevant, very relevant."

"Yeah, I don't believe that life gets any more sad or painful than it does when you are staring at a tombstone that belongs to a deceased parent."

"I'd never try to argue with that."

"I wouldn't expect you to."

"But weren't you scared that you might never find your way home in the mental state you were in?"

"No, I wasn't scared. I wasn't scared for a single damn second. As I've already told you, I was in another dimension, a suicidal dimension, a place from which there is simply no turning back. That is the only way I know to describe the way I was feeling. I was in my own sector mentally. And I was afraid that I might go on living with all of the pain I was experiencing. I could not imagine enduring such pain any longer. That bus could have burst into flames or careened off a bridge into a ravine and it wouldn't have mattered to me one bit. I was just plain sick and tired of being sick and tired. I was tired of hurting the way I did, of hurting the way I'd been hurting for years. And I was going to see my mother's grave before I ended my life no matter what."

"I am sick and tired of being sick and tired, too, Jocelyn. Jesus, am I ever."

"Yeah, I already know that."

"So what brought you back here, back to the hospital?"

"Well, after I got off the bus, I wandered down street after street after street in search of the cemetery where my mom had been interred."

"You did locate her grave, right?"

"I did. I found my mother's grave for the first time since her funeral. I cried when I saw it, Hunter. I collapsed onto the damp earth and leaned against her cold tombstone. I sat there whispering into the darkness. I whispered to my mom how much I missed her. Even though it was obviously much too late for her to help me, I told her that I was both depressed and suicidal. I told her that I wanted to kill myself and that I wanted to be with her."

"That must have been difficult for you."

"It was very difficult, talking to my mom's ghost I mean. Still, I sat on my mother's grave for a long time. I sat there and watched the sun rise. I blew my mom a kiss."

"And?"

"And then something inside of me, some 'force' I could not see, propelled—or pushed—me down the longest of streets and into the lobby of an old hotel.

"What were you doing there?"

"Let me remind you that I am not trying to sound profound or anything, but, to answer you as best I can, I was just following my very own path to the land of self-destruction."

"You really did want to die, didn't you, Jocelyn?"

"Yes. I wanted to die more than I wanted to live, much more. I was already being moved along by a genuine whirlwind of thoughts of being with my mom again wherever she was. Thoughts of my own death, my own suicide were prevailing over rational thinking. I wandered off the street and into that old building and smack into a dead end."

"A dead end? That's a strange play on words."

"It is and it isn't. You see, I knew without question that there was no way I could alter my true direction no matter how hard I tried changing it. I had reached the end of my journey."

"You call a late-night bus ride to your mom's grave a journey?" I sounded skeptical.

"Well, no, not in a physical sense anyway. I was roaming in my head, waiting for my chance to die, waiting for an opportunity to kill myself. The fact that I had ridden a bus to my mom's burial site, a place I am now striving like hell to forget, doesn't matter. I could have ridden that fucking bus anywhere in the world and it wouldn't have made any difference to me whatsoever. I was going to kill myself whether I got off that bus in St. Louis or Cleveland or Pittsburgh or Omaha or Idaho. The destination is of no real consequence now. And it wasn't then."

"So what happened next?"

"Events are just a little foggy from the time I entered that hotel, I can tell you that. As I recall, the decor reminded me of my great grandmother, a woman who killed herself when I was only ten years old."

"She did?"

"Yeah, she did. She hanged herself in the attic of her house one night."

"That's some memory to have to carry with you, Jocelyn."

"It is. But, you know, my memories of my great grandmother's house are clearer than my memories of my great grandmother herself, much clearer."

"And the hotel lobby reminded you of her house, huh?"

"It did. The lobby gave me the feeling that I had stepped directly into a time machine, a time machine that had transported me right back to my great grandmother's living room, a place I had never felt welcome *before* she ended her life or comfortable *after* she had killed herself. I felt out of place and out of time while I stood there in the very center of that antiquated lobby all by myself among strangers."

"What's the next thing you recall? Or can you remember any other details?"

"Well, I recall that I sat on an ornate burgundy bench near a tall fountain that was adorned by small silver angels. I briefly considered wading into the pool at the base of that fountain and drowning myself. Eventually, I changed my mind because I didn't think that the water was deep enough. Besides, I had another plan."

"What was your plan?"

"In a minute, okay?"

"Sorry."

"I want to tell you that I am not sure how long I sat on the ornate burgundy bench next to the tall fountain in the lobby of that old hotel undisturbed by any of the staff or guests. Maybe I sat there for minutes. Maybe I sat there for hours. I probably will never know. I suppose you could say that I have succeeded in blocking that particular detail from memory. Anyway, the next thing I did was enter the ladies' room. Once there, I collapsed. I collapsed onto a champagne-colored vanity chair, and stared into a mirror so large I thought at first that it might be a window. It's odd that I can still see all of the colors so well, don't you think, Hunter?"

"Yeah, that is a little odd."

"You know what else is strange?"

"What?"

"Except for the ornate burgundy bench and the champagne-colored vanity chair and my bone-white face in the mirror, everything else, everything I saw, appeared in simple shades of black and only black. Even the people milling about in the lobby had looked monochromatic to me."

"That's odd, too, Jocelyn."

"Oh, I know it is."

"What happened after that?"

"Well, as I sat in front of the mirror and stared at my dieing reflection, I reached for a bottle of aspirin I'd stowed away in my travel bag. Actually, that was about all I had packed, in case you are interested, except for a very small amount of cash, an extra sweater and some cough drops to suck on."

"That's all? You pack lightly."

"Yeah, that's all. I didn't need anything more where I was going; I was carrying too much with me the way it was."

"You swallowed the aspirin, didn't you?"

"Yep. I dry swallowed them. I swallowed them one at a time, two at a time, three, four and so on. I felt every single one of those little suckers glide down my throat until they were gone."

"And what was going through *your* mind as you swallowed those pills, Jocelyn? I think that maybe you did believe that you had a final reason and I think I know what that conceived final reason was, namely your mom's death, but what was it that was going through *your* mind?" I had to have an answer to that question. That particular answer was an answer Jocelyn had promised to provide and I was determined to obtain it.

"That's just it, Hunter. I can honestly tell you that, like you, nothing was going through my mind, nothing at all. I was in some kind of a stupor, misplaced inside some kind of haze, in some kind of gloom from which I innately understood there was no possibility of escaping. I can describe what I was thinking or what I was not thinking in no other way."

"My God, Jocelyn."

"I definitely mean what it is I am saying to you, Hunter. Please understand."

"Then how in the hell did you end up here at the hospital, here at Lakeshore?"

"Maybe you won't believe this, but I was discovered lying in a heap on the restroom floor by a girl I'd once gone to school with."

"You were?"

"Yeah, I was. Can you believe such unfortunate luck? I was so close to death—at least that's what I believe today—when this girl I hadn't seen since junior high school finds me unconscious, picks me up and, well, dusts me off."

"So you identified the girl from your past life in the mental state you were in? That's hard to believe."

"I recognized her immediately. I saw my friend Marie standing there as if she were my own first cousin. I identified her and she identified me."

"What did you say to her?"

"I can tell you that asking her for help out of the suicidal mess I was in did cross my troubled mind, but only temporarily. I did not ask my old friend for help, as I probably should have done. Instead, as disoriented as I was, I opted to lie. Yeah, I lied to her. I lied as best I could. That's what I did."

"So what did you say to her?"

"I told her that I had been on my way to see a friend and that, except for the travel bag I was still clutching, all of my luggage had been lost. I told her that I'd fallen asleep while waiting in the pink vanity chair for my dad to come and take me home. I told her that I could not afford a room or a ticket."

"That doesn't make any sense. You were waiting for your dad to come for you *and* worried that you couldn't afford a room or a ticket home?"

"Yep."

"And she bought a lie, an excuse, as flimsy as that?"

"Yeah, she did. She bought it. She fell for my fucking lie, and, somehow, never seemed to suspect a thing. And if she did suspect that I was bullshitting her, she never told me."

"I wonder why she never doubted you or let on that she thought that something was wrong with you—if she thought that something was wrong with you that is."

"I often ask myself the very same thing, Hunter. Sometimes I think that her ignorance, her naivety, or her intentional avoidance of the obvious had everything to do with the notion that we had once been equals. There was a time when we'd been 'straight as arrows' *together*. Marie had known me during a period in my life's timeline when I had been doing very well and she never would have suspected that I was capable of attempting to take my own life. I truly believe that."

"And what happened next?"

"Marie gave me a ride to the nearest bus depot, that's what happened next. Once there, she bought me a ticket and saw to it that I got on the right bus. Just like that, I had stepped out of the suicidal dimension and back into the real, tangible world. And, just like that, I was homeward bound. What's really weird is that I know I will never see Marie again."

"Yeah, that is a little weird."

"Oh, don't I know it? She appears out of fucking nowhere, rescues me from what I believe was my very own 'death chamber' and reverses my direction, putting me on a fast track back to this place. And here I am."

"But of course the bus did not drop you off here at Lakeshore General?"

"No, of course it didn't. My dad did. He took one look at my shivering self as soon as I stumbled through the front door of his house and concluded that something was very, very wrong with me—again. So my dad carried me to his truck and drove me to the emergency room for the second time in less than a year."

"Oh yeah, the second time. I forgot."

"I remember, Hunter, that there was a nurse standing outside smoking a cigarette when I arrived. She took one look at my disheveled self and said, 'Looks like this one has come back to see me' in a voice so matter-of-fact it scared me."

"What about your dad?"

"What about him?"

"What did he say to you?"

"He didn't say much, nothing worth repeating anyway. I can tell you that he did appear to be very upset with me. He was probably hurt, pissed, you know. I will also tell you that I haven't heard anyone mention my mother's death since I arrived here in mid-October."

"What do the doctors say?"

"They all say the same thing, that I have made a 'remarkable physical turn-around,' etcetera, etcetera. They all say that I am 'lucky to be alive.' This is the second time they have saved me, Hunter, and this attempt was as lethal as my first attempt. Well, that's what the doctors tell me anyway."

"If you are recovering so well then why haven't you been released? If a person is supposed to be evaluated, medicated and vacated, as you stated earlier, then why are you still here?"

"I'm an exception, a medical exception."

"Meaning?"

"Meaning that my physical 'situation' is dire enough that I must remain here for 'the time being.' You see, Hunter, my body is poisoned, too."

"Does that mean that I may be here as long as you've been here then?"

"Truthfully, it could mean just that."

"I hope that you are wrong, Jocelyn."

"Me too."

"So what was your reason for attempting suicide the first time then?"

"As you've already articulated, Hunter, that is definitely a story for another time, another day."

"I can accept that."

"You'll have to for now. There is one thing of which I am sure, though."

"And what is that, Jocelyn?"

"I never should have survived that long October night."

CHAPTER 8

❀

Late at night, when I was usually the most manic, my mind and my body seemed to operate out of control, on autopilot. So, robbed of sleep, I would usually fix my gaze for hours at a time on the unnatural shapes that danced across my bedroom ceiling in varying shades of amber light while random, senseless notions zipped through my head like luminous meteors. Equally as often, I would pace the floors of my attic bedroom, restless like the moths at my window, waiting, waiting and waiting urgently for nothing, so that I would be prepared for whatever happened next.

Rarely did anything ever happen next. Even the starless night I pried open my bedroom window, removed the screen, and considered jumping to my death turned out to be uneventful. That night proved to be as uneventful as any other manic night I had ever tolerated because simple deduction told me that the distance from the window to the ground was not enough to guarantee a deadly crash landing. I understood all too well that the distance from the window of my bedroom to the ground was insufficient. I wanted more than two broken ankles. I wanted to be dead. So, instead of jumping, I crawled onto the rooftop and considered the pros and cons of killing myself one day soon. From three stories above the earth's edge, I watched with reserved emotion as the morning sun glided across the sky. That is where my parents found me, if you can believe it, roosting alone on the roof of their house in the a.m. sunshine, hanging onto the chimney with one hand and onto a cup of coffee with the other, barely balancing.

I remember that my parent's disciplined me with a string of harsh words I had heard many times before and ordered me back inside my room with a few more. I can tell you that my dad wasted no time nailing the screen back into place. Then he screwed the window down as if he were preparing for a tropical storm.

Meanwhile, I fell asleep with the overhead light on until the sun was gone only to awaken with a renewed interest in doing absolutely nothing for an entire night with vigor. Upon awakening, I felt as if I had acquired a new outlook on life, but I was really floating on a sky-high mania, an emotional free-for-all. Each night, I was playing with a plethora of emotions. And each and every night nothing productive happened. Not a goddamn thing.

"Stay off the roof tonight, Hunter!" my mom hollered at me from the kitchen the next night, as I screwed the cap back onto the toothpaste, as I ostensibly prepared for bed. And as I rinsed, it occurred to me that I was more likely than not the only child on the planet who had to be reminded before turning in for the night to stay off of the roof of his parents' house.

"Okay, I will!" I yelled back at her. "Besides, Mom, the window and the screen are now nailed shut!"

"Well, stay off the roof anyway!"

Except for the isolated incident in which I sat atop the roof of my parents' house until it was nearly noontime, most of my nights consisted of the same pathetic and dull routine, the pacing and the ineffective attempts to busy myself. My mind wandered and wandered, essentially doing nothing, and no matter what the task at hand might happen to be, my mind and my body would not function as one, in unison. Rarely was I able to accomplish anything constructive. Then, very suddenly, and usually by early morning, I would "crash." I would crash hard and "land" in pain. I would crash with such force that I'd find myself missing the precious nocturnal highs and fearing the worthless daytime lows, and even fearing myself to a degree.

Differentiating between those highs and lows, the peaks and the valleys, the two extremes that are the hallmark of manic depression, was easy to do after I had crashed. After I had crashed, I was able to view reality just a little bit better, just a little more clearly than I was able to do when I was manic and flying high. I was also more suicidal after crashing. And when suicidal, I knew for certain that there was a manic, almighty side of me that I liked and missed very, very much.

In a nutshell, I was living a double life, a divided existence. I was trapped behind the swinging pendulum of my ever-changing moods. It was as if a separate "part" of me was fighting for control of my mind. One part of me was both depressed and suicidal at the same time another part of me was both manic and, well, happy. One part of my person wanted badly to die and another part of my person wanted badly to live.

I have no doubt that cycling between the manic highs and the depressive lows interfered with my quality of life. As I have already stated, I achieved very little—if anything at all—the majority of the time. I was unproductive. I was numbed and dormant. I was apathetic and unforgiving. I was constantly elated and constantly bored. Confusion overwhelmed me often. It is tragic and true that I could not concentrate. I simply could not focus. I suffered from a strange loss of memory. My creativity—if I can call it creativity—slowed and came to an unfortunate standstill. I was unable to write, the one pursuit in which I had always excelled and loved more than anything. No matter how hard I tried, I could not compose a single sentence. While writing fiction had always been my salvation, my saving anchor, words escaped me when I was highly manic or when I was severely depressed.

On the rarest of occasions, those rare occasions when I did manage to gain an adequate amount of focus and mental sharpness to actually write something, I was convinced that I was in the same class as William Shakespeare himself. When manic, I was convinced that my prose—if I can call it prose—really was that good. Then I would wake up after a brief, dreamless sleep or come down from a manic high, to the reality that the words I had managed to piece together were nothing more than typing.

Because manic depression casts such a large shadow, many activities fell prey to my suffocating illness. Voices on the radio sounded muddled and made little or no sense to me. The electric faces on the television screen looked pathetically disfigured. Something as basic as reading a magazine article became next to impossible. My ability to be decisive was practically nonexistent. To a degree, I lost control of my mental faculties. I became intoxicated by my lack of sleep and by spurts of glaring mania and sobered by my unrelenting depression so harshly that I could not operate on an even keel. All too often, I searched with zest for a happy medium between the highs and the lows, but, no matter how much effort I put forth, I could not find one. Sadly, I became a miserable zombie, alert but comatose all at the same time. Sadly, I became a reclusive and depressive member of the living dead.

It was not long before I grew accustomed to the certainty that depression has a tempo all its own. Always my depression would "lift" as the hours ticked away. By midnight, I was definitely more "up" than I was during the daytime hours. And by dusk, depression would have taken a virtual backseat to full-blown mania. Mania would have "come of age," violating my small world like an overgrown weed, congregating with only an occasional bout of depression, and I would inevitably waste away the nighttime hours gazing out the window at my parents' moonlit garden, waiting like an expectant father for the long-lost specters of cemetery lawns to come and take me away, to liberate me from my manic yet somber existence. Despite the red curtains of fatigue that always seemed to be hanging in front of my eyes, sleeplessness would hold me captive while I contemplated the meaning of life or, worse yet, while I contemplated suicide.

CHAPTER 9

Jocelyn departed as soon as she had finished telling me about her most recent suicide attempt, saying that she was going to watch some television and take a short nap. She assured me that she would see me soon and promised that we would definitely make time to talk about our "suicidal experiences" again. Jocelyn also reminded me not to sweat the psychiatrist. She reminded me that he was just a man, "a man like any other man," a man doing his job.

So now the plan called for a psychiatrist to see me at any time. Regardless of what Jocelyn had said to me about him being a man like any other man, I was really having trouble accepting that he was scheduled to see me of all people. I could not believe it. I asked myself if I actually was crazy or whether Jocelyn was actually incorrect. I wondered if I was psychotic or whether I was a sociopath. I tried to decipher what those words truly meant and whether they applied to me or not. It occurred to me that I might be losing my mind in a place in which I might really belong.

That is when I recalled Jack Nicholson's superb portrayal of the resistant Randall McMurphy in the movie "One Flew over the Cuckoo's Nest," taking bet after bet and risk after risk and fighting Fletcher's Nurse Ratched at every turn, while confined to a place he himself did not seem to belong. McMurphy's "predicament" and all of his foolish pranks and exploits reminded me of my own fragile situation and of all of the bets and risks I had taken over the years and how none of those bets or risks had ever paid off for me but had always gotten me into trouble or had nearly killed me. I quickly realized that I was definitely in a cuckoo's nest of my own and, like Nicholson's McMurphy, there was no way I was going to be able to run from the psychiatrist. I had never felt so empty inside. Life had never looked so strange to me.

Life was looking so strange to me that I closed my overworked eyes and tried to sleep for the first time in days. And as I lie there with my eyes closed, I recalled a homeless man I had seen sleeping on a bench at a downtown bus stop nearly a week earlier. I soon considered my own singular position, my body lying bloodied and nearly naked in a hospital bed. I wondered which one of us was better off, which one of us had the most to gain, the most to lose. I tried to guess which one of us was the loneliest. I tried to calculate which one of us was the closest to death's door, the homeless man or myself. Regardless of how close we were to dieing, I wanted very badly to trade places with the homeless man at the bus stop. But trading places with that broken man was not an alternative because I was being monitored. I was under surveillance. For the first time in my life, I was confined to a locked psychiatric ward. And I was under a suicide watch. If I attempted to leave the hospital, I would be arrested. Yes, it really was that simple.

Needless to say, it did occur to me that I might be the one man who was closer to death. I recalled the single cardboard sign that was propped against the wrought iron bench where the homeless man was lying in a fetal position. In a large black script the sign read: "Need food. Need shelter. Anything helps." I considered how my own cardboard sign might read if I had one. I decided that it would say: "I need to die."

It was not long before it occurred to me that the homeless man and I were useless, forgotten objects, burnt out stars lost in a galaxy that no longer held any purpose for us, a galaxy that was no longer a safe or secure place for the two of us to inhabit. It also occurred to me that the homeless man stretched out on the bench at the bus stop was still hanging on, still pleading for one last chance to live in the very world I was abandoning. Having concluded that I was at least one step closer to death's door than the homeless man, I held my breath and tried willing my mind and body to die but, again, I failed to kill myself. My mind and body just would not quit.

At the exact moment I continued to live, I accepted fully the sobering fact that a psychiatrist was on his way to see me and that I would not be able to avoid him. It was also at that moment I pictured my own funeral service as clearly as I had pictured it when I was only a child. And that is when I remembered that I could always imagine my own funeral, the ultimate symbol of my having died, when nothing else was working for me. Imagining my own funeral was the next best thing to being there. Imagining my own funeral was an escape from reality's shores, a place that had never been all that safe or pleasant for me.

I conceived my own funeral for the first time when I was only four years old. I was at preschool eating vanilla wafers during snack time when I happened to envision the ceremony I believed would ultimately follow my very own death. For me, my imagined funeral was not a somber event, but a celebration instead. For my parents, my imagined funeral was a solemn, intensely lonely affair and not a celebration at all.

Through the mist that shrouds the vision of my funeral, I see my mom first. She is dressed in the blackest black. She weeps openly for her oldest son, as her shadowed form struggles to remain standing. Through the same mist, I see a single tear run down my dad's wrinkled cheek as he stares at the rain-soaked ground, his arms hanging limply at his sides. I search for my brother John, but he is not there. Finally, I picture my own casket. It is open and my lifeless body is sharply dressed in a black store-bought suit, which seems odd to me because I have never owned a suit of any kind or of any color. But there I am, lying in my very own open casket, a contented smile frozen upon my ashen face. The cause of death is unknown to me but the vision of my funeral is always the same. Year in and year out, the vision is always the same.

"What is it you were thinking just now, Hunter?" The gravelly voice of a concerned Miss Grady, my preschool teacher, interrupted the lurid thoughts of my funeral and snapped me back to the present. "Is there something troubling you today?"

"No." I quickly wiped some crumbs off my desk and pasted a smile on my face.

"Are you feeling okay?"

"I'm fine," I lied. I felt as if Miss Grady had just caught me stealing extra cookies or engaging in some other kind of illegal activity.

"If something is bothering you, Hunter, I'd like for you to tell me what it is, okay?"

"Okay. But nothing is bothering me. Really."

"Really?"

"Yes. Really," I said. Miss Grady stopped pressing me.

Nearly one year later, on the first day of kindergarten as a matter of fact, I discovered a note of encouragement my mom had signed with hugs and kisses folded neatly away in my metal lunch box. Moved by my mom's act of kindness and by her obvious love for me, I found my five-year-old mind thinking about my own funeral again and about how my mom would ultimately react when I was finally dead. Trying to decide how my mom might live her life after I was gone was like trying to solve a complex riddle or a brainteaser for which there seems to be no explanation. It is fair to say that I could not conclude how my mom might react to the loss of a son. That is how truly sickened by depression I really was.

"Close your eyes like everyone else, Hunter." My curiosity was instantly interrupted. Mrs. Dunbar, my overbearing kindergarten teacher, was now standing directly above me. "And take a nap please."

"All right then." I closed my eyes for a moment or two, for as long as it took to be rid of Mrs. Dunbar and then, while my classmates napped away the afternoon, I stared at the ceiling and contemplated for the first time sharing with them how badly I hurt for my mom and how badly I hurt for my self. I decided that it would not be poor strategy to explain my sorrow during show and tell or share with my counterparts crayon sketches depicting my torment. I contemplated spelling out my hopelessness on the chalkboard or, better yet, during story hour. Surely that would win me the attention and help I was craving so badly.

However, I did none of those things. Instead of disclosing my suffering, I opted to keep my grief a secret that day and for many days thereafter. Then one night, as I stood at my bedroom window awaiting the specters I hoped would come for me, I had an idea: I would paint my own grave and tombstone on canvas and hang it on the bulletin board at the front of the classroom for all of my peers to see. I had little doubt that such a depiction would gain their full regard. I felt that it was more than a decent plan. I was positive that every one of my fellow students would be able to sense my personal hell and would see that I needed help. The decision to paint was an easy one. So, later that night, while my parents slept, I finished the portrait exactly as I had planned.

So there it was in molten shades of fiery red and shadowy gray acrylic, my masterpiece, proof of my obsession with my own death. The painting featured a likeness of my own bloodstained hand reaching from my own grave toward the angriest of skies. I had made it appear as if my bloodstained hand was grasping, or clawing, for the very help I so desperately needed, the help I so desperately wanted, the very help for which I was afraid to ask.

The subject of the macabre painting was no accident or fluke. The blackened sky looming over the gravesite, the undated tombstone and the bloodstained hand were all intentional. Each one of them was crafted by design. All of them were joined together to form an impressive whole. And combined, they formed a consolidated plea for help.

I was positive that no one would be able to overlook my sorrow now and so, early the next morning, I smuggled my most recent composition to school.

Without delay or Mrs. Dunbar's permission, I mounted my prized work on the bulletin board for all of my classmates to see. I waited with a rare rush of excitement for their reaction. It was now just a matter of time. I now felt that help was just a heartbeat away.

I was sitting alone at my desk prior to first bell when Mrs. Dunbar hastily removed my grim painting from the bulletin board. Mrs. Dunbar removed my painting from the bulletin board long before my classmates had a chance to see it. Therefore, I never had a chance to see their reaction. I suppose you could say that I had not succeeded at sharing with them my pain, but had failed instead.

"I assume that this is yours, Hunter?" Mrs. Dunbar hissed at me, as she stuffed my painting into a brown paper sack.

"Yes it is," I said quietly and with apparent hesitation. I swallowed hard. Mrs. Dunbar walked quickly out of the classroom with the brown paper sack tucked under her arm.

I was called into Principal Evans' tidy office sometime before school let out for the weekend. Dr. Evans shook my hand and told me to take a seat.

"How are you feeling today, Hunter?" He leaned back in his tall oak chair. He clasped his hands behind his balding head. He closed his sleepy black eyes and exhaled. I smelled tobacco in the air.

"I'm okay, I guess," I responded. I noticed a wooden paddle hanging on the wall behind him. I wondered if he ever used it. I decided that he probably did. I wondered if he was intent on using it on me.

"You are not feeling too good, huh?"

"Just 'okay' I think."

"Is there anything at all you'd like to talk about, Hunter?"

"I can't think of anything." I was too nervous and too scared to tell him what I was really feeling. Sure, I could paint my suffering on a scrap of canvas for the entire world to see, but given the ideal chance, I could not—or would not—explain it.

"Is that true, Hunter? There's nothing you would like to discuss with me?"

"No. Nothing. Really." Then Dr. Evans fell silent for a minute or two, maybe even longer. Meanwhile, I sat there waiting for whatever was going to happen next.

"Well, Hunter …" He placed his giant hands on his desk.

"Well what?" I asked him, feigning confusion. Dr. Evans grabbed onto a black pencil and tapped it against a single manila folder that was laid open on his desk. "So what about the painting, Hunter? Would you like to talk about that?" He was now studying the contents of the folder. I wondered what damaging information the folder might contain about me.

"Well, what about it?" I asked, simulating confusion for the second time since being seated.

"Don't you want to talk about the painting, your painting?"

"No, I do not," I said at the exact moment the final bell sounded. Just like that, I had been saved by the bell. Being saved by the bell was something that had never happened to me before. I must say that I was grateful for that bell. I quickly stood up to leave. And as I stood in front of Dr. Evans' large desk, I got a glimpse of my painting leaning against the wall directly below the wooden paddle. I do not know why, but my painting looked much different leaning there against the wall in Dr. Evans' tidy office. My painting, I realized then, looked like simple child's work and not at all like the masterpiece I originally thought I had created. How Mrs. Dunbar and Dr. Evans were able to conclude that something might be troubling me after viewing my odd painting I will never know. Like I said, my painting resembled simple child's work and nothing more.

"Well, we will leave it at that then," he stated matter-of-factly, looking me up and down, seemingly searching my person for the very answers I had failed to provide. Then he reached across the expanse of his desk and shook my hand again. His grip was much stronger the second time.

"Goodbye, Hunter." he said in a serious tone. "Have a nice afternoon and a good weekend."

"Goodbye … and I will," I said. Dr. Evans did not appear to notice that I left his office in tears that day.

CHAPTER 10

❀

I was mindful of my younger brother John's presence before he entered the room where I lie trying to sleep. It is possible that I sensed his arrival or that I had overheard him speaking with a technician or a nurse or a doctor while I waited with my eyes closed tightly for the psychiatrist to show. Regardless, I knew that he was there, standing in the doorway before he uttered a single goddamn word to me.

"Hi, John," I whispered at him at the same time I opened my eyes. I was still thirsty, thirstier than I'd been when I'd swallowed the Haldol and my broken voice proved just how badly I needed something to drink.

"I need a glass of water or a Coke or something, John," I implored. John stood motionless in the doorway, his hands stuffed into the pockets of his khakis, his intense brown eyes bearing down on nothing in particular, on anything but me.

"There is no way I can help you with that one, Hunter," John responded, obviously disinterested in helping me quench my insatiable thirst or helping me at all for a reason, or reasons, still unknown to me. But such behavior, a certain macho-moodiness, was typical of John.

"Why can't you?"

"I think that you need to ask a nurse that one," he responded with unparalleled conviction, as he extracted a large worn duffel bag I had never seen before from the shadows behind him and dropped it near the head of the bed and looked directly at me for the first time since arriving at Lakeshore General. I could see that he was furious with me. John had never been good at hiding his emotions, especially when he was mad.

"So what's the bag for?" I asked him. I was as suspicious of the duffel bag as I was fearful of his angry disposition. He did not respond. He shook his head instead. That was when I took a good look at the t-shirt I was wearing. The shirt was red where it had once been white. I glanced back at John. Again, he was staring at nothing in particular, but it was obvious by the expression on his face that he had seen my bleeding shirt. How could he have missed it?

"It gets better, you know," he said, his eyes locking with mine for a nanosecond. Then he turned his back on me and silently left the room and the ward. John left the hospital as quickly as he had arrived I think. Just like that, my brother was erased from the newest page of my life's story. I tried to speculate as to whether he would return or not. I could not decide when I might see him again—if ever.

I was no longer trying to sleep, but praying for death to draw the final line, when the telephone next to the bed rang for the first time since my deliverance. I discerned immediately that my parents who lived thousands of miles away in a small town in Germany had just been connected with the hospital where I lie cringing from the likelihood that my life might actually be salvaged.

"Hello, Dad." I answered on the first ring, still speaking in a painful, parched whisper.

"Hello? Hunter? Hunter, this is your dad." His voice sounded untroubled and it comforted me. His smooth, level voice reminded me of safety, of law and order and of my parents' house so faraway and of all of the well-traveled pathways winding through the furniture. My dad's voice reminded me of the home I had left behind so many years before when I was a much different man, a much "healthier" man.

"I know, Dad. I know that it's you. How are you?"

"How are you doing, Hunter?" I tried my hardest to think of a decent answer to that question. I could not find one. I honestly did not know how I was doing. "Hunter?"

"I'm okay, Dad," I responded after a half a minute or more of nothing but silence.

"Good."

"Do you want to talk to mom?"

"Okay." My mom was crying excessively. I had never heard her cry like that before. Her sobbing made me uneasy. In fact, it frightened me.

"My god, Hunter, what if I never had the chance to see you one last time or say goodbye to you?" Somehow, I had been able to understand her tearful question. Again, I tried to think of a decent answer to a question I did not want to answer in the first place. Again, I could not.

"I am doing as expected, Mom," I said in the most upbeat tone I could muster, my voice nearly failing me for the umpteenth time since my deliverance into the hospital. "Don't worry, I'll be alive for Thanksgiving." Even now, I honestly do not know where that particular statement came from. I do not know why I said the word "alive" when I should have said the word "home," but it worked somehow; my mom's crying came to an abrupt stop. I heard her exhale with force and I found myself wondering if she was smoking again. I envisioned my own troubled, grieving mother hiding in her bedroom blowing smoke rings out the open window. I remembered my mom's fragile heart and her pacemaker, the pacemaker I strongly suspected would not last much longer. I also remembered that my mom was, like me, probably dieing a very slow death.

"Do I need to be there, Hunter? I have already checked with the airlines. I could fly out of Frankfurt as early as tomorrow." My mom sounded as lost as I felt.

"No. You do not need to come, Mom. You do not need to come. Please stay home. I will be fine. Really. Trust me on this one." If there was one resolution I had made to myself the night before, it was that I was going to do whatever I had to do on my own—live or die. I was very aware that I had already involved enough innocent people.

"Well, are they helping you, Hunter?"

"Yes, they are helping me."

"Have you seen a psychiatrist yet?"

"I will see a psychiatrist in a while, soon, Mom. I will meet with the psychiatrist soon," I said in a reassuring voice.

Before I knew it, I was tired. I was so tired that I tried to decide whether I had been administered a sleeping agent via my IV drip without first being told, without my permission. Was my sudden fatigue a side effect of the acetaminophen I had ingested, of the Haldol, or of something else? Regardless of the cause, or causes, of my exhaustion, I was beginning to lose power.

"I need to go now, Mom. I did not sleep last night. I have not slept in days and I think that I can sleep right now," I said, exhausted and weak and cognizant that I was drifting fast. Our conversation had been brief but I could not talk to my mom any longer. I could only sleep. At least sleep would be a diversion.

"Okay, Hunter, I will call you later then, after you've had a chance to rest, after you've spoken with the psychiatrist."

"I'll talk to you later, Mom," I said in a low, indistinct tone.

"I love you Hunter," my mom said with a sigh. "I think you know that." Those words echoed through the most distant chambers of my brain. I ascertained that my mom's composure had improved. So had mine. That was a good thing, you know. Thanksgiving was only weeks away.

CHAPTER 11

❀

I believe it is odd the way a dream can often expose answers and uncover the true state of affairs. Even while I slept for the first time in more than 72 hours fleeting impressions of the terrible crimes I had been suspecting I had committed on the eve of my deliverance onto the psychiatric ward gradually mingled with a new reality. The true-to-life impressions created by that new-found reality convinced me that the emergency room at Lakeshore General, the tetanus shot and the stare of the deputy sheriff had all been real, very real indeed.

I was sleeping fairly soundly I think when it occurred to me that The Image and all of its distressing contents were all crucial parts of a real, aggregated whole. Yes, The Image had been living inside of me for several hours now and, yes, I had really been there, shivering in that frigid emergency room. I was the man who had been strapped to a stretcher barely alive, receiving a tetanus shot, as a deputy sheriff stared me down. The Image was, I now knew, as real as was the blood that discolored my body. And now The Image itself was unmasked, out in the open. The Image was a certainty, a proposition from which there was no running or escaping.

I awoke abruptly from my revealing dream and watched as The Image exploded into a million pieces or more inside of my head, right in front of my eyes. The Image burst as if it were a see-through ceramic balloon being struck by the full force of a sledgehammer. The Image had died a very sudden death. With The Image dead and gone, my head felt much less weighted. Without The Image invading my thinking, my eyesight was much clearer, much less cluttered. I could now see my life without all of the grayness. I could now see my life for the bloody, bloody mess that it was.

The third nurse to enter the room since I had been admitted to the hospital had been sent expressly to clean away some of that bloody mess. She tiptoed up to the bed without speaking a single word to me. Maybe it was the unenviable task of scrubbing the blood from my body that caused her to be so silent. Maybe she feared me to a degree and was walking on eggshells. Regardless, she began to diligently wipe the dried blood from my person with tact and precision.

The nurse who seemed determined to scour the blood from my outer self without speaking to me smelled like a cheap German perfume, a perfume I knew I had smelled at least one time before. I wondered if she might be of German origin. I searched her person for clues. I saw that she was wearing a nametag, but I could not make out the text on it for the folds in her blouse.

"So tell me, miss, are you by any chance German?" I asked her.

"It is true. I am German by chance," she responded, with the slightest hint of a laugh in her bold voice. It was the very first laugh I had heard since Jocelyn had laughed at me earlier that same day. I realized at that moment, as the German nurse rubbed the soft cloth across the surface of my bloody arms, that laughter is a priceless fringe benefit on a psychiatric ward.

The German nurse was immediately hushed again. She was dabbing painstakingly at my wrists and stitches when I saw that the cloth she was using was slowly turning various shades of scarlet. I also saw that her gloveless hands and her bare forearms were speckled with my blood. I stood and leaned against the bed so that she could wipe down my legs and feet. I studied the bloodstains on my favorite pair of gym shorts. I studied the blood on the tiled floor.

"So you can speak German fluently then?" I asked her at last, as she quickly redressed the wounds on my wrists. Of course, I had already concluded that she could. Several years before, I had been a student at a small American university in Germany for a couple of semesters and had picked up enough of the language to appreciate that her accent was definitely genuine.

"I am," she answered without making any eye contact with me whatsoever. The German nurse worked fast. In what seemed like only minutes, she had finished removing the blood from my exhausted body and had attired my wrists in new white bandages.

"What happens to me now? I want to go home." I was definitely missing my one room apartment and the freedom that came with it.

"Be patient, Hunter. The psychiatrist should be in to see you soon. You'll be able to know more then." That was the last thing the German nurse said to me before she turned and walked out of the gloomy room as soundlessly as she had entered it. I never saw her again.

I ran my fingers over my forehead and through my hair as best I could. My fingers tripped over the ridges of dried blood the German nurse had missed or had intentionally skipped. I still felt dirty inside and out, but especially on the inside, the one place where water would never cleanse me.

I wanted to shower badly. I peered into the shower and considered standing beneath the cool water and washing my hair while I made every effort to rinse away the evil memories that preoccupied my disordered thoughts. I considered pacifying myself in the shower's spray but I was as tired as I had been when I had talked to my mom, so I crawled back into bed and fell asleep for only the second time since landing on the psychiatric ward, for only the second time in three long days.

Even today, so many years later, I can recall that I dreamt for what seemed like hours of a place I had once called home. I dreamt of a place that was far removed from me when I was awake, a place that was reborn only when I slept, a place that flashed across the walls of my mind like a slide show or a video in a series of undaunted colors. I dreamt of a small village in Germany where I had spent my formative years, a locale that had, at one time, made me feel alive and, even more important, secure. The German village I had lived in as a young man was situated in a valley not far from the Rhine River. Glorious mountains flanked the town on nearly all sides.

Without a doubt, those mountains made me feel safe and protected. Those mountains rose from the earth and aided in my defense against enemy thoughts of suicide and lent me some faith that I would be okay for good someday. That is when things changed. One day I faced the realization that those mountains were not enough to protect me from me, to protect me from steady feelings of depression. In time, the mountains crumbled inside of my imagination and I soon departed for new shores, to a place I hoped would protect me from the frightening essence of depression forever more. I awoke from the dream of that distant German town, my former home and prayed for my independence from my depression once again.

PART II

THE ARRIVAL

CHAPTER 12

❦

I have never understood why, but I muttered to myself a small prayer as soon I awoke later that morning, which was, I think, quite sometime after the German nurse had left me alone and still feeling dirty. Why I put my trust in a prayer that day when I never had before I do not know. Maybe praying to a god I had only ever shouted at was a sign of how scared I was or how desperate I had become or how manic I was. Maybe I was running low on serenity and courage and wisdom all at the same time. Perhaps I thought that a prayer might help me get out of the strange and confusing situation in which I now seemed forever trapped.

About an hour or so after I awoke, a short, squarely built woman with streaks of gray in her auburn hair entered the room with a little too much bounce in her step. She introduced herself as Jane without offering to shake my hand. Then, with obvious effort, she picked up the sizeable duffle bag John had left for me and commanded that I follow her. Without a word, I grabbed onto a chrome-colored "pole" that had an infusion pump attached to it, the same pump I was connected to via IV and guided it beside me as best I could. Although the entire apparatus was rather awkward to maneuver, it rolled along soundlessly. Meanwhile, Jane lugged the duffel bag down the extended corridor to a removed wing of the ward as if she were an out-of-shape bellhop.

"I welcome you to Seven Southwest, Hunter," she said in a semi-hushed tone, practically panting, as we passed through a pair of thick doors and into an expansive quadrangle and coasted to a stop in front of a rather large center island where several nurses sat seemingly awaiting my arrival.

"Hunter Kraven," Jane whispered. A pretty woman in a navy blue sweater with a laminated nametag I could not read pinned to it looked at me briefly, studied a computer monitor and then glanced back at me.

"Hello, Hunter," she said with a slight tilt of her head and an even slighter smile. Then she nodded at Jane a single time and said, "Room number seven." Jane nodded in return.

"What's room number seven?" I whispered at Jane.

"That room over there is yours, Hunter," Jane said, pointing a stubby index finger in the general direction of a corner room off to the left of the nurses' station. "I think that the first thing you will notice about this particular space is that it resembles a hotel room to a degree or maybe even a small dorm room," she said, leading me again, still struggling with the duffel bag while I struggled to keep the infusion pump on course without pulling the catheter to which it was connected out of my left hand even though I was really very tempted to rip myself free from it once and for all and disappear through the thick doors forever.

"That is not *my* room," I insisted from just outside the room's only entrance. "This cannot be happening," I said out loud. "This can't be happening to *me*," I stated with determination. "Please, Jane, let me go home *now*," I pleaded. "I really need to go home *now*. Take this thing out of my hand and let me go."

"Explore if you want to, Hunter," Jane whispered with a broad smile, a smile that seemed too broad to be the real thing, ignoring entirely my declaration that the small room in the corner of the quadrangle on Seven Southwest inside Lakeshore General Hospital was not mine. That is when it occurred to me that Jane always spoke in a very bothersome frequency, as if she were a school librarian with an impatient attitude. The inflection of her quiet voice grated on me. Without a doubt, I missed the bold accent of the German nurse or the untroubled sound and confident diction of Jocelyn's own untroubled speech.

I glanced into the room that was significantly larger than the room I had been assigned the previous night. Feeling defeated, I stepped carefully over the threshold and immersed myself in neutral colors that soothed me unexpectedly.

"Hunter, it's really okay if you want to look around. Explore."

And so I explored. From just inside the doorway, I studied the more-than-ample space, taking a cognitive inventory of its contents. A bed not much wider than a cot or a stretcher occupied the largest area of the boxed-shaped room. There were two nightstands on either side of the bed with skinny lamps on them. Directly opposite the bed, a relatively large television set had been built into the wall. To the immediate left of the television, there was a dresser that appeared to double as a desk. That dresser/desk combo also had a skinny lamp on it. Facing the television, there was a sepia recliner that beckoned me to sit and rest and reflect on my atypical life. I resisted the urge to sit however. I remained standing instead, mindful that I was, to a small degree, being anchored by the sheer weight of the infusion pump and the chrome-colored pole I was still clutching as well as my desire to be set free.

The room that had been reserved for me was separated from a dozen or so other rooms that constituted the rest of the quadrangle by a "wall" made of the thickest glass. That glass wall served as a barrier between my newest room and the center island where, I noticed, the nurses were still sitting quietly staring blankly into the blue-white light of computer monitors. Except for the glass wall, the space did resemble a clean, well-kept hotel room or maybe even a small dorm room outfitted with the bare necessities just as Jane had initially suggested. The room that was destined to serve as my "home" for a yet-to-be-determined amount of time was, in all honesty, a rather nice space. Regardless of how nice the space was, I quickly made up my mind to hate it.

"I don't like this place and I want out!" I shouted at Jane. "Cancel my fucking membership! And do it now!"

"Please keep it down, down, down, Hunter." She leveled her intrusive gaze at me. "And don't forget that this room is all *yours*," she stressed, still trying to sell me on the one room I was now fearing more than anything. "You should really feel very comfortable here. Anyway, I really do hope that you feel at home." By this time, she was busy searching through my possessions, carefully placing each item on top of the narrow bed as she unpacked it. I asked her for a toothbrush. She tossed me a gray t-shirt and a pair of black sweatpants instead. Both the t-shirt and the sweatpants smelled of laundry soap, a scent that reminded me of a not-so-distant world I believed still existed somewhere.

"I don't think that I will ever feel at home in this lousy room," I informed her.

"And why not?" she asked. I noted that she did not sound as concerned for me as I believed she should have sounded.

"Because I am normal, that's why," I responded, intentionally slipping the sweatpants she had chosen for me over my blood-stained gym shorts.

"Here, let's take off that t-shirt." Jane stepped around the end of the narrow bed and, with a pair of scissors, cut the bloody rag from my body and tossed it into a nearby trashcan. Then she shut off the IVAC and removed the line that was attached to the catheter. As if on cue, I put on the clean t-shirt glad to know that I was not putting on a straight jacket. In what seemed like only a fraction of a second, Jane reattached the catheter and restarted the IVAC. Then, opting to explore on foot, I quickly made my way to the room's only window.

Once there, I was relieved to discover that there were no bars crisscrossing the small glass opening. I peered out in hopes of seeing the lake or the stream that flowed through the very center of town but I saw only the concrete walls of a multi-level parking garage instead. I wanted my freedom more than ever.

"There's not much of a view from this room is there, Hunter? I'm really very sorry about that."

"No, I guess not." I answered, extremely disappointed. Yes, I had wanted to see the lake or the stream or maybe some sky but had discovered that it was not going to happen that morning.

"Well, Hunter, there are other things that require your focus and attention right now."

"That's redundant, Jane."

"I mean what I say. You need to pay attention to some other things besides the view from this room."

"Such as?"

"Well, making every effort to get along with the staff is one."

I ignored her stuffy, assuming answer and shuffled away from the small window and its perfect view of the parking garage and stood near the foot of the bed. That is when I spotted the shining mirror that would, I knew, ultimately depict the present state of my situation more clearly than anything else had so far. I considered what might happen if I called together the courage necessary to look into the mirror that seemed to be waiting explicitly for me.

"That's your own private bathroom, too, you know," Jane said, apparently unaware of the inner terror—yes terror—I was now experiencing. "Maybe you should wash your face. Don't you think that would be a good idea?"

That fixed the arrangement. There was no way I would be able to avoid looking into the mirror now and, somehow, I mustered enough strength to take a single step in the direction of my private bathroom and the mirror I knew would soon contain my own bloody counterpart. Then I took a second weighted step toward the mirror I wished I had never discovered in the first place. I limped toward that mirror and the blood-smeared reflection I was certain I would find there. A few more steps and there I was, face to face with that fucking mirror, staring into the contaminated eyes of a living dead man. The blood that still coated my face, the same blood the German nurse had failed to wipe away, appeared as if it had been intentionally applied there, like a vermilion shade of sunscreen. No wonder I still felt dirty on the inside and, especially, on the outside.

"Are you feeling okay right now?" Jane called out in a loud whisper. Evidently, she found my silence disturbing. So did I.

"No, I don't think I am," I answered. My pupils, which were dilated to nearly two times their normal size, stared back at me from the flawless exterior of the mirror, from within the margins of my own bloodied facade.

"Why not, Hunter? Why aren't you feeling okay?"

"Because my face is the face of death, that is why."

"Well, do you think that you might have anything in your bag that you could use to harm yourself?" she inquired, changing the topic once more.

"Just a Ginsu knife and an axe," I responded flatly, a slight sneer forming on my lips, as I stepped away from the mirror and my own blood-smeared likeness, the blood-smeared likeness that seemed to characterize more than anything else my sad, sad life and back into the small room. It did not appear as if I were going to be the free man I had originally vowed I would be and I was resentful, very resentful. I was infuriated that I was being hospitalized, doing time on a fucking psychiatric ward, doing time on fucking Seven Southwest. I was mad, very mad. Jane was undoubtedly the first victim of my anger, the first victim of my towering rage.

"I don't like this place, Jane and I want out!" I hollered at her.

"Well, we can't let you go just yet, Hunter. And please keep it down. I won't ask you again. There are people trying to rest right now. Your shouting will only disturb and maybe even frighten them."

"Exactly how long am I going to be a prisoner here?" I was as frustrated as I had ever been.

"You are going to be with us for a while." I wondered what constituted "a while."

"And just how long is that?"

"I'm really not sure. However long it takes."

"Can't you be more specific? I want to go home *now*, this morning. God, won't you get me out of here? I do not belong in this place, plunging into foreign waters, sinking. Seven Southwest is not for me."

"But this *is* where you belong. You have been officially admitted to this hospital. Accept that fact now and you will be better for it later."

"Bite me, Confucius!"

"Careful."

"Tell me then, how long is 'for now,' Jane?"

"However long it takes to assess you. The staff needs to assess your mood and your behavior, not to mention how your liver is doing. Maybe you will be here for a few days, Hunter, or for a few weeks. I'm really not positive. It could be much longer. It could be much less, too. I have no real way of knowing just yet because the doctors aren't sure just yet. Realize, Hunter, you are somewhat defenseless right now. Also, realize that your life has been severely disrupted. You just can't step right back into your old routine. No, not anymore."

"I want to go home *now*! You can't keep me here, you know. No one can. Besides, I need to be home in time for Thanksgiving. I promised my mom that I would be home in time for Thanksgiving, in case you are interested."

"Well, maybe you will be. Maybe you will be. Just be careful what kind of promises you make; you may not be able to keep them."

"I could leave right now, Jane. I could walk right out of this goddamn place right this minute and I would be fine!"

"No, Hunter, you would not be 'fine'. Without an IV drip and proper medical treatment, your liver and maybe even your kidneys, would shut down. Yes, they would shut down completely and you would die. Left unchecked, acetaminophen poisoning can kill a person, Hunter. I suspect that you knew that already."

"That can't possibly be true." I was stunned. It was the first time anyone had bothered to mention my "predicament" from a medical standpoint. Jane's unexpected revelation reduced the intensity of my anger tremendously. I was instantly humbled.

"But it *is* true, Hunter. Besides, do you really want to go on living like this, depressed and suicidal all the time?" Do you want to go through life being stalked by suicidal impulses, depression eating away at you constantly?"

I had not thought of that specific angle yet. I had never considered the notion that I might be depressed and suicidal for as long as I lived, for the rest of my life. That notion sobered me more than I am able to explain, more than I am able to convey right now.

"No, I don't think that I want to continue living that way," I admitted. "I just want to return to my apartment and my life—not to mention my privacy—as soon as possible. And I want to see my family on Thanksgiving—before I die. That's all. Honestly."

"I think that you probably will go home to your apartment and your life. Realize, though, that your life will not be the same as before. Life will now be very different for you."

"Just give me an estimated time of arrival, Jane. Please."

"I'm sorry, but I can't do that, not right now anyway."

"So be it," I mumbled. Clearly, questions were getting me nowhere. I fell silent. Jane was silent, too, as she persisted to meticulously sort through every one of the items John had packed for me, disregarding completely all of the anger I was exhibiting. She invested the time needed to unfold each one of my shirts, seemingly in search of anything I might use to harm myself, or for contraband, or for both, before she refolded them with deliberate care and proceeded to search the pockets of my blue jeans with the same thoroughness.

"Why am I here, Jane? Of all the places I could be right now, why this room? Why am I stuck on a psychiatric ward?" I asked, searching for clues I had never searched for before.

"You should already know why, Hunter. You should also know that it is really very important that you come to an understanding with yourself."

"And what in the hell does that mean?"

"Well," she began, her hands now resting on the small of her back, her eyes aimed directly at my own, "you need to understand, Hunter, why you did the things you did so that you will be better prepared to explain to your friends and, even more important, to your family exactly why you did the things you did. You need to explain to them why you tried to kill yourself."

"What is there to explain? They already think that they know everything there is to know. They have already drawn their own damn conclusions. I know they have. I am sure that they already believe they have all of the answers they'll ever need. I shouldn't have to talk to them about anything. What is there to explain to them that they don't think they already know? Answer that one, Jane."

"Well, for one, you need to *clarify* for them *why* you attempted suicide. Give them your own version in your own words. I don't think for a minute that they know what that version is."

"And why do I need to do that?"

"Because they have the right to know, that's why, Hunter."

"Maybe my own version of what I attempted to do to myself is none of their goddamn business. They had plenty of opportunities to help me before I ended up locked away in this goddamn place."

"Oh, Hunter, but it is their business. The events leading up to your attempt and the attempt itself were all really very serious. I think you know that already. I hope so anyway. You are fortunate to be here, very fortunate indeed. The pain that pulsates from inside your stomach right now should serve as a reminder as to why you are here even if nothing else does. That said, I think that you need to tell your family something." Jane was no longer whispering like a pissed-off librarian, but, for the first time since she had introduced herself, was speaking like a "regular person" instead.

If I was to put my faith in Jane, I was to believe that I was lucky to be alive, but I did not feel the least bit lucky. I felt as if my luck had run out long ago, long before I had been delivered to Seven Southwest. Furthermore, I actually felt unlucky because I was still alive, still holding onto a depressed life I had never really wanted.

"So what is my diagnosis then? Or do I even have one?"

"It's much too soon to know."

"Well then, do you know if I will ever get better?" Is there any chance at all that I will be cured of my suicidal thoughts, my 'suicidal impulses,' as you refer to them?" I was aware that my anger and bitterness had subsided almost entirely. I had calmed down significantly.

"Yes, Hunter, with proper medical treatment you will probably get better. There is definitely a chance that you will get better." Jane was whispering again.

"Probably?"

"Probably. Hopefully. Yes, *hopefully*." She tossed a pair of white socks in my direction. With my right hand, the hand that did not have a catheter stabbing into it, I snatched the socks out of the air effortlessly and quickly pulled them onto my tender feet.

"But will I ever be *cured*?"

"The one thing you need to understand, Hunter, is that there is no cure for depression. There is no one-size-fits-all remedy for depression. There are certainly no magic antidotes. For now, depression can only be treated—not cured. That does not mean that if you are suffering from depression—and I think that maybe you are—that you can't lead a healthy, relatively normal life. You probably can. Things will probably get better for you. You will have to put forth some effort of your own, push yourself, but things will probably get better."

"Probably, huh? Probably …" The word "probably" was starting to bother me a lot, almost as much as the words "for a while." "Jane, why are you so damn uncertain?"

"Because it's still too early to know exactly where you stand emotionally and medically. You'll have to trust me on this one, Hunter. You'll just have to trust me."

I was not sure that I could trust Jane. I knew without a doubt that I could not trust her the same way I trusted Jocelyn. What's more, I was not sure that I wanted to trust her. I did not even know who the woman who called herself Jane really was. All I did know about her was that she carried duffel bags, sorted clothes and answered questions poorly.

"How do you even know that I have depression?" I asked after a few minutes of quiet introspection.

"I don't. However, I do think that is something you need to ask the doctor."

"What kind of depression is it? Is it your basic 'garden variety' of depression? Is it manic depression? Is it temporary, a phase I am going through or something more? What is it? Please tell me. Am I bipolar, a manic-depressive? I need to know. What's more, I deserve to know."

"Yes, Hunter, you do deserve to know. It could be that you are bipolar/manic-depressive. Then again, maybe you are not. At any rate, you need to ask the doctor those questions. Save those questions for the doctor. He will be here soon enough."

"You know, I have been labeled a manic time and again. And, you know, Jane, I thought for years that I was perfectly healthy. But maybe I'm not at all perfect.

"No one is perfect, Hunter, no one."

"Please realize, Jane, that I am not running from the likelihood or the possibility that I might be sick, that I might be mentally ill, that I might actually be a manic-depressive."

"I know, Hunter. And that is very good to hear. Really it is."

Jane had finally finished going through my personal effects. She was now clutching my belt in both hands. I grabbed my favorite baseball cap from the top of the pile. No way was she confiscating that. I pulled the cap down over my forehead as far as it would go. From where I was standing, I saw that I was now able to glimpse the mirror without having to reenter my private bathroom. I also noticed that my favorite baseball cap cast a shadow over my forehead and made my cheeks appear long and hollow, more long and more hollow than usual anyway. Except for the blood on my face and my furrowed brow, I looked like Boris Karloff as Frankenstein's monster. I looked like an exhausted, unsmiling, blood-stained Herman Munster.

"Now, Hunter, is there anything else you'd like to say to me before I go? Is there anything you feel I should know? Anything at all?" She picked up a clipboard from the nightstand nearest her and pulled a pen from the only pocket on her light gray polo shirt. She appeared to be standing "at the ready" like a waitress in a highway diner. I considered her unexpected questions. Her words rang through my head to the very spot the late Lord Byron called "the palace of the soul."

"I think so. I think I have something to say to you."

"Well, what is it? You can tell me. Don't worry. You'll be fine. Tell me whatever you can, whatever you want to tell me. I am here to listen. I am here to help you, Hunter." As she spoke, I could feel her hazel eyes studying me. I sensed their ardor. Despite their unwavering heat, I summoned all of the things I wanted to say to Jane or to anybody else who might ever want to listen to me. I summoned all of the things I wanted to say to all the people who might feel a need to understand, to all of those people out there who might actually *dare* to understand what I had been through so far.

I tried to shove aside all of my lingering bitterness as well as all of my frustration. I wanted to seize this opportunity to grasp Jane's attention and share with her my forlorn tale, the narrative of all of the manic and depressive events I had been a part of over the years, the same events that had been a part of me. I wanted to explain to her my own interpretation of what I had survived during the past two decades, let alone the past few nights. I wanted desperately to compare notes with her and to share with her all of the details of my manic freefall onto Seven Southwest.

All of the sleepless days and sleepless nights came rushing back to me. The pain I associated with those days and nights was there as well. Composites of my depressed life flashed like lightning across the surface of my memory. So many tattered pictures screamed at me. So much damaging evidence of how terrible my undiagnosed illness had truly been stabbed me in the back as if it were a dirty knife and crashed to the floor.

I searched through the piles of mental photographs that were strewn across my life's path like so much confetti, searching for a picture suitable for framing, the one picture that would be worth a thousand words, the one picture I could show to Jane. Unfortunately, there were far too many pictures from which to choose and I did not know where to start, where to begin.

I have never fully comprehended why I thought about him just then, but I did. While Jane stood there waiting for me to communicate, I recalled the solitary man I had seen walking alone down the very heart of Center Street a few hours earlier, sometime after I'd been placed on the psychiatric ward, sometime after the bar crowd had retired for the night. The man with his hands tucked into the pockets of his long overcoat and his head bent low against the nighttime shadows reminded me of both Mr. Leonard Mead, the lone nightwalker from Ray Bradbury's short story "The Pedestrian," and of myself.

Both men—Bradbury's fictional man and the real, unidentified man I had seen moving silently down the deserted street—seemed to have been forgotten by society. Both men were walking alone in the outer chill. Both men were walking alone against the entire population or so it seemed. Maybe that is why I thought of the stranger on the street when I did. That stranger was as silent and lost as Bradbury's pedestrian and me. And, like me, both men were all alone and moving forward into the darkness that was confronting them.

While Jane stood next to my bed waiting for me to say something, I considered the cognitive street I had traveled, the street that had led me to the gates of Lakeshore General and to the series of rooms that comprised Seven Southwest. That street was dark and blanketed by discarded snap-shots of my so-called life, a street that had been under construction for many years now, a street that was accented by flashing red lights, red lights that had always stopped me from moving forward, the same red lights that had always prevented me from progressing or sent me traveling down unforeseen detours.

I realized then that I had been making my way through the mess that constituted my private boulevard or, as I've already stated, through my private underworld for many years now. Even while I had been sick and had probably been suffering from the mental illness manic depression and the highs and lows that came with manic depression, I had been able to survive somehow. And now, I had to forge ahead. I had to move forward, even if moving forward meant stepping into the darkness and speaking to Jane. I had never been very comfortable talking to strangers and yet I knew that I had to tell Jane something, anything, for my own good. I also knew that I did not want to stay silent any longer. I had been silent long enough, you know. And so I ran through a veritable series of red lights and bypassed all of the mental detours along the way and made the decision to speak to Jane.

"Are you scared of me, Jane?" I blurted at last. I have never understood why I asked that particular question. I don't think that particular question had anything to do with what I had been planning to say. Nevertheless, I noticed that Jane took a small step backwards.

"Should I be afraid of you, Hunter?"

"No. Please do not be afraid of me, Jane," I practically begged. In that single moment, as I spoke those words, I concluded that I was more scared of myself than I was scared for Jane, more than Jane was scared of me. I also realized that Jane was a very patient person.

"Then I am not afraid of you, Hunter."

"Okay. Good."

"And is that really all you want to say to me?" This time I did not have to think twice about what to say to Jane. This time, I knew right away what I wanted to say to her.

"Have I lost my mind, Jane?"

"No, Hunter, you haven't lost your mind."

"Then why is this happening to me?"

"I don't know yet, Hunter. I really do not know."

"I feel so alone right now."

"I know you do, Hunter. I know you do. Remind yourself that, no matter how alone you might be feeling, you are not alone by any means."

"Then that is all I have to say to you, Jane."

"Are you sure?"

"Yeah, I'm sure. You can go now and get on with the rest of your day."

Jane did not ask me another question that morning. Instead of questioning me further, she walked out of my room on Seven Southwest and left me alone to sort my jumbled thoughts, which was, I now understand, the very best thing she could have done for me at the time.

CHAPTER 13

✿

I believe that the media often plays a key role in the manner in which a depressed person's views on suicide are shaped, reinforced. Movies and television depict suicide regularly and undoubtedly contribute to a depressed person's overall understanding—or misunderstanding—of suicide. Radio talk shows cover the topic of suicide just as often. They too shape a person's overall outlook where suicide is concerned. The printed media makes reference to suicide, ultimately bolstering in people, I tend to think, the belief that suicide is commonplace. I would certainly argue that, in aggregate, the mediums I have just mentioned frequently lead people to conclude that death by suicide is not as rare an occurrence as it actually is. As for me, it was a book I read at a very young age that managed to do just that, mainly bolster in me an attitude that suicide is indeed quite common.

I was only six years old when I read the children's book "The Five Chinese Brothers" by Claire Huchet Bishop and Kurt Weise for the first time. "The Five Chinese Brothers" is a book I would refer to repeatedly over the years. Perhaps you have read that particular book as well but in case you have not, it is an old Chinese tale about five Chinese brothers who all looked exactly alike, exactly the same right down to their scant clothing. But outside of their matching appearance and attire, each brother had his own unique talent, or ability, an ability that always rescued him from execution, an ability that always saved him from death.

The First Chinese Brother could swallow the sea in order to catch fish for his family to eat. The Second Chinese Brother had an iron neck that prevented him from being beheaded. The Third Chinese Brother could stretch his legs so that he could not be drowned. The Fourth Chinese Brother could not be burned. Lastly, the Fifth Chinese Brother was able to hold his breath indefinitely.

The abilities that enabled the Five Chinese Brothers to survive a death sentence were truly special. Every single time the judge sentenced one of the Five Chinese Brothers to die, the executioner always failed to kill him. For example, when the First Chinese Brother was condemned to have his head cut off, he went home and sent the Second Chinese Brother back to the village in his place on the day of the execution. Remember: the Second Chinese Brother had an iron neck, an iron neck that could withstand a mighty blow from the executioner's sword. Therefore, the executioner could not behead him. The Second Chinese Brother survived his own execution and in doing so had saved the First Chinese Brother from an appointment with death as well. Please understand that each brother could trade places with another look-alike brother and outwit the judge, the executioner and all of the people of the village no matter what the judge's prescribed death sentence was.

I know that "The Five Chinese Brothers" sounds like one hell of a children's story, but I remember the story vividly. I remember the story correctly, accurately. Some thirty odd years after having discovered the story of those five Chinese brothers for the first time, that story is still with me, still making an impression on me, although that impression has changed drastically from the time I was six years old. And yet after all of these years, I can still recall how that story made me feel the first time I read it, how it persuaded me to think that death is a normal part of living, that death is always looming just beyond a person's range of vision, especially the range of vision of a depressed person. Even now, today, right this minute, I can still recall how the story of the Five Chinese Brothers caused me to consider my own mortality. And even now, I can see, quite plainly, how severely the story of the Five Chinese Brothers ultimately served to confuse me.

I should mention that I read "The Five Chinese Brothers" many, many times when I was young. Every single time I reread that classic story, I somehow got to thinking that death by suicide, like the death associated with being executed, or dieing of natural causes even, is a regular "facet" of life's overall process and that death, especially death by suicide, is as common as the flowers and the trees and the sky. Don't ask me how I became so confused or how I managed to confuse both myself and the "issue." I just did. I accepted that distinct "angle," you know, the angle, or view, that suicide is normal and that death by suicide should be an accepted "solution." And so, with that in mind, I simply came to believe, wholeheartedly, that if a judge could legally condemn another man to be executed, then why couldn't I condemn myself to be executed and therefore execute myself? Yes, the book "The Five Chinese Brothers," the story I had read for the first time at the young age of six, had definitely confused me in more ways than one.

Many years after initially reading "The Five Chinese Brothers," I was lying in a hard bed in a cold room on a lonely psychiatric ward staring at a desolate ceiling when I was reminded of those Five Chinese Brothers who could not, would not die no matter what type of death sentence was handed down to them, the Five Chinese Brothers who simply could not be killed, the five brothers who ultimately reminded me of me.

I want to tell you that I thought about the Five Chinese Brothers a lot during the days after I was delivered onto Seven Southwest. Their unusual tale reminded me of all of the occasions in which I had tried willing—yes willing—myself to die. More important, their tale reminded me of the two occasions in which I had actually attempted suicide and had failed. The way I saw it, I was all of the Five Chinese Brothers rolled into one because, in spite of all my efforts to end my own life, I could not execute myself. No matter how hard I tried to terminate my own life, my aim always "missed the mark."

I was still lying in a bed in a numbing room on a psychiatric ward when I remembered that I had missed that very mark at the young age of seven when Lonny Raye, a deranged kid who lived a few houses down the street from me, defied me to jump my bike over a very large mound of dirt near a construction site. I had never been one to turn down a dare. To me, a dare usually represented an opportunity to flirt with death or, better yet, a chance to die outright. So, without any hesitation whatsoever, I accepted Lonny Raye's challenge. Yes, I accepted his dare in hopes that I would die.

Shortly after accepting Lonny's dare, I pedaled as hard and as fast as I could. I aimed my bike at the massive heap of dirt and the makeshift ramp in the distance. I raced toward the horizon and disaster. That is when the horizon line seemed to undergo a change. The horizon line blurred and, just like that, misfortune seemed inevitable. As countless images of colorless scenery rapidly flashed by me, I realized—not for the first time—that I honestly did not care whether I survived the jump or not. I honestly did not care if I self-destructed in midair or if I slammed into the concrete and cracked open my skull and died on the spot. Truthfully, I hoped that I would do just that.

Seconds before I was thrown from my bike and only moments before I smashed into terra firma, I saw a sickening smile creep across Lonny's wicked face in my peripheral vision. I felt myself smile, too. I saw the planet rushing up to meet me but I did not try to break my fall. I caved instead. In the single fleeting moment before I collided with solid ground, I collapsed emotionally and I gave up on both life and living for what seemed like the final time. I was as ready to die as I had ever been and as I somersaulted through the air I prayed that the impending crash landing would be enough to kill me once and for all. But, unfortunately, the crash landing was not enough to end my ever-present pain. My smile disappeared in an instant. My once-flawless smile was now permanently disfigured and I was still alive, bleeding, but alive. I had flirted with death and I knew that, above all else, another opportunity to die, another opportunity to kill myself, had been wasted.

I sat up on the unforgiving mattress, checked my bearings and rolled out of bed. I moved to the recliner and stared at the television screen that was a troubling gray-black color. I stopped myself from thinking about the Five Chinese Brothers and the deranged Lonny Raye and his dare and my broken smile and tried to focus on the present. Both Jocelyn and Jane had been gone for quite some time and I was now glad to be alone. My wrists were still on fire and I still had a burning sensation where the catheter pierced the skin of my left hand, pumping N-acetylcysteine, or NAC, into my bloodstream in order that the production of glutathione, a powerful liver-detoxifying antioxidant, might be enhanced to ward off the toxins that were now "roaming freely" in my bloodstream. I do not know why I thought about my dad and the Vietnam War just then, feeling the way I did and all but, as I stared at the gray-black television screen from my vantage point in the recliner, I did just that.

I was eight years old when my dad returned from Vietnam for the first time in three long years. It was the summer of 1975. President Ford had called the Vietnam War "finished," and I believed that there was at least a small chance that my dad's long-awaited homecoming might make my own hellish life seem more bearable, more normal. You could say that I was hoping for some "mental stability" in my life. But despite the actuality that my dad had returned from a war that had always perplexed me to no end, my underlying depression continued to manifest itself. My desire to die was still present, still seated in the back of my troubled mind, eating away at me little by little, bit by bit. The so-called end of the Vietnam War and my dad's return had not extinguished my inner sorrow, as I had hoped they would. I was still sick with depression, doubtless that I might actually be beyond help.

Although President Ford had declared that the war had finally come to an end and my dad was now home for good, I was still fighting an internal war of my own, a war with depression I suspected I might never ever win. Therefore, shortly after my dad's return, I made up my mind that if I could not win the war that hemorrhaged inside of me outright, I at least wanted to win a modicum of inner peace and a sense of normalcy badly, more than anything. A new era had been ushered in and times were changing. Why couldn't I change with them?

The summer of 1975 was a tough one for me. My moods were fluctuating badly and I was able to discern that my moodiness was pissing off my family and many, many other people who were closet to me. My dad's homecoming had brought me no relief from my anguish. In fact, his homecoming had only served to worsen my distress because I had observed firsthand the awful manner in which he had been mistreated by the locals for having served time in a war he had never wanted to be a part in the first place. I looked on helplessly as my dad was shunned by the very people he had once regarded as friends. But my dad maintained that he had done his job in Vietnam, the job he had been asked to do and he acted as if nothing were out of the ordinary, as if nothing had even phased him.

My dad was simply doing his newest job, acting as if he was not bothered by the verbal jabs of others, and I was doing mine by acting as if I was not bothered by depression. Despite my proliferating depression and the "rough treatment" my dad was receiving, I was acting as "normal" as I possibly could, making every effort to appear as normal as the next guy. As a young man sickened by depression, I was astute enough to know that acting normal truly was my job, especially if I was to avoid being shunned by my contemporaries as my dad had been.

The sordid pictures of my dad being constantly ignored that were stored in my mind's photo album, as well as the sordid pictures of the fall of Hue and Saigon that were being replayed regularly on the evening news and depicted in the oversized pages of many magazines that long summer, haunted me as violently as did my feelings of depression. Those pictures invaded my hurting self while I was awake and, even worse, while I was trying to sleep, causing my feelings of depression to intensify. Those pictures invaded my life and interfered with my thinking and terrorized my outlook. Maybe that is why the summer of 1975 was the same summer I asked my dad if he had ever killed anyone while on his tour of duty in Vietnam. Maybe that is why I asked my dad one day during the summer of 1975 if he had ever contemplated turning his M-16 on himself. Two very, very callow questions to ask, even for a severely depressed eight-year-old boy I know.

You should be made aware of the fact that my dad never answered those two questions. Actually, he never shared with me any of his experiences of his tour in Vietnam. I suppose he had his reasons. I just wanted to know what those reasons were. I wanted the scoop, the full story. I wanted the facts because here was a man who, I adamantly believed, had been closer to death's door than I had ever been and I envied him for it. Nevertheless, my dad just sat there in his oversized chair, as silent and unmoving as a stone sculpture. He closed his eyes. I left the room. I never mentioned the Vietnam War or any other war to him ever again.

Suddenly, the gray-black television screen melts into nothing. I have managed to fall asleep again and yet I am fully aware that I am lost in the vastness of a dream, a dream I have experienced too many times before, a very twisted dream from which there seems to be no possibility of escaping. The incredibly vivid dream is of my dad and I. We are lost somewhere in the jungles of Vietnam. Try as I might, I can not shake that fucking dream. No matter how hard I try to dream a decent dream and no matter how hard I concentrate on sleeping a restful sleep the dream starring my dad and I stalks my slumbering conscious repeatedly.

So there I am, a sad and perplexed and depressed little eight-year-old, lost in a dream of which I want no part. I am standing with my dad in a silent, unfamiliar region somewhere in Vietnam I believe. We are facing one another. Only a few feet of humid air separates us. As I stare at him, I am startled to find that there is a hole in the very center of his right hand. Blood as dark and thick as chocolate syrup gushes from the gruesome wound. For some reason, a reason I have never been able to discover, my dad holds his wounded hand in front of his chapped lips. Behind all of the chocolate blood, I see his mouth through the hole in his hand. His lips are moving, but there is no sound. No matter how hard I concentrate, I cannot hear a single goddamn sound.

That is when I reach out to touch him. And that is also when he begins to fade away. Very slowly he is becoming one with the trees, one man trapped within the dense jungle. I want very badly to free him. I want to tear him away from the perils of a war I have only read about or glimpsed on the evening news, a place that I frequently see in my gloomy sleep visions, but I cannot free him from that fucking jungle, or from the fucking war, or from my goddamn dreams because my arms aren't long enough. I come up short. Again, I miss the mark.

Then, after enduring so much deafening quiet, I hear my dad shouting at me. Yes, he is shouting at me. His shouts sound very much like the night screams I will hear years later, the screams of the people who are whiling away their days and nights on Seven Southwest, unintelligible, uncertain and indefinite. My dad's words are as useless to me as they are unclear and, no matter how closely I listen, I cannot make out what it is he is trying to say. Yes, his words sound foreign.

I do get the impression that he is trying to warn me about something. Yeah, that's it; my dad is trying to share with me a warning, a message only he seems to comprehend and, as I stare into the television screen and dream away what is left of the morning, I suspect that his mysterious message has something to do with my depression and, maybe, the causes of my suicidal behavior. However, I really can't be positive, so I am left with a general understanding, an understanding that his cryptic message contains clues to my suffering I may never decipher.

His screams continue to echo, as he recedes into the jungle's depths. Then, just like that, he disappears from view altogether and the dream-world falls completely silent again. Yes, all sound is muted. I feel drained and discouraged. I feel vacant inside. I awaken from the eerie dream feeling lost and, yes, alone. That is when it occurs to me that the painful dreams of my dad and I standing in the Vietnamese jungle together always rob me of meaningful sound when it is meaningful sound I need the most. There is dead air when I pine for the clamor of life, when I yearn for sensible answers regarding my own depressed life and, more than anything else, the answers I believe will fully expose the enemy that is my elusive depression. The warped dream of my dad and I trapped in the Vietnamese jungle is devoid of the color of blood and ultimately shows me the blackness that is my bleak, bleak existence. More than anything else, though, my arcane dreams of my dad and I standing opposite one another in the jungle leave me feeling more disheartened and panic-stricken than I am when I am fully awake.

CHAPTER 14

❁

"So how are you doing, Hunter?" Jane has returned as promised. The television screen is now a disturbing gray-black color again, my nap and the perplexing dream officially over—at least for the time being.

"I think that I am doing okay considering. Anyway, I believe I am ready to go home," I respond, still running from the likelihood that my acetaminophen overdose was as serious as Jane had initially advised, seemingly lacking any real interest in how Jane might react to such a statement.

"Well, at least you are smiling," she says, ignoring my stance that I am ready to leave the hospital once and for all. Smiling? That is news to me. I do not feel as if I am smiling, but maybe I am. Maybe. Maybe I am smiling on the outside, on the surface, but, on the inside, below the surface, I am doing my best to conceal my pain. And maybe I am as unsmiling as a dead body. After all, I am still suicidal.

"So tell me, Hunter, on a scale of one to ten, ten being best, how would you rate your mood right now?"

"A five or maybe a six, I guess," I say, intentionally inflating my score in order that I might get myself released sooner than later.

"Okay ... is there anything you need then?"

"What would you say if I told you that I haven't eaten in three days?"

"I'd feed you. You must be starving."

"Yes."

"Then I'll order something for you. I assume that you'd like something to drink also?"

"Yes, I would. I'm thirsty as hell."

"Then continue to rest and I will be back in a few."

Again and not for the last time, I am left alone with my severed thoughts and the gray-black television screen. I am left alone with various mental pictures of my past life, the moving pictures from my childhood. I am alone with my racing thoughts when a clone of my younger self steps forward from the pictures of that past life and dominates the television screen entirely.

I was only nine years old when I had what I now consider was my first true "brush with death." I was in the backyard playing near the swimming pool. I had convinced myself that I could fly and I was turning rapidly in the tightest of circles, my arms extended from my body at near-perfect forty-five degree angles. I was pretending that I was the stressed pilot of a United States Army helicopter that had been struck by a rocket-propelled grenade, or RPG. The direct hit by the imaginary RPG had sent my imaginary helicopter spiraling helplessly and hopelessly out of control somewhere over the barren landscape of my parents' backyard. It was just a game, typical child's play. It was a game I played by myself on a regular basis. But little did I know how soon the game would end—forever.

Time ticked away and I continued spinning, getting dizzier and dizzier. It was not long before I became so dizzy I stumbled headfirst into the deep end of the swimming pool. I was no longer operating in pretend mode; I understood that the game was over. Real, genuine water was engulfing me and, within a matter of seconds, I was drowning fast.

I had always hated the water. I was a poor swimmer and, what's more, I had never been in the deep end of the pool before and now I was, sinking closer to death with every breath that escaped my tortured lungs. I was staring into death's passageway, sinking into the one place I had often longed to be during the most depressed periods of my life.

Why I reached for the pool's tiled edge that day I cannot say. I should have let myself drown, but I did not. Instead of giving up on life, I pulled my small figure from the cool water. I saved myself. Another opportunity to die had been wasted and I felt like a cat who has just used one of its nine lives. I felt what it must be like to be the Third Chinese Brother, the one Chinese brother who could not be drowned.

From that moment forward, whenever I went near that damn swimming pool, or any other swimming pool for that matter, I trembled and twitched. I shook from the frustration of knowing that I should have let myself drown. I shook from the frustration that I should have let myself die. Even then I was sure that I would not have another opportunity to die for many, many years to come.

"Hello, Hunter. How are you doing today?" An attractive brown-haired woman walked directly into my flashback and into my room carrying what turned out to be a ham and cheese sandwich, a small bag of Doritos and a wax paper cup I prayed contained caffeine on one of those plastic trays you see in a school cafeteria or at a cheap buffet. The pretty brunette looked like my runaway angel. The resemblance was incredible and I quickly snapped a cognitive photo of her for my ever-growing collection.

"Can you stay and talk to me?" I asked her without thinking, without hesitation. "I need to talk to someone, anyone. Do you have a boyfriend?" I was suddenly stating out loud every thought that was crossing my overworked mind without taking the time to process such thoughts before speaking them. It was extremely embarrassing and awkward.

"Yes, I have a boyfriend, Hunter," she smiled not at me, but for me I think. I surmised that she was feeling sorry for me. I was suddenly uncomfortable. "And I apologize, Hunter, but I cannot stay," she added.

"Well, what's your name then?"

"Pam." She smiled once more, as she placed the tray on a small table that now spanned the recliner like a miniature bridge. Then she turned and left the room. I never saw her again.

I devoured the ham and cheese sandwich and the Doritos and drank the Coke before Jane reentered my room a minute or two after Pam had departed.

"Feeling any better?"

"Yes," was all I said. Then I made a silent vow that I would never again ask another female if she had a boyfriend.

Jane turned on the television and left my room with another promise that she would be back soon. The local news was just beginning and I wondered if the account of my second suicide attempt in nearly eleven years would be the top story. I listened with undaunted concern until a meteorologist came on and gave his seven day forecast, a forecast that called for more low temperatures and several inches of snow before the end of the week, and then I quickly turned off the t.v. The screen went from colorful to colorless in a millisecond. This time, however, the television screen took on the appearance of an imposing window, a window with a view into my most recent past.

Almost instantly, I saw another ghost of my troubled self standing within the borders of that fucking screen. This time, however, the vision was one of me as a suicidal twenty-seven-year-old man and not a seven-year-old boy crashing his bike or an eight-year-old lost in the denseness of a Vietnamese jungle, or a drowning nine-year-old. I saw, in that goddamn screen, my twenty-seven-year-old self standing on the balcony of my one room efficiency apartment, four floors above the ground, watching a bald eagle circling low over the lake as a police cruiser pulled up in front of the building. I studied for a moment the officer who, I knew, had come expressly for me goose-step his way up the stone walkway like a lone enemy soldier before I was able to slip back into my apartment undetected.

Once inside my sparsely furnished apartment, I contemplated what I was going to do next. I thought that I might try climbing down the fire escape and hiding in the bushes that lined the parking lot on three sides. I pictured my body attired in military fatigues, crouched low behind the shrubbery, my face dabbed in camouflage colors, an olive drab helmet adorned with small green branches secured to it strapped to my head. I scrapped that plan because I owned no fatigues or face paint and the only helmet I possessed was an old leather football helmet that had once belonged to a great uncle who had committed suicide long before I was born. In addition, I did not think that I could possibly make it down the fire escape without being found out. I would have to think of something else. I would have to think of a plan.

I remember thinking if only I could stretch my legs, as The Third Chinese Brother had done when the executioner had tried to drown him in the ocean, I would step right off the edge of that goddamn balcony and, in a single fluid motion, step over the stream and disappear into the lake. I would stand in the lake with my head just above the turbulent waves until the officer finally gave up on me. Then again, maybe I would just fill my pockets with stones as author Virginia Woolf had done and plunge into the lake's deepest waters and drown myself. A police officer was banging on my door and there I stood, manic and suicidal as hell, wishing that I was one of The Five Chinese Brothers or the late Virginia Woolf. God how I needed to grasp a hold of my life that was on the verge of reeling violently out of control and face some semblance of reality. God how I needed to face the truth and accept the consequences of my terrible actions of the previous night, the very actions that had ultimately made me a wanted man.

I do not know why, but even before I had a criminal record, the police had always upset me. I had nothing to hide as they say. I was guilty of nothing and yet the police still upset me to no end. The police had bothered me for as long as I could remember. I can still recall how profoundly the police officer who came to visit my kindergarten class one day bothered me. I can still recall that he had given me a turn at sitting in the back seat of his cruiser for a couple of minutes as if I were the "bad guy," as if I were America's most wanted five-year-old. Way back then, my first encounter with the police had left me feeling ill-at-ease. Maybe my uneasiness had something to do with the fact that I had been seated in that damn cruiser for only a few seconds before I envisioned my adult self handcuffed and stowed away in the cramped back seat of a police cruiser on my way to a real jail, a scene I believed very strongly would one day come to fruition.

A loud, forceful knock on the door to my apartment and I was suddenly caught up in the moment. I considered hiding in my empty closet from the police officer who was now waiting for me to show myself. There I would crouch, trembling and alone, holding my breath indefinitely, as only the Fifth Chinese Brother was able to do, until the officer finally left but, of course, I did not possess an ability such as that, so I considered suicide instead. For what seemed like the billionth time in my life, I tried willing my mind and my body to shut down, to stop functioning altogether and die. I imagined my own death and thought about my own funeral and even wrote my own brief obituary on the yellowed pages of my mind and pleaded with God that my heart might finally explode, but my mind and my body resisted all commands to execute itself. God ignored my frantic pleas and I continued to breathe and suffer the same as always. Try as I might, I could not willfully execute myself. Like each one of the five Chinese brothers, I could not, would not die. I simply could not put myself to death and end my misery.

Seconds after I had tried willing myself to die, it occurred to me that a gun would definitely do the trick. I made a mental note to buy a gun as soon as possible. Now there was an idea. Yes, a gun was definitely the answer, especially when nothing else had ever worked for me. My own death, my own suicide, would outsmart any police officer and end my suffering to boot. No one—not even the fucking police—would be able to touch me then. Even the damn stalker that is depression would be unable to catch me because, as far as I knew, not a single one of the five Chinese brothers could outrun a bullet. And neither could I.

The door to my small world vibrated violently when the officer pounded on it a second time. I stood motionless, as motionless as I could under the circumstances. It was much too late to hide in the closet and hold my breath. It was much too late to climb down the fire escape and hide in the bushes or in the lake. It was much too late to drown myself. And finally, it was much too late to buy a gun.

It was while that goddamn police officer pounded on the door that I brought to mind the occasion my parents had taken me out to dinner to celebrate my thirteenth birthday. As the officer stood in the hallway waiting for me to surrender myself, I remembered the fateful evening in which I became a teenager, the fateful evening I discovered just how bizarre my depressed inner life truly was.

On the evening of my thirteenth birthday, an evening that should have been special for me, my parents ordered salads and steaks and made small talk. I am not exaggerating when I say that their eyes shone with unparalleled admiration when they looked at me. I had no doubt that my parents loved me. Each word they spoke was accented with a smile. It was obvious that they were proud of whom I was, of the man they expected me to be one day, of the man I strongly suspected I would *never* live to become.

But my attention was soon diverted. You see, the four men who were seated at a large round table just behind my parents were now holding my attention. My parents were still talking, but their words were lost upon me. I was preoccupied by the actuality that I could see the ivory skeletons of the men seated across the room from me. I saw those four strangers as skinless frames of men, and I was terrified.

"Hunter, what is it?" My mom had always been the first person to notice when something seemed awry or out of place. Fooling her this time was going to be difficult.

"Could I please have a sip of your wine?" I asked, trying like hell to distract her, trying like hell to distract myself. It was the best I could do on such short notice.

"No, you may not, young sir," my mom said with a frustrated sigh and a displeased look on her face.

"Then how about a sip of yours, Dad?" I asked, mindful that the four skeletons had also heard my odd request for wine and were now laughing at me.

"Maybe next year," my dad said at last. Like the four skeletons, my parents were laughing at me now, too, but I was not laughing at all.

The four skeletons seated at the table behind my parents had lit cigars and I noticed that I could see the smoke entering their lungs each time they inhaled and exiting their lungs each time they exhaled. No matter how hard I tried, I could not shake the imagery of those goddamn smiling, smoking skeletons. I glanced away from them several times, as if I were driving at night on a two-lane highway, temporarily blinded by the glaring headlights of oncoming traffic, but each time my gaze returned to those otherworldly guests, I saw their shiny skeletons the same as before.

I saw those fucking skeletons again and again and again that night, even after my parents had paid the bill and we had left the restaurant. I concluded without any reservations that I was still depressed. I concluded that I was seeing the bones of depression itself. I also concluded that I was still seeing life in its most basic terms just as I had done when I was three years old, just as I had done when I had pictured for the first time the nurses and doctors working feverishly to save me from my depression.

Finally, the enemy police officer stopped pounding on the door. I knew, though, that he had not quit on me. I knew that he would be back soon enough. Still, I stood motionless. I did not know what I was going to do next. I was stumped and I knew that I now needed a plan more than ever before. But a plan would have to wait because just then there was another knock on the door.

"Hunter? Are you there? It's Lisa. Open up!" someone called out. Then there was another knock on my apartment door and then another. If it really was my neighbor Lisa who was now doing the knocking, she did not knock with the same force the police officer had employed. Still I was afraid to move. I thought, *What if it is a trap?* Then the person who was claiming to be Lisa knocked a fourth and a fifth time, punctuating each knock by calling out my name. I stepped toward the balcony and peered out over the railing from which I wanted to dive headfirst. The police officer's cruiser was gone.

"Hunter, please open up. It's just me, Lisa. Don't worry, Hunter, I'm alone." Today, I do not know how I gathered the necessary strength or the necessary courage but I made my way to the door and opened it with extreme caution. Yes, it was Lisa standing there by herself in the brightly lit hallway.

"It's just me," Lisa repeated. I promptly ushered Lisa inside and slammed the door. I turned on the only lamp I owned. I inspected Lisa and her shadow under the dim light. I noticed that she looked as if she had been crying for quite some time. Even through the lenses of her eyeglasses, I could see little red circles under her eyes. Those red circles looked like miniscule bruises.

"So what happened to you?" I asked, knowing all too well that I really did not give a damn what had caused her tears. Lisa touched lightly the corner of each eye with a tissue. Her mascara was smeared across the expanse of her cheeks and across the bridge of her nose.

"My dog died."

"Oh, I see," I said without any apparent emotion. I moved away from Lisa and turned my body at an angle. I was trying to keep one eye on Lisa and one eye on the street below. Lisa lit a cigarette. For whatever reason, only my good friend Tim ever smoked in my apartment, but, for the first time, I did not care if Lisa smoked in my apartment or not. I think that, at the time, I preferred it. There is, I often think, something quite comforting about the smell of a lit cigarette, even to a nonsmoker, although I believe that the majority of nonsmokers would never admit it. "Oh. Oh, you have a dog? I didn't know," I said, devoid of any sentiment whatsoever. I reached for the only ashtray I owned, an ashtray Tim had left there, and handed it to Lisa. Then, more paranoid than ever, I turned away from Lisa completely. I was now focusing on the street with both eyes, giving it my full attention.

"Well, my parents' dog anyway."

"Oh I see," I said for the second time, detached, my thoughts preoccupied by the vision of the fucking police officer who was hunting me and by the dense clouds that were moving in from across the lake, casting the blackest shadows onto the street below. The sky was definitely threatening rain, the kind of rain that only depresses.

"Hunter, are you listening to me?"

"I'm sorry, Lisa," I said, glancing away from the darkening waters and the darkening street and staring at Lisa's small, round, make-up-smudged face with both eyes.

I do not think that Lisa heard me. She was looking out the window now. It was obvious that Lisa was staring at the blue-black waters of the lake and the blue-black mountains that rose to meet the upper limits in the distance. It was obvious that Lisa was searching that place high above, the very place Willa Cather had articulately referred to as "the roof of the world." Lisa was, I knew, searching the narrow line where the earth and the sky were joined together. She was searching beyond the surging whitecaps, as if she were waiting for her dead dog to step out of the heavens alive and well. Lisa's eyes filled with tears. Yes, death is always looming, even when it is just a dog that dies.

"You know, Lisa, when I was fourteen, I took a job one summer washing dishes and bussing tables at a restaurant on the beach, in a restaurant that is now long gone. I saved my tips and wages for weeks on end and bought a puppy."

"What are you getting at?"

"Nothing. Just making conversation, sympathizing with you I guess and letting you know that I can identify with what it is you are going through right now. At least I think that I can."

"Oh."

"That dog died of a heat stroke while we were out hiking one day, before he was even a year old. He was still a pup, and he died so suddenly, so painfully. I never should have taken a puppy on a hike in the mountains. I guess you could say that I know now what I did not know then, and that is that puppies can't always stand the heat."

"That is a horrible story, Hunter. Truly it is. And I'm sorry that your dog died that way."

"His death tore me to pieces. I felt as if I had let him down in some terrible way. I felt that I was solely responsible for his death. To be truthful with you, Lisa, I felt as if I had murdered him. That is how I felt. I could not view his premature death any other way. And, you know, I still can't."

"But you can't blame yourself. It isn't right for you to think that way. It isn't healthy for you to think like that."

"But I *do* think that way. And I always will. I always will." Again, I was reminded of my belief that death is always looming. I also recalled that it was Aristotle who said, "It is the mark of an educated mind to entertain an idea without accepting it." Standing there in my dark apartment with Lisa, I concluded that Aristotle was incorrect. Aristotle did not watch my dog die.

"So what's wrong anyway, Hunter?" Lisa inquired at last, changing the subject, as I knew she eventually would. "A police officer was here just now, knocking on your door. Did you know that, Hunter?" Her tears had disappeared, evaporated.

"Yes, I know."

"So what's up then?" Lisa had always been one to gossip. She was, I realized, gathering new information for her grapevine. But she was the last person I was going to trust. I knew all too well why the police officer had been there and I was not going to share any information with Lisa or with anyone else.

"Nothing, Lisa. Nothing is up," I said after a brief silence.

"Are you sure," she pried. I did not answer her a second time. Instead, I looked out over the water, the water in which I wanted to hide or drown myself and searched for the bald eagle I had seen gliding over the whitecaps minutes earlier.

"Hunter, it's starting to rain." Lisa had always had a flair for stating the obvious. "Maybe I'll go now."

"Yes, I know it is," I responded, still staring out through the mist and the fog and the falling rain that seemed to represent my troubled life, still staring at the lake as best I could, attempting all the while to avoid the sly smile of Lisa, the resident gossip, and locate the eagle one last time. But the eagle was gone, instinctively driven away by the rain I suppose. And just like that, Lisa was gone, too.

I never saw Lisa leave my apartment that day. I don't think she ever said goodbye to me. Maybe she did and maybe she did not. However, I do recollect the loneliness that crept into my body as I stood in the center of my apartment all by myself while I began plotting my second suicide attempt in little more than a decade, the very attempt that would ultimately land me on a psychiatric ward at Lakeshore General.

I knew that it was my brother John banging on the door to my apartment this time. I knew why he had come and I was not looking forward to hearing his version of the manic crimes I had committed against my former girlfriend, Kate, the previous night. Hearing John describe why the law now wanted me would release me from my semi-safe state of semi-denial and I was somewhat comfortable there, in denial I mean. I froze, waiting for John to leave, just as I had done when the police officer had pounded on the door.

"Hunter!" John's baritone voice thundered through the wooden door and into my apartment like a shot from a cannon. I leaned forward and eyed his red car parked in the same space where I had seen the police officer's cruiser parked.

"What, John?" I mumbled to myself and only to myself, conscious that if I had my way John and Lisa and the fucking police department and everyone else I knew would never ever hear me mumble another word.

"*Hun-ter!*" John shouted at the door much more loudly the second time. From inside the blank walls of my apartment, I could hear the stressed syllables of my first name echo throughout the stairwell. "Call your father, Hunter! It's urgent!" John shouted. And then his voice was hushed, the door to my apartment no longer vibrated and the disturbing echo was gone.

From my own eagle's nest high above the shore of the lake, I watched John's red car speed away from the curb through the fog and the falling rain. I wasted no time stepping to the door. Once there, I double-checked the locks, giving both deadbolts a good try, before I dropped the chain securely into place. No one would be able to get to me now. Then again, I had just one problem: I needed to call my dad. My only brother had said that it was "urgent."

Nightfall had finally arrived when I made up my mind to call my dad. Yes, I knew that I had to call my dad. I now had to be, as John would have said to me if given the opportunity, a "real man." But being a real man had never been all that easy for me, especially considering how sickened by depression I had been throughout the years and considering how I had run away from every single challenge that had ever come my way.

"Hello, Dad. It's me, Hunter. John said that it was urgent that I call you. What's wrong, Dad? Is it mom? Is it her heart?"

"Kate called us today, Hunter." *Oh that fucking two-faced, conniving bitch*, I thought.

"And?" I asked him, waiting for the one response I knew was coming.

"Kate told your mom and I that you kicked in the door to her apartment and claims that you spray painted her car last night. Is that true, Hunter? Did you do those things to that girl?" My dad had called Kate, my on-and-off girlfriend of more than four years, "that girl." I thought it rather strange of him to refer to her that way.

"That's not true!" I shouted, pure hatred for Kate and myself now seething throughout my tired head, as I lied to my own dad for what just might prove to be the last time ever. "I would never do those things!" I yelled at him, slamming the phone down full force, ripping the cord out of the wall and crying violently, crying for my slaughtered ego, aware that the jig was up, knowing that I would soon be caught and that the police would soon own me like it or not.

CHAPTER 15

❦

Even today, so many years after the fact, and as each word courses forth from my rested, medicated mind and becomes one with the electric glow of the computer monitor, I realize that I was in an unfamiliar cognitive locale the night I hung up on my dad. I now understand that I was imprisoned in an "altered state of consciousness" that evening, the very evening my subdued self slipped out of my body and out into the pouring rain and proceeded to walk a straight line to the nearest convenience store as if it were on a mission, the mission of a lifetime. Looking back, it is painfully obvious to me that I was trapped in the suicidal dimension Jocelyn would speak of only hours later, not long before I would follow Jane down the long corridor and through the thick doors to a territory that was new to me, to that territory that would house me for three extended weeks, to the place known, quite simply, as Seven Southwest.

How naive I must sound when I insist that life just beyond my troubled vision seemed to be moving in slow motion that rainy day, but I know of no other way to describe the way life was happening to me at the time. And even after I had stepped out of the steady rain and back into my apartment, my suicidal thoughts were idling at the slowest, most relaxing of speeds. Then my suicidal thoughts stopped moving forward altogether. Very suddenly, I had become frozen in a sort of "zone," a zone I did not fully recognize or comprehend at the time. That is something I can remember quite clearly, you know, being so "zoned out" by my preoccupation with my own death, by my own aspirations to commit suicide. Except for my sheer desire to be dead, nothing else mattered to me. Nothing.

Once I had returned to my apartment, I turned off the lamp and stood in the semi-glimmer of a streetlight, a glimmer that had managed to find its way into my private domain as if it were a shadow looking for a body to cling to. The faint glimmer of light warmed me even though I was rain-soaked right through my clothes to my skin. And even though I was soaked through and through, I still recall that I was really feeling quite warm on the inside. And I was at ease, content. I have not experienced an inner peace such as that one since that crucial, life-changing day, the one day that would forever alter my extremely afflicted existence.

As if I were acting on cue, I picked up a photograph that had been gathering dust since the day I moved into my apartment. I tilted the photograph that captured a lost era toward the incandescence of the lone streetlight. There I stood, studying the photograph, the slightly faded depiction of my mom as a child playing near the shore of the lake and I thought, *How strange it is that my mom will outlive me.* I held the photograph in both hands, practically caressing it. I held onto that photograph for several minutes before I placed it in an empty drawer and gently pushed the drawer shut.

I believe that my heartbeat slowed down a beat or two even before I choked down all of the acetaminophen capsules I had purchased at the convenience store with the last dollars I had to my name. A calmness I had never experienced before—not even during my first suicide attempt—took refuge in my body as I positioned myself at my desk in my one-room world intent on stealing my own soul like a twisted burglar.

"Hunter?" The unmistakable voice of a human being calling out to me from somewhere far, far away in the hallway. "Hunter, are you there? Are you okay, Hunter?"

"Yes, I am fine," I whispered to myself. "I am fine." Then the voice was gone and my depressed surroundings turned silent again.

Soon after I had swallowed all of the acetaminophen capsules, I stretched out on my bed to rest for what I believed would be forever. I felt strongly that this time, the second time, the second attempt on my own life, would definitely be the last. And as I lie there bleeding inside of the mental haze that shrouded me, I thought of the terrible crimes I had committed the night before, during the very night in which I officially became a criminal, the same night in which my mental illness, the mental illness that was still undiagnosed, became its ugliest ever.

Terrible pictures of the crimes I had actually committed the previous night clung to me and, as I have already told you, no matter how hard I tried, I could not shake them. Those awful pictures would not go away. Those goddamn pictures pestered me incessantly. They stayed with me no matter how hard I tried evicting them from my conscious and I knew deep down that I would be carrying those pictures with me long after I was dead.

It is true that I smiled as the last moments of my life faded to the darkest black, as sharply defined visions of me vandalizing Kate's car and kicking in the door to her apartment floated through my head and came to rest within the walls of my frazzled brain. It is also true that I smiled a smile of "pure relief" as I endeavored to block out those fucking visions and failed. Those visions sickened me so severely that I apologized to God for all of the bad things I had ever done, especially those bad things I had recently done to Kate. And still I smiled.

While I did feel extreme regret for the unforgivable crimes I had perpetrated against my ex-girlfriend, I smiled because I was no longer a trespasser on her property or anywhere else for that matter. I should tell you that I also laughed. As I lie in my bed in the dark, I laughed. I laughed because I had concluded that the police would have no need whatsoever for my fingerprints or my mug shot any longer. Then I laughed because I knew, without a doubt, that I was on the verge of outsmarting, of escaping, my depressive emotions and my suicidal dementia. To me, that was the best joke of all.

I am not exaggerating when I tell you that I do not know how long I slept the dreamless sleep that followed my overdosing or how close I came to slipping into a coma but I did awaken that night. And upon awakening, I touched my hands to my sweaty forehead and felt the sensation of warm blood trickling into my eyes. I reached for the lamp and knocked it to the floor by accident. I heard the lamp's only bulb explode upon impact.

I stood in front of the window, a window that appeared to have no glass in it whatsoever. I peered out that opening in search of the lake and the stream that were usually swathed in grades of silver by the light of the moon. This time, though, the lake and the stream and the moon were not there. The lake and the stream and the moon had vanished as if by the hand of a cruel magician. Only the faint glimmer of the streetlight and the dark line of its long shadow remained.

Next, I listened intently for the distinct rhythm of the stream I could no longer see, the stream that progressed into the lake from just beyond the property line, from the point where the woods edged the town, but I heard no sound at all. I could not hear the stream I had been listening to for so many, many years. I could not hear the stream that flowed through the very nucleus of town and through the very nucleus of my memory and that disturbed me to no end. The slight commotion of that rolling stream was gone now and I heard absolutely nothing, except for the rapid beating of my heart and the humming and buzzing sounds of my own brain trying to solve equations it had never before computed.

Then there was another indistinct rap on the door to my apartment. I had another unwanted visitor. I surmised that the person who was doing the knocking was not the police officer who had knocked sometime before I had fallen asleep, but Lisa instead. Then another bothersome knock ruptured in my aching ears. Yes, I was certain that Lisa was back. The goddamn gossip simply could not stay away.

"It's me, Hunter, Lisa," I managed to hear her call out over the din of my irregular heartbeat and the humming and buzzing sounds that were reverberating loudly inside of my clogged head. That is when I prayed to god that I might actually be left alone to die in peace.

"I know it's you, Lisa," I whispered to myself. "Who else would it be?"

"Hunter, can you hear me?" Lisa called out.

I froze. I stood motionless in front of that fucking window, a drugged and bleeding mannequin waiting for Lisa to leave me alone, my mind and my body clinging to my life for reasons I simply could not decode. Hours seemed to pass but, in reality, only seconds had expired because it was after the third or fourth or fifth knock that Lisa finally gave up on me. And now I knew that I was officially abandoned, lost in seclusion, lost in a troubling universe that had always been much too brutal for me. Just like that, I was standing all alone on the barren landscape of my personal wasteland, my private war zone, my body stranded beneath tiers of my own blood, waiting for whatever might happen next, wanting desperately to die, aware that I might actually continue to live. I was in limbo. Clearly, I was waiting for death to send me away to heaven or for death to lock me away in hell or wherever it is a man is destined to go when he takes his own life.

I leaned forward into the shadows of an unwanted dawn, accompanied by the dull grayish hues that are a dreary early morning sunrise when death is looming nearby. Slivers of glass that were once a light bulb sliced into my bare feet as I stumbled into the bathroom. Once there, I ripped my jeans from my body and threw them to the floor. Then I stepped up to the white sink and vomited and pissed into it. My urine seeped out of me in disturbing shades of violet.

I was not prepared to see my reflection just then because I was not even supposed to be alive. Be that as it may, I braced myself for what was coming next and peered into the mirror that was mounted above the sink, the sink that now reeked of my own vomit and urine. I stared into a face that was the blood-covered mask of demise, a face that simply was not my own.

I can tell you that I looked savage, inhuman. My high forehead was "painted" the darkest shades of crimson I had ever seen, as were my thin, angular cheeks. My eyelids were also painted several shades of disturbing crimson and my eyelashes were colored by a "mascara" so thick I knew I could not wipe it away just then no matter how I tried. More blood stained my lips and teeth. The blood that had drizzled onto my once-pallid face and into my mouth while I had been sleeping signified death to me more than anything I had ever known. Just like that, I had an idea of what death tasted like. Let me say that death tasted harsh and cruel and very, very bitter.

I stepped away from my own glossy representation and made my way back to my bed, more shards of glass cutting sharply into my sock-less feet, my body aching severely. I plunged into my bed, expecting to die any second from the toxicity of all of the acetaminophen I had ingested or from a loss of blood or from a basic combination of both. Then I succumbed to sleep.

For the very first time, the dream starring my dad and I appears in vivid spectrums of scorching color. In the latest version, my dad has stepped forward and out of the stupid jungle for what will ultimately prove to be the next to last time. He stands so close to me I swear that I can hear the sound of his heart beating. The wound on his right hand has managed to heal itself and he is no longer bleeding chocolate blood. More important, he is no longer screaming at me senseless words, but speaking real words in a confidential voice instead. This time, for the first time, my dad's speech comes through clearly and I suspect that it may finally mean something to me.

"*What is it, Dad?*" I ask him, touched by the likelihood that I will, at long last, be able to obtain the truth behind my enigmatic dreams and touched by the reality that this particular dream is coming to me in color and stereo all at the same time.

"*Depression runs in my family, Hunter,*" he says to me seemingly without regret. "*I mean bipolar disorder, manic depression.*"

"*What does that mean?*" I ask him.

"*It means that you are genetically predisposed.*"

"*I don't understand, Dad.*"

"*Hunter, you are a candidate for manic depression. Fight the illness. Fight it.*" he says, practically begging me to confront something I have never confronted before, at least not knowingly.

"But, Dad, how do I fight something I don't understand, something I can't even see?"

"Accept that something is wrong and seek help."

"Okay, but I need something to believe in now, Dad. Give me something now."

"Believe in yourself, in your doctors. Believe that life is worth living."

"Please stop speaking in clichés, Dad!" I holler at the olive drab form that is my dad. And as I holler those words at his vanishing body, it occurs to me that my plea for him to speak more clearly is much too late. My dad's ragged silhouette has already become one with the denseness of the greenest jungle I will ever see. *"Come back, Dad, come back,"* I whisper into the trees. My dad does not respond. All color disappears and all sound is muted.

Today, so many years later, I suspect that it was late in the afternoon of the day after I had force-fed myself a dangerous dose of acetaminophen when I stirred from the latest edition of that goddamn dream, the version in which my dad had finally spoken to me in words that were not foreign or inaudible but halfway intelligible instead. And it was, I now believe, late in the afternoon of that same day when I stepped on the glass of the broken light bulb again while on my way to the bathroom to vomit and piss into the sink one last time, which was only a short time before John would return and try to enter my apartment by force.

"Hunter?" I heard him holler my name. "Hunter!" I heard him shout. Then he tried turning the doorknob. Then he tried kicking at the door, but the heavy wooden door would not budge. The locks wood not give. "Have you seen him lately?" I heard him ask.

"No, I haven't. I haven't seen him since late yesterday, when it was beginning to storm." It was Lisa again. They were out there now, Lisa and John, the two of them, conspiring against me in the hallway. I was sure of that. They were whispering about me, speculating about where I might have run, speculating about what I might be doing. I was conspiring, too, you know. I was begging God to, at long last, set me free from my depression. I had gulped down so much acetaminophen, and my stomach was hurting so badly, I had concluded that I was finally closing in on death, and so I was pleading with God to make my death a reality this time. But, as always, God did not respond to my pleas. The only voices I heard were the voices of my brother John and my neighbor Lisa. And very soon, their voices became dead air and I stumbled back to my bed and fell back to sleep after vomiting on myself and pissing into the sheets.

I now think that it was shortly after midnight when I awoke and stumbled out into the hallway and down a single flight of stairs to Chan Allen's doorstep, still reeking badly of my own vomit and urine, blood dripping from my body onto his sisal welcome mat, staining it permanently. I also figure that it was shortly after midnight when Chan Allen dialed 911. And finally, I believe that it was also shortly after midnight when I heard the unmistakable sound of a siren shatter the nighttime stillness and discerned that paramedics were finally coming to save me from myself.

I would like for you to know that Chan Allen had served alongside my dad in Vietnam for a single year before he was shot twice in the shoulder by a Vietcong sniper while on patrol in a war he claimed he would never forget. Unlike my dad, Chan had always provided answers to my many questions about his own experiences in Vietnam and I had no doubt that Chan had seen the true blood of combat. Chan, like my dad, was one of my few heroes. I held him in high regard. What's more, I trusted him. Chan had shown me his scars and his medals and, on at least one occasion, bared his heart to me, a man young enough to be his own son. Maybe, just maybe, that is why I sought him out the critical night something inside of me, some sort of life-force over which I did not seem to have any control, fought for my very survival.

Chan threw me high onto his scarred shoulder and hauled me back upstairs to my apartment and turned on the overhead light and laid me out on what I was positive was my very own deathbed. Chan held my arms high in the air, high over my head that was still filled with the humming and buzzing sounds and the echo of a single blaring siren that was, I somehow understood, getting closer to me with every life-breath I stole.

"Hang on, Hunter. Hang on, man. Hang on," Chan said to me in the calmest of voices, in a tone I suspected only a war veteran of Chan Allen's caliber could speak, as he knelt over my poisoned body. "Hang on, man." Then, despite the fact that I am now fully awake, a new vision of my dad comes to me from the distant edge of the dream that once plagued me only while I slept one last time.

"*Hang on, Hunter. Hang on, son. Your life is important,*" my dad yells at me. His words are banal, stereotyped and I try to tune them out altogether so that I might die in silence, but my dad calls out to me a second time from the dream's edge, boring me again with his ridiculous platitudes. "*Your life holds a purpose,*" he shouts at me from the dream in which his likeness seems to be forever cornered.

"Whatever you say, Dad," I respond. "Whatever you say." Chan stares at me, trying to fully comprehend what it is I am babbling about. Then the poor likeness of my dad vacates my person altogether. I realize that I will obtain no more answers from him. The dream closes down one final time, for good, forever. The dream dies as suddenly and silently as The Image will die only hours later. And I see, with certainty, that I will never dream any version of that disturbing dream again.

"Hello?" All of a sudden, there was a new voice in the night. "Hello?" Suddenly there was a new voice in the hallway. "Hello?" And finally there was a new voice echoing inside of my blighted apartment. And this time it was not Lisa or John or Chan or my dad.

The paramedics shoved Chan aside and pieced me back together on the spot. They induced vomiting while a heavy-set woman stood at my desk and asked me questions I could not answer, such as my name and my age and so on and so on. I recall that I whispered "I'm sorry" to every single one of the those paramedics as they hauled me to the ambulance that was parked where the police cruiser had been parked late the previous day. "It's okay, Hunter," one paramedic responded to a single apology. "It's okay, Hunter." *But it is not "okay,"* I said to myself and only to myself. "*It is not okay.*"

CHAPTER 16

The ride to Lakeshore General in an ambulance was a relatively long one. I had lived within walking distance of the hospital and the emergency room entrance for quite some time, but the ride there seemed to take forever. To tell you the truth, the ride to Lakeshore General had taken many long and painful years. Regardless of the time I had wasted—yes wasted—getting there, I had finally arrived. And there I was, shivering in an emergency room, a nurse hovering nearby, waiting, ever so patiently, for me to stop vomiting so that she could move in close enough to give me a tetanus shot.

The nurse who administered the tetanus shot while I was restrained to the stretcher that had been used to transport me to the semi-frozen compartment in the semi-frozen emergency room at Lakeshore General, as The Image was being conceived, as The Image was being born somewhere deep inside the core of my person, was named Carrie.

"Have I seen you here before, Hunter?" she asked me rather casually.

"No ... not yet," I responded rather flatly, without any obvious sign of emotion, foreshadowing the possibility that she might see me again one day if I did not die this time.

That is all the nurse named Carrie said to me before the deputy sheriff ambled in and stared at me as if I were the Elephant Man, which was only minutes before I was removed from the emergency room and transferred to the psychiatric ward four floors above Main Street. Hardly a handful of minutes would elapse before Little Nurse and Big Nurse would show themselves for the first time, which was only a few minutes before Big Nurse would bribe me into swallowing a single Haldol pill with a single cup of water. Shortly thereafter, an imaginary angel would spend the night with me before deserting me for eternity. Sometime after that, Jocelyn would amble into the room where I was being held against my will and introduce herself and tell me that depression needs outside incentives, reasons, to lead a person to attempt suicide. A short time later, and without bothering to shake my hand, Jane would introduce herself and lead me through the thick doors to the secluded ward known throughout the region as Seven Southwest.

My brother John did return to Seven Southwest later that morning, the same morning he dropped off the bag of clothes and other "necessities." And as soon as he entered my room, he pushed a small yellow button on a remote control I had not seen before and a beige curtain glided in front of the immense glass wall, obstructing my view of the nurses' station as well as my view the other rooms on Seven Southwest. I thought it rather strange that he felt the need to close that curtain.

"Why did you do that?" I asked him.

"You need your privacy," he responded in a serious tone, a tone that could best be described as "businesslike," his fervent eyes searching out my own.

"I do?"

"Yes, you do."

The closing of the curtain made my small room seem much more confining, but I did not bother protesting John's decision to keep it closed. I knew that it was pointless to try to change his inflexible mind, to challenge him. For now, the beige curtain would remain closed no matter how claustrophobic I felt.

John positioned himself in the recliner. For the first time I could recall, he was holding onto a cup of coffee instead of a cigarette. He looked unbothered and that surprised me more than a little bit. I asked him what was going to happen to me next. I asked him when I would be going home. I assumed that he was now equipped with answers to those two questions. But my assumption was wrong; John told me in a callous tone that he did not know anything. He suggested that I wait for the psychiatrist to arrive. Then he reminded me that if I did try to leave the hospital without "proper clearance" I would be arrested. John told me to "keep my chin up." Those particular words were the only words of encouragement John spoke to me the entire time I was locked away on Seven Southwest. Those particular words were also the last words John spoke to me that morning before I fell asleep next to the yellow light of the skinny lamps on the nightstands.

While I was lost in what seemed to be my most unsettling sleep in years, it was quite apparent to me that I had traveled all the way to the gates of hell and back. And as I slept, isolated within the chill of that gray November morning, I came to understand that the so-called path to recovery was going to be a lengthy one, a path that would probably wind uphill for painful mile after painful mile after painful mile. I was, however, unsure whether I would opt to follow that winding, uphill path, the path that would become increasingly difficult with every precious step I took because I knew that if I did survive the frightening aftereffects of my second suicide attempt I would have to face the burning glare of reality. And facing that particular glare meant that I would have to admit to the police that I had indeed vandalized Kate's car. Probably more important was the fact that I would have to admit to myself that I was mentally ill, a manic-depressive.

Facing the fact that I was mentally ill meant that I would have to face both my broken past and my dismantled future, irregardless of my deteriorating health. I was not convinced that my current medical state would allow me to do that, to walk the mental path that now lie ahead of me. And it was that particular suspicion, the suspicion that I might never recover physically—let alone mentally—that grabbed onto me with the sharpest of fangs and ate away at my insides and gnawed at my tired bones, the one spot where it always seems to hurt the most.

As I slept a shallow kind of sleep that November morning, I was able to contemplate the emotional journey I would have to undertake if I was ever going to have even the slightest chance of being home in time for Thanksgiving. That journey to a more "stable state of being" would be a trek through the darkest of woods. And while I psyched myself up for the mental expedition on which I might actually embark if my mind and my body actually allowed me to explore life again, I felt less depressed, less frustrated, less angry and much less bitter than I had felt during the fateful days leading up to my second suicide attempt. For a reason, or reasons, I could not identify, I now had a vested interest in both myself and my life and, as I lie there barely sleeping, I was less suicidal and much more hopeful for the future, my future. Being hopeful for my future was a new sensation for me and, strangely enough, I welcomed that newfound feeling openly.

Voices were resonating from the nurses' station. Those voices soon awakened me and I saw that the recliner was now empty. John had slipped away from my room and, more likely than not, from Seven Southwest while I had been asleep. With my view of the ward obstructed by the curtain, I stared at the ceiling that was just as empty as the recliner. I do not know why, but I have always hated "popcorn ceilings," and I especially hated the popcorn ceiling that was above me now. The ceiling's expanse of little "hills" and little "valleys" reflected the desolate hills and valleys that stretched on inside of me. Nevertheless, that is where my conscious was trying to hide when the psychiatrist finally entered my room for the very first time.

The older, silver-haired doctor with a lean build wasted no time shaking my hand. He informed me that his name was "Goodwin." Dr. Goodwin slid his narrow frame into the recliner with ease. It was obvious that he had sat there many times before. And as he settled into the recliner, I recalled that Jocelyn had suggested that I be truthful with him, that I work with him. I decided then and there that Jocelyn's advice might prove to be accurate. I decided that I would level with Dr. Goodwin. But first, I would have to level with myself. I would have to admit to myself that I had by all means committed serious crimes against my ex-girlfriend the night prior to my being admitted onto the psychiatric ward. Yes, I would definitely have to face the burning glare of reality.

Within seconds of Dr. Goodwin's arrival, I decided that I wanted a better look at him. I pressed a button Jane had shown me earlier that morning and my bed began to rise. I felt a smile sneak across my face, albeit briefly. I do not know why I smiled just then, but I did. Dr. Goodwin stared at me as I guided the bed into position. From my new vantage point, I noticed that he had a stare that rivaled that of the deputy sheriff's. His stare was almost as intense.

"So, you didn't expect to be here …" I could not discern whether Dr. Goodwin was asking me or telling me, but his slow, punctuated speech had an effect on me that could best be described as "calming." His level speech erased many of the horrid pictures that had occupied my conscience throughout the night and the early morning hours and I was relieved to be working with a fairly clean cerebral slate. Almost immediately, I realized that I was on the verge of getting the help I had desperately needed for so many, many years.

"No, I guess I didn't," I stated, reality racing up to meet me like the ground had raced up to meet me when I had crashed my bike when I was seven years old. But this time I did not "cave." This time I did not want to die. For the first time in years, for the first time since I had knelt at the end of my bed when I was three and for the first time since my dad had returned from Vietnam, I felt that I might actually want to live. I felt that a modicum of normalcy might just be obtainable.

I was more relaxed than I had been in days. It was a very special feeling, feeling so calm. It is possible that my new mood had something to do with the Haldol I had taken and not with Dr. Goodwin's unruffled presence. Maybe it was a mixture of the two. I had no way of knowing for sure. The one thing I did know for sure is that I was suddenly fully awake, fully alert. I was the most awake and alert I had been in a very long time.

"So tell me what you are thinking, Hunter."

"I'm thinking that I want to go home. Can I leave now?"

"Hunter, it's not that easy. It doesn't work that way."

"Well then, I guess that I'm thinking that I can't even kill myself properly."

"So you didn't expect to be here then?" This time I knew it was a question Dr. Goodwin was aiming at me.

"No, I did not."

"Fate had other plans for you maybe?"

"Maybe it did and maybe it didn't. Maybe fate had nothing to do with my survival."

"Would you say that your hospitalization has something to do with what you did to your girlfriend's car the night before last?

"You mean ex-girlfriend, don't you?"

"Ex-girlfriend then. So what happened?"

"I don't know what it is you are talking about," I lied. In that single manic instant, I had turned my back on the truth. I had perjured myself. I had marred my fragile credibility. And in an instant, I was discouraged, less hopeful because I now understood if I was ever going to get out of the loony bin, I needed to work with Dr. Goodwin and not against him, just as Jocelyn had suggested. After so many years of doing nothing for myself and after all of the sleepless nights and all of the physical and mental pain I had withstood, someone was finally prepared to "hear me out." Dr. Goodwin was willing to listen to me exclusively. It was his job to listen to me.

"No, Hunter, I think you know exactly what it is I am talking about." Dr. Goodwin was practically glaring at me now. I glared right back at him, trying without much success to hide my bruised feelings. I also tried to see right through his skin to his skeleton. Despite my efforts, I could not see his skeleton as I had seen the skeletons of the men in the restaurant on my thirteenth birthday and still I got the feeling that Dr. Goodwin's skeleton was not smiling.

"When do I get to go home?"

"Not for a while." God was I ever getting sick of that answer.

"So you know what happened then?" I asked him, sounding ashamed of myself.

"Yes, I know what happened, Hunter, but I want to hear it from you. So tell me ... what happened?" The prospect of admitting to Dr. Goodwin what I had actually done to Kate, owning up to the crimes I had committed, was much more difficult than I had expected. The road to recovery was proving to be a bitch all right. Now I wanted to sleep more than ever before. I wanted to die, right then and there.

"I'm not ready, I stated matter-of-factly."

"Well, you let me know when you are." Unexpectedly, Dr. Goodwin stood, quickly buttoned his suit jacket and left my room without speaking another word. Frustrated, I stood and settled into the recliner, fully prepared to gaze into the television screen and witness another period of my former life unravel itself.

"Hello, my name is Kendra," was the first thing the young-looking, freckle-faced redhead said to me, as she strode into my room and stood directly in front of the t.v., obstructing my view of the gray-black screen completely. "I'm an aide here and I have some questions I'd like to ask you."

"Hi, my name is Hunter, but you already know that, don't you?" I asked, doing my best to sound upbeat and conceal my suicidal feelings in order that I might get myself released soon, still upset that Dr. Goodwin had left me by myself with so few answers and still upset that I had lied to him.

"Yes, I know your name, Hunter. And how is your mood right now?"

"That's becoming a popular question," I responded, cognizant that I was already being studied quite closely.

"So what's your answer?" Kendra seated herself on the corner of my bed and placed an overstuffed black binder on top of a small table she had extended alongside the bed like a miniature "bypass."

"Maybe a seven or maybe an eight," I lied. I had inflated my score even higher than I had done when I had last spoken to Jane. "Maybe it's even better than that."

"Well, your mood is definitely improving then. That's good."

"Why did Dr. Goodwin leave so soon? I thought that he was going to assess my mood or something like that and let me know when I'd be leaving, when I'd be going home." I glanced back at the blank television screen and braced myself for her answer.

"I don't know why he left when he did, Hunter," was all she said. I looked at her a second time. I watched as she opened the glossy black binder and grabbed onto a pen. She looked much too young to be staring into that binder, the binder I suspected contained top secret and damaging information about me."

"God, nobody will tell me when I'm leaving."

"I'll give you an *idea* as to when you'll be leaving us." She gave my blood-smeared face a good once-over before she focused on the binder exclusively. "You are here, Hunter, for at least 72 hours. Frankly, I think that you may be here even longer than that." Then she mumbled something I could not hear and jotted what I thought might be a small note about my current mood.

"Goddamn it!" I shouted.

"And what's your middle name, Hunter?" she asked in a serious whisper, a whisper that sounded a lot like Jane's.

"Scott." Again, she scribbled something into the black binder.

"And your age?"

"Twenty-seven goddamn it!" I stared at her petite body. I attempted, with all of the internal energy I could summon, to see her skeleton. Try as I might, I could not see it.

"So how long have you felt this way, suicidal I mean?"

"Years goddamn it!"

"Stop shouting please." I turned my eyes away from her small form and concentrated on the television screen. I stared at that screen. I stared directly through it and into the television itself. I focused on the television's insides, the mess of thin, multi-colored wires and the circuitry that could only comprise the skeleton of something electronic.

"First attempt?"

"Second attempt. What are these questions for? What could they possibly mean to you?"

"Hunter, these questions will help Dr. Goodwin and his colleagues determine what type of mood disorder you may be experiencing."

"Mood disorder? I don't have any type of mood disorder." I protested.

"Well, let's focus on the questions anyway. Okay?"

"Yes," was all I said. I felt reluctant to allow Kendra to ask me another question. I felt very strongly that the prying questions she was asking might tell me something about me, something about myself that I had needed to know for a very long, long time, but still wasn't quite ready to accept.

"Are you married, Hunter?"

"No. Never have been."

"Any children then?"

"No. None."

"Okay. Can you say whether you have any plans to commit a violent crime or whether you are planning to harm yourself again anytime soon?" Kendra looked at my face for only the second time since the impromptu "interview" had begun.

"No plans. Not right now anyway."

"Good. Any family history of depression or suicide? Have any of your blood relatives ever been diagnosed with bipolar disorder, manic depression?"

"I think that my fraternal grandmother was a manic-depressive. That's what they tell me anyway. I had an uncle on my mom's side, an uncle I never knew, who committed suicide. They say he was mentally ill, but what do they know? Maybe he was. Maybe he wasn't. My cousin Michelle took some pills several years ago. But she lived. I'm not sure whether she is bipolar or not. Maybe she is. Maybe she isn't."

"Have you been hearing voices lately, Hunter?"

"Hell no. I haven't been hearing any voices. Really, I haven't." That is when I remembered the occasion I had dropped a touchdown pass in the division championship game. Just prior to the start of the play, I had heard a series of voices echoing inside my head. The voices of mania told me that I was invincible, unstoppable, that I was the greatest receiver to ever play the game. I wasn't experiencing a daydream; I had honestly heard the voices of manic ghosts ricocheting inside my head, telling me how to behave. Those manic voices blocked out the sound of the crowd and nearly muted the signals being called by the quarterback.

I was sprinting toward the end zone. Once there, the manic voices instructed me to turn and face the line of scrimmage. I did what the voices told me to do and within seconds the ball intended for me was in flight. The manic voices commanded me to jump into the air. Again, I did as I was told. Very soon, I was floating through the air, on a course with destiny, about to haul in the game-winning touchdown. I was on the verge of becoming a hero. That is when the manic voices told me to drop the ball. Yes, they told me to deliberately drop the ball. Sadly, I did as I was told one final time. I obeyed the manic voices despite the fact that I was harboring suspicions that the voices were of sinister origin. The football fell out of my hands and onto the field and rolled out of bounds. And that is when I heard the manic ghosts laugh at me. Their teasing laughter rang through my brain and died away. Now I could only hear the home crowd booing me from the stands and nothing else.

I wasn't sure whether or not the voices I had heard that particular day were the kind of voices Kendra wanted to know about. Actually, I thought that she might be looking for something more revealing or something more foretelling or something more ominous. That in mind, I decided not to share the story of the dropped pass with her. After all, I never heard any voices telling me what to do ever again.

"Why all the questions, Kendra? No one told me I'd have to answer questions such as these."

"Yes, I know that. I just have to ask you these questions, Hunter. I have to ask. It's my job to ask you these questions. That's all."

"Yeah, well I wish you didn't have to ask me a goddamn thing."

"We're almost done."

"Promise?"

"Promise. So tell me, has there ever been a period when you were not your usual self and you felt so good or so hyper that other people thought that you were not your usual self?"

"Absolutely."

"Were you ever so hyper you got into trouble?"

"Yes, there have been many times I've gotten into trouble. It was small things mostly. I think that hyper behavior was definitely an accomplice."

"Okay then. Have you ever been so irritable that you shouted at people or started fights or arguments?"

"Yes," I said after stalling for many seconds. The questions were reaching me now. I was seeing visions of sides of me I did not want to see anymore. The questions were beginning to wear me down. They were exhausting me to the point I did not feel like answering another. Also, I really did not want Kendra or Dr. Goodwin or his colleagues to have the answers to such meddling questions in the first place. I only wanted the answers for myself. "How many more of these personal questions are there, Kendra?"

"Just a few."

"Like what else?"

"Have you, Hunter, ever experienced a period of time when you felt much more self-confident than usual?"

"Yes, I think I have. But not lately."

"What about sleep?"

"What about it?"

"Have you ever experienced periods when you got much less sleep than usual and found that you didn't really miss it? Does that sound familiar to you?"

"Still another yes."

"And what about your speech, Hunter? Do you ever find yourself speaking much faster than usual?"

"Sometimes. Sometimes. But not lately."

"Do thoughts ever race through your head so quickly you feel that you can't slow your mind down?"

"All the time. All the goddamn time. Why?"

"I have to ask these questions. Now, would you say that you are easily distracted by things around you and that you sometimes have trouble concentrating or staying on track?" Immediately, I thought of my aspirations to become a writer and how I'd never been able to "stay on track" well enough to accomplish anything in the literary field.

"Yes again, especially when I try to write." I said at last.

"Okay. Good. Thank you. Any periods of increased activity such as periods when you do more things than usual?"

"Yes, yes, yes. You know, I'm answering 'yes' to every question? I must be flunking this test."

"This is not a test, so you aren't flunking anything."

"What is it then?"

"It's a Mood Disorder Questionnaire, or an MDQ."

"A Mood Disorder Questionnaire?" I asked. Now I was scared.

"Yes, Hunter, but you are doing just fine. Really you are."

"So what else then?" I was sounding scared and bitter again. "So what other questions do you have for me?"

"Just a few more."

"Such as?"

"Have you ever been much more outgoing than usual?"

"Yes. But why?"

"I have to ask you these questions of you, Hunter. I have to ask you these questions."

"Whatever."

"I also have to ask you if you have ever been much more interested in sex than usual?"

"Who thinks up these questions, Dr. Ruth?"

"I'm really not sure, but they are standard questions. Do you have an answer for me?"

"No. No, I don't have an answer for you."

"Is there anything else you'd like to tell me?"

"Yes. I want to be home in time for Thanksgiving."

"Maybe you will be." And with that, the prodding questions that had been upsetting me stopped coming. Kendra thanked me again and strolled out of the room carrying the black binder in both arms as if she were nuzzling an infant against her chest. I never saw her again. I was left alone for another hour or so before Jane returned.

"Well, what do you say, Jane? What does Dr. Goodwin have to say?"

"I have spoken with Dr. Goodwin."

"Yeah, I figured as much. And what does he say?"

"I know that he will provide you with better answers than I am able to give you, but I can tell you that Dr. Goodwin thinks that you are very alert. He thinks that you seem to be involved in your own body."

"Meaning?"

"That means that you are aware of who you are, aware of any and all activity happening around you, things like that."

"Is that a good thing?"

"Of course it's a good thing."

"And?"

"He seems to think that you are able to distinguish between past, present and future. That's also a good thing."

"I am? You actually believe that?" That particular revelation surprised me. I had felt extremely "lost in time" lately.

"Tell me, Hunter, don't you feel that you can tell the difference between yesterday, today and tomorrow?"

"Well, maybe I can I guess."

"Just maybe?"

"Maybe I can tell the difference between the three. The again, maybe I can't."

"Why not?"

"Because I am as scared of yesterday as I am scared of today as I am scared of tomorrow."

CHAPTER 17

❀

I have felt for quite some time that there is not a single moment in a manic-depressive's life that does not profoundly affect him in some manner, be it good or bad. I also think that when a manic-depressive looks back on past events, the reason things happened the way they did seems obvious to him. However, it is when a manic-depressive is caught in the middle of a manic period, a period of manic elation, a manic high, as it is unfolding, that he is unable to comprehend exactly what it is that is taking place.

Today, I understand that I truly was caught in the middle of a manic period each time I attempted to take my own life. Today, so many years after the fact, I can see quite clearly that I was unable to comprehend what it was that was happening to me as my first and second suicide attempts unraveled right in front of me. Sure, I had planned for each attempt, but my preoccupation with my own death was incomprehensible to me each time I tried to kill myself.

Prior to both of my suicide attempts, I could not get "psyched up" for living my life no matter how hard or often I tried. I simply was not operating correctly. I did not know it then, but my brain's chemistry, my brain's "internal wiring," was experiencing a short circuit and was steadily working against me. A chemical imbalance was chipping away at my ability to reason properly. Finally, suicidal ideation was living inside of me just as The Image would be living inside of me nearly eleven years later, shortly after my second and final suicide attempt.

Looking back, I can see how confused I was during the crucial days leading up to each one of my suicide attempts. I can see that suicide seemed to be my only "option." I knew of no other "solution" for dealing with my problematic life. I was so depressed I just wanted to drop through a hole in the earth's surface and disappear forever. And I do mean that. I believed that my life was over and I wanted a "fresh start." You see, I had already purchased my ticket to nowhere, to a place far, far away from the sad world I knew and now I just needed to have it validated. Many years would pass before I would fully understand that suicide is *not* an option or a solution by any means.

I can still remember my first suicide attempt almost as clearly as I can remember the second. That was the night I choked down an entire bottle of aspirins I had smuggled from my mom's purse. The night had been like any other night really. Nothing in particular spurred me to the so-called "breaking point" other than steady feelings of depression that would not subside or leave me alone. There was no outside force behind the attempt itself, nothing I can recall anyway. I just felt extremely demoralized. I felt that it was finally "time to go," time to "check out." I was, quite simply, on a secret crusade to kill myself.

The day of my first suicide attempt had been routine. The day had been as conventional as it could have been. That day had been like any other day to be honest. I had made it to all of my classes, eaten lunch with some friends and had participated in track practice as usual. Nothing had occurred during the course of my day that would have pushed me to what Jocelyn would refer to so many years later as "the brink."

Regardless of how routine or conventional my day had been, nothing was bringing me pleasure anymore. Depressive lows were creeping in and replacing comforting highs. This time the depressive lows seemed to be permanent and it seemed as if I would never again ride upon the emotional updraft of a manic high. My spirits were low, very low. My spirits were so damn low in fact, that I was convinced that nothing could bring me out of the depressive rut in which I seemed to be forever lost. And I was confused. I was so confused I decided that the only thing I wanted from my depressive existence was for an angel to carry my wretched body away and bury it in a distant place where nobody would ever find it or throw it in a ditch. That is how truly hopeless I was feeling the day I tried for the first time to end my own life.

In his classic song "Manic Depression," the late Jimi Hendrix referred to manic depression as a "frustrating mess." The first time I heard that song, I knew that Hendrix was right. Yes, I knew then, as Hendrix's music and lyrics flowed through my head, that manic depression is a frustrating mess indeed. I understood that manic depression is a mess so frustrating and sinister—yes sinister—it can kill a person. I still think that way today because manic depression almost killed me—twice.

The mess that is manic depression was definitely messing with me my sophomore year in high school, the very year I tried without success to take my own life for the first time. Manic depression was messing with my mind and my body, slowly wreaking havoc on me from the inside out, slowly destroying me. However, I did not know the true source of my gloom at the time because I would not be diagnosed manic-depressive for many years to come.

I was a lonely young man stumbling through the darkening shadows of an illness I did not realize had such a strong hold on me. I existed in the shadows where that illness was concerned and I felt as if I were fighting a battle against an unidentified enemy, an invisible enemy I believed I had little or no chance of defeating. I was too unstable emotionally to realize that I was mentally ill and too naive and misinformed to know that the greatest danger a mentally ill person presents is the likelihood to hurt himself. As I have already stated, I believed that aspiring to commit suicide was a "standard element" of everyday living for all people. I thought that it was a kind of "phase" everyone went through, something that everyone on the face of the planet wanted to do whenever life seemed to be too difficult to endure. Remember: I believed, quite naively I should point out, that death, especially death by suicide, was extremely common. I thought that suicide was an accepted option, an accepted solution. Today, I know that it is not.

I once read that Lord Byron, also a confirmed manic-depressive, described his own mental state as "a chaos of the mind." I believe that I could have described my own mental state of mind in much the same manner. During the fateful moments leading up to my first suicide attempt, the moments in which I emptied a bottle of aspirins into my stomach, I was lost in a chaotic galaxy all my own, lost in the disorder that was my mixed-up, messed up life. I was extremely irritated. I was sad and resentful. I was mad. I was mad at myself and at God. I felt that God had cheated me in some terrible way and I simply could not see a way of escaping the depressive hex he had cast upon me.

I can still recall how the minutes before my first suicide attempt unfolded. I was standing alone in my bedroom sometime after sunset. In my frustrated mind, I bid farewell to my family and friends. And then, strangely, I took one last look around me, one final look at all of my possessions, all of the curious things I had collected over the years. I bid farewell to the entire assemblage, the entire eclectic assortment.

I was not overly sentimental that night, the night I seemed to self-destruct. I did not cry a single blessed tear. Also, I did not leave a note of explanation, which, I believe, was testament in itself as to how serious I was about dying.

Instead of drowning in my own maudlin sentiment, I thought back to a time when I was twelve years old and had gone roller-skating with several friends from junior high school. On that particular evening, I had stepped up to the snack bar and innocently ordered a Suicide, a drink consisting of all of the soda flavors mixed together, mixed into one, suicide in a wax paper cup.

Several years later, as I reflected on that single memory of that Suicide drink, I ripped through the protective seal on a plastic bottle of aspirin and inhaled the one thing I believed was the real suicide concoction, the authentic suicide in a cup. With a single glass of water, I swallowed small handfuls of aspirins until the bottle and the glass were completely empty, until the last pill was gone. The next thing I did was close the blinds. Yes, I deliberately blocked out the moon and the stars. Then I turned off the lamp on my desk. For the very first time in my tormented life, I ushered in the shadows. I welcomed the darkness. Then I stepped slowly through the blackness to my bed and let my body fall onto it. I stretched out on top of a quilt my mom had made for me years earlier and folded my arms across my chest. I braced for my eternal demise. I waited.

While I was lying on my mother's quilt waiting to die, miscellaneous visions of my short life pierced the susceptible barriers of my brain. Visions of any positive things I might have done over the years were nowhere to be seen. However, the negative pictures of terrible manic crimes I had committed over time came and went freely before they scattered like leaves in a nighttime breeze. The negative pictures flew past my feverish eyes with ardent zeal before they exploded into an infinite number of pieces.

I briefly relived the time I had tricked a much younger John into drinking from a can of motor oil. I saw an image of my manic body deliberately dance across a public street during rush hour, against the signal, against the steady flow of traffic, inviting the speeding cars to smash into me, to grind me into the pavement. The autographed baseball I had stolen from a friend's collection without any motive whatsoever sailed through the air in front of me and disappeared. I remembered several instances in which I had smuggled my dad's wallet from his dresser drawer on a whim and spent his money on candy and ice cream. The mental photograph of me secretly pouring water onto a computer keyboard owned by a former friend in a vengeful tirade smashed into me and bounced violently into oblivion.

Random impulses raced through my head so quickly I could not keep pace with them. A lifetime of horrid, manic memories came and went. I tried like hell to get away from them, to escape them. I tried like hell to run across the terrain of my consciousness, but I tripped and stumbled over all of the bad things I had ever done. And there I lie, buried almost entirely in the muck and the mud of my manic life, my future life nowhere to be seen.

The manic visions stopped coming. The bothersome cognitive slide show ended almost as quickly as it had begun. My mind's screen was erased, turned blank. My eyesight blurred. The sound of my heartbeat faded. I felt my body shutting down, "closing up shop" for good. Hardly a minute elapsed before I felt what I believed was the "serene rush of death" overtaking me. I was suddenly certain that my first suicide attempt was going to be a success.

Dawn's early light filtered through the seams in the blinds of my bedroom window, scorching my eyes that were burning inwardly. You can probably imagine how surprised I was when I awoke. At first, I did not know where I was. I thought that I was dreaming from some foreign location, another mental country maybe, but as soon as I perceived that I was surrounded by all of my collections, including several familiar pictures of my family hanging on the wall, and recognized that I was still posing in those pictures with John and my parents, I knew that I had survived my first suicide attempt.

To say I was shocked that I was still alive would be an understatement of tremendous scale. I was stunned, you know, amazed that I was still functioning at any capacity. I was also upset, upset that I had failed to kill myself, and, because of my failure, I felt badly. I felt extreme guilt. I felt what it must feel like to be "society's biggest loser" because I had managed to botch the job for which I thought I had planned so damn well.

Despite my "perfect planning," I did not know what to do next. I doubt that very many suicidal people know what to do next, after they realize that they have failed to end their life, once they are forced to face the actuality that they are still living when they ultimately expected to be dead. I was, quite suddenly, stuck in a predicament I had never known before. Just like that, I was a partner with life in a venture I understood I no longer had any business being a partner in whatsoever.

Physically, my ears were heavy. I know of no other way to describe the way they felt. "Heavy" is the only word that comes to mind. Also, my head hummed and buzzed with the deep sounds of my breathing. I was chilled through and through and I was as numb as I had ever been. And even though I had swallowed all of the aspirins only hours before, I had a headache. Yes, I had a headache.

I tried to hide from my pain in the landscape of the popcorn ceiling that was now hanging extra low above my bed but it was spinning rapidly in maddening circles and I could not maintain focus. With all of the spinning, I felt that I was going to vomit any second. I tried to sit, but I felt too weak to move. I felt the weight of what seemed like a million tons of concrete pressing down on my chest.

After several unsuccessful tries, I was finally able to sit on the edge of my bed. Then, once I felt that I was ready, as ready as I would ever be, I tried to stand. I was standing for little more than a second I suppose when I became acutely aware of just how dizzy I really was. I fell backwards onto my mattress and rolled into the wall with a dull-sounding thud. I wondered how I was going to walk if I couldn't even stand.

"Hunter?" An unfamiliar voice in the distance reverberated in my heavy ears. "What are you doing? What was that loud noise?" Process of elimination told me that it was my mom who was now speaking to me. "Wake up, Hunter. You are going to be late if you don't get up now." I glanced at the clock on the nightstand. Although the clock was a digital, I could not make any sense of the numbers.

"What time is it?"

"It is almost seven. Get up, Hunter." I had tried to stand already. Standing had not worked out for me. I needed a new itinerary.

"I'm sick," I whispered. My whispering voice echoed through my heavy ears, through my humming, buzzing head.

"Why are you shouting? I'm standing right here," my mom whispered back much too loudly.

"I didn't know that I was shouting," I said, fully conscious that I was slurring my words, aware that I sounded drunk. I never would have suspected that an overdose of aspirins could have such an intoxicating effect on a person's speech.

"You look horrible, Hunter. How do you feel?" My mom was slurring her words, too. She was standing only a few feet away from me and yet she sounded as if she were speaking from somewhere in outer space, from the planet Mars for example. She sounded as if she were speaking to me through a tube made of cardboard or from the bottom of an abandoned well.

"I don't feel right." I declared.

"What do you think it is?" She looked concerned. She looked worried. She simply had to sense that I was hurting. She had to see that whatever it was that was ailing me was not some ridiculous ploy to shirk my responsibilities that day, namely school and track practice.

"I'm not sure what it is," I called out. What is strange is that I really was not sure. I had swallowed all of the aspirins expecting to die and now that it was fairly apparent that I was going to live I expected everything to be satisfactory, okay, back to normal. Despite all of the aspirins I had ingested, I could not comprehend or admit to myself or to my own mother, why I felt the way I did.

CHAPTER 18

The day after my first suicide attempt is one mammoth blur. Years later, I can remember only remnants, handfuls of the sparsest details. I do remember that my dad left for work early that morning with hardly a word to anyone. Nothing out of the ordinary there. Then my mom told me to "get some rest" and soon departed for work as well. And that is how the day began, my tired mind left alone to contemplate the emptiness I was feeling as I lie on my bed frustrated and exhausted by my failure to kill myself.

I do not know how I was able to do it as sick as I was that morning, but I rolled out of bed and slid out of my pajamas without breaking any bones. Next, I crawled slowly to the bathroom where I collapsed onto a pile of dirty towels. Several minutes later, I stood and staggered into the shower with tremendous effort. Looking back, I realize that it was one of the most difficult tasks I have ever performed. I am not even sure how I turned on the water as weak as I was, but I found just enough strength to pull the handle into the required position.

I sat under the cool water for what I now believe was a "fairly long time." Once I got up the nerve, I stood and leaned against the wall of the shower in a vertical push-up position as if I were a human praying mantis and vomited as the water sprayed down over my body. Several minutes later, I turned off the water on the third try, fell out of the shower and landed on the pile of dirty towels a second time.

The water's chill had been comforting, but my ears were still troubling me. They still felt heavy and, what's more, my head still hummed and buzzed inside. Despite the pain in my ears, I crawled very slowly back to my room and knelt at the edge of my bed just as I had done after I had refused to eat my supper when I was three years old. I was still kneeling at the foot of my bed, trying to think of what to do next when it occurred to me that I needed to dry myself. Shivering, I tugged at the bedding and wrapped myself in my mom's quilt until I was certain that all of the water had been absorbed from my body.

It was then that I heard a faint ringing sound. I quickly narrowed the list of possible sources of that bothersome noise to either the inside of my parents' house or to the inside of my own humming, buzzing head. Then I honed the list of possible sources to a doorbell or, possibly, to a telephone. The upsetting noise silenced itself for a few moments. Then it started bothering me again. I concluded at last that it was in fact a goddamn telephone that was emitting such a disturbing noise. I concluded that my mom might be calling to check on me. I also concluded that I would never locate the phone in time to answer it, so I let it ring and ring and ring until, at long last, the disturbing noise it was making died away.

I glanced at the digital clock on the shelf above my desk. This time the neon numbers made sense to me. The digits read "7:44," which was, I somehow recalled, the exact time of day I was born approximately sixteen years earlier. At 7:44 of the morning after my fist suicide attempt, I realized that if I hurried I could still catch the school bus. In an effort to shave precious minutes, I dressed myself in the same clothes I had worn the day before. Then I drank a glass of milk—the only thing that appealed to me—for breakfast and made my way to the bus stop, practically stumbling along as if I were a blind man crossing the street without his cane.

I can't seem to remember very much about the bus ride to school that morning. I just remember that the scenery outside my window appeared to be moving much, much faster than the bus was moving. Houses and sky streamed in front of my eyes like a video stuck on fast forward. Sometime later, after the disturbing bus ride, I was sent to the school library for refusing to participate in calisthenics. I had informed Mr. Van Dorn that I was sick, very sick, but he did not believe me—not for a single damn second. If only he had known how sick I was, how suicidal I was. I felt as if I might collapse at any time and he still banished me to the library in much the same manner my mom had banished me to my room for refusing to eat my supper when I was only three years old.

I took refuge at a small table in the most remote corner of the library. But I was not alone for very long. You see, from the time we were in junior high school, Erica Ashwell had had a crush on me. And from the moment I sank into a chair in the library, she was there. She nearly pounced into the seat across from me. I just wanted to be alone with my thoughts and serve the sentence Mr. Van Dorn had dished out, but Erica Ashwell would not have it.

"You look horrible, Hunter," she said in a kind of pitch I could barely hear. Are you feeling okay?" Regardless of her obvious concern, a grand smile was plastered across her lovesick face. I came to the realization that I despised that smile; Erica Ashwell had far too many teeth.

"I have a headache. That's all," I announced, the fervor of life missing from my voice.

"Are you sure?"

"Yes, I am sure." I responded, realizing that a headache and the humming and buzzing sounds in my head were not my only problem. I was lying again and I briefly considered letting Erica know the true source of my pain. I briefly considered telling her about all of the aspirins I had secretly swallowed the previous night if for no other reason than to make her stop talking to me. I thought that maybe, after all these years, that would get rid of her for good, for the first and last time. But I did not tell her a damn thing about the aspirins because I did not think that I could trust her. I was afraid that she would tell someone else what I had done or had attempted to do. I was afraid that she might tell one of her friends perhaps and by the end of the period word of my first suicide attempt would be featured on the front page of the school newspaper or in the local press or on the national news or maybe even on "Nightline."

"Just a headache? You look so white, so pale, Hunter. Your skin looks like porcelain," Erica informed me. I wondered, *Couldn't she say anything without that fruity smile glued to her face?*

"I just have a headache, Erica," I repeated, sounding both beaten and intoxicated at the same time. I was trying with tremendous difficulty to keep from slurring my words. To make matters worse, my head was still humming, still buzzing inside. My ears still felt heavy and I was still having trouble hearing because of it. I noticed that I could not hear any external sound other than the steady drone of Erica's voice, a low-pitched voice that sounded as if it were being generated from another star system.

"So what did you do last night, Hunter?" she asked me. Even her eyes were smiling at me now. I could see that she wanted details. Again, I considered telling her the truth. I considered telling her that I had attempted suicide, but I resisted the urge.

"I did absolutely nothing last night," I nearly shouted at her, employing a manufactured glare in hopes of shutting her up for the remainder of the period. At that moment, I saw that her skeleton was even whiter than her toothy grin.

"Hunter, weren't you wearing those same clothes yesterday?" she asked, this time without a smile. Leave it to Erica Ashwell to notice a detail as minute as that.

"No!" I shouted.

"Are you sure?"

I never heard the bell ring, the very bell that saved me from my racing thoughts, Mr. Van Dorn's stupid punishment and Erica's incessant questions, but I knew that it had rung because Erica suddenly stood, prodded me from my seat with a playful right jab to the ribs and, you guessed it, a smile.

"That's the bell, Hunter. Let's go." I stood and waited for all of the bookshelves to stop revolving. At the exact instant they came to a stop, Erica grabbed onto my shirtsleeve and led me down the darkly painted hallway like a bellhop with a little too much bounce in her step. I followed her closely. At one point, I reached out to hold her hand, but I missed it. She threw my jacket over my shoulder.

"See you later, Hunter," she said with her identifying smile, as she abruptly changed direction and disappeared from view entirely.

Yeah, if I'm still alive," I called after her, still slurring my words. I do not think she heard me. Honestly, I do not think anyone else heard me either. In fact, I am now positive that no one heard me call out in pain.

I was propped against a wall in the vacant school cafeteria talking to my dad on a pay telephone when I told him that I needed to go to the hospital as soon as possible. His voice sounded as if it were being transmitted over a string connected to a pair of empty soup cans and still I managed to hear him say that he would be by to pick me up in a few minutes. I excused myself from school that day and stood outside in front of the guidance counselor's office and waited for my dad to arrive. My head was humming and buzzing worse than ever before and my ears seemed to be dragging on the ground when my dad finally pulled up to the curb.

"What is it, Hunter?" my dad asked me as soon as I had fastened my seatbelt.

"I can't hear anything," I stated without hesitation.

"But you can hear me, right?" he asked as he turned onto Lakeshore Boulevard and aimed the car in a southerly direction.

"Yeah, I hear you, Dad, but barely," I answered in an upsetting drawl. I had a hunch that I was slowly going deaf. I was now certain that my inability to speak and hear properly were the first phases of dieing. I was also certain that I did not want to die in that manner, slowly I mean. The fact that I had asked my dad to drive me to the hospital was veritable proof that I was trying to save myself, just as I had done the day I had reached for the swimming pool's tiled edge when I was nine years old. I really cannot explain why I wanted to save myself.

"Well, what do you think it is then, Hunter?" Instead of focusing on the street in front of us, he glanced at my face in a manner that could best be described as "concerned fascination." I could see quite plainly that he was dreading what I was going to say next.

"I overdosed on aspirins last night, Dad." I stared out the window at the moving scenery that bordered Lakeshore Boulevard. A rather large orange sign with the words "Road Work Ahead" printed on it in bold black letters soon came into view. My dad let off the accelerator and the car lurched forward as we passed a small group of men in bright orange vests standing on the far edge of the street holding mud-caked shovels in their hands.

"Are you suicidal, Hunter?" My dad sounded skeptical and worried at the same time. The car steadily regained speed until my dad turned onto Center Street. I could now see Lakeshore General Hospital, the hospital that would one day be my residence for three long weeks, looming in the distance.

"No!" I responded emphatically, my one-word answer forever committed to memory.

My dad stopped asking questions and parked the car not far from the hospital's front entrance. How I was able to get from the car and into the lobby I do not know. I suspect that I stumbled along well enough that I did not need anyone's assistance. Regardless, that particular detail is not committed to memory.

The next thing I recall is being pushed into a large soundproof chamber by a stocky male nurse with an impatient demeanor. I remember that the nurse barked out some very basic instructions. As per the instructions, I was to raise my right hand if I heard a sound in my right ear and raise my left hand to signify that I heard a sound in my left ear. If I heard a sound in both ears at the same time, I was to raise both hands.

The instructions were simple enough, but I was nervous as hell. I was nervous that I had done permanent harm to my hearing. I was also nervous that I might flunk the test upon which I felt my entire future depended. I did not like being semi-deaf. I could not begin to fathom what living would be like if I was to become completely deaf.

A short time later, the nurse reported to my dad and I that I had passed the test. Then he reported to my dad in a voice that was semi-audible to me that I had appeared to be "very nervous" while I was taking the test. Well, it was true; I had been very nervous. I was afraid of what my dad would say to me as soon as the nurse left us alone. He still had not asked me about the aspirins I had claimed to have swallowed or why I had claimed to have taken them. I was glad for that. I was relieved. I was also upset, upset by his apparent lack of interest in what was now happening to me.

I was sitting next to my dad in the hospital's overcrowded waiting room reciting to myself my ABCs as if I were a bored kindergartner when my name was finally called. I was relieved to know that I could hear again without much difficulty and I was beginning to suspect that my hearing might recover completely. As I stood and began moving with a slight forward lean in the general direction of the person who had called my name, I was grateful that my dizziness had subsided altogether and that I had learned to walk a straight line again. I had no desire to crawl across the waiting room floor in the same manner I had inched my way to the shower earlier that morning.

I followed another nurse—a thin female this time—into a small room where she casually went about taking my vital signs. I remember asking the nurse for the various numbers, but I cannot say today whether my blood pressure was too high or too low. I just remember that the numbers differed greatly from the norm, my norm. I also remember that the nurse shot me a rather strange look and shook her head. I speculated as to whether I had just insulted her mother by saying that she wore army boots or something along those lines. Considering the state I was in, I could not be sure whether I had or not.

"What is it?" I asked, upset by her standoffishness.

"What have you been up to?"

"Nothing. Not a thing. Why?" The nurse shook her head again. Then she tugged the thermometer from beneath my dry, swollen tongue. She studied it briefly and shook her head a third time.

"Why do you keep shaking your head?" I asked.

"Your blood pressure is a definite concern, your temperature is far from 98.6, your breath has a stench I can't identify and you are hyperventilating. Now you tell me why I keep shaking my head."

I did not bother asking the nurse whether my temperature was too high or too low. I do not think I cared enough to ask. I knew why I was there and now that I had passed the fucking hearing test and was walking upright again I figured that I would eventually be all right, despite the fact that I did not feel "all right" at the time.

My dad drove me back to school shortly thereafter. He drove the entire distance from the hospital to school in a bothersome kind of silence. I waited for him to say something, anything, but he just stared straight ahead, like a distracted man trying to solve something, some puzzle, or brainteaser for which there seems to be no plausible solution.

We had to take an alternate route when my dad missed his turn and we ended up on a dead end street. He remained mum as he put the car into reverse and put us back on course in the direction of Lakeshore Boulevard.

"So has your hearing improved any, Hunter? Can you hear me any better now?" my dad asked me at last, as we pulled into the school parking lot. I could hear my dad's words, but nothing else. I concentrated on hearing the steady whir of the car's engine as I had done many times before, but I heard nothing except for my dad's semi-slurred speech and a faint rendition of the humming and buzzing sounds inside of my aching head. Although my hearing was steadily improving, my ears still felt heavy and I was so tired I could barely hold my head above my shoulders.

"I don't think it has," I lied. My dad stopped the car just outside the guidance counselor's office.

"Well, you'll be okay. Just give it time."

"Yeah ... just give it time," I said. "Just give it time." The words I had reiterated bounced off of the dashboard and smashed into my skull as soon as I released them. Just give it time.

CHAPTER 19

I did return to class that day. How I did it I will never know, but there I was in fourth period algebra as if nothing had ever happened, as if I had never swallowed those fucking aspirins in the first place. I made a feeble effort to follow along with the rest of the class, but because life was now more meaningless to me than ever before, I could not concentrate. Maybe that is because I wasn't supposed to be tardy or in fourth period algebra class. I was supposed to be dead. No wonder the numbers on the chalkboard meant absolutely nothing to me.

Soon after class had begun, Emily Ryan, a pretty little thing I had known for years, pushed her desk next to mine.

"So, Hunter, tell me what do you want to be when you grow up?" she asked me in a soft voice, setting her gaze on Miss Riggs, the teacher the two of us despised the most, the teacher who was now busy scribbling miscellaneous information on the chalkboard.

"I'm still trying to solve that one." I said to her, also staring at Miss Riggs' back. "Truthfully, I don't know that I ever will grow up."

"And what does that mean?" Emily sounded confused.

"It means nothing."

"What do *you* want to be when you grow up?" I asked Emily, turning the tables on her.

"Normal. I want to be normal." With that, Miss Riggs asked the two of us to please stop talking.

I have no memory of any of the classes that followed algebra that day. It is as if the rest of the school day was never even recorded in my mind's journal. The next entry in my mental diary is a rather brief conversation I had with Coach Leyland just before track practice was scheduled to begin.

"What is it, Hunter?"

"I'm done, coach," I informed him, as I placed the uniform I had once felt privileged to wear on his cluttered desk. Being rid of that damn uniform ushered in a feeling of relief, a kind of relief I had never experienced before. Coach Leyland was visibly stunned.

"But why?" was the first thing he said. He glanced at the uniform on his desk Then he glanced back at me.

"I just feel I have to go now, Coach. I'm tired." I knew, however, that my reason for quitting the track team was the same reason I had given myself for quitting life when I had overdosed on aspirins the night before: it was simply time to go. I was worn out. I was beaten, defeated and depressed. And I knew that I could not run any more races or run at all any longer.

"Are you feeling okay, Hunter?" Coach Leyland grabbed onto the brim of his cap and pushed it high on his forehead.

"Yeah, I'm fine," I lied. I have noticed over the years that manic-depressives tend to lie a lot. It is in our genes I think. Or maybe it's the way we are wired. Perhaps it's a medical problem, a condition, an illness in itself. But, then again, maybe genes and body chemistry have nothing at all to do with a manic depressive's tendency to lie. Maybe a manic-depressive's tendency to lie has more to do with the situations in which he often finds himself cornered than anything else. Then again, maybe there is no logical explanation in the first place. It could be that my imagination is simply working overtime.

"But you've been running so well," Coach Leyland stated, sounding as if he had just heard that a close relative had died. He was right, you know. I had been running well, very well. Just recently, I had set three school records in three different distances. I had set record times in the 600-meter dash, the 800-meter run and the 1,000-meter run. But I knew that I could not run any more races. The stress of having to perform daily was simply too much for me to bear, much more than I could handle. Quitting track was a "way out" in its own right. Given the opportunity, I would have quit school, too. And why not? I had already quit life.

"Well, why don't you think about it? Take the weekend. We'll talk again on Monday. What do you say to that?"

"Coach, I'm finished," I said without any reservations. I turned my back on him, nearly sprinting for the door.

My quitting the track team had nothing to do with my having swallowed so many aspirins. My ability to reason might have been impaired to a degree, but, as I have already told you, I had given up on track and every other activity in my life long, long before I had swallowed a full bottle of aspirins. I am certain that quitting track had everything to do with my interest in living having been depleted. Because my life no longer held any joy for me, there was simply no joy in running track anymore. My tired body seemed to have stopped producing "happy endorphins." And something deep inside of me seemed to be broken, busted, beyond repair.

I missed the school bus that day while I was talking with Coach Leyland. Emily Ryan had missed the school bus while waiting to talk to me. She was waiting to tell me that I was sick, that I was, of all things, bipolar, that I was a manic-depressive.

"Are you feeling okay, Hunter?" Emily asked, moving in front of me, forcing me to come to an abrupt stop.

"I just quit the track team, that's all."

"So the all-star quit the team ... Feeling a little sorry for yourself today?"

"No, not at all. I'm relaxed now. Now I can rest." I stepped around her slender body and lengthened my stride. "Now I can rest," I repeated.

"Rest?" she asked, still managing to follow close behind me. "What does that mean exactly?"

"It means, if you must know, that I can now escape the dullness, the boring course of action that is my monotonous life."

"You poor, poor boy. Life is just one damned thing after another, isn't it?"

"So who's responsible for those words?" I asked, mindful that the quote that had just been shared with me did not belong to Emily Ryan.

"Elbert Hubbard, I think. That particular quote belongs to some dead guy, that I can tell you. There is a lot of truth in those words, Hunter."

"And who is Elbert Hubbard?" I asked, glancing back at Emily, still walking, still staying in step or keeping pace if you will, with my own disturbed drummer.

"Hell, I don't know anymore. Maybe Hubbard was a politician or a soldier. Maybe an author. Yeah, an author. No, he was a renowned lecturer or something I can't recall right now."

"Does it really even matter, Emily? I don't think it does." I didn't know it then, but the words Emily had attributed to Elbert Hubbard would cross my mind time and time again over the years.

"No, it doesn't *really* matter what Hubbard's occupation was. It's what he said that counts. So tell me, Hunter, what did you mean when you said earlier today that you weren't sure you would ever grow up?"

"Nothing! I meant absolutely *nothing*!" I shouted.

"I am sick, too, you know! I am sick and so are you!" Now Emily was shouting. I stopped walking. I turned and stared down at my misshapen silhouette on the sidewalk. Emily raced up to meet me. "I'm sick just like you, Hunter."

"And what makes you think that I am sick?" I looked into Emily's eyes. I couldn't see my reflection there, but Emily was definitely beginning to see through mine.

"You are sick, Hunter. You are a sick man. Trust me." Emily handed me her textbooks and placed her small hands on my shoulders and tilted her head far back and studied my face. "So what have you been thinking lately?" Her words seemed to bounce off my chest and into oblivion.

"Nothing."

"Yeah, right, Hunter," she released her grip on me and stared into my eyes. "You've been moping around here for weeks. You are missing school and your grades are slipping because of it. You are withdrawn, irritable and not yourself. This is not a bad dream you are having. Something is wrong. And I know what it is."

"So what is it then, Emily?" What's your opinion, or diagnosis, of what's wrong with me, Dr. Ryan? And please, be specific."

"You are depressed. To be completely honest, you are beyond depressed. You are suffering from bipolar disorder. I believe that you are a manic-depressive. I can see it in your actions, in your posture, in your eyes that betray you. It's vicious what a depressed person can do to himself. It really is."

"And just how do you know that?" I asked, searching the pages of my mind for a definition of bipolar disorder.

"Because, Hunter, I *have* depression. Yes, I have depression. Truthfully, I was diagnosed manic-depressive, or bipolar, two years ago, while we were in junior high, while we were still in the eighth grade. You never knew it, that I was a sick individual I mean. I kept my diagnosis a secret from everyone and, for the record, I have been watching you closely ever since. I've been watching you, Hunter."

"I am not a manic-depressive, Emily."

"Hunter, do you even know what manic depression is?"

"No. Nothing is wrong with me, though. Nothing is wrong with me. I am fine. Really I am."

"But something *is* wrong with the way you are behaving. You simply are not thinking clearly. You are sinking, drowning. And you are in trouble, more trouble than you know. You have an illness, a mental illness."

"Maybe I'll see you later, Emily Ryan. Then again, maybe I won't." I dropped her books onto the concrete and turned my back on the first person to ever openly allege that I was sick, that I was mentally ill, and simply walked away from her one last time.

I made up my mind to take the long way home that afternoon. And as I roamed the darkening streets, I thought a lot about what Emily had said to me. I couldn't help thinking about the direct manner in which she had accused me of being a sick man, a manic-depressive. Emily had maintained that I was suffering from bipolar disorder, a mental illness I knew next to nothing about, and I was upset by the probability that her analysis might be correct, even if I didn't fully comprehend at the time what it was she had said to me.

Eventually, I found myself walking along the stream that flowed steadily through the center of town. I was trying to think of an explanation as to why I was the way I was. I was trying to justify to myself all of the strange ways I had ever acted, all of the strange ways I had ever behaved. I searched the closets of my tired mind for answers. I wanted to know the reason, or reasons, behind my first suicide attempt, if a real reason actually existed that is. I also wanted to know why little Emily had called me a manic-depressive, which was, without a doubt, an awful-sounding name I simply did not understand at the time. But more than anything else, I wanted to know why I operated the way I did.

I thought a lot about life and death, but mostly about death that strange day. And, as the sun began to set on the western edge of the lake, I thought what it must be like to be a member of the animal kingdom, unable to imagine death by suicide as only a human being is able to do. I also considered the actuality that I had seen my first suicide attempt coming for several years. On one cognitive level or another, I had dreamt of it. I had planned for it. And after I had finally acted out my morbid plan, I was faced with an unparalleled sense of failure I could not deny. I was really having trouble accepting the fact that I had missed out on a most ideal opportunity to die.

CHAPTER 20

❁

Another nurse strode into my room on Seven Southwest. Her silent disposition along with her preoccupation with the machine I was connected to made it apparent that she was there for the sole purpose of checking my IV drip and not to chat. She traced the line with a thin finger, checked that the connections were tight and punched a few buttons on the infusion pump without speaking a single word. She did not even make eye contact with me. She was essentially there for my benefit and yet she went about her business as if I were not even present, as if I did not even exist.

The silence between the two us was upsetting to me. I was tempted to say something, anything that might shatter the quiet, but I was afraid I might make an out-and-out fool of myself by asking her whether she had a boyfriend, as I had done earlier with the nurse named Pam. Besides, what could I possibly say to this nurse that would make any sense? Where would I begin? I considered asking her what was going to happen to me next, when I would be going home, et cetera, et cetera, but none of the other nurses I had spoken to so far had been able to answer those basic questions, so I let the moment pass. The nurse turned away from me and left the room. I never saw her again.

A short time later, Jane came to escort me to lunch. I saw by the analog clock on the wall at the nurses' station that it was a few minutes past twelve. I was hungrier than I had ever been. I had not eaten anything in the three manic days prior to having been admitted to Lakeshore General and since arriving I had eaten only a small sandwich and a small bag of Doritos. I believed that my hunger was justified.

"Are you still hungry, Hunter?" Jane asked me. Of course I was, but I had my reservations about dining with the people of Seven Southwest, especially the woman who had screamed the previous night from the opposite end of the ward. I still hadn't seen their faces and, truthfully, I did not want to see their faces now.

"No, Jane, I'm not," I lied, as I peered cautiously into the dining room, searching with a hunter's eye for Jocelyn among all of the unknowns. Much to my disappointment, I saw that she was not there.

"You'll be okay, Hunter. Trust me. Please don't be scared of these people. They are harmless. Really they are." Clearly, Jane had read my mind.

"Then what are they doing here, Jane?" I was still under the impression that, except for Jocelyn, they were society's defectives. I believed that they were all criminally insane and that I did not belong in the funny farm with them, let alone in the same dining room. As I had stated earlier, I was going home soon, very soon in fact. Everything had been a mistake, a mix-up, a misunderstanding. Eating lunch with the psychos of Seven Southwest was not on my agenda.

"Many of them are here for the same reason you are, Hunter."

"And what *reason* is that, Jane?" That word, the word "reason" was beginning to bother me … a lot.

"Most of them have recently attempted suicide the same as you. You have that in common with most of them."

"Are they manic-depressives, Jane?" I must tell you now that the prospect of seeing a real, live manic-depressive up close terrified me. After all, the only manic-depressive I had ever known outright was Emily Ryan and she was now a distant icon from my semi-forgotten past.

"Well, yes, they are manic-depressives."

"Then I'm not ready, Jane. And I think that I've lost my appetite—what little appetite I had anyway," I lied again.

"Hunter, do you even know what manic depression is?" Jane asked in a patronizing voice.

"I have an idea."

"Then what is it?"

"It's an illness, a mental illness," I whispered, unsure of myself. I tried to remember every time I had ever heard the term "manic depression." My mind shot back to that day years before when I had quit the track team and Emily had claimed that I was sick, that I was a manic-depressive like her. "It's a mental illness," I repeated.

"That's true. Manic depression is a mental illness. But it's much more complicated than that. Manic depression, or bipolar disorder, is a major affective disorder in which an individual alternates between states of deep depression and extreme elation. Manic depression is an illness that is probably caused by a chemical imbalance, by electrical and chemical elements in the brain not functioning properly. Yes, it is an illness, Hunter."

"That does not sound very complicated to me, Jane."

"That is a very basic definition."

"Yeah, you sounded like a dictionary just now."

"Manic depression affects thoughts, feelings, behavior and even how a person feels physically."

"Now you're sounding like a medical journal, Jane."

"Maybe."

"Jane, if you know so much about manic depression then what causes a person to become a manic-depressive? What causes the illness itself?"

"No one really knows. More likely than not, the causes of the illness are a combination of several factors. Multiple factors come into play. You see, Hunter, there are physical, mental, emotional and even environmental factors involved. More likely than not, inheritability is involved as well."

"Whew!"

"More complex than you thought, I know."

"Yeah, more complex," I admitted.

"Well, Hunter, you asked me. I feel now that you've had the chance to visit with Dr. Goodwin that it is really very important that you receive adequate answers to any questions you may have."

"Then when am I going home? Give me an 'adequate' answer to that one."

"I'm sorry, Hunter. That is the one question I still do not have an answer for."

"Kendra told me that I am here for 72 hours at least."

"Yes, I think that might be fairly accurate."

I was eating lunch in my own room, mulling over the possibility that I might actually be a mentally ill reject, when Dr. Goodwin reappeared. "Why aren't you eating in the dining room with the rest of the group?" he asked me, a trace of what I instantly discerned was frustration or maybe even anger in his voice.

"So I am part of a 'group' now, huh?" I shoved the tray of food aside just as I had done when I had shoved aside my roast beef and mashed potatoes when I was three. The probability that I was being classified as one of *them* by Dr. Goodwin himself disturbed me.

"Yes, Hunter. You are a member of a group now, that group." Dr. Goodwin pointed in the general direction of the dining room at the opposite corner of the quadrangle before he turned his gaze toward me. He was studying me closely, looking me up and down and side to side. Maybe he was seeing my skeleton. Then again, maybe he was not. "From now on you will eat in the dining room with everyone else. Do you understand?"

"Yeah, I get it."

"I had some time so I thought I'd stop in and see how you're doing, how you are feeling. It will give us a chance to talk." He was staring at my baseball cap now. I considered taking the cap off, but I knew that my hair was still caked with my own blood.

"Okay."

"So Jane tells me that you still want to go home," he stated with conviction, as he assumed his regular position in the recliner. Again, I could not decipher whether the doctor was asking me a question outright or merely telling me something. I responded anyway.

"I need to go home."

"Where is home?"

"I live right here in town, just beyond the stream, on the other side of the bridge."

"Just beyond the stream and over the bridge, huh?"

"Yes."

"Do you have any roommates?"

"No, I live alone. The only person I have to take care of is me," I said, cognizant that I had not been doing a very good job at that, especially lately."

"Siblings?"

"One younger brother. He lives here, too."

"Do the two of you get along?"

"No. Why do you ask?"

"Just curious. What about your parents?"

"What about them?"

"Where do they live?"

"They live overseas."

"Overseas, huh? So far away ... no real support ... you are lucky, Hunter, luckier than you may know."

"Yeah, I guess that maybe I am lucky," I said with a nod, although I had not thought of it that way yet, although I really did not feel very lucky at all.

"So, Hunter, why don't you tell me a little about your life so far or, if you prefer, a little about your childhood?" That quickly, Dr. Goodwin had changed the tempo of our conversation. His unexpected question sounded as if it were right out of the movies, one of those movies in which the patient is lying on a couch while a distinguished-looking psychiatrist is nodding his head and jotting the patient's spoken thoughts onto a legal pad.

The question inviting me to elaborate on my youth threw a switch that controlled a rare bright light inside of me, a light that shone through the haze of the most recent years, months, weeks and days onto some of my earliest memories like the brilliant beacon from a lighthouse. It was as if something I can't quite describe, some new way of looking at life, was suddenly born, or reborn, inside of me.

I reflected on my early childhood with very little effort. With tremendous ease, I transported my inner self and my memory all the way back to a time when I was three years old, to that time when I had refused to eat my supper and had missed out on dessert. My memory froze at the exact spot where I had knelt at the edge of my miniature bed crying and then, as if a gentle wind were propelling it, my memory moved quickly forward again, bouncing off of happy remembrance after happy remembrance.

For the very first time in a long time, cheerful memories consumed me. I was suddenly reminded that almost every aspect of my life until the age of thirteen or so had essentially been good—not great, but good. Sure, there was an inner vacuity that I could not explain as well as the underlying feelings of depression that had pestered me almost constantly, but my life as a young boy had essentially been better than acceptable. Despite my having been aware on one mental level or another that something about me was not "quite right" with my way of thinking from the time I was only three years old and despite my having been obsessively suicidal from the time I was thirteen, there were those in-between years when my life as a kid had been pretty damn good.

"Are you still with me, Hunter?"

"Yes."

"Then tell me what you were just thinking."

"Well, you know, I was thinking that I wasn't always depressed to the point that I was suicidal. I was thinking that there was a period, a period of several years when I had never viewed life through suicidal specs at all. Well, not on a regular basis anyway. I was also thinking that life was treating me pretty well considering…"

"Considering what?"

"Considering my feelings of depression and my occasional desire to be dead."

"Why do you say that?" Dr. Goodwin sounded untrusting. Also, he was now staring at my face and not at my favorite cap that was, I knew, stained with my own sweat and blood. I wondered if he thought that I was lying to him. Of course I knew that I was not.

"Well, from the time I was three years old until the time I turned thirteen, my family lived in a small town in Germany. Let me tell you, there was something about that small town and the mountains that surrounded it, something about the manner in which those mountains encircled that small town that made me feel safe, protected, alive and even normal. I miss that small town and those mountains especially."

"And how did those mountains make you feel, Hunter?"

"Normal. Yeah, normal. I'd thought about death a few times, imagined my own funeral even, but, relatively speaking, those years between the ages of three and thirteen were the most 'normal' years I have ever known, especially when compared to all of the years that followed my thirteenth birthday, especially when compared to the way I feel today, the way I feel right now, right this minute. I was more at ease back then, more satisfied with life, my life."

"And why do you think you were 'more at ease' back then?"

"I've asked myself that same question many times before."

"So what's your answer then?"

"I've never been able to come up with a suitable explanation as to why I felt the way I felt when I was a kid."

"Well, take a guess then." Dr. Goodwin glanced casually at his watch.

"I guess it could have something to do with the fact that I was young and still somewhat hopeful. I was not depressed all the time—not like I am now anyway. As I have already stated, *most* of my depression surfaced *after* I turned thirteen and not before. Plus, there were fewer stressors and a lot less pressures on me then.

"What do you mean? Try to explain."

"Well, I mean that I did not know a single thing about holes in the ozone layer or global warming or manic depression or having to work to pay the bills and the rent. Living was just easier, more pleasurable when I was a kid. Life was not nearly as complicated in my younger years as it was in my later years, as it is now, as it is today. Ignorance is, as they say, bliss."

"Do you honestly believe that?"

"I think so, but then I don't know. I have trouble with that one. I guess that sometimes I do believe those words and sometimes I don't."

"In what other manner was your childhood less complicated?"

"Hell, I don't know. Maybe because peanut butter and jelly came in separate jars and tasted better because of it. Maybe it could have something to do with the fact that I ate white bread instead of wheat bread without feeling any guilt."

"Are you joking, Hunter?"

"No, I am leveling with you."

"Okay then."

"That things seemed less complicated for me when I was younger could very well have something to do with my being held prisoner in this god-awful place, if that makes any sense to you.

"It does."

"That things seemed less complicated when I was younger might very well have something to do with the fishing line that now binds my wrists together and the fact that I am now undergoing treatment to repair my seemingly-doomed liver, that makes my former life—my childhood—seem so appealing to me again."

"So now let's consider what you've said so far."

"Okay."

"You said that you were depressed enough to occasionally think about your own death and depressed enough to imagine your own funeral even, but not depressed enough to think about suicide? Is that right?"

"Yeah, that's right. I thought about death now and then, which I felt was not entirely out of the ordinary, but not about suicide. There were times I wanted to die, but I did not know what suicide was. You see, I had never encountered suicide firsthand. Suicide was something I had heard of, but did not fully understand. I had heard the word used in conversation, but did not understand the concept of suicide itself."

"What about all of the times you wanted to die?"

"What about them?"

"Give me an example of one."

"Like I just said, 'suicide' was just a word back then, a word without an actual definition."

"But, Hunter, what about all of the times you wanted to die?"

"I can recall one particular example right now."

"Share it with me."

"Well, once, when I was ten, I sat in the middle of a highway that ran through town and prayed that a truck would come along and turn me into road kill."

"Why did you do that?"

"I don't know for sure. I just wanted to be dead I think. Sometimes, I question my own recklessness. Most of the time I don't get an answer."

"Wouldn't you say that such recklessness—your word—would be classified as suicidal behavior?"

"No, I wouldn't. Like I already said, I didn't even know what suicide was. It was just a word back then, a word like any other word."

"Were there any other instances in which you were as reckless as the time you sat in the middle of the highway?"

"When I was eleven I jumped out of a moving school bus on a dare."

"On a dare?"

"Yep. I did it on a dare. Someone dared me to do it, so I did it."

"You just did it, huh?"

"Yep. And, Dr. Goodwin, I think I know what it is you are thinking right now: you are thinking that if someone dared me to jump off a bridge or a cliff today, would I do it?"

"So what—if anything—were you trying to accomplish when you jumped out of that bus?"

"Nothing. I was dared to do it, so I did it. That's the truth, Dr. Goodwin."

"Weren't you thinking of the danger involved or were you feeling as if nothing could happen to you?

"The danger involved crossed my mind—briefly."

"Hunter, you know you could have gotten yourself killed."

"Yes, I know that. Actually, the probability that I might get myself killed was an incentive to jump."

"Oh really?"

"Yes. Really."

"If given the chance or if dared to do it again, would you make that same jump today? Would you jump out of a moving school bus a second time?"

"No, I would not."

"Why not?" Dr. Goodwin leaned forward.

"Not enough chance of dieing. I don't think that the odds favor me dieing in a situation such as that one, especially since I already tried it once and can now speak from experience. Besides, I feel much less impervious today."

"So you still want to die then, Hunter?"

"Yes, of course I still want to die, but not nearly as badly as I did last night."

"Not as badly as last night?"

"No."

"Why not?"

"Can we change the subject?"

"Tell me about your parents." Dr. Goodwin glanced at his watch a second time.

"I love my parents. I always have. I think they did a very good job overall. Sure, they missed some signs. They missed some red flags along the way, in my teenage years especially, but, all things considered, I think they were the best parents anyone could have had."

"What 'signs' and what 'red flags'?" Dr. Goodwin was now cleaning his eyeglasses on the sleeve of his white shirt.

"Well, for one, they failed to notice that what should have been good times for me were almost always veiled by depression. They did not notice that I suffered from a strange inability to cope with the 'regular challenges' of everyday living. You know, Dr. Goodwin, I have suspected for years now that feeling overwhelmed the way I did then is common among people who are suffering from feelings of depression."

"I think that is a very insightful assessment on your part, Hunter."

"Yeah, I think so, too."

"Then, Hunter, give me an example or two of how your parents did not see that you were unable to cope with the 'regular challenges of everyday living,' as you put it."

"Well, the fact that I hardly ever slept is one example."

"Sleeping was a 'challenge' for you?"

"Yes. And it still is."

"And you are telling me that your parents did not notice that you were having a hard time sleeping?" He stretched his glasses over his ears, sliding them onto the bridge of his nose with an index finger.

"They did and they didn't."

"What does that mean?"

"It means that they witnessed occasions when I could not sleep. It also means that they did not take those occasions seriously. My mom told me once that even as an infant I hardly ever slept. Also, as an adolescent, I'd often fall asleep at, say, 3 o'clock in the morning only to wake up at, say, 7 o'clock in the morning. I would wake up hating myself and my parents and everyone else I knew because I had slept for only four hours. I would blame anyone and everyone for my trouble sleeping."

"And your parents didn't know that?"

"Like I already told you, they knew that sleeping was a problem for me. They just did not know how bad, how significant, the problem was. They did not know to what extent it affected me.

"Would you say that you were sad most of the time? Or were you happy most of the time"

"I was sad, very sad, very low the majority of the time. I do not think I smiled too often back then because my parents and my friends were constantly telling me to smile more, to laugh more. What was odd, though, is that I could not see why smiling or laughing was such a big deal. I could not see what was so funny or why everybody else appeared to be smiling and laughing. I must have missed the joke more than once. But, then again, there were those times I was happy and higher than a kite. There were those times I felt as if I were God himself I was so high.

"Okay … So what were some of the other signs, or red flags, your parents did not see?"

"I don't think I can list them all, Dr. Goodwin."

"Try to list a few."

"Well, they never seemed to notice how lonely I was in my mind, if that makes any sense to you. They didn't seem to notice how I was often alone in a crowd. I think they should have questioned my loss of interest in the activities I usually enjoyed, but they did not. I also think that they should have taken notice of my steady periods of self-loathing, but, again, they did not. There were a lot of other signs they missed.

"Such as?"

"My extreme temper is definitely one. They did not appear to notice just how unpredictable my temper was."

"You temper was pretty bad then, huh?"

"Yes, it was 'pretty bad.' It truly was. Hell, it still is."

"Apparently it is or you wouldn't have vandalized Kate's car the other night. Wouldn't you agree with that, Hunter?"

"Yes. I believe that's true."

"Any other signs that were missed?"

"Yeah … they did not discern, or take heed of, how disinterested in life I was and how I hated myself most of the time. They simply failed to see that my life lacked any real semblance of what I'd call a 'normal' life. And that pains me—a lot. I was hurting badly on the inside most of the time and they simply missed the signs."

"Did you ever try sharing with your parents how you were feeling? I think it would have been a good idea."

"No, I never did. Regrettably, I kept my feelings a secret."

"So you soldiered on?"

"I faked happiness. I maintained a false cheerfulness. I took on the dubious role of a happy person, acting as happy as I possibly could. It was a difficult part for me to play, but I think I pulled it off ... for the most part."

"And why do you think you did that?"

"Several reasons really. First, I think that I was waiting for a solution of some kind to present itself. In addition, I honestly did not believe the way I was feeling was worth mentioning—to anyone. I figured I was doing 'okay.' I figured that the occasional thoughts of dying with which I had been burdened off and on between the ages of three and thirteen were simply an unpleasant 'side of life' for all children. I believed that the more severe thoughts of suicide I had after the age of thirteen were also a 'natural fact of life.' Plus, I don't think that I wanted to burden my mom and dad with my emotional baggage, my emotional pain. My parents were great, you know. I definitely did not want to tell them that I was envisioning my own death now and then. I could not see myself putting that kind of pressure on them."

"But don't you think that you've put them under some pressure now, Hunter?" Just then, the phone next to my bed rang. Dr. Goodwin stood and started to make his way to the door.

"Let's talk some more," I said.

"There's a friend on the line for you. He pointed at the phone. He stepped quickly out of the room. The phone was still ringing.

CHAPTER 21

❀

"Hunter, how are you feeling, Hunter?" my mom asked. She was no longer crying, but I could sense that she was still in pain. Briefly, I considered my mom's question. I tried to rate my mood, but I couldn't. I really was not aware of how I was feeling exactly. I had my suspicions that I was unwell, but suspicions usually aren't enough to draw a bona fide conclusion, especially when it comes to rating one's mood. To put it another way, my outlook was way out of focus and the crusted blood on my wrists reminded me that I would be forever scarred. The same blood was making it difficult for me to highlight the positives in life, something my mom and dad had always told me to do no matter how messed up my life seemed to be. Highlighting the positives was my parents' best advice. Truthfully, highlighting the positives was the only real advice they ever gave me.

"I'm fine, Mom," I said many seconds later. But I knew that I was anything but fine. I knew that I had just lied to my mom for the umpteenth time in my life.

"No, Hunter. Really, how are you doing right now? Tell me, *how are you doing?* What does the doctor say?" Yes, my mom's tone sounded much, much better considering the actuality that one of her sons had recently attempted suicide.

"Dr. Goodwin says that I'm doing relatively well," I lied again.

"Well, Hunter, you need to give Dr. Goodwin permission to speak with your dad and I, so that we know what's going on with you, so that we can help you get back to normal." *"Yeah, sure. Back to normal,"* I said to myself.

"Okay, I will then," I lied once more. I did not intend to grant Dr. Goodwin permission to speak to my parents—not ever.

"Good, Hunter. So has John been by?"

"Yes. He dropped some stuff off this morning, clothes mostly. Lots of clothes. He's mad at me, Mom."

"Why?"

"I don't know why, but he's pissed as hell."

"But I don't know why he'd be mad at you."

"Maybe, maybe, maybe he's mad at me because I tried to kill myself. You need to think about that. Just try and think about that."

"He's not mad at you, Hunter. He's just very worried about you right now. He's concerned. He loves you. He's your brother."

"His love for me is not the issue. He's mad at me for doing it. He's mad that I am here. He's mad. Really. What he doesn't understand is that this is the one place I knew I would eventually end up one day if not six feet under."

"Hunter, don't say that. Don't talk like that." Now my mom sounded as if she were on the verge of crying—again.

"Well, it's the truth." Yes, my bitterness had returned.

"Why, Hunter?"

"Quit asking me 'why' all the time, Mom. I don't know why."

"You haven't really thought that you would eventually be in a hospital, on a psychiatric ward, have you?" At that point in the conversation, I noticed a marked change in the tone of her voice. She had never sounded so skeptical of me, so disbelieving, so determined to disagree with me.

"Yes, I have. I honestly have. I have had a hunch on and off for a very long time now that I would be hospitalized one day. I have wanted to die for almost forever. I am telling you the truth. You need to know that I am telling you the truth." This time I was not lying.

I do not remember saying goodbye to my mom that crucial day. I do not even remember how that particular conversation ended for that matter. Maybe my mom stopped arguing with me and told me that she loved me and reminded me one more time that I needed to permit Dr. Goodwin to speak with her and dad. Maybe I promised her a second time that I would be going home for Thanksgiving and we simply said goodbye with promises to talk again soon. Perhaps I simply hung up on her. Regardless, the real-life conversation between my mom and I was quickly replaced by a conversation from a corrupt dream, a dream I still remember.

The verbal exchange in the dream is an awkward one. In the dream, I am at odds with my mom as to whether I will eventually commit suicide or not.

"*God, why do you think that way, Hunter?*" she asks me in a detached manner, a manner that does not sound as distressed for me as I think it should.

"*I just want to be dead*," I respond, oblivious to the strangeness of that statement. I declare that I want to be dead as casually as if I were letting my mom know that I was running an errand, going to the grocery store for a gallon of milk for example.

"But, Hunter …" she says in return. She says nothing else. "But Hunter" is all she says.

"*I am going to kill myself someday*," I inform my own mother. The dream is definitely an odd one, to say the least.

"*Then do it!*" she shouts at me from the other side of that goddamn dream, from the other side of reality.

"*Okay, I will then!*" I shout back at her. Then silence sets in. There is silence, dead silence, the kind of silence that seemingly cannot be broken, that kind of hardened silence that is only audible in dreams or in nightmares. But, surprisingly, the hardened silence is short-lived.

"*You were once so happy, Hunter, weren't you? Weren't you ever happy?*" Her frightened voice breaks into the silence. Somehow, the silence I had thought was unbreakable is violently shattered.

"*Sometimes I was happy.*"

"*Tell me then, when were you happy? Help me understand.*" As if beckoned by mom's demanding question, a handful of blissful memories slam into me as I sleep, as I dream the day away. Those happy memories slam into my conscious with fervor. There they are, in full view, the good memories, the memories of my dad and I playing catch in the front yard on a Saturday afternoon. So many good memories are spinning in my head. So many, many memories of birthday parties and Christmas presents and summer nights spent camping in the backyard dance through my brain.

Then, without a moment's notice, the good memories become bad memories. The bad memories crash into me with a force that terrorizes my slumbering mind. Inescapable, undeniable memories of so many bad things that actually happened to me play on in my sleeping conscious like an unblemished video. There are memories of me hiding in the closet on a Saturday afternoon in an effort to avoid my life for a reason, or for reasons, I cannot define. There are memories of birthdays parties missed out on because of a depression that will not subside and sad, sad memories of Christmas presents forfeited to steady, unshakable feelings of melancholy. I am cheated out of glorious summer nights by aspirations of suicide I can not control. The good memories are wiped away by the bad memories like dirty words being erased from a chalkboard. And just like that, the good memories are turned into a worthless layer of dust.

"*I have wanted to be dead for a long time,*" I respond just as soon as the bad memories finally fade out of my dreaming head.

"*Why do you think that way?*" my mom asks again from the most faraway corners of the bothersome dream.

"*How I wish I knew,*" I tell her. That hardened silence that is only audible in dreams and nightmares returns. I awaken. The revealing dream is no more.

Believe it or not, my first suicide attempt gradually slipped to the back of my mind and fell from view almost entirely. My first attempt to kill myself became a blip on the radar screen that was my fractured existence. Eventually, I thought of that day as just another dark period in my dreary history and, eventually, my days became routine again, as routine as they could be for a suicide survivor that is.

My dad did send me to see our family doctor that day, the day that ultimately turned out to be anything but routine, the very same day my hearing was tested by the gruff male nurse, but, strangely enough, Dr. Lyon found nothing, absolutely nothing wrong with me. I sometimes think that Dr. Lyon might have had his suspicions that something was "not right" with me—physically or mentally or both—but I will probably never know. Whether he suspected that something was not right with me or not, Dr. Lyon dismissed me back into my old life without a single word of advice, or a single diagnosis, or a single prescription. It is safe to say that I lost all faith in nurses and doctors, as well as medical science that day. Perhaps that is why, so many years later, I regarded Big Nurse and Little Nurse as enemies and nothing more.

The pressure that had weighed heavily on my ears dissipated shortly after my appointment with Dr. Lyon. My hearing returned. The headaches and the steady feelings of nausea went away, too. Very soon, I concluded that I was fortunate that I had not done permanent harm to my hearing or any noticeable harm to my body. I also considered myself fortunate to have been able to survive my first suicide attempt virtually undetected.

As for Coach Leyland, I never did speak to him the following Monday about staying on the track team, as he had originally suggested, which was, in a matter of speaking, both upsetting to me and a tremendous relief. In fact, I never went out for high school track again. The team would carry on, winning meet after meet after meet without me.

Coach Leyland never spoke to me again. One of the few people who was in a position to acknowledge that something with me was "faulty" and get me the help I needed so badly, missed all indications that something was askew with my overall way of thinking and behaving. Sadly, he did not realize that I was in an unfortunate state of disrepair where my psychological make-up was concerned and he simply chose to ignore me. He shunned me and it was not long before I stopped bothering to say "hello" to him altogether. It was not long before we passed each other in the school hallways or on the street, like two broken acquaintances.

My parents never did ask me why I quit the track team. I think that they should have said something, anything, but they never mentioned my having quit track a single goddamn time. Again, I decided that they might have thought that I was simply acting like an average—or typical—teenager, somewhat reckless, somewhat indecisive, searching for my identity. Regardless, one more occasion in which my illness could have or should have been detected, let alone brought out into the open, was overlooked, blatantly missed. Another warning sign had passed undetected.

My dad never did mention to me my admission that I had swallowed the aspirins or the day he drove me to the hospital to get my hearing tested. Simply put, the subject of my having overdosed on aspirins was never brought up again. My dad treated that day like any other day really, as if it had never even happened in the first place. Maybe he was in denial that his oldest son had claimed to have overdosed. Maybe he simply thought that I was just being overly dramatic when I informed him that I had swallowed so many aspirins. Perhaps he thought that I was looking for attention, that my claim was in fact an attention-getting device or, even worse, that I was lying.

I am certain that my dad never shared with my mom the details of how he had driven me to the hospital that strange day because, had he told her, I have no doubt that I would have heard more, much more. At any rate, the day I attempted suicide for the first time in my life became a memory lost deep within the shadows of my depressed mind. In time, that very memory had virtually disappeared from view altogether and by the time I attempted suicide for the second and last time in 1994, the memory had faded so far into the distance I no longer gave it any substantial consideration whatsoever.

I think most unsuccessful suicide attempts end that way, you know, overlooked and shrouded in secrecy. I also think that the majority of undetected suicide survivors hush themselves and ultimately try to regain some degree of "normalcy" in their troubled lives. Those survivors try to move forward, giving life another "shot." Some survivors of a suicide attempt may find their lives again, despite the emotional scars that weigh heavily upon them. Other suicide survivors, however, simply fail to attain true peace within themselves. And it is those survivors that travel the road to their own private hell and attempt suicide a second time as I did, as Jocelyn Layne did, as have far too many other clinically depressed people.

I believe, more often than not, that the second attempt is much more serious than the first attempt. I believe that the second attempt is the one attempt that ultimately exposes the suicidal person as the person he or she is, a hurting person in dire need of medical attention. Because the seriousness of the second attempt usually surpasses the seriousness of the first attempt, the second attempt is usually much more difficult to conceal. The survivor of a second suicide attempt is often "found out," or discovered, all alone and in pieces. And that is, to put it mildly, a good thing.

Fortunately for me, I was found out, discovered. Why I opted to knock on Chan Allen's door after my second suicide attempt I still can not say. Regardless, I believe that fate intervened and sent me to his door in order that I would be discovered and rescued. And, as I have already told you, that is precisely where I was found. Yes, Chan Allen, the Vietnam War veteran and unique friend of mine found me standing alone and in pieces, bleeding at his doorstep. Shortly thereafter, paramedics discovered me in my apartment clinging to a life I truly no longer wanted, a life I had essentially discarded and hastily pieced me back together and transported me to Lakeshore General, a place I did not want to be in spite of the fact that I had envisioned myself on a psychiatric ward on countless occasions. There was simply no running from my second suicide attempt or from Seven Southwest. I could not run away from that particular attempt or that particular place no matter how badly I wanted to hide. I had been found out. Yes, fate had seen to that.

CHAPTER 22

❦

"What did Doctor Goodwin have to say?" Jocelyn definitely had a talent for making an entrance.

"Why weren't you at lunch with everyone else?" I asked her, feeling both betrayed and abandoned.

"Dr. Goodwin gave me a day pass, a ticket to freedom, a ticket to the real, tangible world. So, what the hell, I went to McDonald's."

"Oh," was all I said in return. I was a little jealous. McDonald's represented autonomy. The independence from Seven Southwest that I wanted so badly had never sounded so appetizing, believe it or not.

"You didn't answer me. What did Dr. Goodwin have to say?"

"He said that I have one week to live. Lord, let us celebrate!"

"Hallelujah, smart ass! Tell me, what did he say? Or don't you want me to know?"

"Truthfully?"

"Of course truthfully."

"He asked me a lot of questions, most of them about my childhood, that sort of crap."

"That's par for the course. Give it time and you will be asking him all of the questions."

"Asking what?"

"Oh, things such as, *What is depression? Why do I behave the way I do? Why did I do it?*"

"I think I know what depression is already."

"Maybe."

"So you think I have depression, don't you, Jocelyn?"

"I do. Remember, though, I'm definitely no expert on the subject. We both know that."

"When will I know for sure?"

"Well, the psychiatrists have to observe you for a while, for at least 72 hours I think. You don't know it, but you are under their careful observation right now."

"Am I on camera?"

"No, but they are watching you just the same. And they'll be watching you for a while."

"What I would not give to know how long 'a while' is."

"Seventy-two hours. I just told you that."

"Yeah, but you weren't sure. And you sounded just like Jane. That's the same thing Jane tells me every time I ask her when I'll being going home."

"Jane's a bitch. Don't compare me to her."

"I don't think that she's all that bad. Actually, I think she means well."

"Hunter, you will start hating her soon enough. No matter what a person's dilemma is, she believes that she knows everything there is to know about a person all of the time, all of the fucking time. And I mean that. No matter what a person says to her, she has an answer, '*the* answer,' and it is always the very opposite of what you tend to believe yourself."

"Really?"

"Really. Someone in her position, with her job I mean, should be a much better listener. It is so annoying the way she speaks as if she were a psychiatrist herself. She gets under my skin."

"What is her position by the way."

"She's a nurse. Right now, she is your primary nurse. And mine, too."

"I take it you don't care for Jane then?" I asked, smiling, trying to get Jocelyn to 'lighten up' a little.

"Of course I don't care for Jane. Listen to what it is I am telling you."

"I was only kidding."

"All right then."

"So does Jane give *you* any idea as to when you will be released?"

"No, she doesn't. It's really not her place to say."

"No idea whatsoever?"

"Jane doesn't say, but the doctors do."

"When?"

"Soon. Real soon I think. My discharge could be only hours away, Hunter."

"Out of here now, Jocelyn." It was Jane. Her identifying whisper was gone—again. She was now sounding like an angry drill sergeant.

"Ask me nicely," Jocelyn sassed her.

"Group therapy is in ten minutes. You will see Hunter then."

"Then I guess I will see you in ten minutes, Hunter." Jocelyn dragged her feet and smirked at Jane before she left my room.

"Hunter, you need to get cleaned up. You need to wash your face *now*. I will be back shortly to take you to group therapy."

"I don't want to go to therapy of any kind, Jane. I'm not ready. And I never will be. You can count on that."

"You don't have a choice this time. This isn't lunch we're talking about."

"But I *don't* want to go to therapy! Goddamn it, Jane! Listen to me for once!"

"Oh, but I am listening to you and you *are* going to therapy, Hunter."

"So be it," I said too weak mentally—and physically—to argue with her any longer. Reluctantly, I let Jane win.

"Thank you, Hunter. You'll be okay. Really you will."

I decided then and there that if I had to go to group therapy I would make myself look more presentable, as Jane had suggested. Of course that meant that the blood on my face would have to go. I stepped into the bathroom and up to the mirror with much more determination and confidence than I had demonstrated the first time I had peered into it. I pulled my cap from my head and managed to hang it on the rounded edge of the mirror. Light thrust itself onto the bloody range that was my face. I studied multiple streaks of blood, the ultimate proof of my battle with my self.

I wondered if my skin would be yellow under all of the red. I also wondered whether I would indeed appear jaundiced. I knew all too well that if I was jaundiced I was probably going to face a very slow, painful death. I also knew that I did not want to die slowly, gradually, in pain. If I was going to live only to die a slow death, I decided that I would definitely find a better, quicker way to kill myself.

I splashed some water onto my painted face. Droplets of red water colored the sink. More water on my face, more red droplets in the sink. More water, more water. More blood, more blood. Blood flowed in miniscule streams down the sides of the sink and into the drain. Then the blood mask I had been wearing for many hours was gone. My face was clean of blood for the first time in more than a day. I turned away from the mirror and rubbed a soft towel over my forehead, over my eyes, over my nose and over my lips. I stepped back into my room.

"The hour is at hand, Hunter. It is time for me to take you to group therapy." Jane had returned earlier than I had expected. She was standing alone in the doorway. "Let me see you. Yes, you look so much better now. It's nice to finally see your face. Honestly."

I had rinsed the blood from my mug with much success and, in the process, had discovered that my complexion was a blanched white and not a deep, troubling yellow, as I had feared it might be. Nevertheless, I still felt that I was not prepared to join the crowd of misfits or attend the session itself—at least not emotionally. I knew that I was still too unstable emotionally to take part in such an event and, again, the thought of coming into contact with all of the suicidal psychos, not to mention the woman whose chilling scream I had heard the previous night, upset me tremendously. I wanted absolutely nothing to do with any of them and I told Jane so, challenging her once again.

"I'm not going, Jane."

"Hunter, group therapy is an important—even basic—part of the healing process. Besides, everyone attends group. There are no exceptions, so let's go. Now! Okay?"

"I'm not ready. Besides, you sound like an infomercial for a psychiatric hospital or, worse yet, for a regional center." I was suddenly determined to defeat Jane at her own game.

"You're not ready for what?" The drill sergeant shouted at me.

"I am *not* ready to stand in front of a bunch of unknowns with intentions of explaining why I ended up on this *goddamn ward*, sergeant!" I shouted.

"It's not like that," she flinched. "That may be the way it is in the movies or on t.v. or at other psychiatric facilities, but that's not how things work on Seven Southwest. We do things differently here. You will stand in front of no one and if you do not want to speak, you can always listen. There is therapy in listening, too, Hunter."

"So tell me then, how often do I have to attend group therapy?" I was hoping that attending group therapy was a one-time affair.

"There are two sessions a day, five days a week. And participation is mandatory."

"That sounds like a lot. Besides, Jane, I'm leaving soon. Remember?"

"I remember, Hunter. I remember." So I went to my first group therapy session in protest, against my better judgment, under the sergeant's watchful eye. On the way down the long corridor, I reminded myself that I might be forced to attend only a small handful of group therapy sessions since I would be leaving the hospital in less than 72 hours. I made up my mind that I would skip as many of the remaining sessions as I possibly could before I was discharged. That way nobody would have a chance to get to know me very well—patients and staff included.

"Everyone, this is Hunter. Hunter, this is everyone. These people are your fellow travelers, Hunter," Jane said to me in her trademark whisper, the drill sergeant having vanished altogether. "Hunter arrived here late last night," she announced to the circle of faces, still whispering. "Please introduce yourselves as time allows and make him feel welcome." Then she departed, leaving me standing in the doorway by myself. That is when all eyes centered on me for what seemed like forever—if not longer. I stared back at those eyes, the same eyes that were now searching, I suspected, for my skeleton, for my true identity.

While I stood there staring, frightened by the very people I figured society had branded defectives, I noted that a few of them actually cast wary smiles in my direction. A few others glanced away from me as if they were embarrassed to be there or embarrassed of themselves or embarrassed to have met me. Others waved halfheartedly. One old man nodded at me. He nodded at me as if he had placed me from another period in his life, as if we were old war-time buddies reunited for the first time in years. I soon saw that Jocelyn was seated by herself on a long sofa to my left, directly across from the man who had nodded at me. Our eyes met and, with the slightest tilt of her head, she motioned for me to sit beside her. Without hesitation, I stepped out of the bashful state I was in, entered the solitude of the carpeted room and sat next to her diminutive figure. I stole several more glances at the timeless, seemingly-defeated profiles of the entire group. I tried to put a face to the woman who had screamed at the ghosts of depression the night before, but I was unable to make a connection. If she was there, I had no way of knowing it.

"How are you feeling right now?" Jocelyn murmured. Her breath smelled like mouthwash, like Cepacol.

"I don't want to be on this ward," I said to her. "I don't want to be in this room. And that is the truth. You have no idea how scared I am of being in here with these freaks," I intoned. I was telling the truth.

"There's no need to be afraid. I'm here with you." She handed me a piece of gum and smiled the kind of smile that comforts a person in an inexplicable way. Then she clasped my right hand, the hand that did not have a catheter jutting out of it, in her own. Her touch warmed me more than I am able to articulate right now. Let me tell you, there is nothing like the touch of another human being when you are suffering on a locked psychiatric ward waiting to see if your own survival is obtainable, let alone worthwhile.

The unmistakable tones of nurses and various other staff members muttering in the corridor soon flooded my thoughts. I asked myself whether they were whispering about me. Again, I could not think of a decent answer. Then the flooding voices stopped, Jocelyn's warm grip tightened just a little and a rather striking blond woman with emerald eyes strode into the room with a clipboard tucked under her arm. A balding man with a rather wide mustache called out, "Hi, Kris."

"And how are you doing today, Ernest?" Kris asked, smiling.

"Good," Ernest responded with marked enthusiasm. "I'm good, real good."

"That's very nice to hear, Ernest." Still smiling, Kris withdrew a chair on wheels from the shadows just beyond the group's perimeter and positioned it in the very center of the room, within the confines of the human circle. It was obvious that she had sat there many times before.

"So how is everyone else doing this afternoon?" her eyes examined the dozen or so silent faces for a response. "Come on, someone speak to me. Please. It is another glorious day, a new beginning. Someone must have something to say to me."

"I have something to ask you, Kris," said a man at last, a man who possessed a movie star's face complete with blue eyes and sand-colored hair, hair that fell freely and touched the collar of his denim-blue shirt. The man who claimed to have something to say was seated directly opposite from where Jocelyn and I sat holding hands. I noticed that he was clutching a clipboard of his own.

"Hi, Mr. Mann. Go right ahead. Share with all of us what it is you are thinking today," Kris responded in a voice so sweet it nearly sickened me. I noticed that her see-through smile was suddenly replaced by a frown. The rest of the group also seemed to be frowning as they too awaited Mr. Mann's question, a question I suspected would catch Kris entirely off guard or offend her or both.

"Call me 'Ayden.' I prefer Ayden. You should know that by now, Kris."

"Okay then. I'm sorry, Ayden. I forgot. So what's on your mind today, Ayden?"

"Well, Kris, how is it that you can assume that you know what we are all going through when you are not even living what we are living right now?"

"I'm not following you, Ayden."

"You think you know so much about manic depression when you actually know very little."

"So that's what's on your mind today, Ayden? Kris responded with measurable calm, dignifying with an answer a question that sounded too vague in nature to deserve an answer in the first place, a question she could have easily ignored.

"Yes. I want to know your answer to that one." I heard a small hint of hatred for Kris in Ayden's low, distinct voice.

"First, I'm not 'assuming' anything. And second, Ayden, I can say that, essentially, I only know what it is you tell me—as individuals and as a group. I have my own 'theories' as to what you are living, as to what you are going through. I have my own guesses, educated guesses I think, as to why you act or behave the way you do. I have been doing this kind of work for years and years now, Ayden. And while I cannot *force* you to have confidence in me, it would be nice if you could trust me just a little, don't you think?" A tone that was as tense as I was stunned had replaced Kris' sugary voice.

"But how *can* I trust you? You have never walked in my shoes or, more important, stepped inside my head?" I felt Jocelyn's grip tighten around my hand like a soft leather glove that is too small to do the job for which it is intended. And yet her fragile hand warmed me in a manner in which I had never been warmed before.

"Those are really very good questions, Ayden. Yes, they are all very good questions, very good questions indeed. And I can appreciate your concern, but I also know a lot more about your illness than you may realize, than you are willing to admit, than you are willing to give me credit for."

I glanced at Ayden. Since being delivered to Lakeshore General, I had been asking myself the very same questions of the entire staff, including Jane and the almighty Dr. Goodwin. Until I had heard Ayden speak, I had assumed that all mental patients—with the exception of Jocelyn—were a bunch of sick idiots. But now I was beginning to see things differently and I silently applauded Ayden for asking Kris the questions I knew I was still too shy and too afraid to ask of anyone.

"You know, Kris, you are like an astronaut who knows every single thing there is to know about space flight, but has never actually walked on the moon. You may have been educated to deal with manic depression, but you can't possibly know what it truly means to be as sick and depressed as I am, as we are." He was now staring directly at Kris's thin, sharp face and, I was fairly certain, right through her outer body to the bones of her skeleton. Again, I silently applauded him for being so open, so blunt.

"Does anyone here agree with Ayden?" Kris rotated her chair in the tightest of circles, her tiny feet propelling her and surveyed the faces of the silent people who, I was sure, were also staring through her outer body, through her pale skin at her freshly marred skeleton, searching for who she really was. Jocelyn nudged me with an elbow and I froze. I think I knew what was coming. Jocelyn, like Ayden, had an agenda.

"I do," Jocelyn responded. She sounded so confidant I was glad to know her. She raised her free hand and waved it at Kris.

"And what did you want to add, Jocelyn? Kris asked with apparent caution. "Why do you agree with Ayden? And speak up, please." From just beyond the confines of the human circle, Ayden was beaming. He had an out-and-out abettor and he knew it. He knew without a doubt that he was not alone. Just that quickly, Kris had lost control of the group. And, just that quickly, Ayden had found it.

"Well," Jocelyn said, taking time to clear her throat, "because only a depressed person can truly know what it is like to be a depressed person. Only a depressed person can honestly know what it's like to live a single day stigmatized by the better part of society and seemingly dead on the inside. There is no way you could have peered into hell's flames, as we've often done."

"Hell's flames? That's a bit dramatic, don't you think, Jocelyn?"

"No, not really. I don't think so."

"So is that to say that I cannot learn from you, from your experiences, especially your depressive experiences, as you might learn from my own life experiences?" I shot a glance at Ayden. He was now staring at the carpet at Kris's feet.

"I think that Ayden is onto something. All the education you claim to have and you're still 'out of tune,' or 'out of step' with us."

"I am a clinical psychologist, Jocelyn, and not the naïve gal next door. That should be worth something, don't you think?" Kris was beginning to sound frustrated.

"So what! Your degree, your education, is worth *nothing* to me. You are a facilitator of this group and *nothing* more!"

"Well, I think that you need to get your facts straight before you criticize me."

"I am not criticizing you!"

"Then go ahead and make your point. And lower your voice please."

Jocelyn cleared her throat a second time. "Just let me say that when Ayden compared you to a well-trained astronaut who has never had the opportunity to walk on the moon, an astronaut who is lost in space, he was right. You cannot possibly know what it is like to be as sick as we are. You cannot speak from experience, but only from what you have read in textbooks and learned from a few other 'bogus' sources."

"Hey, Jocelyn, what about all of the information I have gleaned from you and all of the other depressed people I have ever counseled. Doesn't that matter? Isn't that worth something? I believe it is."

"It's not enough."

"Then you tell me what it is I need to know in order to help you, in order that I might better serve you, so to speak. And you tell me too, Ayden. And anyone else who wants to have his or her say, please tell me exactly what it is you think I need to know. More important, you tell me precisely what it is you *want* me to know."

"The list is a long one, Kris," I blurted, very surprised that I had said anything at all. In my peripheral vision, I saw Ayden jerk his head in my direction. His movie star grin had widened again. He realized that his posse was growing.

"Well, Hunter, we still have lots of time." Kris said, turning her chair slightly and aiming her eyes directly at my own.

"No, we do not have that kind of time. *You*, Kris, do not have that kind of time. And if you weren't so lost in outer space, you would probably understand that."

What happened during the remainder of group that day is hazy at best. Today, many years after that particular group session took place, I am relatively certain that Kris never regained control of the group because I seem to remember that Ayden took a few more very powerful verbal jabs at her before she dismissed us. I also remember that Ayden shook my hand as we left the room. "It's good to know you," he said with a smile that appeared to be genuine. Until Ayden had smiled at me, I had no idea that a manic-depressive could smile that way. There was a measurable amount of hope in his smile.

CHAPTER 23

❧

I thought of my first group therapy experience as a bad joke and nothing more. I thought that Kris was a sad, sad pushover. To be more specific, I thought of her as a pathetic pushover lost, as Ayden had initially suggested, in outer space. Had I only known what my own illness actually was, more about the mental illness with which I would soon be diagnosed and more about myself from a medical perspective, I would have shoved my shyness aside and had more to say to her. But, as Jane had stated just prior to group, there is therapy in listening and listening to Ayden and Jocelyn had been therapeutic to a degree and had opened my eyes for the first time to the notion that manic-depressives are not at all crazy or defective.

We found ourselves in her room this time, Jocelyn and I. I was quick to note that both the layout and the decor of her room were identical to mine, right down to the sepia recliner. However, unlike my own room, Jocelyn's room was embellished with balloon bouquets and get-well cards and a large assortment of stuffed animals from well-wishers. Jocelyn's warm room made my own room seem dark and desolate.

"Park it," Jocelyn commanded. I sat in the recliner without hesitation. Jocelyn knelt on her bed, facing me. So there we were, just the two of us, trading glances in a peaceful kind of silence. That is when it occurred to me that I did not know what Jocelyn's diagnosis was. Of course I suspected that she was suffering from manic depression, but I wasn't certain.

"Jesus, Hunter, what is it you are thinking about? You look so troubled and confused. Plus, you're staring."

"I'm thinking nothing," I lied.

"You *are* thinking something. I can tell that you are. You definitely do not possess a 'poker face.' Come on, you can share your thoughts with me. What's on your mind?"

"Well ... I'm thinking that I don't even know what your own diagnosis is. I'm also thinking that I am in no position to ask you what mental illness you are ... suffering from."

"I am bipolar, a manic-depressive. My official diagnosis, Hunter, is Bipolar 1," she said with gusto, obviously unafraid to openly identify her mental illness to me. "I am a manic-depressive. Just realize this: that's *what* I am, but not *who* I am."

"Okay."

"You didn't know that already, Hunter?"

"No, I didn't. You never said."

"You never asked. Plus, I thought that you would have figured that out by now, especially after what I said to Kris in group today."

"Well, maybe I wanted to hear it from you."

"Well, now you have. You have heard my own diagnosis straight from the heart. And now you can tell me what your last name is, don't you think? Remember: fair is fair."

"Jocelyn, why is my last name so important to you?"

"I'm just curious. That's all. Really. And don't forget that you already know mine."

"It's Kraven. My last name is Kraven."

"Hunter Kraven, huh? I never would have guessed that—not ever. I like it, though. I like it a lot, Hunter Kraven."

"Well, I'm glad that you like my last name," I said with a laugh and a sigh, having noticed that I felt especially good when talking to Jocelyn—even when talking about nothing in particular.

With Jocelyn's diagnosis now officially revealed to me, our trust for one another seemed to be solidified. Endeavoring to build on that trust, the two of us soon discovered that we had even more to share with one another than we had originally thought. We talked candidly for a considerable amount of time, for a couple of hours I think. We remembered. We shared. We remembered and shared some more. This time, however, we spoke mostly about our respective childhoods, the periods in our lives when we had both felt somewhat happier and much less depressed and didn't feel like dieing quite so often.

We examined some of the bad times, those times when we had missed out on various life-events, such as school dances, family picnics and sunsets due to our depressive emotions having taken control of our ability to think clearly and make "proper" decisions. We talked about some of the good times as well. We reflected on the first time we had discovered rainbows after a summer rain. We called to mind weekend afternoons spent making mud pies in our mothers' gardens and spoke of snacking on cookies and milk after school, many of the "better things" in a child's life.

We also acknowledged one last time the wounds on each of my wrists, the wounds that were now indelibly stamped upon me, the wounds that would soon turn into scars and mirror Jocelyn's own disturbing scars. We recognized that concealing our scars from the public's intrusive and judgmental gaze would be an "obstacle" we would have to face together *and* alone if we were to earn a "fair chance" at living a happy, productive life. Then we speculated how wounded and scarred our psyches might be if and when we reentered the world beyond the immense walls of glass and the thick doors, the same doors that separated Seven Southwest from the rest of the human race.

Furthermore, we owned up to the fact that we had any number of obstacles to overcome if we were ever going to reintegrate into society. We made a short list of some of those obstacles, the hurdles that would inevitably present themselves, taking turns scribbling them on the back of a Hallmark card. We understood that we would lose forever some of our most trusted friends. We understood that there would be that faction of people who would reject and abandon us. We decided that losing friends would be the most difficult aspect of living among the populace as a manic-depressive suicide survivor. But we also decided that we could "make it" as a team and individually—if my injured body managed to survive the aftershock of an acetaminophen overdose that is.

Our efforts to share our experiences with people who would try not to listen to us speak of our days and nights spent on Seven Southwest would surely be thwarted. And then there would be the 'challenge' of dealing with the rumors that would undoubtedly circulate throughout our public and private worlds, to the places we would do our best to deem off limits to others, the curious places we would eventually dub "safe harbors." Yes, rumors of our strange, manic journeys would definitely circulate. And then we would be labeled.

"We'll be targets for ridicule and so we'll have to beat the fucking odds," Jocelyn said to me that day. "We'll have to face ourselves and each other as well as the rest of society head on. We will have to summon a kind of strength we've never summoned before."

"I'm not sure that I can," I said as soon as Jocelyn had recorded the last obstacle—our need to highlight life's positives—on the back of the Hallmark card. "I'm really not sure that I can."

"I'm hurting, too, Hunter. You need to understand that."

"I know that you are hurting, but you aren't dieing as I am." As soon as I spoke those words, the ache that had been pulsating from my abdomen, from my liver itself, seemed to worsen. The pain became more pronounced and any thoughts of a future life quickly slipped from view, giving way to the present and the likelihood that my greatest obstacle of all would be surviving liver poisoning.

Having decided that we could "beat the fucking odds" if my body did manage to heal itself, the two of us sat in Jocelyn's room hurting in ways that were unique to us. Each of us answered a steady stream of questions as accurately and as honestly as we possibly could. I shared with Jocelyn various details of my distressing life. I shared with her the truth that I still wanted to die, especially if that was my fate. I shared with her my self, breaking boundaries and barriers and crossing lines I had never crossed before.

Then we talked about Jocelyn, Jocelyn the person, the only daughter of a troubled and over-protective army colonel and an elementary school teacher. Jocelyn told me about her life as a military brat and how, by the time she had turned ten years old, her family, which included a pair of well-disciplined older brothers, had relocated five times. Jocelyn had lived on military bases as far away as Munich, Germany and Fort Hood Texas, among others.

Jocelyn had been doted on by her brothers and a mother she described as being "downright over-protective" and still she insisted that she had suffered from a loneliness that was brought about by her family's traveling lifestyle. "I was afraid to make friends with people I might never see again," Jocelyn confided in me. "And, at the same time, I was really very scared of the loneliness that was living inside of me, the loneliness I was a part of."

Even though she possessed stunning attractiveness and obvious intellect, Jocelyn gradually became withdrawn from her family and her peers. Over time, she became increasingly uninvolved in her own life. She became lost in self-absorption. Tragically, she began to "lose her grip." Very slowly, she was slipping, sinking. And while Jocelyn was gradually failing at life those days, she did manage to excel in the classroom, a place where she had always felt "at ease" and "comfortable." A straight A student from the time she was in grade school until she graduated with honors from an Ivy League university, she had almost always felt ostracized from the life she led outside the classroom.

After earning a bachelor's degree in Communication Studies in just three years, Jocelyn briefly considered pursuing a career in broadcasting, but she was so depressed and suicidal she could not hold down an entry level position for any considerable amount of time. "I was so depressed I could hardly put together a simple resume," Jocelyn reflected. "The jobs I did get hired for, my father had found for me through a myriad of contacts and connections."

"And you lost them?" I asked, concerned.

"I lost several jobs because of my manic depression. Today, I am positive that manic depression was the major cause, the main culprit. But it wasn't just manic depression that was interfering with my ability to function and my ability to find a semblance of a so-called 'normal life.' Suicidal thinking, a product of depression, was also to blame. And because I wanted to die so badly, I was having an especially hard time finding out who I was and who I wanted to be. I was out of touch with myself. I had a very respectable degree stowed away in a cardboard box in my parents' basement and a family that supported me to no end and yet I did not support myself. You could say that my depression was running amok. Suicidal ideation was secretly dominating my thinking and my overall outlook, my perspective on life, my life."

"Did you ever think of asking your parents for help?" I asked, sounding, I noticed, a little like Dr. Goodwin.

"Once I did. I remember that I was a freshman in college the day I cried out to them for what would turn out to be the very last time. I told my mom and dad that I was sick inside, that I was sick emotionally. I described to them exactly how I was feeling, how I felt as if nothing was working for me. I told them that something was not 'clicking' inside of me. I cried tears I'd never cried before, Hunter, I was so upset."

"And what did they say to you?"

"My mom threw a fit, called me "ungrateful" and stomped out of the room."

"Ungrateful, huh?

"Yeah, ungrateful."

"And your dad?"

"He walked out of the room in silence."

"And then what happened?"

"Nothing. Neither one of them spoke of my claim that I was sick ever again."

"In denial, you think?"

"Oh yes."

At that point in our conversation, Jocelyn was called out of the room by one of the many techs, apparently to take her meds, or to see any one of the many psychiatrists, or both.

"See you later?" I asked her.

"See you later."

I sat alone in her room for a few more minutes, studying more closely the tokens from her various supporters, the people who were "pulling" for her until a tech chased me out. I returned to my own quiet room, trading one kind of loneliness for another. I turned on the pair of skinny lamps. I sat in the recliner in front of the gray-black television screen and reread the list of obstacles we had written on the back of the Hallmark card until I fell asleep.

A short time later, I was awakened by a hollow knocking sound. I opened my eyes and saw that Ayden was standing in the doorway. "Are you up for company?" he asked.

"Of course."

"That's good. I know that I could sure use a little companionship myself right now."

"Yeah, so could I."

"You arrived just last night, huh?" Ayden sat down on the end of my bed and rested his hands in his lap. He looked intense sitting there, like a man searching for his own lost soul, like a man who is searching for an inner peace he cannot seem to find no matter what stone he uncovers.

"Yes, last night. And you?"

"I arrived the night before you did. But I'll be leaving soon."

"How do you know?"

"Because I was diagnosed a manic nearly twelve years ago, at the age of eighteen actually. My illness is already well-documented. Until now, I was really doing very well."

"Then, if you don't mind, how did you end up here?"

"Well, kind of strange really … On a whim, and after I had a few beers inside me, I tried to cut myself with a small pocket knife and announced to some friends that I wanted to die. They took me seriously. I didn't really want to die at all and still they took me seriously. They threw me into a van and drove me to the emergency room. I suppose I can't blame them for reacting the way they did. They were only trying to help me."

"On a whim? I have no idea what you mean by that."

"I mean that I did it without thinking it through. I'd never cut myself before. Actually, I didn't even cut myself. I dragged the dull pocket knife across my forearm, barely leaving a mark, and declared to a few of my closest buddies that I wanted to die."

"Why would you do that?" I asked, aware that I was probably being overly critical of a man who had almost done the very same thing I had done to myself.

"I was drunk and acting stupid for the most part. Plus, I think I needed some attention that night."

"You did it for attention?" I was instantly reminded of the painting of my own grave I had created years earlier for precisely the same reason, to get attention.

"Yep."

"And you'd never done anything like that before, Ayden?"

"Never."

"What in the hell happened then? What went wrong?"

"Well, I'm not sure that anything did go wrong. All I can say is that I was feeling so good, so good about myself and the way my life was going, I decided that I didn't need them anymore, my medications I mean. So, one day, I just stopped taking them altogether. I dropped them into a trash can and walked away. It wasn't long before I started feeling depressed again."

"Quitting your meds wasn't a very smart move on your part, huh?" I asked, both confused *and* worried about my newest companion.

"Not a good move when you consider I knew better."

"So you'll be going home soon despite the fact that you abandoned your medications?"

"I believe so. I've promised the doctors and myself that I'll take my medications for good this time, especially if it means distancing myself from this place. Still, I'm afraid."

"Afraid of what?"

"Afraid that my medications might interfere with my creativity, with my ability to write well, with my ability to actually sit down and write a novel."

"You mean you're a writer?" I was impressed by the prospect of being in the company of a "real writer."

"I'm an aspiring novelist, a would-be writer, a 'writer-in-training,' if you will."

"What does that mean?"

"It means that I'm still searching for my story and my voice, among other things. It also means that I'm unpublished."

"Is being unpublished such a bad thing, Ayden." It was a stupid question and I wanted badly to take it back, but Ayden answered anyway.

"Yes, being unpublished is a bad thing. I suspect that it always will be. Hunter, we live in a society that only views a 'writer' as a 'real writer' after he has published something. It is a frustrating dilemma, man, especially if the aspiring writer wants and needs affirmation that what he is doing is legitimate and worthwhile."

"I have to admit that makes a lot of sense to me. It's sad that our society thinks that way."

"Yeah, it is."

"So how do you search for a story? And how do you search for a voice?"

"I'm not sure just yet. I make up the rules as I go along mostly. I listen. I observe. I spy. And then I listen, observe and spy some more."

"Is that all there is to it?"

"No, of course not. Because I'm still searching for the do-it-yourself method to becoming a writer of fiction, I understand that there is much more to becoming a novelist than just being a spy."

"Have you always wanted to be a writer, a novelist?"

"Yes, I have. From an early age, I knew that I was different. I think I sensed that something was amiss deep inside me and that I would be writing about myself someday. Would you believe I was reading at age four and writing my own stories by the time I was five?"

"I can believe that. If you don't mind, what have you written?"

"A lot of short stories, a few poems. Some of it is shit, but some of my writing is actually pretty damn good. When I'm having a depressive episode or stuck in what I refer to as a 'black mood,' I can't write at all. I can't write when I'm manic either. I write my best stuff when I'm hypomanic, feeling not overly depressed or overly manic, but somewhat lucid instead. My productivity increases tremendously when I'm in a hypomanic phase. Unfortunately, I've never been hypomanic long enough or often enough to write an entire novel. I have bunches and bunches of notes I pieced together while I was hypomanic, but virtually nothing to show for the time I invested in writing those goddamn notes. I've lost a lot of valuable time, Hunter, a lot of very valuable time."

"And now, with your new meds inside of you instead of beer, you are going to write the Great American Novel, huh?"

"I sure as hell hope so. At least then I'd be leaving my mark, if you know what I mean."

"I don't know that I follow you," I stated. With that Ayden let out a frustrated sigh and, suddenly, I pictured him sitting in front of an antique typewriter in a big city somewhere, a pencil tucked behind his ear, crumpled sheets of paper at his feet, the page in the typewriter as white as snow.

"Well, I'd be leaving this life having made my mark. I'd be leaving this world a success."

"Sounds as if being recognized and remembered as a published author is really very important to you."

"It is."

"Why?"

"Well, you see, I never really knew my father. I knew him as a dad before he died, but I never knew him as a man, as a writer. That's what he really wanted to be, a writer, a novelist."

"Was your dad killed in the Vietnam War by chance?" I asked. "I have had my suspicions since I was eight or so that my dad *almost* was."

"No, he wasn't killed in any goddamn war."

"But your dad was a writer, Ayden?"

"He was definitely a writer. He never published anything worth noting, but he was a writer through and through. He was still working on his novel when he was killed by a drunk driver while crossing the street to buy a carton of cigarettes."

"My god. How tragic."

"I know. His death still makes me shudder."

"How old were you when he was killed?"

"I was only six at the time. I could definitely use a cigarette right now, man, but these damn fools won't let me smoke in here when I want to. I can only go for a smoke three times a day. And that sucks."

"Stressed, huh?"

"Only when I'm not writing."

"So you are really going to write a novel? I'm sorry, but I just can't believe it." I was awestruck by the man I was sitting next to. I was also taking extra care not to pry as to what the subject matter would be, acutely aware that writing of any kind is a very personal thing.

"I have to write a novel. I feel it swelling inside of me, breathing. I need to get it out of me, out of my system. I need to put it on paper once and for all. Plus, I feel a dire need to follow through with my dad's failed mission."

"Mission, Ayden?"

"Mission."

"How hard it must be for you to feel the need to follow in your dad's literary footsteps, especially when you never really had a chance to know him as a man, let alone as a writer. What I mean to say is how do you measure up to a man you've never really known?"

"I publish. Would you believe I still see him, Hunter? I still see him staring out the window in silence, looking for those answers that never seem to come to a writer very easily, for the same answers he never had a chance to find, the same answers I'm still searching for myself." Having made that statement, Ayden stood and stretched.

"I think that maybe I see him, too, Ayden," I said, taking a cognitive snapshot of the profile of Ayden Mann, the aspiring writer, and adding it to my ever-growing collection before he exited my humble room and disappeared down the corridor without speaking another word.

CHAPTER 24

❀

For whatever reason, and to my disappointment, Jocelyn did not answer the call to dinner and so Ayden and I shared our own table in the dining room that evening. Ayden picked at his food while he described various abstract details of a life he openly referred to, quite simply, as his "disrupted and fractured existence." At first, ours was a conversation having little to do with any one thing in particular. But then, as if he had been nudged in the back by an impatient school teacher peering over his shoulder expressly to check that his homework was complete, Ayden became strangely serious and spoke in a confiding tone about the highs and lows, the moodswings, he had experienced throughout the years. And as he reflected, I could only imagine the novel he would write one day. His talent for putting his thoughts in order was evident. His flair for describing that which mattered most to him—his desire to write for example—was obvious—even to me, a wannabe writer who had never published anything at all. And while he too had never before been published, I got the distinct feeling that Ayden was already a member of a special literary league that was, more likely than not, shared by a very limited number of extremely talented "writers-in-training."

Ayden revealed that he had essentially lived two very different lives. First, he claimed to have lived a roller coaster life, a painful life, a life of disjointed emotions that had unfolded at a rapid pace prior to his diagnosis having been made "official." He explained that he had lived a life that began soon after his having been "properly" medicated, a new life that had unfolded much more slowly and with much less pain than the first life. "I felt better after I'd been on my meds for a couple of months," Ayden said to me that night in the dining room. "There were those days I actually thought that I was truly defeating my mental illness. There were those days I believed that I was going to lay bipolar disorder at my feet—forever."

"So you did feel better then, while medicated, didn't you?" I asked him, somewhat confused.

"Almost," he answered in an unconvincing whisper. "Almost."

"How can a person 'almost' feel better?"

"Well, because I'd definitely become less manic and less depressed while medicated. And, also, because I certainly wasn't cycling nearly as much as I had cycled during my first life. That was a victory in itself, Hunter. However, at the same time, my writing was suffering tremendously. You see, I simply wasn't writing anything that was worth anything. And I could not stay focused. I concluded that I was overly medicated and, therefore, I felt that I was *almost* winning the war I was waging against bipolar disorder. Yeah, almost. Almost."

"That must've been a difficult time for you."

"It was. It was a difficult time. In retrospect, I can see that I had been living my first life almost solely for my next manic high, my next rush, my next thrill. A short time later, after having accepted my diagnosis and my need to be medicated and after what seemed like an eternity of counseling, I was living a second life, a life that was actually much better than the first. In fact, I was living that second life almost exclusively for a new tomorrow so that I could, at long last, write effectively and tell my own bipolar story." At that moment, Ayden shoved his plate of food aside and motioned to a nearby tech that he needed a cigarette by holding his thumb and forefinger to his pursed lips. It was a gesture that was wasted on the one man in the room who would see to it that there would be no more smoke breaks until the following morning. The tech simply rolled his eyes and shook his head before he turned on a ceiling light that was a disturbing kind of yellow and left Ayden and I sitting alone together.

"But now you've stopped taking your meds," I said. "Ayden, that's one of the reasons you're on Seven Southwest. You told me so."

"That was just a stupid stunt, an experiment at best, Hunter. I thought that I might write better without them, but my mind raced so badly I couldn't write at all. Like I said, I couldn't stay focused. Now I've started taking them again. Truthfully, I'm taking a new and supposedly 'improved' regimen. This time my doctor will be watching to see that my creativity isn't jeopardized by medications. I'll be watching, too, you know. And as long as I can write well, write with a renewed passion and stick with it, I'll stay with them. And then my third life chapter can and will begin."

"So, Ayden, would you say that your manias got you into trouble?" I asked, pushing what was left of my cold meatloaf away from me. I was secretly crossing my fingers that he would answer such a personal question.

"Yes, they did. I definitely got into trouble from time to time and more often than most people I think."

"If you don't mind, what were some of the worst things you can remember doing when you were manic?" I asked. As I posed that question, I was instantly reminded of the recent night I had vandalized Kate's car.

"The list is a long one. God, Hunter, the list is a long one. Truthfully, I remember doing many bad things while I was manic. But one thing in particular stands out." With that, he leveled his gaze on me. He stared directly into my eyes. He was searching for both my skeleton and my inner self I was certain. And I knew, more than anything, that Ayden was searching my character to see if he could trust me. After all, if he was going to trust me with any more information related to his manic and double-sided life, I understood all too well that he would need to know why I wanted to know what I wanted to know.

"Well, I've got time." That is when Ayden's focus appeared to become diverted. He stopped staring at me altogether. His dark eyes began to explore the void behind me, the void just over my shoulder, and I was thinking that his intense vision was focusing on a segment of the life he had lived prior to his having been diagnosed manic-depressive.

"I've got to trust you, Hunter." Now his eyes were frisking my person again.

"I know that you do. And you can."

"Okay then."

"Okay, Ayden." And with that, the flood gates opened and Ayden let the truth flow out.

"From a fairly young age, I had felt hyper in my brain," he said with a heavy sigh. "My jumbled thoughts confused me often. Almost all the time I was feeling so hyper in my head I was fearing what might happen to me next. Even worse, I was afraid of what I might happen to do next."

"So how old were you when you noticed such feelings?" I asked, sounding, I realized, like a meddling writer conducting an interview for a cheap teen magazine. I was upset that I was acting that way and so I made it my goal to sound reserved, nonchalant even.

"I was just a kid, Hunter. I don't remember an exact age. I only remember that I was still a little kid when I experienced such awkward feelings."

"Were you ever afraid that you might harm yourself?" I felt as if I were prying again so I tried to calm myself. I wanted to play it cool, but I also wanted information—badly.

"Of course I was afraid that I might harm myself. And I was also afraid that I might harm *someone* else. To be honest, I was afraid either way."

"So *did* you ever harm yourself, Ayden?" I asked, glancing over his shoulder and studying closely his silhouette on the wall. His upright silhouette looked unflawed, as if it were a statue, a statue of a great, great man, both strong and secure and not at all like a man who was mentally ill and sitting with a stranger on a psychiatric ward discussing particulars of a life that had been anything but normal. Briefly, I contemplated showing Ayden his own broad and perfect shadow on the wall, but I knew that if he turned to see his shadowed likeness it would be forever altered by his movement. His silhouette would be broken.

"No, except for the other night, the night I dragged a pocket knife along my forearm, I had never harmed myself."

"And had you ever harmed anyone else?"

"No, I hadn't. I've been accused of harming another person, a woman, but I never did harm her, as she had maintained. I never touched her but, in a single, manic, manic, manic instant, I once admitted that I had. And as a consequence of my manic admission, I was ticketed for assault for the first and last time in my life. It is, Hunter, horrific what a single moment of mania-ridden panic can do to a person. It's fucking horrific. God is it ever frightening, scary. And that is the moral of the story I am about to share with you. That is the goddamn moral."

"So what happened, Ayden? Want went on?" I asked in a zestful kind of whisper that would have embarrassed me had Ayden not been so distracted by his obvious desire to confide in me.

"First of all, you need to know, Hunter," he said, lowering his own sturdy voice, "that I realize right now, right this moment, before I explain to you what transpired the crucial day I admitted that I had actually hit a woman I had never ever hit before, that the words that are to follow will be the most difficult I have ever had to share—with anyone. I know, Hunter, that you may not believe what it is I am about to say to you. However, the account I am about to spell out for you is the truth and nothing less. The chance you may not believe me is a chance I feel I must take, though. Regardless of the stance you will ultimately assume once I have spoken my peace, I feel very strongly that I must present to you this particular segment of my life's story."

"And you've never told anyone what it is you are about to tell me?" I asked, still whispering.

"Not anyone. Not any of my doctors. No, not even Goodwin."

"Well, what happened then?" I asked, as Ayden reached deep into his pocket and pulled out a small, dirty ball of clay and began to roll it between his fingers with precision.

"It was several years after I had moved out on my own when I had my first run-in with the law. Until that particular encounter, I had never been ticketed for anything. No, not even for jaywalking. My earliest confrontation with the law would nearly destroy me emotionally and would prove to be, without a doubt, the single-most frightening and manic period in my life."

"So what happened?"

"A police officer came to see me while I was at work."

"And that frightened you?"

"It did. Isn't that pathetic? I think that maybe it is."

"No, not really. I don't think it's pathetic anyway. I believe there are some people out there who would be frightened by the prospect of being visited by a police officer while at work, especially if the 'visit' was unannounced."

"Yeah, I agree, especially since his visit was in fact unannounced. Suffice it to say, I was petrified from the moment he arrived. I didn't know what I had done—if anything. I considered myself innocent of any charge, or charges, the officer could bring against me, but the stone-cold look on his face told me that he believed that I was guilty of one crime or another."

"That would be scary."

"Yeah, like I said, it really was a frightening time for me. It still frightens me to think about it. I still shudder when I see his picture hanging in my mind. And I am thoroughly aware that as I explain what transpired that distressing day, and during the days following, that I make myself sound rather defensive, or even guilty, especially when I was so quick to conclude that some type of offense or illegal activity might have occurred in the first place. Nevertheless, Hunter, a police officer was now seated across from me, prepared to interrogate me I was sure."

"What did he say to you?"

"He asked me if I'd hit a girl, a girl named Vicki, a girl I'd once dated, a girl I'd once lived with and even slept with on occasion."

"Well, did you hit her, Ayden?"

"Never. I didn't even know why she would've gone to the police in the first place, but, nevertheless, I felt my muscles tighten the moment Officer Taylor—that was his name—asked me that question."

"And did Officer Taylor believe you when you said that you'd never hit her? Evidently, he did not."

"Oh no. It was obvious by the grave look on his face and by his serious demeanor that he didn't believe me—not for a single goddamn second. And let me say that I was clueless. I was fucking clueless."

"Well, what had she told him? What are the details?"

"She'd alleged that I'd grabbed a phone from her and, in doing so, that I'd hit her."

"And that wasn't true?"

"Yes and no. Part of what she'd said was true. You see, I had tried to take my phone away from her, but I'd never hit her, not a single goddamn time. We hadn't even come in contact with one another when I'd tried to retrieve my goddamn phone. Not once. Not a single fucking time. Vicki had lied to Officer Taylor."

"And did she press charges?"

"No, she never did. That was the first questions I asked. Officer Taylor answered by saying that, while she hadn't pressed charges, the police had an 'obligation to step in and clean things up.'"

"So why were you trying to take your phone away from her?"

"I didn't want her using it. That's all. I just didn't want her using it."

"Why not?"

"I don't know. I just didn't want her using my phone. We were living together, but she had her own line and her own phone. The way I saw it, she didn't need to be using mine."

"So what happened after that?"

"Well, when I asked that she not use my phone, she started shouting at me and, in an apparent effort to keep my phone away from me, she took a quick step backwards and tripped over the phone cord itself. She stumbled, but never fell down. She regained her balance almost immediately, remained standing somehow, and then promptly accused me of hitting her. I never hit her, though. Never. Not once. I don't even know why she would have accused me of hitting her to begin with because I never did. There had been no physical contact between the two of us whatsoever. That's what happened. That is the truth, Hunter."

"And why were you trying to take your phone away from her?" I asked a second time, fully aware that I was stuck on that particular point.

"I just didn't want her using it, but she'd insisted. It really was odd the way she kept insisting on using my phone—especially when she had a phone of her own."

"Then why do you think she insisted?"

"I'm really not sure why. I'm really not sure. Honestly. Hunter, I am sounding increasingly upset with each word I speak, huh?"

"A little."

"I am?"

"Yes."

"Do I sound manic to you?"

"I don't know what manic sounds like, Ayden," I admitted.

"Well, if it's all the same, I was upset—as upset as I'd ever been—as I sat there answering Officer Taylor's barrage of questions. I had tried to remain as collected as I possibly could, but extra adrenaline was surging through me and I was becoming increasingly tense with each breath that liberated itself from my shaking body. I sensed that I was about to lose my composure completely, entirely. I also sensed that I was becoming manic—as manic as I'd ever been.."

"You actually 'sensed' that you were becoming manic? Really? I didn't know that was possible."

"Oh, I knew I was on the verge of becoming manic, very manic. I could feel it, my oncoming mania. I just couldn't control it. I tried to control it, to sequester it, but I couldn't. I was becoming more panicked and more agitated by the second. Plus, again, it was quite obvious that Officer Taylor did not believe me; he just kept pressing me and pressing me. That only compounded the direness of the situation, stressed me more and more and, ultimately, caused me to become increasingly upset. And, yes, like I said, I was definitely becoming manic."

"What was it like knowing that you were unable to control the rushing mania?"

"It was strange, troubling even."

"Do you think that Officer Taylor noticed how upset, how manic you were becoming?"

"Probably not. I remember that he was paying close attention to his notes. He just kept staring at his damn notes. And I realized, as he concentrated on those goddamn notes, that he had not made eye contact with me a single time since the two of us had sat down together, since his arrival. I doubt very much that he noticed how manic I was."

"What did he say to you next?"

"He told me that he believed that I had actually been 'mistreating' Vicki for quite some time. He had used the word 'mistreating,' which seemed vague to me."

"And why would he think that?"

"Because Vicki had also claimed that I'd threatened to kick a hole in her t.v., that's why. It wasn't true, Hunter. I'd only told her that I was going to put her belongings, a list of belongings that included her t.v., out on the street. We'd only been living together for a couple of weeks. I'd needed a roommate and she'd needed one, too. I think the main reason she'd said such things about me was she didn't like that I'd told her to go, to get the hell out. What's more, and probably most important, is the fact that she couldn't accept that I'd been seeing a girl named Angie. She'd wanted Angie out of my life. Retaliation was her motive. I didn't know that then, but today I am sure of it."

"And you are telling me that you never hit Vicki a single time *and* that you never threatened to kick her t.v.?"

"Hunter, you are sounding just like Officer Taylor. And yes, that is exactly what I am telling you."

"Sorry, Ayden. I did not intend to come across as a police officer."

"It's okay."

"And then?"

"And then he asked me about what he referred to as 'the time on the street,' which was another occasion in which Vicki had asserted that I'd hit her. Actually, he didn't ask me; he *accused* me of hitting her a second time. Once again, I was confused, locked in the dark. I asked him for specifics as to what she'd said. That's when he explained that she'd told him that I'd hit her once while we were walking down the street. Needless to say, I was stunned that someone could tell such lies and that another person could believe such lies. But, then again, Officer Taylor was there to 'clean things up.' He had an obligation. He'd said so himself."

"Now you were really scared *and* manic, weren't you?" I watched as he gave the ball of clay a good squeeze. The clay disappeared in his trembling fist.

"You know, Hunter, how people often describe how frightened they were at a given moment by saying that they almost pissed their pants? Do you have some idea what it is I am talking about? I assume that you do. Anyway, as soon as Officer Taylor accused me—yes, accused me—of hitting Vicki a second time, I pissed my pants.

"God, you did?"

"I did."

"So what did you say when Officer Taylor asked you about the time on the street, the second time?"

"Well, I confessed."

"Shit! You confessed? But why? Why would you do that? You told me that you'd never hit her."

"Please believe me, Hunter, when I say that the word 'yes' jumped from my manic brain and off my tongue in a single, manic instant, long before I could stop it, long before I realized what it was I was saying exactly, long before I realized that I was confessing to a crime I had never committed in my life. Then my trembling voice fell silent. Right then and there, Hunter, I knew that my manic answer, my manic confession, would change my manic life from that point forward. At the same time, I felt that my manic admission would earn me nothing more than a slap on the wrist, so, in a single moment, I made the poor choice to go along, to accept what was not true and to live with my dubious 'confession.' I acquiesced and walked straight to my desk to fetch my driver's license for Officer Taylor in a very painful kind of silence. Let me tell you, it was a long walk to my desk that day. And I noticed, as I approached my office, that a handful of my coworkers had been eavesdropping. And as I moved passed them, they avoided all eye contact with me and tried to feign disinterest by acting busy, by acting as if nothing out of the ordinary had taken place, but I knew that they had heard every single fucking word."

"I just don't understand why you would confess if you weren't guilty, Ayden," I said, perplexed.

"Mania. Sheer mania. Being confronted by a police officer triggered in me a mania I still can't explain or justify."

"You really believe that, don't you?"

"Yes, I really do. I've absolutely no doubt that I was manic when I admitted that I'd hit Vicki. I know that I was manic because I'd simply been unable to handle the pressure of such an interview rationally, in a manner in which a 'normal' person would have handled it."

"But don't you think that you might just be blaming your illness when, in reality, your illness had nothing at all to do with your unfortunate response?"

"No. No, I do not think that at all. I was manic. I was a manic mess."

"Ayden, what happened after that?"

"Without having to think twice, I requested that Officer Taylor drive me downtown to the two-bedroom apartment I shared with Vicki, the same woman who now maintained that I had hit her when I honestly had not. Yes, it is the truth that I had not hit her—not a single time. And still, I requested that I be escorted to my apartment by a police officer who had just ticketed me for assault. It was a very strange request on my part, especially under the circumstances, I know."

"I agree. That is a strange request."

"Hunter, let me say that I was mute during the entire drive and, as we approached my apartment building, I found the nerve to con Officer Taylor into parking in the alley behind the building by telling him that space in front of the building was limited."

"But why?"

"The prospect of being seen getting out of a police cruiser scared the hell out of me, so I simply lied. I lied. But that was the only lie I told."

"That makes some sense."

"Would you believe that I had never felt more confused than I did when I entered my apartment with a police officer following behind me so closely I could feel his shadow on the back of my neck?"

"I can believe it."

"Then Officer Taylor asked me if he could trust that everything was going to be "all right" until Vicki was finished packing and moving her things. Even in the shocked state I was in, I was able to assure him that I would leave her alone and he left the apartment without another word."

"So she was moving out, huh? I guess that's not surprising."

"Yep. About a half dozen of her friends were already there, rapidly stuffing cardboard boxes with her belongings. You know, I glanced at each one of those people, but every one of them avoided eye contact with me. Vicki, on the other hand, stopped packing a box long enough to look at me. Her crying eyes were the crying eyes of a pathetic liar, a liar searching for vindication. Her tears were fake, Hunter. I know they were. It was obvious she knew that she was the guilty one. She said nothing to me and I said nothing to her. I knew, though, that if I had given her the chance to speak she would have."

"She really looked that guilty?"

"Yeah, she did. I'd never seen her looking so guilty—not ever. And today I see that I should have hated her for what she'd done to me but I didn't harbor any hatred for her at all, at least not then anyway. I think I pitied her more than anything. I pitied her for wanting to hurt me as badly as she did. The hatred for what she had done to me would come much later. That is how confused—and manic—I was."

"And then what?"

"And then I moved passed her tear-filled eyes toward the phone in my bedroom. We were definitely crippled acquaintances now, Vicki and I, and I could not think of a single thing to say to her. I stepped with mitigated care in the direction of my phone and my ruptured future."

"Ruptured future?"

"My own ruptured future. See, Hunter, I knew even then that it would all come down to a single phone call."

"Ayden, I'm not following you."

"It was her idea, but I was the one who had made it happen."

"Made what happen?"

"Why I went along with her deceitful plan I will never know. Looking back, I think that I was definitely manic because I was acting strangely, saying and doing strange things. I had told Officer Taylor that I'd hit Vicki when I never had. I'd lied to him about the parking situation in front of my building and now, when I should have told her to just take her things and go, to get the hell out, I struck with her the worst deal I'd ever made."

"But why would you make a deal with her, Ayden? Could she even be trusted?"

"I guess you might say that I have been far too sensitive for far too long. I have put too much stock in the careless, callous words of others. I think she knew that when she told me that if I would call my parents and admit to them that I had hit her, she wouldn't tell anyone else that I'd hit her, even though I already knew that I had done nothing to her at all."

"So that was the 'deal' the two of you made?"

"That was the deal."

"And what did your parents say when you told them that you'd assaulted another human being, a woman?"

"I talked to my dad actually. First, he asked me if she was okay. And, of course, she was."

"Man, Ayden, how difficult it must have been for you to confess to your dad that you had hit another person when you never had."

"Of course it was difficult. What made the whole situation worse was the fact that my dad believed that I had assaulted another person. But why wouldn't he? What kind of person would claim to have committed such a crime if he was genuinely innocent?"

"Where was Vicki while you were talking to your dad?"

"She was still there. She had positioned herself on the bare floor in front of me. She was, I knew, listening to every word, making sure that I fulfilled my end of our twisted bargain. You know, I saw then just how fucking satisfied she was with herself. I could see the look of satisfaction in her eyes that were now tearless. I swear that she was smiling to herself and silently laughing at me all at the same time, as my hurting voice traveled miles and miles to my dad's unsuspecting ears. God, how that spiteful grin of hers hurt me. Her intentional smirk hurt me worse than having to lie to my dad did. Yes, she'd definitely gotten her revenge."

"Did you say anything else to your dad?"

"That was all I had the strength to say to him. I'd said precisely what Vicki had bribed me into saying to him, which was more than enough, so I hung up the phone immediately after I shared with him a single 'I love you,' and left it at that. I was too sick inside to tell my dad anything else, to tell him the real truth and risk the possibility that she might go to my coworkers and verbally attack my wounded character not to mention my crumbling ego."

"So did she go to your coworkers with her allegations?"

"Yes. Yes, she did.

"She really did?"

"I went to work very early the next morning believing emphatically that I could definitely smooth everything over with all of my peers, especially with those peers who had eavesdropped, but I was much too late. She had reneged on our deal and, by the time I had arrived at work, she had already wreaked havoc on my reputation. She had maimed me with words. There was no doubt that I had been tricked and I was a wreck because of it."

"Jesus ..."

"She had taken it upon herself to make it known to everyone at my place of employment that I had assaulted her, even though, as I've already told you, Hunter, I had not. According to my good friend, my best friend, Tim, the only person besides Angie who believed that I was innocent, Vicki had placed a few strategic phone calls to a couple of the office bigmouths and the word of my supposed wrongdoing had spread rapidly, long before I had any chance to implement any form of damage control. My coworkers grabbed a hold of the lies she had told them and whispered about me from behind my back for the first time in my history. Yeah, they believed Vicki the same way my dad had believed me."

"Man, that's rough."

"For the very first time in my life, I was playing the part of a criminal. The role was painfully awkward for me and I left work within minutes of arriving that day."

"I don't blame you, Ayden."

"Several hours later, Tim stopped by my apartment, as planned, to help me pack the last of my personal property. Of course, Vicki was gone now and, because I had been filling boxes for hours since I had returned from work earlier that morning, I was nearly finished by the time he got there."

"What did Tim have to say about the whole ordeal?"

"Like I said, he knew that I was innocent."

"How did he know?"

"Because she never pressed charges against me and, far more important, because she had, according to Tim, once made very similar allegations against a former boyfriend only to deny them shortly after making them. Man, that revelation stunned me more than the revelation that she hadn't pressed charges did."

"How did Tim know she had accused another guy of assaulting her?"

"Because she'd told him that once."

"She actually told him that herself?"

"She really did. But here's the clincher: the same morning that Vicki defamed me, she admitted to Tim that I'd never hit her—not once, not ever."

"She said that, too?"

"She said it. She confessed, plain and simple. She told Tim over the phone that she'd had a 'score to settle' with me."

"She sounds like a bad person. And I think I can say, Ayden, that had you stayed away from Angie, none of this would have ever taken place. The police don't ticket you, nothing. And I mean that."

"I should have stayed away from Vicki—that's what I should have done. And it is true that a voice inside of me always told me that she was not a good person but, for whatever reason, I never listened to that inner voice or to my instincts. Then I started seeing Angie while Vicki and I were still living together and, well, Vicki, as injured as she was, got even with me."

"She really was settling a score."

"Like I already said, I know now that revenge was her only motive."

"That's what it sounds like."

"Well, with Vicki anything was possible."

"I think that she is a very vindictive person."

"She's more than a little strange, if you ask me. I'm surprised that I never picked up on that sooner, her strangeness I mean."

"You realize it now, don't you?"

"That I do."

"You should have gotten the hell out of there, Ayden. You should have left her alone."

"I think I always knew that, too. You are not the first person to tell me that by the way. Several people told me to stay away from her from the beginning. But I never did."

"Jesus, why not? Why didn't you listen?"

"I think that I had become too dependent on her emotionally and, even though we were just roommates, maybe I'd even become too dependent on her sexually, physically."

"You know, if you were sexually involved, you were probably more than just roommates."

"I know that. That very point has occurred to me more than once."

"Then maybe you were sending her mixed signals?"

"That is a possibility."

"And maybe, just maybe, you were behaving somewhat recklessly?"

"I think I was. In fact, I know that I was behaving recklessly. In retrospect, I know I was manic the entire time I was living with her and, Hunter, that scares the hell out of me."

"It scares me, too. It's all so odd, so weird."

"What really seems odd to me today is the fact that I was never very angry with Vicki after she had broken our deal—not at first anyway. I was so busy trying to protect my self, my person, from the verbal bashing she had doled out I don't think I had enough time to get mad at her. Rather than getting angry at her, I simply accepted—yes accepted—what it was she had done to me."

"Maybe you'd accepted what she'd done to you then, Ayden, but you don't accept it today, right now."

"Yes."

"I get the feeling what happened then still bothers you now."

"Well, it does."

"I assume that's not the end of the story. I get the feeling that Vicki resurfaced after she'd moved out. She did, didn't she?"

"She did. I remember moving into a new apartment a few days after I'd been cited, a couple days after she had gone to my work place and had tried to destroy me, which was only a few days after she'd left for what was supposed to be for good. But somehow, some way, she'd been able to get her hands on my new unlisted phone number and, only hours after I had carried the last box into my apartment, she called me. I was unpacking a box of books when the phone rang."

"She called you?"

"Yes. And she was in tears, man. She was in tears. She was also openly confessing that she had lied to Officer Taylor about my having hit her."

"So she confessed?"

"Yes. She told me that she had made everything up. She told me that she had lied to Officer Taylor."

"And what did you say to her? Nothing I hope."

"Hunter, have you ever been stunned speechless? Maybe you have been and maybe you have not. All I can say is that when Vicki confessed that she had lied to the police by claiming that I had hit her when I honestly hadn't, I was stunned speechless. And then, after having regained a small portion of poise, I explained to her that the damage had already been done. I reminded her that there was no fixing things now—not that I wanted to. I reminded her that there was simply no turning back—not that I would have turned back. Then I slammed the phone down before she could utter another goddamn word. Then, for the first time in little more than a year, I began to arrange everything I owned in a foreign apartment all by myself."

"She surfaced again, didn't she? I know she did."

"She showed up at the door of my apartment later that same day, not long after she had called and owned up to the fact that she had indeed lied to the police."

"How in the hell did she find you?"

"I've never been able to answer that particular question. I asked her, but she ignored me. I have no idea how she found me but, nevertheless, she did."

"So did you slam the door in her face?"

"Not until I'd made it clear to her that I knew that she'd wanted to hurt me, that she'd wanted revenge because I had opted to see Angie exclusively. And would you believe, Hunter, even after I told her that, she asked if she could come in. She still wanted to talk."

"Now that is the definition of 'pathetic,' Ayden. Did you tell her to go screw herself."

"I did, in so many words anyway. First I informed her once more that the damage had already been done. I reminded her that the ticket for assault would shadow me forever."

"How did she respond?"

"She begged for forgiveness. She begged, begged, begged. That's when I slammed the door in her pitiful face and locked it."

"So was that the end of it?"

"Not even close. In the days following, she would 'materialize' seemingly 'out of nowhere' several times."

"Materialize?"

"Materialize. The first time she appeared out of nowhere was while Angie and I were shopping. I turned around to look at a display and there she was standing a few feet away from me with tears in her eyes."

"That's almost scary."

"I know it is, man."

"And that happened more than once?"

"Yep. The second time Angie and I were driving to a neighborhood restaurant. When I happened to check the rearview mirror, Vicki and a woman I'd never seen before were in the car behind us. Vicki was driving. They followed us for several city blocks before they vanished. A few weeks later, I found out that she had rented an apartment on the same street as me, only a few blocks away."

"You know, it almost sounds as if she was obsessed with you."

"Yeah, I think that maybe she was. At the same time, I think that's beside the point."

"There is one point that stands out, Ayden."

"What is it?"

"Well, if she never pressed charges against you, why did you feel that being ticketed for assault would shadow you forever? Couldn't you just get on with your life?"

"Not really. Remember: my manic confession was enough to get me ticketed. And a confession is all the police really need, whether charges have been pressed or not."

"So you went to court, didn't you?"

"No, I didn't. I went through a pretrial diversion program instead. I had no prior arrests, so I was eligible for pretrial diversion. Pretrial diversion made sense to me because I was trying to earn a dismissal."

"And did you?"

"Yes."

"So that's the end of it, don't you think?"

"Yes and no. Maybe that's the end of it and maybe that's not the end of it. Please understand that the memory of admitting that I'd committed a crime I honestly had not while in a manic 'frenzy' and being subsequently ticketed for assault still haunts me. To some degree, I believe it always will."

"I'd just let it go."

"I try, but I can't."

"I'm sorry."

"There is one more thing you should know."

"What's that?"

"One night, shortly after I had completed the pretrial diversion program, there was a message for me at work to call a woman who called herself Renee. I didn't know anyone named Renee, but I dialed the number anyway."

"And?"

"And once I had identified myself, she told me that she knew that I had never hit Vicki. 'I know you didn't hit Vicki,' the woman stated matter-of-factly."

"God, who was she?"

"Just some lady named Renee. That's really all I've ever known. I've never been able to discover any clues other than her first name and the fact that she'd actually believed that I was innocent."

"So did you ever hear from the woman named Renee again?"

"No, I never did. There were no more messages at work, no more phone calls, nothing."

"Was it Vicki herself?"

"I'm know that it wasn't. This voice wasn't Vicki's. This time the voice belonged to someone who wasn't crying or hurting in any way. This woman's voice cared for me I believe. This time the voice on the other end of the line belonged to someone who understood my situation, my dilemma. The voice belonged to a person who not only felt for me but had wished that I'd stood up for myself to Officer Taylor."

"How can you be so sure?"

"Because that voice knew something. I could sense it then and I can sense it now. That voice knew something."

"What did Renee's voice sound like?"

"Like I said, her voice sounded like someone who cared for me, like someone who was looking out for me. That voice was the voice of a person who seemed to understand my plight, a voice that was all-knowing."

"Your plight, Ayden?"

"My plight, Hunter. The woman named Renee, whoever she was, knew that I had been wrongly accused. She also knew that I was hurt, injured. She knew that I'd been wounded emotionally."

"I wish that you knew who she was."

"So do I, Hunter. What I would not give to know that woman's full identity."

"Well, it's all behind you. I hope you realize that."

"Sometimes I do. Just remember, Hunter, it's horrific what a single moment of mania can do to a person. One moment of mania can alter a person's life … forever." With that, Ayden returned the small, dirty ball of clay to his pocket. He reached across the table and wrapped his hands around my forearms, giving them a firm squeeze. "Thanks, man," he said with just a trace of a smile. "Thanks." That is when he glanced away from me. His eyes were, I could tell, looking to the future, his future. He stood up tall and strode out of the room and back into Seven Southwest, the one place he would soon be leaving once and for all.

CHAPTER 25

Jane and a phlebotomist woke me the next morning. The clock on the wall near the nurses' station read 8 a.m. I did the math and was quick to note that only hours had elapsed since I had sat listening to Ayden describe what he had referred to as the most frightening period in his problematic life.

"So I hear you and Ayden had quite some conversation last night," Jane said, as she seated herself on the very edge of the recliner, her hands placed neatly in her lap. As soon as she sat down, I made a conscious decision to tell her nothing.

"We did," I responded, my voice the rough-sounding voice of a man who has, at long last, found a small amount of decent sleep in his life. I made a half-hearted fist and the phlebotomist went to work.

"Well, it's nearly time for breakfast and I'd really like to see you there with everyone else, with the rest of the group I mean. You need to eat something, don't you think?"

"I won't be eating breakfast today, Jane. I'm just not hungry." I was telling the truth. I was not the least bit hungry. That is when Jane's token broad smile, the same smile that seemed too broad to be the real thing, a strange smile I'd already seen many times before, quickly disappeared and I made up my mind that I would not bother arguing with her that day. It was obvious by the determined look in her eyes, eyes that were practically daring me to argue, that she was much more prepared to "spar verbally" than I was.

"Hunter, you need to eat something. I want you in the dining room in five minutes."

"Okay, okay. Jesus, I'll be there then. I'll be there." The phlebotomist glanced at my face before he taped a cotton ball onto the inside of my arm and removed the tourniquet. I wrapped my right hand around the cotton ball, determined not to lose anymore blood. I applied pressure until my five minutes were up and then I walked with deliberate care to the dining room.

At breakfast, I was both surprised and miffed to see that neither Jocelyn nor Ayden were in attendance. In fact, the only faces I happened to recognize were the grizzled-looking faces of Ernest and the anonymous man who had stared at me in group the day before as if I were a semi-forgotten buddy from a semi-forgotten war from long, long ago. Neither man appeared to have seen me so I took a seat at a small empty table in the most remote corner of the room near a window that, sadly, also framed a perfectly boring view of the same parking garage that was visible from my own boring room.

"This isn't a restaurant, you know," I heard someone say after I'd been staring at the side walls of the concrete parking garage for a few minutes, or longer. Until I heard that voice, I had been lost in a daydream. My daydream of a walk with my dad through the snowy woods as a young boy having been entirely disrupted, I looked away from the parking garage in search of the source of the statement that had broken my concentration and shattered the dining room's morning quiet, strongly suspecting that the remark had been intended for me and only me.

"Who are you talking to?" I asked the faces that were busy studying their cereal bowls, seemingly devoid of any emotion whatsoever, apparently feigning disinterest in my question. I'm still not sure why, but I was instantly afraid for myself.

"Yeah, you, stupid." I heard the voice say. It was now evident that the words were coming from an opposite corner of the dining room where sat a large woman with hair so black it glistened in the room's dim morning light. It was also evident that the words were meant for me. "Yeah, you," the black-haired woman, a woman I'd seen in group the day before, said with a sly smirk, her black eyes filled with disdain, her speech laced with anger.

"I didn't think it was a restaurant," I responded, trying to sound confident and unbothered in spite of the fact that I was feeling somewhat defensive, a little insecure and afraid of being embarrassed by the stranger who was clearly biding her time by making my business her business. I now understood that I was on a collision course with the woman who had just called me "stupid."

"You must learn to serve yourself in here. So what are you staring out the window for anyway? Planning your escape?"

"I'm not staring at anything," I told her. Before the woman in the opposite corner had called me "stupid," I had been daydreaming about a distant day, a single day that was decades old, a day my dad and I had hiked far into the woods beyond edge of town to a location where the stream was born from an above-ground spring, to cut down a Christmas tree, but I wasn't telling her that.

"There's nothing out there for you either," she practically shouted.

"And how in the hell do you know that?" I was suddenly cognizant that the others were watching me, too. I swear I felt a chill run through my self. I wanted to flee that room but I knew that the infusion pump I was attached to would only hinder my exit, slow me down. I also knew that if I fled the dining room I would be a marked man for the duration of my stay. While I had every intention of ending my stay on Seven Southwest as soon as possible, I did not want to run from someone who was nothing more than a mentally disturbed bully.

"Because you're just another goddamn misfit, a misfit like the rest of us, that's why. You might as well quit your daydreaming because you aren't going anywhere anytime soon."

"How do you know when I'll be leaving? Are you a medical doctor?" I asked. "Is your last name Goodwin?" I sassed her, cornering her with a logic all my own. I heard the group gasp collectively. They were definitely watching me now, those unfortunate victims of mental illness, the very people the bully had just labeled "misfits." There was no doubt about in my mind.

"Fuck you, man!" she hollered after the briefest pause.

"No, fuck you," Ayden said as he entered the room, quickly taking my fire. His hair was still wet from having just showered and I realized at that moment, the very moment Ayden had defended me, that I needed to shower as soon as possible. I needed to cleanse myself of the group's piercing eyes. I also needed to cleanse my skeleton. "You think you're the authority on who goes and who stays? Hell, you don't even know his name, let alone his medical history. And, by the way, you aren't a goddamn doctor." Ayden tilted his head in my direction. His hands were on his hips now and, standing there in the doorway, he looked both brave and strong. I was relieved to know that he was on my side. I knew that I was ill-equipped emotionally to be arguing with mentally disturbed bullies all by myself.

"Well, do you even know *my* name?" the woman in the corner asked, a trace of surrender present in her speech, a hint of hatred for him in her tone.

"No, I don't know your name, but I heard you screaming the other night. I heard you crying. So I think I know enough about you to know that you are hurting. And I don't think you should be taking your pain and resentment out on Hunter."

"I know your name, Donnie," Ernest interjected, casting a shy, shy smile in the bully's direction. Heads turned and laughter filled the room, albeit briefly.

"Shut up, Ernest!" Donnie commanded. Ernest was immediately silent, as were the others, their eyes staring into the shallow depths of their cereal bowls once again.

"Screaming?" she asked Ayden. Now it was Donnie who was on the defensive. I was starting to feel pretty good about myself.

"Yeah, screaming and crying."

"So I had a dream, a nightmare. Big goddamn deal." Her black eyes followed Ayden as he crossed the room and seated himself at my table, directly across from me, his back to Donnie. I wondered if she was trying to see his skeleton. I decided that she probably was.

"Ignore her, man," Ayden whispered. That was when the black-haired bully named Donnie stomped out of the room in a hurry, nearly knocking over a tech who had just entered seemingly to put an end to the early morning shouting match.

"So you heard her screaming, too, huh?" I asked Ayden in a kind of whisper I knew the tech would never be able to comprehend just as soon as Donnie had disappeared down the corridor.

"Yeah, it scared the hell out of me to hear a person screaming like that."

"Scared me as well," I said. "What do you think her problem is anyway?"

"She's a psycho I think. Hell, Hunter, I don't know. I have no real way of knowing. Maybe she was only dreaming that night, having a nightmare after all."

"Maybe." I was instantly upset that Ayden had chosen the word "psycho." I thought that calling Donnie a "psycho" was a little harsh.

"I'd leave her alone, man."

"Oh, I promise you that I will. I'll be avoiding her no matter what, at all costs. I don't want any more trouble—with anyone. I want to go home. I want to get the hell out of here."

To be safe, I did avoid Donnie. The two of us would pass each other in the corridors without a sound, without making eye contact, several times the very same day she had tried to pick a fight with me. Later that day, I would see her up close for the final time. Unable to look away, I would stare directly at her as she was being rolled away on a stretcher by a couple of paramedics, a stillness I had never before witnessed in anyone possessing her. Even now, as I describe my experiences on Seven Southwest bits at a time, the stillness of her unmoving body upsets me. I believe it always will. Try as I might, I cannot look away from the memory of her dead body no matter how much effort I put forth. Sometimes memories are like that, harassing I mean.

I ran into Ernest at dinner the next night, my fourth night on the ward, the evening after I'd seen Donnie being carried away to a place I would never be able to name. He would tell me, in his own bashful way, that Donnie had somehow managed to take her own life. How she did it, he honestly did not know. Or he simply would not say. All he would say is that it was a suicide. That is all anyone would say about Donnie's death and so that is all I would ever learn about her unfortunate exit.

"From Jocelyn." Ayden slid a wrinkled piece of notebook paper across the table's smooth surface.

"What is it?"

"Love note."

"A what?" I asked.

"Read it." I unfolded the wrinkled note.

Hi Hunter,

PLEASE do not be upset, but I had to go. I wanted to say "goodbye," but Dr. Goodwin and Jane thought it best that I let you sleep. I will call you as soon as I'm settled in at Dad's. That is where I will be staying for a while, or at least until I take care of a few routine particulars anyway. Listen to Dr. Goodwin, Hunter. More important, listen to yourself.

J.R.L.

The note was definitely a brief one. There was no phone number. There was no address. There were no details about her overall well-being, her mood. Immediately, I found myself wishing that she had provided some background as to why she had been discharged so suddenly, seemingly in secrecy. Sitting there in the dining room at breakfast, Ayden had read my mind.

"They told her it was time to go, Hunter. They were very determined to send her home."

"Was she prepared medically? Or do you even know?"

"Hunter, she didn't say and, of course, neither did they."

"She couldn't say goodbye to me?"

"You were sleeping."

"Well, where were you?" I asked.

"I was reading a book in my room. She tiptoed in, hugged me and handed me that note."

"That's all?"

"She did say she would call us both soon."

"Ayden, how was her mood?"

"She seemed to be in a good mood, upbeat even."

"That's something, isn't it?"

"It is, Hunter. It really is something."

Breakfast came to an end shortly after Ayden had given me Jocelyn's note. Escorted by a pair of techs, most of the group, Ayden included, filed out of the dining room and down the main corridor, through the thick doors and outside into the ever-present November chill to smoke. Instead of tagging along, I wandered down the corridor to Jocelyn's room, her former room anyway. The balloon bouquets were gone as were the stuffed animals and the get well cards. Jocelyn's old room looked as bleak and lifeless as mine did. Then I saw him, an elderly man who appeared to be much older than Ernest or my old war-time "buddy," sitting on a corner of the bed. He was staring at the floor, at nothing, his eyes glistening with tears. As I stood there in the shadowy corridor, just out of view of the crying old man, it occurred to me that Jocelyn had been gone for mere hours and yet her room was already inhabited by someone else, a new pained soul.

Jocelyn had been discharged to embrace her illness and face herself. The elderly man had, most likely, been admitted to Seven Southwest to face fears and a diagnosis that would surely be new to him. Standing there in the hallway, watching the old man cry, I realized I had already come a very long way; I was already facing many of my own fears while awaiting a diagnosis that would ultimately bring me some peace of mind and place me on the esteemed road—if you can believe it—to emotional recovery.

I returned to my room before the elderly man had an opportunity to see me. I sat in the recliner. I searched the gray-black television screen for answers as to why Jocelyn had missed both dinner and breakfast. Finally, I tried to figure out why she had been discharged so abruptly, without having a chance to say goodbye. I found no answers in the television screen, though. This time the screen would remain imageless. This time, sitting there in the recliner, I would be faced with the reality that I was, except for Ayden, all alone with the very people the late Donnie had dubbed "mental misfits."

My second group therapy session, a morning session, a session I would learn sometime later was appropriately referred to as "day group," lasted less than half an hour. Jane, the appointed facilitator that particular morning, asked each individual to outline a single short-term goal. She went around the room asking each of us one by one what goal was most important to us that day. Try as I might, I can recall only two of those goals, the goals belonging to Ayden and myself, the goals of the only people present that day who openly maintained that they wanted to write a novel more than anything else.

"And Ayden what goal do you have in mind? What's your goal?" Jane had asked after having already prompted all the other members of the group, except for myself, to share a goal.

"To take my meds religiously, Jane. And to start writing again. And to write well for the first time in a long time." Ayden looked directly at Jane before he looked at me. Jane was nodding. I nodded approval, too. It was a very respectable goal. For Ayden, an aspiring novelist who was determined to stay on his meds and manage his manic depression once and for all, it was the only goal.

"Very, very good, Ayden," Jane said as she scribbled his words into a large black binder, a black binder that appeared to be the same one Kendra had carried with her except for the fact that this black binder was somewhat thinner than Kendra's.

"And your goal, Hunter?" she asked at last.

"My goal is to go to bed every night and get out of bed every morning," I responded without any reservation. "That's my goal ... for now."

"Oh, that's an admirable goal. I'm really glad to hear that you've set a goal for yourself that is so realistic, so obtainable. And that is a goal you can build on." Having openly endorsed my short-term goal, Jane closed the black binder and dismissed the group back into the ward.

Ayden and I stayed behind after Jane had excused everyone from day group.

"You know, Hunter, I'll be out of here soon, too. I'm going to run from this place. I'm going to sprint to my newest life-chapter and write."

"Where will you go?" I had been wanting to ask that question ever since Ayden had introduced himself. "Where does a writer go when he must find both his voice and his life again?"

"No one place. That's why I'm going to hit the road. That's why I'm going to fill a backpack with some books and a few notepads, a handful of pencils and find my potential, my story and, more than anything else, myself as a writer."

"Who will you read?" I asked. "Or do you even know yet?"

"Anyone. I'll read anyone I can get my hands on."

"And then, of course, you'll listen, observe and spy? I asked. "That is, wouldn't you say, your most basic 'rule' to becoming a writer, to becoming a successful novelist. Am I right, Ayden?"

"Hunter, during my search for a 'bona-fide set of rules' to becoming a 'bona-fide novelist,' I've discovered only one thing."

"And what is that?"

"Only three rules exist."

"If you don't mind, what are they?" I asked, suspecting that I was on the verge of hearing something about the art of fiction writing I had probably never heard before. I desperately needed to know the answer to that question. I felt as if my own future as a writer depended on learning the three rules for becoming a novelist Ayden had painstakingly uncovered.

"The first rule is that there are no rules."

"Really?"

"Really, man."

"And the second rule?"

"Read anything and everything. Just read and read.

"Okay. And the third rule?"

"Finally, the third rule is to write something every day, every fucking day. You should know that I invested a lot of time searching for those rules."

"How much time?"

"I searched for years and years, to tell you the truth. All the while I believed that I would eventually find the ultimate set of writer's rules, some sort of writer's code, a code that would guide me along the road to the land of literary prosperity. Then I discovered the rules I just shared with you. Now I just need to apply them. I need to listen, observe and spy but, most important, I need to read, read, read and write, write, write. Hunter, if I am ever going to experience even a small measure of success as a writer, I will have to live by those rules, the only rules I know."

Later that same afternoon, sometime after an uneventful lunch, a lunch I had chosen not to eat, a lunch Ayden had not attended, I was standing alone in front of the only window in a room most often referred to as the "study," the same room where group therapy sessions were usually held, observing the winter world living and breathing seven floors below me. Yes, as I had informed Big Nurse my first night on the ward, life was happening out there and soon, very soon in fact, Ayden, like Jocelyn, would rejoin that world, the world that was still beyond my grasp, the world I had shunned by attempting to kill myself days before and, hopefully, create for himself a brand new life, a life spent managing manic depression, a life spent writing with success. Standing there, so many stories above the frozen earth, I realized that I too could rejoin life if my poisoned liver managed to survive the toxins that were attacking it full force and, like Ayden, write my own novel one day. That is what I truly wanted to do, you know. More than anything, I wanted to write. But first I would have to accept my pending diagnosis, whatever diagnosis that might be, and comply with the staff. If my future as a person and as a writer depended on succeeding at those particular tasks, accepting and complying I mean, I would meet such goals head on. Standing alone in the study, I really couldn't see myself acting any other way.

"What are you looking at, Hunter? What's out there?" Jane's familiar voice crashed into my thoughts of my own pending release.

"A view I'll never forget," I responded, still witnessing the world below me living and breathing, the people passing by, the reflection of flashing neon lights on snow, a memory of the solitary man I had seen moving through the darkness in much the same manner as Bradbury's pedestrian a few nights before.

"What do you see right now? Tell me, Hunter, what's out there? What do you see?"

"I see nothing at all, Jane," I lied. I see nothing at all."

"Nothing? What about that view you just said you'll never forget?"

"It's just nothing, Jane."

But that wasn't the truth. I had seen something out there. I still couldn't see the stream or the lake in the distance for the winter fog, but I could see the hospital grounds far below where shades of the season dominated the landscape. I could see footprints in the snow leading away from the hospital. I could see a procession of cars moving very slowly along Center Street. Finally, I could see an image of Jocelyn standing alone in her bedroom in her dad's house amidst all of her ribbons and trophies and the various memorabilia of her topsy-turvy life. Moreover, I could see that Jocelyn was still hurting. I could see tears of uncertainty in her crystal-blue eyes. Then again, I was only daydreaming; maybe Jocelyn was doing just fine. Maybe she had unpacked, showered and dressed, eaten a lunch she had prepared herself and fed the dog. Maybe life—her life—was becoming routine again. Maybe.

"It's nothing, Jane," I repeated.

"Well then, I'll leave you alone with your thoughts as long as you're feeling okay."

"I'm okay, Jane," I assured her. Jane patted me on the shoulder and left the room.

A nurse I had never seen before soon entered the study. With an inviting smile, the kind of proud and nonjudgmental smile a mother bestows on one of her own children, she placed a small, oblong pink pill in my palm and handed me a cup of water.

"And what is it?" I asked.

"It's 10 milligrams of Paxil, an antidepressant. Don't worry yourself, my dear." She smiled again. This time, unlike the time I swallowed the Haldol, I took the pill without any reluctance whatsoever. This time, unlike the time I swallowed the Haldol, my thirst was quenched.

"I'll feel less depressed after taking Paxil, huh? Sounds magical."

"We shall see, Hunter. In as soon as a week, Paxil will start working for you. You will probably notice a marked change in your symptoms, your symptoms of depression that is, in a month or so. Plus, your chances of sleeping well will, more likely than not, improve in as little as one or two weeks. That's something to look forward to, don't you think?"

"Maybe it is."

"Maybe? Why do you sound so doubtful?"

"Because I haven't slept 'well' for years and years—if ever. I'm not even sure I know what it means to sleep well."

"I have a feeling things are going to be much different for you very soon, Hunter."

"Why so long before I see a 'change' in my depression? A month is an awful long time. I'll be out of here in less than a month."

"A month isn't a long time, Hunter. Be patient and you will see that I am right." Without speaking another word, the nurse who had just introduced Paxil into my life turned and left the room. I never saw her again.

Outside the window, below the confines of Seven Southwest, the city was still zestfully living, still breathing. I was passing time watching its synchronized movement, the flow of traffic for example, when I glimpsed Ayden himself, a large backpack hanging from his wide shoulders, making his way through the ankle-deep snow in the direction of Center Street. His stride was long and animated. It was as if he were trying to imitate a determined running back leaping over a team of would-be tacklers, as if he were running for his very life.

"Ayden had to go, too, Hunter." Jane was standing beside me again, also watching Ayden rushing forward through the snow.

"Jesus! Doesn't anyone say goodbye anymore?"

"That's just Ayden, Hunter. He's a quiet man. You'll see him again. Don't worry. He'll keep in touch with you."

"How do you know that?" I did not agree with Jane that Ayden was a quiet man.

"I just do. I know Ayden."

"You mean he'll really be back?"

"I doubt very much, Hunter, whether you'll see Ayden on Seven Southwest again. He didn't say 'goodbye' to you I know but he'll reenter your life one day."

"He's got a novel lost inside of him. He just needs to find it. Did you know that, Jane?"

"Yes, Hunter, I knew that already. Ayden made that known to me the first time I talked to him. I also know that you have a novel lost inside of you as well."

"What makes you say that?" I asked, surprised by her statement, a statement I had never heard before—not from anyone.

"Ayden told me so, that's why. He made that known to me, too."

"Jane, I never confessed to him that I want to be a writer."

"I don't think it was really all that necessary that you share a confession such as that with him. Ayden is a smart guy. He knows things. He sees things." Jane turned away from the window and looked at me at the same moment I turned to look at her. For the first time since I had been admitted onto Seven Southwest, I felt myself smiling at her. Then her stare returned to the wintry world outside and to a man named Ayden. My eyes refocused on the running Ayden, too. Having already reached the shoveled sidewalk that paralleled the near side of the street, he broke into the boldest run, his stride seemingly undaunted by the piles of snow and chilling temperatures. He was, I realized, running to write. Yes, Ayden was running to write his novel and soon, and without looking back, his sprinting form crossed the four lanes that comprised Center Street.

"Look at him go, Hunter," Jane remarked, practically beaming.

"Yeah, look at him go. See Ayden run," I said, a feeling of happiness that could only be derived from the strong sense of relief that was now welling inside of me, my voice filled with pride. "See Ayden run." I watched his empowered shadow turn down a side street and vanish in the fog of a cold, cold November day.

That is also when it hit me: Ayden had been, I now understood, striving for a very long time to separate himself from his depressive past as painlessly and as soon as possible. The final separating step had occurred when he had shared with me anecdotes from his up-and-down life. Those anecdotes included, primarily, the troublesome account of Vicki having accused him of assaulting her and his conscious was clearer now because he had been open with me and because he had been open with himself. Now, unfettered by such a troubled and manic period in his life, he was hopeful that he could write again. What's even more important is the fact that he was now on the road he had always coveted so much, the road to the land he had once referred to as the land of "literary prosperity."

Before he had fled Lakeshore General, Ayden had stated that the only thing in his life capable of holding him back was untreated manic depression and he was determined, more than ever, to manage—if not defeat—his depression outright. I knew without a doubt that Ayden had promised Dr. Goodwin and himself that he would continue taking his medications no matter how difficult the life that was now open to him might become. One point stood out: the only person with the potential to hold Ayden Mann back was Ayden Mann himself. Something else was also clear to me: with Jocelyn and Ayden having been readmitted into that living and breathing world outside the study's only window, the world beyond Seven Southwest and Lakeshore General Hospital, I was alone with my pained liver—as alone as I'd ever been—once again. Little did I know at the time how poor my odds of survival actually were.

CHAPTER 26

❀

As you may have already surmised, my first four days spent on Seven Southwest are essentially a series of imperfect flashbacks, recollections. Except for my rather lengthy conversations with Jane, Jocelyn, Dr. Goodwin, Ayden and a very brief, but difficult conversation with Kate, my ex-girlfriend, a conversation I will share with you now, those four days expired in a fast-moving and hazy fashion. Despite the haziness, I do seem to remember that new bandages were wrapped around my wounds shortly after my private "session" with Ayden had ended, which was, I think, a short time before I was kicked out of the study and sent back to my drab and monotonous room by a tech with a bad attitude, which was also a short time before Kate called.

"Day group starts in a few minutes, Hunter. You'll be there, right?"

"Yes, Jane," I said at the very moment the phone next to my bed rang for the first time since I had talked to my mom days before. I was in no mood to talk to my mom or my dad. I was in no mood to talk to John—not that I believed he would bother calling. I was in no mood to speak with anyone. As far as I was concerned, everyone I knew outside the hospital had let me down. I answered the phone anyway if for no other reason than to silence it.

"Hunter?" It wasn't my mom or dad this time, or John for that matter, but Kate instead. I wasn't surprised that she had called. I had been expecting to hear from her. Her phoning me was simply inevitable; she had her sights set on obtaining an explanation as to why I had vandalized her car. Plus, she was seeking an apology. And why not? She deserved one.

"Hi, Kate," I said, nervous as hell and extremely embarrassed by what I had recently done to her and by what I had recently done to myself.

"Why'd you do it, Hunter?" She had wasted no time getting to the point.

"What do you mean?" I was stalling. I really wasn't sure why but I was stalling. Stalling seemed like such poor strategy and there was simply no avoiding what was coming next, namely the single question I had just tried to avoid.

"You know what I mean. Why did you vandalize my car with a can of spray paint? I didn't have that coming, you know."

"I was just mad I guess."

"You guess?"

"Yeah," I responded, remembering how Ayden had revealed that he could feel himself becoming manic as he spoke to Officer Taylor. Speaking to Kate from the confines of a psychiatric ward, I realized that I too had been full-blown manic when I had spray painted graffiti on the hood of her car, although I hadn't realized it at the time. I now realized that I had felt that particular mania coming on for days and days.

"Aren't you at all upset, Hunter?"

"I'm upset and sorry, Kate," I stated as the horrid pictures of me frantically vandalizing her car flew through my guilt-ridden brain again. Yes, I truly did feel guilty. Also, I was honestly empathizing with my ex-girlfriend, a woman who would never be quite the same because I had flown into a manic rage and had attempted to destroy a portion of her inner life. I was scarred now and so was she.

"I don't know that an apology will suffice, Hunter." The line went dead and those horrid pictures of how horrid I had behaved that horrid night became permanently captured on my mind's most horrid canvas in the most horrid colors. Yes, those particular pictures would be with me forever if not longer.

I was very aware of how shaken I was after Kate's call. My hands were trembling and there were tears burning in my eyes. What's more, I could feel my stomach churning in a manner I was certain was unrelated to my toxic liver. I had managed to apologize but the pictures of the crimes I had committed against Kate while in a manic frenzy were disturbing me to no end. The guilt I was experiencing was unparalleled. And I knew that the person who had committed such awful crimes was not the "real me."

I tried to get at the root of the guilt that was eating away at my insides and exorcise it from my body by reminding myself that I had in fact apologized but I could not reach deep enough. Then a kind of fear I had never known before made its presence known. I was suddenly dreading the impending visit from the police who I knew were coming to take me away. Kate had left me with no clues as to whether she would press charges or not and so I envisioned myself finally being booked for both vandalism and trespassing. The vision of me being photographed and fingerprinted by the police that was playing on inside of my head brought more and more tears. I was crying tears of fear and frustration when Jane returned to my side.

"What is it, Hunter? Was that your ex-girlfriend on the phone?"

"I think she's still my girlfriend," I responded, wiping my eyes on my bare arms, ashamed of my odd declaration that Kate was still my girlfriend. Jane glanced away and did not offer a reply. The awkwardness of having stated openly that Kate was my girlfriend when she honestly was not served to increase my trembling and I nearly fell out of the recliner. I did not know why I had referred to Kate as my girlfriend but I did understand that I would have to stop thinking of her that way soon.

To my surprise, I was permitted to skip the first group session, day group, that morning because I had been extremely upset with myself after I had spoken to Kate. Truthfully, I had cried myself to sleep. While asleep, I had seen before me for the final time the cognitive film of my dad and I hiking deep into the woods on the other side of the stream to cut down a Christmas tree. Why I dreamt that out-of-place dream again I still cannot say. I can only speculate that my tired mind was trying to escape the boundaries of Seven Southwest as well as flee the police. After all of these years, those are the only viable reasons I have uncovered as to why I experienced that particular dream when I did.

I also missed night group again. A few hours before the night session was scheduled to begin, I had been administered morphine via my I.V. drip to stave off the intense pain I was feeling in and around my liver. I hadn't complained about the pain I was feeling. The doctors who were busy trying to save me and my liver had drawn the conclusion that I was in much physical pain on their own. The morphine did serve to deaden the hurting that had been shooting through my abdomen and I soon fell into one of the deepest sleeps I have ever experienced. My fourth day on Seven Southwest quickly melted into another bleak and foggy day.

On the bleak and foggy morning of the fifth day, more blood was drawn from my body and I was asked to swallow more Paxil. I satisfied Jane that I did not need to eat breakfast. Blaming the morphine, I simply claimed that I was feeling sick to my stomach when, really, I had no interest whatsoever in sitting down to breakfast with the rest of the group. She believed me and so, instead of sitting in the dining room staring out the window at the concrete wall of the parking garage, I sat up in bed next to the phone and waited for Kate to call. I was praying with all my might that she would not be bringing any charges against me. I was also praying for a friend, new or old, to walk right into my room on Seven Southwest and distract me from the pain I was feeling just as Jocelyn had done days before. However, I knew that no friends would show that day. I also knew without a doubt that Kate would never be a friend to me again and that she now wanted us to lead separate lives. Yes, I knew, without a doubt, that is how she wanted things to be.

I had not seen John in days. You may have guessed by now that the two of us hadn't been close for many years and my suicide attempt had not improved our rocky relationship. It was fairly evident, with each passing minute, each passing hour, that John, like my mom, was not coming to see me anytime soon—if ever again. Jocelyn hadn't called yet and neither had Ayden. Truthfully, I would have been stunned to receive a call from Ayden, a man who had become obsessed with meeting his newest future, his third life-chapter, as soon as possible. Sadly, any other friend I could have turned to, confided in, had become absent from my life.

Sometime that same day, sometime after the winter darkness had invaded my desolate room, I focused on the motionless shadows on the walls and inside of my head. I replayed in my mind the brief conversation I had had with Kate. I tried to uncover hints in her tone and in her words as to whether she would be pressing charges against me or not. However, my search turned up nothing, no tips whatsoever, and I became so frustrated I contemplated using my shoelaces to strangle myself. My shoelaces were the only "weapon" I still had in my possession.

"Hunter, are you okay?" I couldn't place the soft voice originating from somewhere near the doorway, the same voice that belonged to a person who had just interrupted my thoughts of another suicide attempt. I knew that the voice in the doorway did not belong to Jane, or Jocelyn, or any goddamn angel. "Hunter, are you sleeping?"

"Who's there?"

"Claire. I'm your nurse tonight. Are you feeling okay, Hunter? Do you mind if I turn on the light?"

"Please leave it off. I'm trying to sleep here." Silently, I pulled the IV line out of the catheter and let go of it. I felt a cool liquid that was probably either sterile saline or dextrose trickling off my thighs and into the sheets.

"Tell me, Hunter, how's your mood right now?"

"Too low to measure."

"Do you still want to die?"

"No, no I don't," I lied. I stared into the poorly lit corridor just behind Claire. The corridor was empty. It appeared as if everyone on the ward, except for Claire and I, was sleeping. I leaned forward and glanced out the window. Cars and pedestrians were nowhere to be seen. Actually, it appeared that everyone on the planet might be sleeping except for myself and a nurse named Claire, another goddamn nurse I figured would never be able to free me from my despair. Yes, everyone was sleeping. Let me say that the world is an especially lonely place when a person is feeling depressed and suicidal on a psychiatric ward when the rest of the world is fast asleep and dreaming.

"Well, I should check your I.V. while I'm here." She turned on the ceiling light without asking a second time. She stepped up to my bed and I watched as a decent smile quickly became a frown. "Oh, what'd you do, Hunter?"

"Nothing," I lied again. She ordered me out of bed and rushed in with new sheets, stretching them over the mattress in a flash. She handed me a pair of clean, dry sweatpants she'd found in the stack of clothes John had delivered days earlier and shoved me into the bathroom to change. She was wiping the floor with a white cloth when I crawled back into bed.

"Do you have children, Claire?"

"Three." She had answered with a single word and I was positive that she was upset with me. I noticed that she was wiping at the metal sides of the bed with the same white cloth she had just been using on the floor.

"Do they know what you do?"

"Of course they do." She reinserted the line into the catheter and punched a few buttons. Everything was functioning normally again—everything except for me.

"So your children know that you work with suicidal mental misfits then?"

"You are not a 'mental misfit,' Hunter. It's clear that you still want to die, but you aren't a mental misfit." She flipped a pair of switches on the wall. The overhead light was snuffed out and a soft light that shone down on my bed almost exclusively was turned on. Then she left my room.

The next morning, after more of my blood had been drawn and I had taken another 10 milligrams of Paxil, my cousin Dana came to see me. Dana, a nurse practitioner, had her own office on the second floor of Lakeshore General and had been the first relative other than John and my parents to discover that I had been admitted into the hospital. She was also the last family member to visit me during the three weeks I was hospitalized.

"So, I hear that you still want to die." Dana stepped up to my bed and briefly rubbed her hand on my back and patted my shoulder, a gesture that seemed to be the next best thing to a hug.

"I do," I admitted. "So how's my mom doing?"

"I think she's doing okay. She is as okay as she can be." She tries to call, but you are always asleep." That statement confused me. The entire time I had been confined to Seven Southwest, I had felt as if I'd been getting too little sleep. I had also concluded that my mom had given up on me. But maybe I was wrong. Maybe she hadn't given up on me at all. "We're happy that you are alive, Hunter."

"You are?" I was still confused.

"Of course. Of course we are."

"How's my dad, Dana?"

"He's okay."

"He's really okay?"

"He's scared for you. He wants to know more about how you are making out medically speaking."

"I wish I knew myself."

"The hepatologist hasn't told you anything yet, huh?"

"Told me what?" I asked, bracing myself.

"Well, I think you already know that, much like your life, your liver function has been severely disrupted. I don't have the numbers in front of me but they are high, extremely elevated. Let's just say that the blood levels of your liver enzymes are high, way too high. Your liver is in trouble, Hunter. That's what the hepatologist tells me anyway.

"He told you that?"

"Yes, he did. Little more than an hour ago. Would you like me to find out more? You know I can if you want him to share with me more of the specifics."

"Can my liver be saved?" I felt a tear run down my face and onto my neck. I couldn't decide if I was crying because I was relieved that I might at long last actually get to die, or if I was saddened that I might actually continue to live.

"I'm not sure, Hunter. I'm not sure whether your liver can be saved. We'll know soon enough, though. The next 24 hours will prove to be critical."

"Critical, huh?"

"Here, kiddo, I brought you a journal, something I thought you might be able to use right now." Dana was changing the subject. "Maybe you should try and write whenever you are feeling up to it."

"Okay, I will." I took the journal. On the cover was a picture of a sunrise or a sunset. I could not tell which but I studied the muddled shades of burnt orange and crimson just the same. Sunrise or sunset, the picture of the sky on the journal looked almost bloody to me.

"I'll check back when I'm free, when I've got more time. See you after a while then, huh, Hunter?"

"Yes."

"Keep your chin up, sunshine. And write something."

"Okay, I will," I said as Dana disappeared down the corridor.

More than ever, I felt an urge to write something. It was a kind of urge I had never felt before. It was as if my cousin Dana had granted me permission to write, or had unknowingly given me a sense of affirmation, a sense of affirmation that my pursuit of literary success was worthwhile, or both. Either way, I knew that writing would be a welcome escape from the here and now, from the borders of Seven Southwest. I also understood that I needed to purge both my brain and my soul of the enigmatic story that had been steadily evolving inside of me over the course of many years.

I grabbed a hold of a pen Jane had left sitting on one of the nightstands and touched the tip to the first page. *Write something* I told myself. Much easier said than done. *What are you waiting for? Write something.* I tried to stain the paper with ink, with my innermost thoughts, but I could not find the appropriate words to tell the story that had been neglected for far too long. Like so many times before, my creativity was at an unfortunate standstill and the story I longed to tell was evading me. I was, you might say, at an utter loss for words. By the same token, I was not defeated—not yet anyway. I had not given up. I was very determined to write something substantial, something worthwhile, something of merit. I just needed an idea, a spark, if you will. Then, suddenly, sitting up in bed, clutching Jane's pen and my newly-acquired journal, it occurred to me that I was already living—yes living—that very story, my story. My story was happening, or unraveling, with every life-giving breath I took. Finally, finally, finally, after so many years of speculation and introspection, I had an idea, the idea of a lifetime.

CHAPTER 27

❁

Dr. Wyatt, the hepatologist assigned to the unenviable task of saving my seemingly-doomed liver, visited me for the first time on the morning of the sixth day. Soon after I had donated another vial of blood and swallowed more Paxil, he walked into my room, stood near my bed and explained in a very serious and direct manner that my liver was indeed suffering from acetaminophen-induced hepatoxicity, something most often referred to as chemical-driven liver damage. My suspicions had been validated. My liver was dieing.

Jane was standing at Dr. Wyatt's side when he confirmed what Dana had already told me, which was the fact that the next 24 hours would likely be the most critical I would ever face. Dr. Wyatt went on to explain that biochemical evidence of the maximal damage to my liver was still not known. The maximal diagnosis of how damaged my liver was really did not matter to me, though. All I wanted to know was whether I was going to die sooner than later, or ever. Ultimately, I wanted to know if I would have enough time to write my story, my novel, before my liver stopped working altogether.

"I will be back this time tomorrow, Hunter," Dr. Wyatt said before he exited the room, leaving Jane and I alone to contemplate what was left of my future, a future that was truly in doubt.

"What's on your mind right now, Hunter? You look so frightened."

"I'm not frightened, Jane."

"Well, what is it then?"

"I just can't believe that my whole life has come down to what will transpire over the next 24 hours. For the first time I can remember, I get an idea, a solid idea for a story, my story, for a novel, my novel, and now this. My life has been reduced to 24 fucking hours, Jane."

"Is that really what you want to talk about?"

"I didn't say that I wanted to talk about anything at all."

"Hunter, you put yourself in this position. You and only you."

"I know that."

"I believe that you want to live, Hunter. I really do."

"What makes you say that?" I sounded as awful as I felt.

"Because there is something in the way you speak, in both your tone and diction, that gives you away. Something about the way you carry yourself tells me that you are still hoping to give life another try. I can't put a finger on it, Hunter, but from somewhere inside of you a voice all its own is crying for your life to be spared ... one last time."

"Jocelyn told me the other day that she believes there is a life-force inside all of us that wants us to go on living even when we feel like dieing."

"I would agree with Jocelyn."

"So do you think there is a life-force inside of me that is still fighting to live?"

"Yes, I think so. Don't you?"

"I don't know whether I have a life-force or not, Jane. I only know that I want to live to write. If I'm destined to die, then I want to go quickly, painlessly. If I am given another shot at living, than I want to live for as long as it takes to write my novel. If that is an example of an inner life-force, then maybe I do have one."

"Maybe so, Hunter. Maybe so." At that point, Jane left the room presumably to check on other patients, or to be rid of me for a while, or maybe both. I was still fully awake when the phone next to my bed rang a few minutes after midnight.

"Hunter?" a familiar voice was speaking to me.

"Is that you, Jocelyn?

"Yes. Yes, it's me, Hunter."

"What's wrong?"

"I can't take it anymore." Her voice sounded lost and hollow. Her voice sounded distressed.

"Can't take what?"

"Living this life of mine."

"My god, Jocelyn ... What is it?"

"Everything."

"Well, like what?"

"My dad won't speak to me. What's more, no one else will talk to me either—not even Richard or Keith."

"Who in the hell are Richard and Keith?"

"My brothers, stupid." Jocelyn began to cry.

"How awful." I noticed that I was on the verge of crying as well. I took a deep breath. I heard Jocelyn breathe deeply, too. I wondered if she was summoning the life-force I was certain was living somewhere inside her psyche. As defeated as she sounded, I decided that she probably was although she probably was not conscious of it at the time.

"What do I do, Hunter? Tell me, what do I do?"

"Ignore them right back," I said, very determined to help my hurting friend. Looking back, I can see how poor an answer that was. Looking back, I can see that I should have given her better advice. And finally, in retrospect, I can also see that I had no other advice to share with her at the time.

"But I have been ignoring them. We haven't spoken in days, not even a simple 'hello.' Ignoring them doesn't work."

"Why not?"

"Because I feel even more ostracized when I ignore them. Besides, I want them to listen to me when I do talk to them. More than anything, I want them to understand."

"Oh. Understand what?"

"I want them to understand why I've done the things I've done. I want them to understand what I am, who I am, understand why I operate the way I do, that sort of shit. Finally, I want them to understand manic depression."

"I'm not sure what you can say to them to make them understand," I blurted.

"Thanks, Hunter. Thanks very much." And then the line went dead.

I was still awake when Jocelyn called back a few hours later. Since her first call, I had been unable to sleep and had passed the time writing—yes writing—in the journal Dana had given me. I had been busy recording what I had experienced the first six days in the hospital. I had also written a rough draft of the poem "Manic," the same poem that appears in its entirety at the beginning of this book. The process—if one can call it that—of creating the poem "Manic" and the process of writing detailed notes of my most recent experiences on Seven Southwest seemed to take a couple of hours at the very least. I was still writing when the phone rang a second time.

"Thanks for answering, Hunter. I still need to talk."

"I'm glad you decided to call back. I'm really worried about you, Jocelyn. You know, I still don't have your phone number and nobody here will give it to me, not even Jane. I almost left to come see you, but I don't know where it is you're staying right now. Where are you staying anyway?"

"Hunter, are you doing okay? Don't ask me how, but I get the feeling that your prognosis is not good."

"Did you talk to Jane, Jocelyn?"

"Of course not. She'd never tell me anything anyway. She can't."

"Right. I forgot."

"So, Hunter, how are you doing?"

"I'm fine," I lied.

"Have you seen Dr. Goodwin lately?"

"Not lately. Jane has been here almost constantly."

"What does she say?"

"Nothing."

"Are you feeling any better, Jocelyn?"

"I'm okay."

"Just okay?" I was getting my own feelings as to how Jocelyn was doing. I felt very strongly that she was not doing "okay." I had my suspicions that she was as suicidal as she'd ever been—if not more.

"Damn you, Hunter, I'm okay. Let's leave it at that. Can't we please talk about something, or someone, else?"

"Sure." That is when I asked the one question I probably shouldn't have asked. "Are you taking your meds, Jocelyn?"

"Why?" A monosyllabic answer and I got the feeling that she wasn't.

"Just curious. That's all."

"Just because I'm a manic, doesn't mean I can't have an off day. I don't have to miss my meds to have an off day."

"So you're just having a bad day then, huh? And you are taking your meds as prescribed? I asked, forging ahead.

"Yes, I'm just having a bad day. I'm also thinking that my meds are none of your fucking business, Hunter Kraven." And with that, the line went dead for the second time that night.

I was fully awake when Dr. Wyatt, Dr. Goodwin and Jane returned only hours after I had last spoken to Jocelyn. It was my seventh morning on Seven Southwest and, for the first time in several years, I was finally writing again. Reluctantly, I closed my journal and laid it on one of the nightstands.

"How are you feeling, Hunter?" Dr. Goodwin was the first to speak.

"That all depends I suppose. What do you have to tell me?"

"First, Hunter, I have concluded that you are suffering from bipolar disorder, manic depression." Dr. Goodwin had gotten straight to the point. I respected his candor very much.

"So how do you know?"

"I've been observing you"

"I know that already. But how do you know that I'm bipolar?"

"Well, for one, John tells me that there is a history of depression and suicide in your family."

"John told you that, huh?"

"That he did."

"And what else?"

"And while observing you over the past week, I've noticed, as Jane has, as your nurses have, that your moods have been fluctuating. You've been up, you've been down. You've been up again. You've been cycling—rapidly. Even your speech is rapid at times. And at times, you seem distracted, unable to focus. You demonstrate a 'flight of ideas' often. Even more important, your MDQ, Hunter, tells me that you are probably bipolar."

"Well, I'm not surprised," I stated rather calmly.

"No?"

"No, I'm not." I was telling the truth this time; I wasn't surprised one iota. I had been expecting that particular diagnosis for several days. All at once, a sense of relief washed over me. Just like that, I had a diagnosis all my own. What's more, I had a new perspective, a new and improved outlook. Yes, I was bipolar, a manic-depressive. Now I could get on with the rest of my life—if my liver continued to fulfill its purpose that is.

"Well then, we will talk again later today. Is that okay with you, Hunter?"

"Right." I watched as Dr. Goodwin, his early morning mission having been accomplished, stepped over the threshold, nodded at a couple of nurses and passed through the thick doors at the opposite end of the ward.

"And what news do you have for me?" I turned to face Dr. Wyatt. I was wondering if he would kill my good mood by telling me that my liver could not be spared.

"It appears, Hunter, as if you are going to manage to pull through," he said, his voice a strange whisper, a whisper I had never heard before, a whisper I have not heard since. I glanced at Jane. She smiled at me rather cautiously, her eyes apparently searching my face for evidence as to how I might respond to such information. I did not bother smiling back. Unlike learning that I was in fact a manic-depressive, the news that my liver would continue to live had come as something of a shock. All through the night, especially while I had been writing the poem "Manic," I had been telling myself that, at long last, my ticket to a place far away, a place unknown to me, was about to be punched, validated.

"I will pull through, huh? I'm going to make it then?" I asked Dr. Wyatt after a few silent moments of introspection.

"Yes, you will, Hunter. I'll say that you are 'lucky' and leave it at that." Dr. Wyatt's lips turned upward forming the slightest of smiles. "We'll get you off the IV very soon." He turned and left the room without speaking another word. I want you to know that I never saw him again.

"So how do you feel?" Jane asked me as soon as Dr. Wyatt had passed through the thick doors.

"Numb."

"I can only imagine. Well, breakfast is in a little while. I'll see you there, okay?"

"Yes, you will," I said. "Yes, you will."

CHAPTER 28

It all made sense to me now. My once-pathetic life, the same life that had seemed anything but fixable, was now making sense to me. I suddenly knew why I had behaved the way I had behaved over the course of so many years. I now realized what I was, a manic-depressive, and who I had been all along, namely a lost man who had been severely mislead by a mental illness he could not identify, a mental illness he did not know how to control. I also realized who I was going to be for the rest of my life: I was going to be, at long last, myself, Hunter Kraven, a manic-depressive who had been granted another precious chance at living.

I understood all too well that I was no longer a lost soul. I had been found—in a manner of speaking—and it was clearly up to me to resurrect myself from the pitfalls of depression. It was up to me to restart my life. I now understood that my life was worth saving. My life, like Jocelyn's and Ayden's and that of every other suicidal mentally ill person on the planet, was worth saving.

"How would you rate your mood right now?" Claire asked me as she strolled casually into the study. I had been staring out the window at the snowy scene seven stories below again.

"An eight."

"Well, that's an improvement since I last talked to you. Are you leveling with me, Hunter?" For the first time, I took a good look at Claire's face. I saw that she wore very little make-up and that she had the most delicate features. Hers was an honest face, the face of a person who could be trusted. Her fine hair, which was the faintest shade of red, was tied in a girlish ponytail. Her youthful brown eyes stared back at me, as she waited patiently for my response.

"I am leveling with you, Claire.

"Okay, Hunter. I wish, however, that you would stop skipping meals. You missed breakfast again."

"So where's Jane anyway?" This time, I was the one who was changing the subject.

"Jane is off for the rest of the day. Actually, she has the next three days off."

"Well, she does deserve some time away from me, away from this place I think."

"Perhaps she does, Hunter. So anyway, how will you go about telling people that you are bipolar? Or will you keep your diagnosis a secret?"

"I am going to tell everyone I know, everyone I meet, that I am a manic-depressive, Claire," I responded without giving her questions a second thought. "I will be keeping no secrets."

"I think that's a good idea."

"So do I," I said. I had arrived at my decision to admit that I was indeed suffering from bipolar disorder on the spur of the moment, without hesitation. And I knew without any doubts whatsoever that I would be standing by that decision for the rest of my life.

"Well, Dr. Goodwin will be by shortly. Day group starts in about half an hour. Everyone else will be there, Hunter. You will have your first opportunity to tell the other manic-depressives that you too are a manic-depressive."

"Yes, I suppose I will."

Dr. Goodwin entered the study only minutes after Claire had departed in what I regarded was a "cheery frame of mind," a zealous voice giving his happy mood away. "Hunter, I want to start you on a medication called lithium carbonate as soon as today," he stated in a fairly loud tone as he positioned himself on a thick arm of a large overstuffed chair and clasped his hands in his lap, the toes of his shoes barely touching the carpeted floor. I turned away from the window. I crossed the room and sat on the same sofa Jocelyn and I had shared during my first group therapy session.

"I've heard of lithium, but I don't really know what it is," I stated.

"Lithium is a natural element that is present in small amounts in the human body. It serves as a mood stabilizer."

"I knew that already ... I think," I told him. I watched him unclasp his hands, stand up, unbutton his sport coat and sit down in the large overstuffed chair. "Dr. Goodwin, if I am going to start lithium therapy, I need to know if it will interfere with my creativity, my ability to write my novel. I've lost enough time the way it is. I guess I need to know whether I will be losing me, myself, my identity."

"We will try to find the proper dose so that your creativity is not jeopardized, Hunter. We will work to 'control' your illness with both Paxil and lithium. We want to provide you with a reasonably 'normal lifestyle,' a lifestyle I honestly believe is obtainable for you. You will you have to stick with it, really stick with it."

"If it does not interfere with my writing, I will." Ayden's own stance on the importance of taking meds to treat manic depression while writing a novel came to mind in an instant. "I'm certainly going to try to stay with the meds you prescribe for my anyway," I added.

"That's good to hear, Hunter."

"Dr. Goodwin, when will I be leaving?" I still wanted to go home. I wanted to run through the snow as Ayden had done. More than anything, I wanted to write in an environment that was more conducive to being creative, an environment that would be more accommodating for me.

"I'd like you to be here for another two weeks, okay?"

"Why? Dr. Wyatt said that I am going to pull through. He said that I'll be off the IV sometime today. My liver is going to make it, you know."

"Yes, I know, Hunter. I know."

"Then why am I staying another two weeks?"

"Because it's important that we set up a dosing schedule for you. And as a part of your dosing schedule, I will want to observe your mood experiences once you have been on lithium for a little while. I'll have you stay here for another two weeks and then, after you've been home for a week or two, we'll meet again in my office and take it from there, see how you are doing. Don't worry, Hunter, I will be sending you home. I don't want you to become too dependent on this hospital. I don't think you need to be here more than two more weeks."

"But if I am to stay here for another fourteen days, I won't be able to make it home in time to have Thanksgiving with my family."

"Hunter, I suspect that you aren't too set on going home to see your family right now anyway. Am I right?"

"How did you know that?"

"John told me yesterday that you have not given any indication that you want to go home for the holiday in several days. Actually, I seem to recall that he said that you turned down his offer to fly to home with him."

"I did."

"Well, I need to know, Hunter, what your plans are."

"So you think that I will see improvement in as little as two weeks then?"

"Improvement is usually gradual, but it depends on the individual. You may feel better soon after you start taking lithium, but I'd say that a noteworthy improvement may take about two weeks or more. I want to watch you for a while, watch your mood. I also want to watch for side effects during the initial phase of treatment. More than anything, I want you to feel comfortable taking lithium."

"Then I am going to stay here for two more weeks." Ultimately, I knew that the decision had been mine to make. It was not a difficult decision; I knew that I needed to get "on track" with my meds so that I could write well. I would simply make other plans for the Thanksgiving holiday.

"Okay. That settles it. Two more weeks."

"What are some of the side effects I might experience?"

"Well, you might feel ill at times, or nauseated. You might notice fine hand tremor, excessive thirst and excessive urination. Those are just a few of the possible side effects, side effects that are directly related to the amount of drug in the bloodstream. You should know that those particular side effects are usually transitory. Usually, they will subside, or even vanish altogether, as your treatment continues."

"Is lithium addictive?"

"Not at all."

"Has lithium worked for any of your other patients?"

"For the majority of them."

"But are any of your patients writers?"

"Not that I can remember. Several of them are artists I think."

"Artists, huh?"

"Artists, Hunter."

"Okay then. Let's do it," I practically shouted.

"Okay, Hunter, we'll do it then. Just don't get impatient. You are doing a good job taking your Paxil and I think we will see improvement soon. You need to give the lithium time to work for you, too. Just keep you chin up, keep writing and let the lithium do its own thing." He stood, buttoned his sport coat and left the room. As soon as he was gone, I made a mental note to do some research of my own on both lithium carbonate and manic depression.

Claire was the first person I would speak to after Dr. Goodwin had informed me that I would soon be placed on a regimen that included not only Paxil, but lithium as well. Originally, I had intended to ask Dana for any information she might be willing to share on lithium but when I discovered that she had written only her home phone number and not her office number on the back of my journal, I decided that my next best move would be to ask Claire, a nurse who had not once closed the blinds on me or reminded me that she had other patients to check on.

Unable to locate Claire on my first try, I made up my mind to see what information I could uncover in the study. Somewhere within the stacks there had to be a book, or a guide, on lithium and manic depression.

"Find what you're after?"

"Not yet, Claire." I was frustrated because I had been searching for nearly two hours. "So far, I've found nothing."

"Nothing?"

"Not a thing. You know, you'd think that a psychiatric ward would have some information on manic depression and lithium at their patients' disposal. You'd think there'd be a whole damn section on mental illness and its treatment."

"Maybe you should take a look at this."

"What is it?"

"A book for you, silly. It's from my own collection."

I grabbed onto the book and studied the worn cover. The words "Manic Depression" were printed in gold on a forest green background. "How old is this book? What's the vintage?"

"It's a few years old. The main thing is the fact that it is still accurate today. Hunter, I think you will learn from it. I know I have. Plus, there are a couple of chapters devoted to lithium treatment. I think you'll learn what it is you want to know. Remember: if you can't find the answers you are searching for in there, I'm here to help you. And so are the other nurses and doctors."

"Thank you, Claire. I'll get this back to you just as soon as I've finished it."

"There's no need. I want you to have it. Keep it. The book is yours. There's no time to read it now, though. Group starts soon. And you will be there." She smiled at me. "But first, we need to disconnect you from that IV."

CHAPTER 29

❃

In day group later that morning, I informed Claire and Ernest and everyone present that Dr. Goodwin had diagnosed me manic-depressive.

"How does that make you feel, finally knowing for sure that you are bipolar?" Claire asked, prompting me to answer openly, honestly, the slightest smile visible on her delicate face.

"Relieved, relieved and more relieved." I watched Claire's smile widen.

"Hunter, now that you've been diagnosed manic-depressive, what will your newest goal be?"

"I'm going to ask for help."

"What kind of help?"

"Help in understanding exactly what manic depression is."

"Help from whom?"

"From you, Claire."

"From just me?"

"And from Dr. Goodwin and Jane and Jocelyn and Ayden and everyone in this room. I will be seeking help from anyone who might take the time to listen and want to help me, from people on the outside for example, people who care enough to support me in my fight against the illness that has interfered with my life for so many years."

"Very, very good. Understanding manic depression is vital to keeping the illness in check, Hunter." Claire set her notes on a small round table and looked around the room, seemingly searching the other members of the group for input.

"Hunter," Ernest cleared his throat. "Share with us another goal, if you don't mind. I think we've got the time." Ernest glanced at Claire.

"We do," Claire nodded.

"Okay, I will." I thought for a moment or maybe a little longer. Then I looked directly at Ernest's ruddy face. "I will also be educating myself on manic depression," I told Ernest and the rest of the group. "I will listen to Dr. Goodwin and the nurses and the rest of the hospital staff. Yes, I will listen. I will listen to all of you, you people who are fighting like I am for understanding as well as for inner peace. That is, Ernest, another goal I will be pursuing. I really hope that makes some sense to you."

"It does," Claire and Ernest said in unison.

I looked at the faces that were now staring at me with expressions that told me they approved of my new-found approaches to 'controlling' my manic depression. "I will be listening," I informed the manic-depressives who were as much a part of the group as I was. "I will be listening." And with that, the people in attendance began to cheer. Some of them even went so far as to applaud me. All at once, I had been fully accepted as a member of the group. It was then that I realized that admitting openly to my peers that I was a manic-depressive and being accepted by them for my honesty was, more than anything else, the very first step to understanding my mental illness.

"Well, we will close this particular session and meet here again this evening at 9:00, as always. And, as always, I'd like to see all of you here. Oh! And by the way, each of you should have thought of a new goal by then." Claire picked up her clipboard as the group members filed out of the study one by one. I was the last manic-depressive to exit the study. "Hunter, I'll meet you in your room in a couple of minutes, okay?"

"Sounds good, Claire."

Carrying a small tray with a pair of pleated white paper cups on it, Claire joined me in my room for the first time that day.

"Here it is."

"Is it lithium?" I asked, feeling just a tinge of nervousness course through my body.

"This, Hunter, is a drug called Eskalith. Eskalith is a brand name for lithium." She held one of the pleated white paper cups, a cup that contained six small capsules that were half purple and half yellow, in front of me.

"How much Eskalith will I be taking?"

"Dr. Goodwin wants to start you out on 1800 milligrams a day for now. That may seem like a big number to you, but once you've responded, we should see your dosage level reduced to 300 mgs 2–3 times a day. So are you ready?"

"I'm ready," I said with a sigh, glad to know that this time I was not lying.

Claire handed me the cup with the Eskalith inside of it. I stared into the cup at the capsules that were, if everything went as planned, supposed to change my life for the better. I poured the capsules into my mouth and caught them on my tongue. I reached for the cup of water, took a single large sip and concentrated on washing down all six purple-yellow capsules. Lithium, the most commonly prescribed medication for treating manic depression, was now, at long last, officially inside my body, presumably to stabilize my mood.

"Nothing to it, huh?"

"Nothing to it, Claire. Could I have some more water please?"

"Sure thing." She stepped outside my room and into the corridor. She reached inside a small white refrigerator, a refrigerator I hadn't seen before. From inside, she extracted a long, clear bottle. She twisted the cap off for me and handed me the cold bottle of water. I put the bottle's rim to my lips and drank until it was empty. That water was the best water I have ever tasted.

So now I was on a medicine regimen all my own. Yes, Paxil and lithium were inside me, in my bloodstream, chipping away at both my feelings of depression and my mania. Also, I was now living within the system Jocelyn had described the day I met her. I had already been evaluated and medicated. In two weeks, I would be, if everything went as planned, vacated. I really had come a very long, long way.

I was sitting in the recliner thumbing through the book on lithium and manic depression Claire had given me, making notes in my journal, when the phone next to my bed rang. I had already received a handful of messages, messages from my parents mostly, the staff had been considerate enough to take for me and I felt strongly that the person on the other end of the line this time was indeed my mom and not a sobbing Jocelyn or a pissed-off Kate.

I thought back to the morning after my first suicide attempt. I remembered how I had been unable to locate the ringing phone that day. This time, on the day I had ingested 1800 milligrams of lithium as prescribed, I located the ringing phone and answered it with a renewed sense of accomplishment.

"Hi, Mom," I said in a voice that was anything but a whisper.

"Hunter, how did you know it was me?"

"You'd left so many messages for me already, I just figured."

"Hunter, how are you?"

"Doing pretty damn well I must say. My depression has lifted—that's probably the Paxil working—and my liver is going to make it."

"Dr. Goodwin told your dad and I that it is still too soon for the Paxil to be taking affect."

"Well, I feel better, much better. Explain that, Mom."

"Dr. Goodwin says that you are simply having some 'good days' right now."

"Whatever. Maybe." That's when I remembered that the nurse who had given me my first dose of Paxil had told me that a couple of weeks would pass before I would notice a marked improvement in my mood.

"How is it that you talked to Dr. Goodwin? I never gave him permission to talk to you."

"Yes, you did. You just don't remember."

"Please don't tell me what I do and don't remember, Mom. You're treating me as if I had been in a coma this past week."

"Dr. Goodwin says that you are now off the IV and taking both Paxil *and* lithium." Just like that, the subject had been changed.

"I am."

"Good, Hunter. Stick with it, the treatment plan Dr. Goodwin has laid out for you."

"I will, especially if the plan 'stabilizes' me to the point that I am able to write again. Hopefully, I will be able to write again, Mom. Just imagine ... "

"Shouldn't you be more concerned with your well-being, Hunter? And don't you think you should pursue something worthwhile?"

"My writing *is* worthwhile. I feel better about myself when I'm writing. Why can't you understand that? Why can't you ever support me as a writer? To you my writing is just therapy, isn't it?"

"I do support you. I always have. Hunter, I just want you to be happy."

"Then let me decide what is and isn't worthwhile. Once and for all, let me make a decision on my own. And let me write. I need to be writing, Mom!" Having made my feelings known, I hung up the phone without another word and returned to my journal and to my note taking, tears blurring the words I had scribbled the day Dana had given me the journal, the words *Write, write, write.*

In the community room, people were passing time playing board games and watching television In one corner, Ernest was playing chess with one of the many staff members, a tech named Bruce. In another corner, several people, including my grizzled war-time "buddy," were playing Monopoly, every one of them counting out loud the numbers on the die, every one of them aggressively moving their pieces across the game board, passing "go" with the same zest they displayed when they were sent to "jail." It was a fun time watching them accuse one another of cheating and I pulled up a chair, hoping to get in on the next game so that I could continue to gather material for my novel.

"So, you're one of us I hear," a smallish man named Pauley said to me. "Maybe you have a cigar for me?"

"Sorry."

"How 'bout a dollar then?"

"Sorry again."

"Any idea as to when I'll regain my freedom, my liberty?"

"Still sorry."

"You want to break out of this joint?"

"No, I don't, Pauley. I want to stay a while."

"Maybe you want to take my place then? I have a phone call to make."

"Have to call your mommy, Pauley?" asked an ultra-skinny younger man who went by the name of "Skeeter."

"No, I have to call your wife back, you jackass!" Pauley sassed him. Everyone seated at the table laughed at Pauley's joke. Skeeter's complexion turned several shades of red.

"Well, up yours, Pauley!" With that, the man called Skeeter stood and grabbed hold of the table's thin, rounded edge. Putting his back into it, he shoved the weight of the table away from his lanky body, managing to tip it over entirely, sending an array of tiny plastic houses and tiny plastic hotels flying, before he stomped out of the room, a pair of techs and several patients, including at least three of the people who had just been cheating at Monopoly, following closely behind him.

"Checkmate!" Ernest hollered from the room's opposite corner, apparently oblivious to the tantrum Skeeter had just thrown. "Checkmate!" he hollered a second time.

I was busy helping Pauley and a woman named Sylvia pick up the game pieces when Ernest strode out of the room, the smile of a victor on his glowing face.

"So what meds do they have you on, or do you even know?" Sylvia asked me, pushing a pair of folding chairs up against the wall. It was a personal question, but I answered anyway.

"Paxil and lithium." I grabbed onto one end of the table and helped Pauley and a tech named Gene drag it back into place.

"Yeah? Well, I'm on Paxil and lithium, too," she said with a nod. And there she was, a woman who just happened to appear as decent as any other woman I had ever met, a woman whose medicine regimen was identical to my own.

"Are you a manic?" I could hardly contain my curiosity.

"We all are," Pauley responded. "Except for a very few space cadets who aren't here right now and that idiot over there." Pauley pointed in the direction of a little man who was sitting alone on the tiled floor next to the television. The man was rocking back and forth and blinking rapidly.

"What's up with him anyway," I asked, recalling that I had walked passed the man Pauley had referred to as an "idiot" on several occasions, neither one of us uttering a single word to one another.

"He's a schizophrenic," Sylvia answered for Pauley. I stared across the room at the little man who sat alone blinking furiously for no apparent reason. As far as I knew, I had never seen a schizophrenic before. The man definitely did not look like an "idiot" to me.

"Cut him some slack," I said. "He can't help it that he's that way." Pauley's eyes widened and then he shrugged as if to say, *What the hell do I know?*

"Yeah, Pauley, just like we can't help being manic-depressives," Sylvia stated, echoing my sentiment. Pauley shook his head and walked away. Over near the television, the little man was still rocking back and forth, still blinking rapidly at nothing.

On my seventh morning on the ward, I discovered that Seven Southwest was definitely a culture all its own, a culture with a very strict schedule. Meds were doled out every morning at precisely 8:00 and then again at precisely 8:00 every night. In between the two dosing times, there were three supervised meals in the dining room and structured activities in the community room in which everyone, everyone including the on-duty staff, took part. There was also time allotted to visit with psychiatrists and other patients and an ample amount of free time, time I usually spent in the study reading both the daily news and the book Claire had bestowed upon me, or in my bedroom working vigorously on my journal, or, after I was rewarded with full ground privileges, exploring the hospital itself. As for the group therapy sessions, day group usually started at 11:00 and lasted approximately one hour, concluding just in time for lunch. Night group usually started at 9:00 and lasted about an hour as well. Lights out was at 11:00 p.m.

Medicated, somewhat rested and alert, taken off of the IV and looking toward my future as a writer, I soon fell into a routine all my own, a routine that was complemented by the schedule I have just outlined for you. A very large part of that routine was devoted to listening, observing and spying and, of course, recording in my journal what I had heard and seen. I carried my journal with me at all times because I was afraid that it might be stolen, or because I did not want to miss out on the chance to document the various behaviors I was constantly witnessing.

The community room was the best place to find material for journaling. Unlike the study and the dining room, the community room was almost always noisy, a place that, surprisingly, was not bereft of laughter. I usually sat in a large wingback chair not far from the television and not very far from the rest of the group. Rarely did I play games. Most often, I would log time listening to the other patients interact. These people were manic-depressives like me and I was quite determined to hear them speak of their lives in "regular" conversations, conversations in which they would speak most often of the trials and tribulations of living a manic-depressive's life.

I recall that there was a man called Davis. Davis was his last name I think and it was also the only name he went by. He was a rather small man, a small man with broad shoulders and rather large facial features, features that looked as if they belonged on a much bigger man's face. His crooked nose appeared to have been broken any number of times and it was obvious to me—and to the other patients I believe—that he was a feisty little shit, a real survivor, as well as the leader of the group. How and why he had ended up on Seven Southwest nobody seemed to know, or at least they simply would not say. Nevertheless, he was looked upon as something of an enigma and what he said was accepted by the rest of the group as law.

It was Davis who told me that Seven Southwest was not such a bad place and not Jocelyn or Ayden or anyone else for that matter. He never did say why but he readily admitted that he liked it there. He also made it known that he understood that he could not stay there forever. "I'm a hard working man," he told me one day, as he laid down a full house and scooped up a large pile of poker chips, much to the dismay of several of the other patients. "I know I can't stay here indefinitely. For me, this place is just a pit stop. I'll be back out there soon enough." Like Jocelyn and Ayden, Davis was hopeful for a future beyond Seven Southwest.

"What will you do once you are discharged? I asked him as he slid his queen the full length of the chess board, checkmating Ernest for what must have been the fifth or sixth game in a row.

"Hunter, I can build a motorcycle from the ground up," he informed me as he pulled from his shirt pocket a small, creased picture of a mint condition Harley Davidson, a Harley he claimed he had restored himself, and dropped it on the table as if it were his last ace. "There aren't too many people who can do that. There just aren't, kid."

"Probably not," I agreed.

"There's no 'probably' about it. So what can you do, Hunter?" Davis tucked the picture of his prized Harley back into the pocket on his white t-shirt.

"I can write."

"Is that why you carry that book around with you all the time?"

"Actually, it's a journal."

"Is that why you carry that journal around with you all the time?"

"Yes."

"What do you write in it?"

"Thoughts, ideas, that sort of stuff."

"Are you going to write a book or something someday?"

"Yes, I think so."

"You can't just think about doing something, Hunter. You have to believe in doing something. Then you have to get off your ass and do it." I watched him as he put each chess piece back in its place. "There is a tremendous difference between thinking and doing. You need to be certain about what it is you want to do. You should try putting your heart in your writing on every page, every word. Bleed a little. Bleed a lot. Get some snot and a little dirt in your eye. Get into the fight—if writing is what you really want to do with your life."

"It is."

"Hunter, if your heart isn't involved in what you are doing, you will ultimately fail. Trust me."

"I'll try and remember that," I told him. Would you believe I have yet to forget a single word Davis spoke to me the day he told me that he could build a Harley Davidson motorcycle from the ground up.

On my eighth day on Seven Southwest, a Saturday, Jocelyn called me on the phone in my room only minutes after day group had ended. This time, she was not crying.

"Hunter, I'm glad I reached you. Really, I am. I keep missing you lately." Her voice sounded alive and hopeful. It was as if she were full of dreams for a better tomorrow. Yes, she sounded that happy but I had my doubts as to just how happy she truly was. I wondered if her happiness was all an act for my benefit. I was still suspecting that she was not taking her meds. I was also suspecting that her current troubles with her family were reaching much deeper than she was willing to admit to me or to herself. I quickly turned my journal to a clean page and readied my pen.

"How are you doing, Jocelyn? How are you feeling? What's been going on?"

"Well, I saw Davis."

"When did you see him?"

"We met for coffee early this morning."

"Where?"

"In the hospital cafeteria. He was discharged today while you were probably still sleeping. He called me to wish me well and I suggested meeting for breakfast."

"You were here this morning?"

"Yes, but it was early, before visiting hours."

"So how are you feeling then?" I didn't dare ask if she was taking her meds, as I was tempted to do.

"I'm okay, hanging in there, busy looking for a job and an apartment."

"Any luck so far?"

"Not yet. I need to get out on my own again, though. It's impossible to be myself in my dad's house."

"Is he speaking to you yet?"

"No."

"I suppose Keith and Richard aren't either?"

"Sometimes they ask me what's up, how I'm doing, but it's obvious they are uneasy around me. They treat me as if the word "fragile" were stamped across my forehead. I think they are fearing breakage. Hunter, how are you doing?"

"I'm taking lithium now and I'm writing again!" I exclaimed.

"Wow! That's definitely a sign of improvement, taking lithium and writing again. So you are working on your book then?"

"I am. I have a very good, very solid idea. I'm journaling that idea now, preparing an outline."

"Well, Hunter, stay on your meds and you will soon be fit for discharge."

"Dr. Goodwin says that I'll be out of here in thirteen days, at the three week mark. Today is actually day number eight."

"That's good to hear. You know, you should ask him for a day pass and come see me."

"Yeah, I really should. In fact, I'll do just that," I said, even though, after spending more than a week on Seven Southwest, I now understood that I was not quite ready to face the outside world—not yet anyway. I knew that I could not run to my future as Ayden had run to his. I simply was not ready to meet the people who would frisk my person for answers or shun me or both. I was not ready to step back into my bloody apartment. I was not ready to sort through the pieces just yet. After all, too much work still needed to be done from the inside. I decided that I would see Jocelyn after I had been discharged for good, forever. Thirteen days was soon enough.

"Come see me in a week, this next Saturday, Hunter."

"Well, I'll try," I lied.

"You're not bullshitting me, are you, Hunter?"

"I promise I will see you on Saturday, in a week." I lied a second time.

"Yeah, come see me on Saturday. I've got to go now but I will talk to you tomorrow maybe."

"Feeling okay, Jocelyn?"

"Yes."

"Then I'll talk to you sooner than later." Just like that, the latest conversation with Jocelyn had ended. I hadn't recorded a single word while we'd been talking but as soon as I hung up the phone, I started writing again. And the words just flowed and flowed and flowed. Manic depression is like that, a flowing stream of undaunted emotions. Sometimes, there is no taming that creative stream, the flow, which is, I strongly believe, more often than not, beneficial to the overall success of a manic-depressive writer.

CHAPTER 30

❀

"Will you be coming home for Thanksgiving, Hunter?" my mom asked early in the afternoon of day number nine, a day that looked and felt like all the others, hazy gray and cold as hell.

"No, Mom, I won't be going home."

"What do you mean? Why not?"

"Well, Dr. Goodwin wants me to stay here for a couple more weeks. Besides, I'm not sure that I want to go home," I admitted.

"Why not? Is it money, the cost of the flight? I'll pay for your ticket if that's what's bothering you."

"No. I want to stay here. I need to see this through, my treatment I mean."

"What's the real reason, Hunter? Why wouldn't you want to come home? Only a few days ago, you were pleading with the entire staff to let you go. And now you want to stay? I don't understand."

"I'm just not ready. Let's play it by ear, Mom. Okay?"

"But what will you do? Where will you go?"

"I'm not sure yet."

"I hope that you'll change your mind."

"Maybe I will. I have to go now, Mom. I have to write. I need to be writing."

"What is it you are writing about, Hunter?" It was a question that surprised me, caught me off guard, left me feeling stunned and numb and speechless. My mom had never asked me about my writing before. Why would she start now?

"I'm writing a novel, Mom," I said at last.

"I know you are. What's it about?"

"I can't say just yet. I don't want to say. I have to go now." The numbness that had crept into my body was still present. That numbness was feeding on my inner self. Without speaking another word, my mom hung up on me. That is when it occurred to me that I was a man who was still much too fragile to be treated that way.

My mom wasn't the only person who had tried to coerce me into spending the Thanksgiving holiday outside of the hospital. My cousin Dana had also extended an invitation. I decided instantly that it was a bad idea for me to accept. I felt that I would be scrutinized and handled with "kid gloves" by the other guests. Simply put, I did not want that. Such treatment, no matter how considerate the intention, would only serve to upset me. I knew, above all else, that I would not be able to handle the extra attention I was certain everyone present would bestow upon me. I wanted to blend in, not stick out, so I tactfully declined Dana's thoughtful invitation.

"So, I hear you are writing a book." Dr. Giles said with a smile as he entered my room. He was a man with a strange angular face that was accented with a short graying goatee. He had the darkest brown eyes I have ever seen. Also, his posture was perfect. He was a person with whom, up until now, I had had very little contact. He was also the first person to ask me what I was doing writing in a journal since Davis had asked why I had been carrying it with me all the time.

"I'm writing a novel about a manic-depressive's life experiences, experiences that include time spent being treated on a psychiatric ward," I responded, tapping my fingers lightly on the journal itself. The revealing of my most coveted secret had left me nearly breathless. Until then, I had kept my subject matter to myself. Why I opted to confide in Dr. Giles that particular day I cannot say.

"Autobiographical maybe?"

"Semi-autobiographical. It's more of a fictional story than a non-fictional story. It's based very, very loosely on actual events."

"I see."

"And what are you reading there?"

"It's a book on lithium and manic depression." I held the faded green book up so that he could see it more clearly. "Claire gave it to me."

"How is it so far?"

"It's very interesting. Actually, it's been very helpful." I was beginning to wonder why Dr. Giles was paying me a visit.

"That's good," he said, smiling. "Hunter, we want you to take a test."

"A test?"

"Yes. We would like for you to take a Minnesota Multi-phasic Personality Inventory test. It's what is known today as an MMPI-2."

"What kind of test is it? What does it do?"

"It's a very basic true or false test that assesses personal or social or behavioral problems in a psychiatric patient. Much more important, the MMPI-2 helps provide relevant information as to what type of treatment you require. The test is used frequently in the psychiatric field and there is nothing to fear."

"Nothing to fear but fear itself, huh?"

"Right."

Minutes later, I was sitting alone in the study filling in tiny circles with a pencil. Unfortunately, I no longer recall any of the questions that were on the test. Maybe it's best that I don't because I might find myself over analyzing them. However, I do remember filling in those tiny circles for nearly two hours. After I was finished, I felt drained, exhausted. I also felt quite strongly that I had been completely honest with myself and Dr, Giles. I knew, without a doubt, that I had answered all questions as honestly as possible. Being honest on a test that would ultimately reveal once and for all my poor morale as well as my overall dissatisfaction with life was a tremendous step forward. Nobody had to tell me that; I already knew that my truthfulness had been a plus.

Early the next evening, the evening of day number ten, I was called into Dr. Giles' office. I was staring at various models of the human brain when he informed me that he was certain that I was "crying out for help" and that I had probably been crying out for help for many years. I did not bother arguing with Dr. Giles. I knew that the MMPI-2 had assessed me correctly. I felt that I had been crying out for help in one way or another for a long time. What's more, I knew that I was still praying to be saved from my melancholy. It was clear to me as well as to the doctors and the rest of the hospital staff that I wanted to be rescued from my depression. An inner life-force was definitely living inside of me.

"So where do we go from here?"

"Hunter, this test contains several trait scales. One of those scales shows us that you are really very depressed."

"But I knew that, Dr. Giles. And so did you. Didn't you?"

"That's true, I did. But I want you to know that your score was indeed high enough to suggest clinical depression."

"Yeah, but you must have drawn that conclusion already. Had you not, I wouldn't have been diagnosed manic-depressive to begin with. I wouldn't be taking both Paxil and lithium."

"The test simply supported our initial diagnosis, Hunter. It has given us more clues as to why you behaved the way you did when you were faced, for example, with the likelihood that you were going to be arrested for vandalizing your former girlfriend's car. Ultimately, the test has filled in some blanks."

"That makes sense. So where do we go from here?" I asked a second time.

"We will stay with the Paxil and the lithium. We also recommend that you seek counseling once you are discharged. I suggest that you see a clinician, or a psychologist, from time to time."

"Dr. Goodwin did suggest that I come see him a couple of weeks after I'm out of here, which would put me on lithium for about a month and Paxil for about five weeks, but he didn't say anything about seeing a clinician."

"I see. Well, I recommend that you see Dr. Goodwin once every two or three months so that he can help you manage your meds. The two of you can work that out soon enough. I also recommend that you see a clinician at least once a month and maybe even two times a month. That way he or she can counsel you on your illness, give you some solid cognitive approaches to dealing with manic depression. I think that you would only benefit from that kind of a treatment regimen."

"Well, I plan on staying medicated. And I will certainly consider seeing a clinician."

"I am happy that you are going to look into it, Hunter."

"It really would be nice to have someone to talk to—someone who understands manic depression better than I do. Talking to a professional, someone in the field, about manic depression, my manic depression, would even be educational I think. Maybe my writing would improve some, a little, or a lot."

"I agree." Dr. Giles closed the folder that contained the results of my MMPI-2.

"Okay, I'll pursue it then," I said. Clearly, our meeting had ended on a solid note.

"I stood and reached out to shake the hand of Dr. Giles, the only person in the world who knew what my novel was actually about. He shook my hand with obvious vigor and told me to keep writing.

"Bring me a book, Hunter." He nodded a single time. His nod was a nod of sincere encouragement. And those words, the words "bring me a book" were the kindest words ever spoken to me—by anyone. To this day, I can still hear their echo from the other side of the stream.

"I will. I will bring you a book, Dr. Giles. I promise." I left his office and reentered the short section of corridor that led back to Seven Southwest, keenly aware that Dr. Giles' request that I bring him a book was the first request I had ever received for a copy of this novel.

As I have already pointed out, I had been having trouble sleeping for a long time, for many years. This was especially true in the days after I discovered the topic of my novel. All I wanted to do was read the heavy book Claire had given me and write, write, write but the strict routine I was now a part of was beginning to take a toll on both my mind and my body. During the uneventful days between day number ten and day number fifteen, I rose early every morning as required after I had been awake late every night writing in my head in the darkness. With my story coming together inside of me at night and on paper during the day, I wanted the time remaining before my discharge to pass in rapid fashion. Yes, I now wanted to go home—permanently. I wanted to go home, clean up all of the blood and write a novel on the plight of a young manic-depressive man. Eight days had elapsed since I had been put on lithium and I had gone from being patient to impatient. Any notion that I might become too dependant on hospital living was now, as far as I was concerned, a myth at best.

Unfortunately, lithium also contributed to my sleeplessness. On lithium, I soon learned that I had to pee many more times a night than usual, which ultimately interfered with even my best efforts to get a full night's rest. On the nights when I was able to stop writing in my head and focus on getting enough sleep so that I could get up at the required 8 a.m. without too much difficulty, I would awake extremely fatigued because I had spent so much precious time going to the bathroom. It was, to put it lightly, a frustrating dilemma. All the same, I was determined to give lithium a chance and so I accepted the fact that I was peeing many times a night and losing sleep because of it without complaining to anyone a single time. After all, Dr. Goodwin had told me at the start of my treatment that a side effect of lithium was indeed frequent urination. Needless to say, I was not at all surprised or worried.

More often than not, I whiled away the nocturnal hours writing cognitively while my body that could not would not sleep logged much time making its way to the bathroom to pee. During the days following the fateful day I had initially ingested lithium, I had come to accept that particular routine. At the time, I felt that I did not have any other choice but to accept such a pattern. However, had lithium been making me sick, I am positive that Dr. Goodwin and I would have made the necessary adjustments, or changes in my drug regimen. But I was not getting sick. And that was definitely reassuring.

My days quickly became rather conventional, ordinary. I invested a lot of time writing and reading and writing and reading. I listened, observed and spied more and more. I made notes, wrote and read some more and then I listened, observed and spied again. I frequented the community room as often as I could. I believed that time spent in the community room was time well-spent because it was an environment rife with original characters and a kind of material that stretched my imagination, material of a "literary nature" to an aspiring manic-depressive novelist.

I received several calls from my mom during those days. Always, she was checking to see how I was doing as well as whether I would be coming home for Thanksgiving. So as not to upset or worry her, I was quick to maintain that I was improving all the time. I was also quick to assert that Paxil was definitely working and that I believed that lithium would soon start working as well. I explained over and over again that I would not be going home for Thanksgiving. I also made it a point to mention that I was writing again. After I had started journaling, I never once missed an opportunity to remind my mom that I was writing again for the first time in years because I felt that writing was as fundamental a part of my treatment as Paxil and lithium were.

Jocelyn also called me during that particular time frame. She usually called late at night, when she could not sleep, when I too was having trouble sleeping. She hardly spoke of herself. She would, however, show interest in how I was doing. When I did try to ask about her own mood as well as her "living situation," her life in general, she would waste no time changing the subject to how I was making out. Therefore, I would have only one more "opportunity," an opportunity I will share with you later, to ask her whether she was taking her meds. It should be noted that Jocelyn never volunteered any information in that regard. It should also be noted that I had strong suspicions that any inquiry in that area would be viewed by her as an invasion of her privacy anyway. Asking Jocelyn whether she was taking her meds as prescribed was, in a matter of speaking, a futile venture.

Jocelyn reminded me often of my plan to get permission from Dr. Goodwin to leave the hospital for a day so that I could see her. I had been hoping since the day I had originally made that promise that she would have forgotten such a dubious vow, but it was obvious that she had a very good memory for such things and I soon understood that eventually I would have to fulfill her request and pay her a visit. I simply could not see a way out of obtaining a day pass no matter how hard I searched for an excuse. I also understood all too well that the world beyond the borders of Seven Southwest was beckoning me to reenter it. Whether I liked it or not, that world was inviting me to give it a new chance. So on my fifteenth day in the hospital, a rather bleak Saturday, just six days before I was scheduled to be released permanently, I forged ahead and asked

Dr. Goodwin for a day pass so that I could see Jocelyn in her own environment.

"Are you sure you want a pass, Hunter?"

"I think so." I did not sound very convincing.

"But are you really sure that you are ready?" Dr. Goodwin's eyes narrowed. His skepticism that I was prepared for such an undertaking was obvious.

"Yes. I think so. I think I'm ready."

"Where are you going to go? What are you going to do?"

"I don't know just yet," I lied. I was hiding from him the fact that I had already discussed with Jocelyn my intention to visit her. I was also keeping a secret the fact that I had left a brief message that I would be stopping by on the answering machine that belonged to Chan Allen, my old neighbor, my old friend, the man who had saved my life by saving me from myself one Friday night little more than two weeks earlier.

"Are you going to return to your apartment?"

"No, I don't think so. Not yet anyway. I will return to my apartment after you discharge me."

"It's short notice, Hunter, but since I will be discharging you in six days, I will let you go. I do suggest that you take things slowly at first, pace yourself, maybe take in a movie, or go to the mall for a while. I expect you back here no later than 5 o'clock."

That was all there was to it. Almost as quickly as I had been admitted to Lakeshore General, I had been granted a "ticket" to reenter the outside world. I had been issued a ticket that would enable me to explore an odd version of my former life, a place that had been troubling me off and on for the better part of fifteen days if not longer.

I retuned to my room and dressed in blue jeans and a heavy gray sweater. I was nervous leaving the hospital but, at the same time, I was now looking forward to seeing Jocelyn again. I was also looking forward to my visit with Chan very, very much.

"See you this afternoon, Hunter?"

"See you this afternoon, Jane."

"Take it easy out there. And put your coat on," Claire said in an upbeat whisper.

"I will. Don't worry, I will."

PART III

THE RETURN

CHAPTER 31

I rode the elevator down to the lobby very aware of my nervousness and the fact that the day I would spend with both Jocelyn and Chan would ultimately mark the very beginning of my return to living a life outside the hospital. I put on my coat and tugged at the sleeves of my sweater until they covered my wrists. Only a few days earlier, the stitches had been removed and I soon discovered how deep my wounds really were. I understood that hiding them beneath the sleeves of my sweater was really the only option I had if I was going to keep them concealed from strangers on the street or from anyone else who might come my way.

Jocelyn had given me her dad's address several days before. Fortunately, he lived only a few blocks away from the hospital on a shady boulevard on the other side of the stream and so walking, my only option, was easy. His house was a house I had passed a number of times and, because I was somewhat familiar with that particular neighborhood, I arrived within minutes of leaving the hospital. Jocelyn answered the door, a strange kind of smile, a smile that did not seem to befit her, hanging on her pale face.

"Hunter! I knew you wouldn't stand me up! So as not to in let the cold winter air, she ushered me inside with a frantic wave of her hand and slammed the door behind me. "Hunter, how are you?" She gave the lock a quick turn. "You got your stitches out, huh?"

"Yes. Finally. It's as if I have been wearing those damn things forever."

"Good. I'm glad they're gone. You are now one step closer to being released. Come on, there's a fire going and you can warm up for a while. Take off your coat."

"I'd rather leave it on." The heat from the fire soon enveloped me. It was a kind of heat I had never felt before, a kind of heat I have not felt since. While I understood that my "freedom" from Seven Southwest was only temporary, I sensed that the warmth I was experiencing was the warmth associated with being a free man out on his own making new decisions for himself. Then again, maybe that kind of warmth had more to do with the fact that I was visiting a new-found friend on a winter day.

"Hot chocolate? Coffee? Just name it, I've got it."

"Anything with caffeine would be good." Days before, Dr. Goodwin had advised that I avoid caffeine altogether. But I was making decisions for myself that day and I decided that a little caffeine couldn't possibly hurt. Evidently, Jocelyn had made the same decision.

"Come on in. Have a seat." I remained standing in the kitchen doorway. I did not feel comforted by the prospect of running into Jocelyn's dad or her two brothers and so I kept my coat on and stood ready to run from the warm kitchen if I had to.

I no longer remember what the interior of her dad's house looked like because I was not inside long enough for it to make an indelible impression on me. Also, I no longer remember what we talked about while I waited for Jocelyn to produce some caffeine. I only recall her filling a large metal thermos with coffee and telling me that she wanted very badly to go for a walk in the woods.

Once outside, Jocelyn claimed that she knew of a place far removed from hospital living, a place near the stream that hardly anyone knew about, a place that would be wrapped in both snow and silence. Jocelyn promised me that we would be able to talk there without being interrupted by meddlesome patients or by techs or by nurses or doctors and so I walked beside her as we gradually became cloaked in the shadows of tall snow-laden pines.

Over the years, I had spent much time wandering in the woods on the edge of town but I had never been to the place Jocelyn led me to that day. I believe it must have taken us more than a couple of hours to reach the aging wooden bridge, a bridge that seemed to have been neglected by the touch of any human being for decades, a bridge that spanned the stream far above the bridge that traversed the stream near Lakeshore General. The long walk in the snow had been calming, relaxing for me. The cold walk beneath the pines had refreshed me to say the least.

"We can sit here, don't you think?" Jocelyn brushed some snow off a wooden bench near the base of a pine that stood much taller than all the others. She produced a small blanket from inside her coat and spread it over the bench. As I sat, it was apparent to me that my ankles were sore from more than two weeks of inactivity. The time I had spent lying in a bed on Seven Southwest had definitely taken its toll on my joints.

I sat as close to Jocelyn as I possibly could, hoping to share with her my body heat, hoping that she would not mind sharing her own body heat with me. She did not hesitate to shift her weight until our shoulders were touching. Yes, I could feel her warmness through my clothes to my soul that was now rejuvenated almost entirely.

She removed the cap from the thermos. The distinct aroma of hot coffee filled my nostrils and I suddenly felt alert and alive. Sitting on a bench in the woods that were hushed by fallen snow on a gray November day while Jocelyn poured hot coffee, it felt extremely good to be alive and living. My old life and my hospital life now seemed far away, distant, and my new life, my life as a writer, seemed to be nearer to me than ever before.

"Cold?' Jocelyn asked.

"I think I'm fine."

"Well this will chase away any doubts you may be having about the chilly weather." She handed me the cup of coffee. I took a small sip and passed the cup back to her. The hot coffee that represented safeness and tranquility more than anything I have ever tasted was delicious.

"How long have you known about that bridge over there and this spot, this bench?"

"I stumbled upon it years ago, when I was a much younger girl. I can't say exactly when. I have been coming here from time to time ever since, though. I love it here." She refilled the cup and handed it back to me. I took a substantial sip and gave it back to her.

"So I see." And then we were lost in the winter quiet again, passing the coffee back and forth in robotic fashion, Jocelyn refilling it as needed. Minutes of solitude, minutes of peaceful introspection passed. Jocelyn was the first to break into the soothing stillness.

"When are you due back at the hospital?"

"At precisely 5 o'clock." Dr. Goodwin's orders."

"So we have some time then."

"We do."

"You are doing well, huh, Hunter?"

"Yes, I feel that I am."

"And you are writing again. What a relief that must be for you."

"God is it ever."

"Taking your meds?"

"Religiously."

"That's good. Where do you think you'll go once you're discharged?"

"Wherever I have to go to write. Maybe I'll rent a new apartment, or maybe I'll just hit the road as Ayden did."

"Ayden's a very special case, Hunter."

"What do you mean." I watched as Jocelyn refilled the cup with the last of the coffee and dropped the thermos into the snow near her feet.

"I don't know. I can't put a finger on it. He just is. I suppose it's because he's been able to separate himself from his depression so well and because he is now following his dream. That's all I'm saying. I hope, Hunter, that you'll be able to do the same."

"That's my most coveted goal of all. I know that if I can pull away from my depression, I'll be following my own dream of becoming a writer. Tell me, Jocelyn, what's your most coveted goal now that Seven Southwest is finally behind you?"

"I'm still not sure. My goals change from day to day. I do know that I want to be out on my own, away from my uncaring father and my uncaring brothers. I want to be self-sufficient, productive. Finish this." She handed me the cup one last time. I swallowed what was left of the coffee and passed the empty cup back to its rightful owner.

"Jocelyn, I don't think that's a bad goal."

"Yeah, well I'm having a little trouble 'breaking free' as Ayden was able to do, as you plan on doing."

"I think that's a natural way to feel. Just look at all you've been through." I was suddenly tempted to ask whether she was taking her meds but, once again, I resisted the urge.

"Hunter, Ayden has separated himself from more than just his depression; he's also separated himself from his troubled past, from one incident in particular." I thought instantly of Ayden having been charged with domestic assault. I wondered if Jocelyn knew about his troubles with Vicki. I concluded that she did.

"You know, don't you, Jocelyn?"

"I know, Hunter. I know."

"But how?" I asked. She breathed deeply, hesitating, deliberating over whether she wanted to say anything more about Ayden.

"Ayden and I used to work together," she said at last. "I was in the office the day the police officer came to see him, the very same day he was ticketed for assaulting Vicki."

"And did he ever assault her?" I asked, glancing at Jocelyn's perfect profile, searching her sharp features for an answer, for a new set of clues.

"No, he never hit her. Ayden is not capable of hitting another human being. Really he isn't."

"But how do you know?"

"Because I knew Ayden back then. We weren't the best of friends, but I knew him well enough to know that he was incapable of harming another person. He's a nice guy. But I knew Vicki as well. Truthfully, I knew her much better than I knew Ayden. And I understood that she was definitely capable of lying the way she did."

"So Vicki did lie to the police?"

"She lied. I just happened to be one of the people she confided in after Ayden was ticketed. She admitted to me that he never once hit her. I really did hurt for him then, Hunter. My heart went out to him. It still does. I think it always will."

"Did you ever let him know that Vicki had confided in you? I hope you did."

"I did. It's just that Ayden never knew it was me."

"Jocelyn, I'm confused."

"Don't be. I called him at work a day or two after Vicki had bragged to me that she had gotten even with him for sleeping with Angie."

"And?"

"And I told him that my name was Renee. And I told him that I knew that he was innocent. And I told him that things would eventually get better. I reminded him that life goes on. Life does go on, Hunter. I suspect that it does anyway."

"You mean you are the woman who referred to herself as Renee?" I was stunned. I no longer felt warmed by the coffee or by Jocelyn's shoulder but ice cold inside instead.

"Yes, I was Renee."

"But why conceal your identity? I'm still confused, Jocelyn. I really don't get it."

"I concealed my identity and disguised my voice because I had to. I used my middle name, Renee, because I had to. I had to get through to Ayden; I knew that he was hurting badly."

"But why hide from him?"

"Because I had to, Hunter."
"But why?"
"Because Vicki knew things."
"What things?"
"Well, if it means that much to you, she knew that I'd embezzled from the company for one. She threatened to turn me in if I ever went to either Ayden or the police with the truth. Talk about being trapped."
"You stole money?"
"Yes, I did."
"Why?"
"I don't know why? I just did it. The money was there so I took it. I wasn't thinking clearly at the time. Maybe I was manic."
"Did you return the money?"
"Vicki did. She claimed that she returned it anyway. I gave the money back to her because I was scared of being caught. I gave the money back to her because I had already quit my job and I now felt as if I were 'untouchable.' You see, I quit the same day she threatened to turn me in if I ever told Ayden what she had told me. Nevertheless, I still felt compelled to tell Ayden something. I tried to reach him at home, but he had already moved and his new number was unlisted. Calling him at work under an alias was my only option if I was ever going to let him know that someone out there knew that he was indeed innocent. Still confused?"
"No, I'm not."
"Good. I'm glad. Please don't tell Ayden what I just told you, Hunter. He'd never forgive me."
"You mean for taking the money?"
"No, for not stepping forward and openly defending him as I should have done."

Our private thoughts soon distracted us and we were quiet again. Let it be said that there is something very comforting about the silent echo of the wilderness when one's future life is anything but certain. Let it also be said that the same silent echo is extremely conducive to examining one's own thoughts and feelings. Although I was strident in the belief that I had finally uncovered the topic of my novel, I was still the poor, unfortunate victim of my own skeptic thoughts, my own feelings of doubt. Emotionally, I was definitely lost in an awkward place.

"Hey, Jocelyn?" It was my turn to break the silence.
"Hunter?"

"You haven't asked me what my novel is about yet. Why is that? Why haven't you asked what it's about?"

"Do you want me to?"

"Yes and no. I want you to ask me what it's about because it will show me that you believe that I'm actually going to pull it off, but I don't want to have to tell you what it's about until I've actually finished it."

"Well, I won't ask then. Besides, I'm sure you'll tell me what it's about soon enough. And, Hunter, I do believe that you'll finish it one day. I really do. However, there is one thing I want to know now."

"What's that?"

"Why did you do it? I mean what happened that night, the night you vandalized Kate's car?"

"I wish I knew. I wish I had an excuse, or a reason for what I did, but I don't. I think about that night all the time. I think about what I did and try to unearth the 'why' behind my irrational actions, but I can't seem to find an answer that fits. How'd you know what I did to Kate's car anyway?"

"I overheard you. I overheard you talking to Dr. Goodwin one day."

"You mean you eavesdropped?"

"Sort of."

"What do you mean?"

"Well, I heard you tell Dr. Goodwin how badly you felt for doing what you did. Truthfully, Hunter, I heard you crying to him one afternoon. I hadn't been trying to listen, but I couldn't stop myself from hearing what you were saying. You should know that your voice carried all the way to my room that particular day. You were pretty upset when you told Dr. Goodwin that you had been mad at Kate and that your act of vandalism had been a product of your anger."

"You heard me say that?"

"Yeah, I did. And let me tell you that it is terrible what you did to her."

"I know it is, Jocelyn. I know it is. I don't deny that for a second, not for a single goddamn second."

"Then why did you do it?"

"Why did you steal the money, Jocelyn?"

"Hunter, they're not the same thing. Stealing money and vandalizing a person's car are definitely not the same thing."

"But maybe their motivation, the forces behind the acts, are the same. Maybe sheer impulsiveness, impulsiveness brought on by mania itself, had something to do with why we behaved the way we did."

"I'm pretty sure that I'm not following you."

"It's really not that difficult to understand. I'm saying that it is very likely that you were manic when you stole the money and very likely that I was manic when I vandalized Kate's car."

"I suppose it's possible. But can mania act alone like that, without, say, drugs or alcohol or other stimulants?"

"I believe that it can. But then again, maybe the impulsiveness, the rash thinking, I demonstrated when I made the fateful decision to spray paint Kate's car was a part of the mania itself. What I mean to say is that there was indeed a measurable amount of poor judgment involved. Could that apparent lack of judgment, that reckless behavior, be an unfortunate side of mania. I tend to think that it can. You see, I just need to know whether my anger toward Kate was a byproduct of mania, or if my mania was a byproduct of my anger."

"I admit that I hadn't looked at it that way yet, Hunter. But I do suppose that there is something to what you are saying. In your case, vandalizing Kate's car was probably the end result of you being mad at her for whatever she did to make you mad in the first place. Once you were really pissed off, your anger and mania mixed in such a manner that rational thinking became nonexistent. And if that is the case, then your rash thinking, your decision to spray paint her car, was probably brought on by your being a manic-depressive who was unable to 'think things through' while mad at someone who did not deserve such treatment."

"That's a good point. Kate would never buy it, though. That theory—if I can call it a theory—would be viewed by her as an excuse and nothing more. Take what little bit I understand about manic depression and realize that Kate, like your dad, probably understands even less about manic depression and what motivated me to behave the way I did the night I damaged her car."

"True."

"Hey, Jocelyn?" I turned to face her. She turned to face me. In her wolfish eyes I thought I saw a tiny reflection of myself flash by. Briefly, I wondered what she could see in my eyes. I wondered what was reflected there—if anything.

"Yes, Hunter?"

"I want you to know that I was not myself the night I vandalized Kate's car. The man who did that simply was not me. I want you to know that."

"I already know that, Hunter," she responded in the softest voice. "I know that it was not you that night. I know that it was not you."

CHAPTER 32

❀

Snow was beginning to fall and shadows were beginning to lengthen when Jocelyn and I decided to make our way back to town. We had grown quiet again, listening to the stillness of the woods, each of us absorbed in our own thoughts, after Jocelyn had confirmed that she was the woman who had once referred to herself as Renee in order to provide Ayden with some much-needed peace of mind and after I had confirmed that I had in fact vandalized Kate's car. I believe our openness that November afternoon left us feeling much too cold to be sitting outside revealing secrets any longer. Sometimes the truth, a chilling entity unto itself, can do that to a person.

The downhill hike out of the woods took much less time than the uphill trek had taken. In what seemed like only minutes, we emerged from beneath the snow-covered canopy and stepped back into civilization cognizant that we had probably not been missed by anyone.

"Hunter, did you know that it's almost time for you to return to the hospital?" We were standing on the sidewalk in front of her dad's unlit house.

"What time is it anyway?" I asked, glancing over her shoulder, searching for a single sign of life in any one of the windows. I was still worried that her dad or brothers might actually show themselves. I was also wondering whether I would have enough time to visit Chan.

"It's almost 4:30."

"Yeah, I guess I'd better be going," I said, deflated. I understood that I would have to see Chan another time.

The snow was falling much faster now and several nearby streetlights were struggling to fend off the hues of a new November evening when Jocelyn gave me a hug.

"Please don't tell anyone about the bridge or the bench," she whispered, still hugging me, still clinging to a man-child she hardly even knew, a man-child she probably felt she had known for a lifetime. "Let's keep them a secret, our secret."

"I won't tell anybody about them," I assured her at the same moment she unwrapped her arms from my upper body. "I promise I won't." Once again, I wanted to ask her if she was taking her meds. Once again, I wanted to ask her how she was making out in her personal battle against manic depression. I wanted her to tell me the truth in the same frank manner she had told me that her middle name was Renee. More than anything else, I wanted her to tell me that she was going to set some goals for herself and make it out of her private woods alive and well. But I did not ask her a single damn question.

"Thank you, Hunter. Thank you for listening. Thank you for today. I'll call you soon."

"I know that you will."

I watched as Jocelyn entered her dad's dark, lifeless house. I waited for her silhouette to emerge from behind the drab curtains, as I knew it would. I stared at her until she waved at me. For a moment, I thought I saw tears in her azure eyes but I could not be sure. Nevertheless, I waved back before I turned my body in the general direction of Center Street and Lakeshore General oblivious to the fact that I would never again walk in the woods with Jocelyn Layne.

As soon as I was back in my room on Seven Southwest, I called Chan to apologize for standing him up. Chan asserted that he had been neglecting me ever since I had landed in the hospital and apologized profusely for not having visited me a single time.

"Hunter, of course I've wanted to see you ever since the day after I rode with you in an ambulance to the hospital but I was told by a bossy nurse that I needed to leave you alone, let you rest. Then your mom called that Saturday, the following morning, sometime after she had spoken to you, and asked that I visit you as often as possible. She needed me, needed my help, as I'm sure you did, but I had a flight to catch; I could not postpone my out-of-state business plans. I tried to push them back but I couldn't. Plus, I figured that you might need some time to yourself, a little time to get acclimated with your new surroundings. And I wanted you to have some time to do some healing."

"But, Chan, that doesn't explain why you haven't visited me since that first Saturday or why you did not call. You know damn well that you could have called, left a message with the staff."

"I know. I know. I suppose I was a little hesitant to talk to you because I truly did not know what to say to you. It was embarrassing not knowing what to say, not knowing what to do, how to act."

"That does not sound at all like you," I stated, slightly miffed that he had resorted to "walking on eggshells" where my well-being was concerned.

"I've seen men die, Hunter. You know that already. But, believe it or not, I have never seen a suicide attempt. I wasn't prepared for what I saw that night."

"What about the guy in your unit who killed himself? What about him? You saw his suicide, didn't you?"

"No, of course not. I never actually saw him do it. I never saw him after he did it either. He just walked into the jungle by himself one day and put a gun to his head. A couple of my buddies found him lying on the jungle floor a day or two later, after it was much too late."

"But you saved my life, Chan. You saved my life after I attempted to kill myself."

"Maybe."

"But you did. There's no 'maybe' about it."

"Whether I saved your life or not, Hunter, I still wasn't prepared to find you barely alive, wanting desperately to die."

"Obviously, Chan, neither was I. I wasn't ready to wake up again. I should have died. Even my doctors tell me that I should have died."

"I wasn't prepared to see a close friend, a young man with a future, in such a manner as I saw you that night. You should have told me that you were hurting, that you were considering suicide."

"What if I had told you how depressed, how suicidal, I had been in the months and weeks and days leading up to my attempt? What would you have done, Chan?"

"I would have kept you safe … from yourself I mean."

"I'm not sure that was possible then."

"Still I would have tried to keep you safe. So how are you now, Hunter? How are you making out?" It was clear that Chan was trying to change the subject. I understood that he wanted to stop talking about my attempt to end my life and discuss the days that lie ahead of me.

"I'll be going home in a week, six days to be exact."

"So you will still be staying at the hospital on Thanksgiving? You won't be going home to be with your family?"

"This is where I have to be, Chan."

"Well, that settles it then. You are coming here for Thanksgiving dinner. Bring a friend if you want."

"Okay, I'll think about it."

"Good. So, Hunter, how have you been doing so far?"

"Pretty well lately. Let me tell you, it's been a strange journey. It's been a strange trip compressed into a small amount of time. I can't begin to tell you all that has happened."

"So what's it like in there anyway? I've seen and heard of the place but I have no idea as to what it's like on the inside."

"It's not so bad. I think Seven Southwest is a fairly safe place to be. I hated it at first, but I have goals now. I'm taking my meds and I have a decent outlook. Had I not ended up here, who knows where I would have landed or what would have happened to me. Medically speaking, this place saved my life."

"Yeah, well don't get too comfortable living that particular life. Remember: you have lots of work to do out here."

"I remember." Instantly, I thought of the blood I would have to wipe away. Then I thought of my writing, of my novel, of my innate desire to create a story, of my strong need to use an imagination that had been trying to escape from inside of me for nearly three decades. I thought of my need to create something out of nothing through writing. "Chan, do you still recall the time I confided in you that I want to write a novel some day?"

"Yes, I do."

"Well, I'm doing it now. I'm now writing a novel, Chan. I'm doing it. 'Some day' is now."

"That's one hell of a project, Hunter. Are you sure that you're up to the challenge? I think that writing, writing anything at all, would be difficult for anyone." Immediately, I was upset that Chan had referred to my novel-in-progress as a "project" but I said nothing. I kept my frustration to myself.

"Yes. Of course I'm up to the challenge."

"Don't you think, Hunter, that you might be wasting your time pursuing something like that, some kind of dream, a dream that might just prove to be nothing more than a dead end?"

"No, Chan. I don't think that at all."

"Hunter, in this life you need to have a plan, a long-term plan, a plan that will keep you occupied and prevent you from becoming a lost man, a drifter. You need to stop drifting through life, Hunter. You need to sink your teeth into something and stick with it. You need to do something for Hunter. I hope you can appreciate what I'm telling you."

"Of course I'm going to be sticking with it. I sunk my teeth into my writing long ago. I've fallen off course, lost my bite, many times already I know, but I am now taking medications to treat my depression and stabilize my mood. Also, I am going to be counseled for depression soon after I am discharged. And I am writing every day, every fucking day. That is my plan and, yes, my dream. No one is going to interfere with my intention to become a successful author, Chan." And that is when it occurred to me that Chan's "have a plan" speech had probably stemmed from a conversation he had had with my parents.

"Hunter, you need to know that Kate stopped by last night." Chan had changed the topic of our conversation a second time.

"Why? Why would she want to see you?"

"She wanted to talk to me."

"But why?"

"She wanted to tell me what you did to her I think."

"You think?"

"Well, I believe that she wants to know why you did what you did. Clearly, she was searching for an explanation, an explanation she must've thought I'd be able to provide."

"I was mad, Chan. All I can say is that I was mad."

"Your being mad does not justify what you did to her car."

"I know that. Dr. Goodwin explained that to me already."

"I was also manic," I asserted. "I was manic when I used an entire can of spray paint on her car." There was an odd silence after I stated that I had been manic when I vandalized Kate's car. For many awkward seconds, neither one of us uttered a single word.

"Are you a manic-depressive?" Chan asked.

"Yes, I am."

"That explains an awful lot."

"Does it, Chan?"

"Of course it does."

"What did you tell Kate about me? What did you say to her?"

"First, I told her that you need professional help because, Hunter, you do need some help. And I do hope that you are getting that help. I also told her that I prayed that she would forgive you some day. Finally, I asked that she not press charges against you."

"You really did that?" I tried to envision the conversation that had taken place between my long-time friend and my former girlfriend. I could picture the two of them sitting across from one another at the table in the dining room of Chan's modest apartment, Kate's posture wilted, but not beaten, her arms hanging at her sides. I could see Chan leaning forward slightly, his eyes locked on hers. I could see—but could not hear—that he was whispering in my defense, practically pleading with her to reconsider, to give me a chance to seek help and rebuild my life in much the same manner she would eventually rebuild hers.

"Yes, Hunter, I did that. I asked that she just let things go."

"Is she going to press charges?" I had my fingers crossed that she would just "let things go" and understand that the pathetic man who had vandalized her car had not been himself that night, or himself for a very long, long time.

"She said that she would not be pressing any charges, Hunter. You should feel fortunate that she is willing to drop it. She said that she has forgiven you. I find that hard to believe but that's what she said."

Instantly, a kind of relief I had never known raced through me, through my veins, through my vertebrae. That relief coursed through every ounce of my recently-medicated mind and through every nook and cranny of my body. Yes, Kate had found it in herself to forgive me. Now there would be no need for the police to obtain my fingerprints or my mug shot. Now there would be no court dates or entries in the local newspaper chronicling the sentence that surely would have been handed down to me by a judge who surely would have ordered that I pay restitution or serve time in the county jail or both.

"I wish I could thank her, Chan. I've already apologized. I just wish that I could thank her."

"Well, you can't. You cannot go near her or contact her ever again. You do understand that, don't you, Hunter?"

"I understand," I admitted. Exhausted by the topic of our conversation, I thanked Chan, assured him that I would see him soon, said goodnight to him and moved to the familiar safeness of the recliner. Day fifteen, the one day that had served to mark my return to the real, tangible world more than any other day since I had been admitted into the hospital, was finally drawing to a close.

If it was true that Kate had actually forgiven me—and I believed that it was—then I was going to make amends with myself once and for all, as soon as possible, and get on with my life. In other words, I would become friends with myself for the first time in many years. If Kate could find the requisite strength to forgive me for the bad things I had done to her, then why couldn't I find a similar strength and forgive myself as well? Hopefully, such an undertaking would clear my troubled conscious of the sordid pictures of me spray painting her car and I would be able to write my story without any disturbing cognitive ripples of regret or burdensome, floating feelings of guilt.

I was now cognizant that making friends with myself was a goal that was as obtainable as it was promising. It was the kind of goal that could only open new doors for me, doors leading to new opportunities. One goal in particular stood out: I would pay less attention to myself and be more considerate of others. Once that goal had been accomplished, I would apologize to my family for not having provided them with explanations as to why I had attempted suicide. A short time after I decided that I would pursue the aforementioned goals, the phone rang. It was my mom.

"Hi, Hunter," she whispered, a hint of caution in her voice that was still bothering me.

"Mom, I'm sorry that I didn't share with you the fact that I was hurting all these years, that I was suicidal. And I would like for you to know that I never meant to hurt you. I only wanted to escape my depression … and the police," I gushed.

"I know that, Hunter. Your dad and I know that."

"How did you know? How?"

"We've pieced some things together. And we see now what we did not see before. There were so many times you wanted us to understand or to be aware of how badly you were feeling, weren't there?"

"Yes, there were."

"But you masked how you were hurting, didn't you?"

"I did."

"Hunter, we only want you to be well, to be happy. Ultimately, we want to help you. You realize that, don't you?"

"I realize that."

"Hunter?"

"Yeah, Mom?"

"Please come home for Thanksgiving. We want you here with us, if only for a few days. John is coming and we want you here, too." The fact that John was going to be there did not sweeten the deal.

"I won't be there, Mom," I whispered with deliberate care. "Mom, it's just Thanksgiving, another holiday. I need to stay here and follow through with the treatment plan Dr. Goodwin has outlined for me. Also important, I need to stay here and work on my writing, on my novel. My novel is my life's purpose I believe. My writing is more than just therapy, Mom."

"Okay then, Hunter. I know that your mental health is at stake, so we'll see you this summer—unless you'd like for us to come back sooner. We can come back sooner, you know."

"I'll see you this summer, Mom. And I'll talk to you on Thanksgiving, if not before."

"Please continue to take your meds, Hunter. And please, Hunter, listen to Dr. Goodwin."

"I will, Mom," I responded, trying to conceal my disappointment that my own mother had chosen to ignore my declaration that I needed to write, that my writing was my life's purpose, that my writing was much more than just therapy.

I remember that Jane and Claire stopped by my room that Saturday night, the eve of day sixteen, to see how my time outside the hospital had transpired, to see what I had done, where I had gone, that sort of stuff. I told them, with no regrets or reservations, that I had gone to see Jocelyn. Both nurses asked how she was doing, concern resounding in their voices. I reported that she was doing fine despite my intuition that she was anything but fine. I did not want them to know that I suspected that she was not taking her meds and that I believed that she was still suicidal. But maybe Jane and Claire knew that already. That's when I asked myself if it was possible for a person to be released from a psychiatric ward still the pathetic victim of suicidal impulses and ideations. I decided that it probably was.

I thought of Ayden next. I was positive that he was takings his meds and that he was now, for the most part, devoid of suicidal ambition. Ayden was moving forward. I was sure of that. But why wasn't Jocelyn moving forward? And why had she been crying when she waved at me from the large picture window in her dad's house? Was it simply depression rearing its ugly head—again? Was it the poor treatment she had received from her dad and her two brothers? Was it their lack of understanding and compassion? Or was it a combination thereof? It was a question I could not answer, a question I was ill-equipped emotionally to fathom completely. Perhaps it was a question only Ayden, an articulate young man who had experienced separation from his own depression, could have answered. Perhaps it was a question for Jane, or Claire, or even Dr. Goodwin.

The phone rang only minutes after Jane and Claire had left me with a single reminder that they expected me at dinner in an hour and at group immediately after that. As I reached for the receiver, I told myself that it was, more likely than not, Jocelyn. After a strained 'hello" sounded in my ear, I knew that it was definitely her.

"What is it, Jocelyn? What's wrong?"

"My dad kicked me out."

"When?"

"Just now, maybe thirty minutes ago. He kicked me out, Hunter. I can't believe it."

"But why?"

"We got into an argument. He was yelling at me to stop lying around, to stop feeling sorry for myself. He called me a self-centered user, a brat and a bum." Jocelyn was now crying softly. I could not comprehend how a father could ever speak to his daughter in such a manner.

"What started the argument?"

"I was sitting on my bed in the dark. He walked in and started ranting about how I was a 'nothing,' about how I never would be anything and about how I was bankrupting him with all of my medical bills. So I told him to leave me the fuck alone because it was obvious that he no longer cared anyway."

"God … Where are you right now?" I was praying that she wasn't calling from a bus stop or from the lobby of an old hotel in a distant town or from a similar place.

"I'm at the house of a friend. She's out right now, buying some groceries. I'm not sure how long she'll let me stay here."

"Does your dad know where you are?"

"No, not yet anyway."

"Well, at least you are safe from his verbal abuse … for now."

"Yeah, but I don't know if Marcia wants me here. I told her that I'm still looking for both an apartment and a job. I promised her that I would pay her back for letting me stay here as soon as I am able. Hunter, Marcia doesn't seem to comprehend my illness either. I tried explaining it to her, in a nutshell, but she just shrugged and told me that I should 'look at the bright side.' I don't see a bright side right now, Hunter. I doubt I ever will."

"But you will, Jocelyn. You will," I reassured her. Once again, I was tempted to ask her whether she was taking her meds, but I opted to listen instead because she sounded desperate to talk to someone. I was that "someone."

"Hunter, do you remember when we talked about how we would have to beat the odds?"

"I remember."

"Well, I'm not beating them. I see the glares from people who have already rejected me. I see their incredulous stares. The reactions of those people are beating me down, breaking me, hurting me."

"They'll come around, Jocelyn. And if they don't, just ignore them and get on with your life."

"You know what I've noticed?"

"What's that?"

"I've noticed that I can't find anyone outside the hospital who understands manic depression." At that point, Jocelyn let out a disturbed sigh. She had stopped crying but her voice sounded weak and defeated. "She's home, Hunter. I'll call you later."

I sat with Ernest at dinner that night. I probably should have sat by myself but I felt that I needed to be close to another person, a manic-depressive—even if that manic-depressive was someone I hardly knew. After a few minutes of awkward silence, Ernest asked me what was wrong.

"Jocelyn isn't doing very well," I stated, pangs of guilt ricocheting throughout my conscious for not having kept Jocelyn's current state-of-being a secret. I understood that I had already said too much. But Ernest surprised me.

"Yes, I knew that, Hunter. Well, I sensed it anyway. She's a bright girl but she is extremely troubled, troubled by mental illness. Brainpower is not enough when a person is trying to stave off manic depression. Believe me. It's more complicated than that." Ernest stared into his soup. Then he looked at me. "Realize, Hunter, that she may not land on her feet this time or ever again."

"What makes you say that?"

"I sense it. That's all. I sometimes think that I have a gift for such things. I know that I can tell when a person is not operating the way she should be operating. But maybe I am wrong. I hope that I am wrong."

"How do you sense things like that?" I wanted Ernest to be more specific. He stirred his soup without looking into it.

"In Jocelyn's case, I can sense that she is not doing well because I know, for one, that she is not doing anything for herself. What's more, I am almost positive that she isn't taking her medications. I can't prove that but I can certainly sense it. I also know that she is not seeking any help right now." Appearing frustrated, Ernest crumpled his napkin and dropped it into his soup and shoved the small bowl away from him. I watched as the napkin absorbed an ample amount of broth to become submerged. "Stay by her, near her, Hunter. She needs a friend right now, probably more than ever. I guess I will see you in group." Ernest stood, pushed his chair in and left the dining room. I glanced around the room. All of the other patients had left already.

Sitting in the dining room by myself, I felt what it must be like to have the weight of the world on my shoulders and I mean that. I felt the weight of Jocelyn's depression bearing down on my own remnants of depression. The weight of knowing that I was, more likely than not, the only person with whom Jocelyn felt she could talk in detail, the only person who would not glare, or stare at her incredulously, was mind-numbing. Even more numbing than that was the manner in which Ernest had "sensed" that Jocelyn was not taking her meds. I had been sensing the same thing for days now and Ernest's admission had only served to solidify my own suspicions. And that scared the hell out of me.

I was able to skip group that night—not that I wanted to—when I confided to Jane that I had reason to believe that Jocelyn was still suicidal. Instead of sitting in group with the people Jane had once referred to as my "fellow travelers," the two of us sat in my room talking quietly. I was on the verge of crying tears of infinite frustration when Jane told me that she had already known that Jocelyn was still suicidal at the time she was discharged.

"And you let her go?" I asked. To say that I now felt "empty" on the inside would be an understatement of immeasurable proportion. There was simply no mistaking the void that was developing inside of me.

"It wasn't my decision, Hunter," Jane whispered. "It was the decision of the doctors."

"Well, it was a poor decision, the worst decision possible."

"Hunter, she was, at times, smiling, laughing even. Plus, none of us wanted her to become too dependent on the hospital. Not only that, we didn't want to help with her grieving any longer. Look at it this way: Jocelyn was taking up space that should have been occupied by someone else, by someone in dire need of help. That person wasn't Jocelyn. Can't you appreciate that, Hunter?"

"No, I cannot. That girl is hurting, Jane. I know she is. She is in danger ... of harming herself." I was suddenly tempted to tell Jane what Ernest had said about Jocelyn at dinner earlier that evening if for no other reason than to demonstrate that I was not the only person who sensed that she was not taking her medications but I decided against it because maybe she was taking her meds as prescribed and the suspicions Ernest and I shared that she was not taking them were just that—suspicions.

On the morning of the sixteenth day, I realized for the first time that I was no longer content sitting in the recliner in my room staring at my past in the gray-black television screen. Also, I was no longer interested in sitting in the community room listening, observing and spying. I was doubtless that I had heard and seen more than enough of the real people who would soon become the basis for several of my literary characters, people who were, like me, waiting for their time on Seven Southwest to finally come to an end so that they could pursue a "new and improved way of living."

I felt quite strongly that I now had an ample number of characters "breathing" inside of me and so I made a conscious decision to abandon the community room permanently. Shortly after I had made the decision to stay away from the community room altogether, it occurred to me that I would have to engage the characters I had created for my novel just as soon as possible. Ultimately, I realized that I would have to reinvent myself as a writer if the characters I had painstakingly created over the years, and especially during the past week or so, were ever going to be brought to life to tell the story I had dreamt of telling for far too long. Yes, I knew that I needed to go home and start writing very soon.

My short ride in the elevator to the lobby was not as unsettling as it had been the first time I had been permitted to leave the hospital grounds. This time I was content in knowing that I would be achieving something, fulfilling a goal. And this time, I was returning with a mission, a mission to see Chan yes but, even more important, I was returning with every intention of reentering my apartment to begin cleaning up the mess I knew I would find there.

As I walked across the bridge that spanned the stream nearest the hospital, I glanced into the blackened water that had become frozen in place, an unmoving icon of the winter season's touch. In the ice I saw not my current reflection captured there, but a reflection of myself that was now little more than sixteen days old. The reflection of a manic man who was determined to damage his ex-girlfriend's car was hard to miss. Also hard to miss was the likelihood that the stream, which was only a few blocks from my apartment, had captured everything that had transpired that frightening November night. Standing on the bridge, gazing into the ice, I watched as another dark flashback careened into view. That flashback was a vision I had seen before, you know, the troubling vision of me being loaded into an ambulance. This time the flashback had its own soundtrack accompanying it and I heard, or reheard, the voice of a single paramedic call out to me just before the doors of the ambulance were slammed shut. "You get better, Hunter," he said, his caring voice providing me with the faintest ray of hope that I might actually get better if my toxic liver managed to survive the days that lie ahead of me that is.

It was not long before I was standing on the front steps of the apartment building where both Chan and I had resided for years. Staring at that old building, I felt the most foreboding kind of silence echo inside my head. And as I entered the corridor, I knew, or sensed, almost immediately that Chan was not in his apartment that day and that I would have to reenter my own apartment by myself. A calmness best described as "bothersome" crept into my chilled body when I noticed that there was no longer a welcome mat in front of the door to Chan's apartment. I had no doubt that Chan had disposed of the bloody thing and I made a mental note to buy him a new one as soon as I was working again.

The same bothersome calm was still with me as I climbed a single set of stairs to the door to my own apartment and glimpsed the streaks of dried blood, my blood, near the door knob. I inserted the key John had left in a side pocket of the duffel bag. A turn to the right and a hard push and I was inside my unlit apartment for the first time in more than two weeks.

Let me tell you that there is definitely something strange about stepping into the past, regardless of how distant or near that past actually is. When I stepped into my apartment that day, I stepped directly back in time. And when I turned on the ceiling light, an ugly yellow beam shone on my most upsetting past, lending the room an eerie kind of iridescence. That is when I saw the blood, the kind of blood that could only signify an extremely low point in my life's disturbing timeline.

Within seconds, the bothersome calm feeling was gone. Within seconds, I fled my apartment and a segment of my recent past. On my way downstairs to Chan's apartment, a flashback of my former self, a bloody, seemingly-defeated self, consumed me. Fearing that bloody vision, a version of me I felt I no longer was, I pounded on Chan's door as loudly as the police officer had pounded on my own door the day I had stood staring at the lake, searching for a way to evade the law, ultimately searching for a way to end my life. But Chan did not answer. My intuition that he was not home had probably been correct.

I maintained a brisk pace, almost running, on my way back to the hospital. I was frustrated that Chan had stood me up. More important, I was angry that I had run from my own apartment and my own messed-up past when I had needed to face them both. How was I ever going to get on with my life and look toward tomorrow if I couldn't even clean up the blood of yesterday? It was a question that resounded inside my head with every labored breath I took. It was a question I simply could not answer.

In group later that same evening, I explained to my fellow manic-depressives that I had made what I considered was a gallant effort to face head on the blood that signified to me how much emotional healing I had or had not done in little more than two weeks. I described what I had seen while standing in my apartment trying to convince myself that I needed to clean things up one final time if I was ever going to move forward, if I was ever going to live to write and write to live.

I painted for the entire group a mental picture of the mess, the shards of glass from the light bulb, the empty gauze wrappers the paramedics had left scattered on the floor. I related the guilt I was still feeling for having inconvenienced every one of the paramedics who had pieced me back together.

"You haven't inconvenienced anyone, Hunter," said Sylvia. "Believe me." She was sitting on one of the sofas with Ernest. When I glanced at Ernest, he nodded.

"I sure feel as if I have."

"And guilt is something you do not need. I'd try to lose the guilt," she added.

"I'll try," I responded, knowing all too well that losing guilt, being free from its constraints, is never very easy. The guilt I associated with my having inconvenienced the paramedics was overpowering and seemed to be unshakable. I still felt extremely guilty for what I had done to Kate and for the trouble I had caused her family. I also felt guilty for the pain and hurt I had brought upon my own family over the years. Finally, I felt guilty for not having been able to forgive myself for all of the crimes I had ever committed and for the fact that I still had not been able to make friends with myself.

"Losing guilt is one tough assignment, Hunter," Ernest assured me. I glanced at Claire, the nurse-facilitator, and saw her ever-present smile. Clearly, she agreed with everything Sylvia and Ernest had said so far.

"Hunter, you now have a new goal," Claire stated, still smiling.

"And what's that?"

"You must make it a goal to return to your apartment and put things in order. Only then will you be able to finally make amends with yourself and, as Sylvia just articulated, lose the guilt."

"But I don't know if I can go back there—ever."

"You will, Hunter. You will. And the sooner the better. I would even make it your agenda to go back tomorrow."

I looked around the room at the faces of the manic-depressives who were, like me, trying to "put things in order." I remember that those faces, every single one of them, appeared to look upon me approvingly and with obvious care. It was as if they were all silently echoing Claire's sentiment. It was as if they were all silently speaking in unison, saying, "You will, Hunter. You will."

Jocelyn called several hours after group had convened. I was lying in bed on my back writing in my head in the dark when the phone rang.

"Are you okay, Jocelyn?" I had known that it was her the minute the phone's ring interrupted the flow of ideas I was experiencing. At such a late hour, who else could it have been? Even before she answered that question, even before she spoke a single word, I knew that she had been crying and that she was not doing well.

"Hunter, I just need to talk to someone, to someone who understands."

"Are you still staying with Marcia?" I was afraid that she had been kicked out of another home, afraid that she was on her way to the nearest bus stop to run away to some place unknown—again.

"Yes, I am. I don't know how much longer she'll have me, though. I'm already getting the feeling, a vibe, that she wants me to go back to my dad's, that she wants me out of here. She might just be as insensitive and naive as the rest of them. In fact, I believe that she is."

"Jocelyn, ask her if you can at least stay there until Friday. Remind her that I am being discharged on Friday, this Friday. Remind her that it's only a matter of a few days and that you promise to stay out of her way. Tell her that, starting Friday, you will be staying with me." A snapshot of my bloodstained apartment flashed across the surface of my brain and I knew that my having Jocelyn as a houseguest would not only make her feel safer and protect her from herself, it would also give me incentive to "put things in order" and enable me to "lose the guilt." "Jocelyn, as soon as I'm discharged, we will work something out so that you don't have to return to your dad's house. How does that sound?"

"Hunter, I don't want to impose. You have yourself to think about. Besides, I can't pay you a goddamn thing ... not yet anyway."

"I'm really not worried about money, Jocelyn. Money is not the issue right now. Your peace of mind and your safety concern me most."

"My safety, Hunter? What do you mean?"

"Do you think that you might harm yourself, Jocelyn?" I blurted. I was aware of how intrusive that question was, but, by the same token, I did not care whether I had violated Jocelyn's private thoughts or not. If she was going to turn to me for help, and it appeared that she was, then I was going to ask whatever questions might provide me with the needed information to assist me in keeping her safe—from herself. As far as I was concerned, any subject, especially the subject of how suicidal she might be feeling, was "fair game."

But Jocelyn did not seem to share that particular logic. No, not at all. As soon as I asked whether she might actually harm herself or not, she began shouting so loudly that her words became incoherent. I tried to make sense of them but, like the words spoken in one of the many dreams starring my dad and I, they were lost upon me. I was definitely in a strange and frustrating position. I had never been shouted at in such a manner before and I was tempted to hang up on her, but I resisted the urge to shun her because I was positive that she now needed me more than ever before.

After a minute or two of listening to her shout, Jocelyn started sobbing profoundly. She was speaking "normally" again, but I still could not understand what she was saying for the sound of her crying. Obviously, she was in pain. Also obvious was the likelihood that I might be ill-equipped to help her. It is true that I wanted to help her. It is also true that from somewhere deep inside me, somewhere so very deep within me I could not trace the origin of such a thought, it occurred to me that she would never be able to save herself from herself. And then, as quickly as that random thought had entered my mind, I banished it from further consideration. I simply was not ready to face the likelihood that Jocelyn would succeed in taking her own life.

Jocelyn hung up on me after muttering a single "goodbye." I wanted to call her back, but the upsetting thing was that I did not have Marcia's number. Equally as upsetting was the fact that I had no way of obtaining it. I did not know Marcia's last name and I was convinced that Jocelyn would not give it to me until she had calmed down. I would just have to wait until she called again. Unfortunately for Jocelyn, I had no way of knowing when that would be.

CHAPTER 33

On the morning of day seventeen, I noted that it was snowing worse than it had since my deliverance, since my arrival, since my return. Once again, I found myself standing in the study in front of the window watching the traffic steadily plow its way up and down a congested Center Street. I was trying to decide whether I would still be permitted to leave the hospital for the day when Jane appeared at my side.

"How's she doing, Hunter?"

"I don't think she's doing all that well. Truthfully, I know that she is not. She is so down, so low, lately. You know, Ayden told me that she was in good spirits when she left this place but she certainly isn't now. She is suffering badly and I'm not sure why. But that shouldn't be at all surprising to you, Jane. Or should it?"

"I figured as much. Her suffering is a product of her manic depression, Hunter. That's one of the reasons she needs medication and counseling—to keep the depressive episodes in check. Then again, maybe she is simply having some bad days. Restarting one's life after a suicide attempt can be an extremely painful ordeal."

"No, her pain runs much deeper than 'bad days,'" I asserted. Seven stories below the study's only window, a yellow taxi was moving cautiously down Center Street by itself. Watching the yellow taxi navigate through layers of snow, I suddenly found myself wishing that I was a passenger on my way to a place far away from Seven Southwest.

"She was really doing very well ..." Jane's voice trailed off and I began to question her vagueness. I wanted to know what she had actually intended to say.

"And?" I asked, glancing at Jane and then back at Center Street again. This time, when I peered out the window, the taxi was gone.

"Hunter, her latest mood change is so sudden, or at least that's the impression I get."

"So what?"

"So, Hunter, most suicidal people experience a sudden or sharp change in mood just prior to attempting suicide. I probably shouldn't tell you that; I really don't want to worry you."

"I believe that her mood did undergo a change, Jane. Sudden? Yes. Sharp? I cannot say."

"If you are correct that Jocelyn is not doing well, that she is 'suffering badly,' then there is definitely room for concern."

"Yes."

"Stay by her, Hunter. That is an awful lot to ask of you, but she is relying on you right now I think. She needs a friend. You can be that friend."

"Yes, I know that, too."

"Well, you should also know that we are here if you need to call on us."

"Sure," was all I said as Jane strode quietly out of the study.

As had been predicted, snow continued to fall heavily throughout the day and well into the late evening hours. After an uneventful night group, I was standing by myself in the study again staring at a Center Street that was now devoid of traffic. I was wondering where Jocelyn was going to sleep that night, whether she would follow my advice and ask Marcia to let her stay until Friday and, ultimately, whether she had experienced a "sharp turn," or not, as Jane had suggested might happen. I could draw no conclusions as to how she was making out, or how I could possibly "stay by her," a woman who seemed to be hiding from me what was really happening in her life, as well as what was going on in her manic-depressive mind.

I was aware that it was about time for the late news to come on when I met a man who looked to be much younger than myself. Upon entering the study, and while shaking my hand quite firmly, he instructed me to call him by his first name, Tyler, and told me that he was a psychologist.

Although I only knew Tyler for a relatively short time, there are several things I remember most about him. I remember that his face was well-defined, much like the chiseled face of a champion bodybuilder. He had an ultra-clean complexion and he smiled an awful lot. He even smelled good. But what I remember most about Tyler is that he definitely knew more about me than any one of the nurses or doctors did, including both Jane and Dr. Goodwin. For example, he knew in detail what I had done to Kate's car and that she had chosen not to press charges. He knew about both of my suicide attempts and about my newly-formed friendship with Jocelyn. He knew about the "frustration" I now harbored toward my parents, and toward my brother John especially, for their apparent lack of support and for their apparent lack of understanding over the years. He knew that I was still confused and hurting inside. And finally, he understood that I wanted to be a writer, a novelist, more than anything else.

Because Tyler knew so much about me, things about my life and the manic depression with which I was suffering and about my undying desire to be a novelist, I felt quite comfortable talking to him. It was almost as if I were speaking about old times with a close relative, or even with my best friend from grade school. Needless to say, I trusted Tyler instantly.

I don't remember everything we talked about that night but I do recall that Tyler brought our private "session" to a close by asking how my last few days had gone, taking a special interest in how I had spent my two days outside of the hospital. I told him about my long walk in the woods with Jocelyn and about how I had stopped by my apartment on the second day only to discover that I was still unprepared emotionally to face the blood, my blood, and the challenge of washing it away.

"My last few days have been going pretty well," I told Tyler that night as I moved away from the window and took refuge in one of the overstuffed chairs that was situated directly across from the end of the sofa where Tyler had seated himself.

"Your days have been going 'pretty well' except for the fact that you were unable to see your buddy Chan and except for the fact that you were unable to clean your apartment, two things you had hoped to accomplish. Isn't that right, Hunter?"

"Yes. Other than being stood up by Chan and being unable to reenter my apartment and face the awful person I'd been seventeen days ago, I was actually doing pretty goddamn well."

"But things have not been going well for Jocelyn and that upsets you. Am I right?"

"That's right. I'd rather not talk about Jocelyn right now, though. It's troubling, what's happening to her." I was slightly miffed that Tyler had tried to talk specifically about Jocelyn but I decided immediately not to hold my frustration against him. I decided that I would continue to work with Tyler in much the same way I had eventually worked with Dr. Goodwin.

"Okay. We don't have to talk about Jocelyn. What would you like to talk about? We still have some time."

"I'm not sure."

"You're not sure?"

"I'm not sure."

"Anything you'd like to show me? Someone told me that you have been writing a lot."

"I guess I would like to show you the poem I just wrote," I said at last. Somewhat nervous, and now feeling obligated to show a psychologist a poem I had originally written for myself and only for myself, I reached for my private journal and opened it to the page where I had recorded the poem entitled "Manic." I studied Tyler's face rather closely as he read my latest poem, the first poem I had written in years. I watched a smile form upon his lips.

"That's really very good, Hunter," he said, pausing to study quite closely the sunrise, or sunset, on the journal's blood-red cover before handing it back to me. Do you have any more like that, poems about manic depression I mean?"

"I think so." At that very moment it occurred to me that sharing the poem "Manic" with Tyler had not only been a good idea, but liberating as well. My depression was definitely "lifting."

"You only think so? Are you saying that you do not know?"

"I say that because I'm unsure whether any of the other poems I've written are strictly about manic depression. At the time I invented them, I was writing them essentially to get them out of my head. That's all. Whether they are actually about manic depression, I can't say right now. I do plan on reading them again as soon as I am able in hopes that I might come to understand them better. You could say that I will be looking at them with a new set of eyes, a brand new perspective."

"And when do you think that will happen?"

"Hopefully before Saturday. Soon anyway."

"Hunter, when do you think you'll be able to reenter your apartment? Before Saturday?"

"I'm not sure," I said, knowing all too well that I needed to have my apartment cleaned by Friday, Saturday at the latest, so that Jocelyn and I had a place to stay.

"So what do you think is stopping you, holding you back?"

"Tyler, when I inserted my key into the lock yesterday, when I stepped into my dark apartment, I saw all too clearly what I did to Kate's car that night, let alone what I did to myself."

"And seeing what you had done was upsetting to you?"

"Of course it was upsetting to me."

"Why?"

"Because I shouldn't have behaved that way."

"You see that now, don't you, Hunter?"

"Yes."

"So the memory of what you did to Kate's car is still on your conscious, still upsetting you?"

"Of course it is. When I tried to reenter my apartment, so many days later, after all the time I'd spent waiting for Kate to forgive me, after all the time I'd spent trying to forgive myself, I discovered that the mental pictures of what I had done to Kate's car were still with me. It really bothers me that I can't figure out for the life of me why I did what I did that night."

"Were you mad?"

"Yes."

"Were you mad at Kate?"

"Yes."

"Why were you mad at Kate? Had she done something to you?"

"She'd broken up with me earlier that same night. I thought you'd already been made aware of that."

"Hunter, I'm simply trying to reconstruct a few things."

"I see."

"And that's what made you so mad, so mad you decided to vandalize her car?"

"I can definitely answer that question for you, Tyler, but I know that you won't believe my response, my reason for getting so angry."

"But maybe I will believe you. Try me."

"More than anything else, I was mad at her for the way she handled the break-up itself."

"I can believe that. I think that makes some sense."

"Good. Also realize, Tyler, that many things had been bothering me for quite some time."

"But, Hunter, you need to understand that your anger does not justify your actions, mainly what you did to Kate and what you did to yourself."

"Yes."

"Then why do you think you behaved in such an irrational and irresponsible manner?"

"I now think my behavior that night had a lot to do with my being a manic-depressive," I said after a few seconds had elapsed.

"And why do you think that?"

"Because that wasn't the first time in my life I'd experienced such feelings of raw anger and acted so irrationally and with such impulsiveness. By impulsiveness, I mean without thinking things through as I usually did. But more important is the fact that I never told myself that I was going to take a can of spray paint to my ex-girlfriend's car. All of a sudden, I was doing it and I could not stop myself.

"That makes some sense, too, Hunter. Impulsivity, the kind of impulsivity brought on by anger that is, can be a very dangerous thing, especially when combined with a bad temper, especially when combined with the bad temper of a manic-depressive." I did not know how to respond to that particular statement. Today, I believe that I was slightly embarrassed, albeit briefly, that Tyler truly knew what I had done to Kate's car. Also, I was now having to openly accept—once and for all—that I had a dangerous and volatile temper.

"But aren't we over-simplifying why I lashed out at Kate?" I asked after another long-sustained silence."

"You tell me."

"I think it's possible that I was acting on impulse. But is it fair to blame my actions that night on both impulsivity *and* manic depression?"

"I think that it might be. I also think that it might be one—not the only reason—but one reason why you attempted to kill yourself once you realized that you would have to take responsibility for the crimes of trespassing and vandalism, the two crimes you'd committed. Hunter, your anger toward Kate and the way you acted that night, were, more likely than not, the byproducts of a number of things, a culmination, a culmination of events." Yes, Tyler had used the term "culmination," the same term Jocelyn had used the first time we met, the time she had argued, rather profusely, that I had garnered more than one reason for attempting to take my own life.

"A culmination, huh?" I was now staring at Tyler's figure full force, trying with all my might to see his skeleton, a skeleton I simply could not find. I was stunned by the manner in which Tyler and Jocelyn shared the same viewpoint that suicide attempts are brought on by a sad series of life-changing events. At the same time, I was still suspecting that depression alone can lead an individual to attempt suicide.

"Hunter, I believe that many things occurred over a very dismal period of time that led you to your decision to attempt suicide. Your suicidal state of mind wasn't formed by any one thing. No, it was not. A number of things contributed to your irrational thinking and your inability to reason affectively having become impaired. And if Kate, or anyone else, is to believe that you attempted suicide only because you had a bad break-up, or only because you vandalized a car, or only because you were running from the police, or only because you are a manic-depressive, then they are mistaken. They are wrong, Hunter. You can appreciate that, can't you?"

I did not answer Tyler right away because I really did not know *how* to respond. Instead of agreeing or disagreeing with him, I found myself replaying in my head the soundtrack from my first conversation with Jocelyn. I heard Jocelyn's well-spoken words echoing inside my brain, resounding, *"I have no doubt that it was your existing depression, depression brought on by any number of events, combined with the actuality that you were running from the police, that motivated you to attempt suicide,"* I heard her undaunted voice say again and again, *"I have no doubt ... I have no doubt ... I have no doubt ..."* And then Jocelyn's words were drowned out by Tyler's own voice of concern.

"Hunter, are you feeling okay?"

"I am feeling just fine." I was feeling fine, quite fine. I was feeling fine because I now understood, without a doubt, that both of my suicide attempts had been perpetuated by a series of occurrences, a culmination of troubling events, and not by any one thing. Sitting across from Tyler in the study seven stories above Center Street and the rest of the frozen outside world, I knew that both Jocelyn and Tyler had been correct. Even more important, I now realized that Jocelyn's current psychological state as well as her distressed outlook, were related to more than just a few medications missing from her depressed life. Jocelyn's moodswings and her poor outlook had everything to do with "any number of events." Jocelyn's pain, her suicidal dementia, had been "formed" by a culmination of mood-altering changes in her head and in her life. Little did I know just how mood-altering those events, events that would remain unknown to me for a lifetime, my lifetime, would become. And I simply failed to recognize the dangerous line Jocelyn was now walking between the real, tangible world and her own suicidal dimension.

You might find it interesting to know that I never saw Tyler again. It's odd how life works sometimes. A person can enter our universe for only a short time and shape our outlook, or a portion of it, until we die. Tyler had succeeded in doing just that. As I have already explained, he convinced me that suicide attempts are brought on by a culmination of events and not just by any one thing, a stance Jocelyn had taken from the beginning of our friendship.

More important, Tyler also awakened in me a new sense of urgency regarding Jocelyn's "situation." I now understood for the first time that she needed a combination of medications *and* counseling if she was ever going to stop her life from reeling dangerously out of control. I also understood that I needed to find her as soon as possible.

The following morning, the morning of day eighteen to be exact, I explained to Dr. Goodwin that I was ready to return to my apartment and finish the cleaning job I had been wanting to finish for days. Late the night before, shortly after I had bid farewell to Tyler, I determined that I was now ready to clean up the mess I had left behind nearly three weeks earlier. I knew all too well that my apartment needed to be restored to its original state. And that is the truth. However, there was something I did not confess to Dr. Goodwin that morning and that was my plan to spend as much time as was needed hunting Jocelyn.

If Dr. Goodwin suspected that I was actually intent on spending my third day of temporary freedom from Seven Southwest searching for Jocelyn Layne, he did not let on for a single moment that he knew what my true strategy was. I was grateful for that because I had a strong, inexplicable desire to keep my itinerary for the day a secret from the entire staff. Yes, I was determined to find Jocelyn on my own. My only real worry was whether a single day would be adequate time to locate a young woman who appeared to be as lost as a person could possibly be.

I marched through the thick doors and into the waiting elevator very determined to find Jocelyn and save her from herself. I did not bother speaking a single word to anyone as I exited Seven Southwest and I was grateful that I had been able to leave the ward seemingly undetected. My mood was serious and, upon stepping into the outside air, it was not long before I became oblivious to the cold November breezes.

I had decided late the previous night that I would first check to see if Jocelyn had returned to her dad's house. But as soon as I walked off of the hospital grounds, I changed my mind. Numbed more by the prospect of having to pay a visit by myself to the home of Jocelyn's verbally abusive dad than I was by the day's low temperature, I decided that I would detour to Chan's apartment instead and enlist his help in saving another human being for what I hoped would surely be the final time.

I arrived at Chan's apartment within minutes of leaving Lakeshore General, my pace having been the brisk pace of a man obsessed with something that is both driving and testing him. Chan was on the phone when he opened the door and so I entered his home without saying anything. With his free hand, he motioned for me to sit at the table that was situated just off the kitchen. As soon as I was seated, he walked quickly out of the kitchen and into the living room and out of hearing range. I admit that I had every intention of eavesdropping on his conversation, but he had left the room as soon as I had positioned myself at the round table where I had sat listening to his war stories so many times before. After a couple of silent minutes had elapsed and after I had calmed down considerably, he reentered the room and sat directly opposite me.

"I suppose you know who that was," he said.

"No, I don't," I responded, my tone marked by a new kind of curiosity.

"It was Jocelyn."

"Why?" I was confused. "What was it about?"

"All she would say is that she's looking for you. She said that she needs to talk to you. I tried to get more out of her but she kept evading my questions."

"Where is she, Chan?"

"I asked her that but she wouldn't say."

"Is she still at Marcia's?"

"Like I said, she would not say."

"Did she leave a number?"

"No, she didn't."

I understood immediately that I did not have time to relate to Chan all that had transpired between Jocelyn and myself over the course of the past eighteen days. I also understood that I had a responsibility to tell him that she was a suicidal manic-depressive and that we—yes we—needed to find her soon. My determination to "go it alone" was now nonexistent.

"Are you sure you want me along?" Chan asked as soon as I told him that Jocelyn was mentally ill and needing help. "I mean I don't even know the girl."

"Yes, Chan, I need your help more than ever. Right now you are the only person I feel I can trust."

Chan's old truck started on the first try. We had no other leads and so I gave him directions to the house where Jocelyn had been staying before her dad had attacked her verbally. Chan drove with diligent care as we made our way through the snow-covered streets to the house that belonged to Jocelyn's naïve father in what must have been a record pace. Looking back, I think we were really very lucky that we did not have an accident.

The first thing I noticed upon arriving at the house of Jocelyn's dad was the fat lamp in the picture window. Dusk was many hours away and still that lamp was on, burning brightly. Surely that meant that someone was home. It also meant that I would have to confront that person regardless of who it turned out to be.

Chan opted to stay in the truck and so I rang the doorbell and stood on the front steps alone. I remember wishing that I was lying on a beach on an island somewhere as I waited for someone to answer the door.

"Who is it?" I heard the unmistakable voice of a man call out just as soon as the sound of the doorbell had died away. I did not bother answering that voice. Instead of identifying myself, as I probably should have done, I glanced back at the truck where Chan was still sitting. He was staring down the snowy street in front of him and I was instantly reminded of a time we had gone fishing together and how he had spent the entire trip staring into the calm water without speaking a single blessed word. I wondered that day what he was seeing in the surface of the lake but I never asked. Maybe I should have asked but I never did. Standing alone on the front porch of the house that belonged to an unknown man I was now fearing, I decided that, this time, I would ask Chan what he had been staring at that almost-forgotten day. I would also ask him what he had been staring at as I waited for the door of a stranger's house to open.

Finally, the door did swing open and a tall, balding man with a graying moustache appeared. He was wearing a burgundy robe that was cinched at the waist and he was barefoot. I got the impression that he had just gotten out of the shower.

"What do you want?" he asked, his tone marked by sheer impatience. It was apparent that I had disturbed him. Also, the few words he had spoken with obvious authority were enough to tell me that I was in the presence of Jocelyn's cold-hearted dad.

"I'm looking for Jocelyn." To this day, I cannot recall whether I sounded as nervous and frightened as I felt. I only recall that I had gotten straight to the point.

"She isn't here, Hunter. That is who you are, isn't it?"

"Yes." I swallowed hard.

"So you are the guy she talks about all the time," he practically growled. I did not know what to say. "She's staying at her friend Marcia's I'm sure. I don't know where that is but Marcia works in a diner out west, on the old highway. Maybe she can help you find the girl that was once my daughter. And maybe, if you see her, Jocelyn I mean, you can tell her that she can come back once she has made the changes we talked about."

"Maybe," I said with a simple nod. "Hopefully," I added a split second before the door slammed in my face. In an instant, my fear of the man who still thought of himself as Jocelyn's dad had dissipated. But I did not mind. I did not intend to speak to him ever again now that I had an idea as to Jocelyn's whereabouts. Needless to say, I was very familiar with the small all-night diner that sat on a hill next to the old highway on the western edge of town.

CHAPTER 34

❀

Jocelyn, or an extremely pale, tired-looking version of her, was seated alone at a corner table near the kitchen of the all-night diner. She was staring at the ceiling and I got the feeling that she might be trying to hide in its textured surface.

"Are you feeling okay?" I slid into the seat directly across from her somewhat embarrassed by the stupidity of that question. In my peripheral vision, I watched as Chan positioned himself on a stool at the counter just beyond her shadow and ordered a cup of coffee and a piece of pie from a pretty waitress whose oversized nametag read "Marcia."

"It's good to see you, Hunter. It truly is. And I mean that. Honestly, sincerely." She took a sip of coffee. Then Marcia approached the table and told me what the specials were. I ordered a pitcher of black coffee and nothing else. Jocelyn looked at her long enough to ask for a smoke. Marcia obliged by producing a cigarette from a pack she had stowed away in the pocket of her pink and white striped apron and tossing it gently onto the table.

"Jocelyn, I didn't know you smoked," I said, confused and worried.

"I don't." She extracted a book of matches from her breast pocket.

"Tell me how are you feeling. And what's been happening?"

"No real place to stay, no job, no money, no family, no friends." She took another sip of coffee. "You tell me, Hunter, how things are going. How am I supposed to beat those fucking odds we talked so much about?" At that point she lit the cigarette and took a long, steady drag. Then she exhaled with force.

"I am your friend and so is Marcia. And so is Chan by the way," I said, as I glanced at Chan's back and studied the remnants of an insignia on his denim jacket that was so far gone I could not discern what it had once stood for. It was my best answer, the only answer I had for her. Clearly, she was hurting, injured, wounded emotionally. Clearly, she needed a friend more than ever.

"I don't know where to go from here, Hunter." And that is when our eyes met. That is when she looked directly at me for the first time since I had entered the diner. Through the vanishing smoke, I saw that the hues of crystal-blue that had once characterized her stare had begun to fade from her eyes.

"You are going to stay with me until you find your own place. I'm going to loan you some money and help you find a job. Things will get better, Jocelyn. But first, I have to go back to my apartment and take care of a few loose ends, do some cleaning, get my hands on another bed, stuff like that." Jocelyn did not respond. She sighed instead. "That is where you will go, where we will go, from here," I added. "And we will beat those fucking odds we talked about."

"Okay." She rubbed out the cigarette she had hardly smoked in a glass ashtray, an ashtray that was full of partially smoked cigarettes.

I waited for her to say something more, but she never did. "Okay" was the only word she said to me before I stood and dropped a fifty dollar bill Chan had loaned me onto the table directly in front of her. I promised that I would call her later that day if she would give me a number where she could be reached. Nodding, she pulled a pen from the same pocket where she had found the matches and scribbled a number across the unwrinkled face of the fifty dollar bill and shoved it toward me. Surprised, I picked up the bill. I studied the seven digits and, after hesitating for a moment, pushed it deep into the pocket of my blue jeans.

"Do you need a ride?" I asked. I waited for her to stand, but she did not stand. She just sat there. Then she looked away from whatever she was seeing inside the coffee cup. She looked at me one last time. "It's going to be all right, huh, Hunter?"

"Yes, it's going to be all right," I said, hoping to soothe away the sorrow I knew she was experiencing. "Everything is going to be all right. Trust me." I turned my back on her and stepped back into the winter world with Chan Allen, the tested veteran of life itself, at my side.

Without the images of the crimes I had committed against Kate dancing in my head, my apartment did not appear to be nearly as bloody as I had initially thought it might be or nearly as messy as I had remembered it. In less than three hours, Chan and I had managed to put practically everything I owned back in order. Some items, including several pieces of clothing, had to be thrown away. We also threw away the broken lamp I had knocked over while on my way to the bathroom on what was definitely the saddest, most frightening night of my life. Truthfully, that was a fairly easy thing to do because things were finally coming together for me. I had succeeded at cleaning away a painful part of my past and I was now progressing because of it. Furthermore, I was now fully prepared mentally to have Jocelyn as a houseguest and help her put her self back together piece by piece, little by little in much the same way I had been rebuilding my own self.

After we were finished cleaning, Chan dropped me off at the front entrance to Lakeshore General. On the way to the hospital, he made it known to me that Jocelyn and I were welcome at the home of his parents for Thanksgiving dinner and that they were actually expecting us. Without giving his invitation a second thought, I accepted. I would now have a safe, neutral place to go on Thanksgiving day and so would Jocelyn. That she would be in the company of others who would treat her as an equal during such a difficult period was a source of tremendous relief for me.

I walked straight to the phone in my room and dialed the number Jocelyn had given me. I let the phone ring and ring but there was no answer. I dialed the number again but, again, I did not get an answer. On the third consecutive try, I got a busy signal. I decided that a busy signal was a good sign, a sign that she was trying to call me. I hung up the receiver and waited and waited but the phone in my room did not ring. I would try her again later that night, sometime after group.

In night group, I told the few people present that I had made plans for Jocelyn and I to attend Thanksgiving dinner at the home of Chan's parents.

"That means, Hunter, that you will have two Thanksgivings. First, you will spend part of the day celebrating with us and part of the day celebrating with Chan and Jocelyn," Sylvia said, smiling. "That's really very fitting because you have so much to be thankful for."

"You are telling me that you have no place to go for the holiday?" I asked Sylvia.

"Well, Ernest and I don't," she responded with a convincing nod. "We are the only ones, except for Pauley. And who the hell knows what his intentions are? Maybe he'll join us and maybe he won't. I doubt that he will, though."

I asked myself why both Ernest and Sylvia had no place to go for the holiday other than the dining room on Seven Southwest. It was a question I could not answer, a question I would not ask of them.

"Pauley is certainly welcome to join us," Ernest said.

"Where is Pauley?" I asked.

"He is not feeling well right now," Claire answered before Ernest or Sylvia could field the question. "Being away from home and loved ones during the holiday season can be especially hard on a person."

"Yeah, I suppose it can be," I agreed. Briefly, I thought of my own family. I thought of both John and my parents celebrating without me a holiday we had always celebrated together and I knew that I was not ready to go home for Thanksgiving just yet.

Ernest and Claire spent the remainder of the group therapy session listening to Claire talk about cognitive approaches to dealing with depression, especially during the holidays. Although I was positive that Claire knew what she was talking about, I soon tuned her out completely. I was much too busy thinking about Jocelyn and what it might take to save her to listen to anyone speak about anything.

Spending a small part of Thanksgiving day with Ernest and Sylvia would probably be a nice break in my routine, but the day would only be solidified as a happy day, as a happy memory, if I managed to find Jocelyn. That said, I knew that I needed to find her sooner than later and long before I made any more preparations for her to stay with me after my discharge on Friday. Clearly, everything I would do during my final days on Seven Southwest would hinge on whether I could locate Jocelyn one more time.

I was awake most of the night, worrying about Jocelyn, waiting for her to call and trying, without any success whatsoever, to write in my head. But she did not bother calling. The phone in my room never rang and, because I was so concerned about her, I was unable to write anything at all.

The ward was practically deserted on my nineteenth day on Seven Southwest. It was Wednesday, the day before Thanksgiving, and the number of staff had been cut by half or maybe more. As for the number of patients on the ward, only a handful remained. That handful included Ernest and Sylvia as well as the schizophrenic man who was almost always found sitting next to the t.v. in the community room blinking rapidly. Pauley would also stay behind that day and would end up skipping the holiday meal by spending hours in his room watching football by himself.

Jocelyn still had not called and several attempts to reach her were unsuccessful. After I had tried calling her for what must have been the fifteenth time, I was recruited by Ernest and Sylvia to help decorate the dining room in a Thanksgiving motif. We invested a lot of time taping one dimensional turkeys that had been painted on construction paper days before by some of the other patients on the walls and scattered cut-out paper leaves on the tables and folded burnt orange and dusty brown napkins into clever shapes and placed them with precision at each place setting. Although we had added some much-needed color to the dining room's boring interior and had warmed the space up in the process and were now looking forward to Thanksgiving for what seemed like the first time since being admitted, not one of us had forgotten that I had been unable to get a hold of Jocelyn. While none of us mentioned her name while we had been hanging multi-colored streamers from the ceiling, each of us was worrying about her I was sure.

I was tired and needed a nap badly, but I also knew that I needed to place a call to my parents. I needed to let them know that I was improving daily. I felt a dire need to remind them that I would be released in two days, on Friday. Plus, I wanted to get their advice as to how I could best help Jocelyn. You see, I had an inkling that they might just know how I should approach Jocelyn's current state of affairs and, ultimately, how I should approach Jocelyn herself. And in the off chance that they did not know how to help me deal with her, I would still have an opportunity to let them know that I loved them. That was reason enough to call.

I let the phone ring many, many times but I did not get an answer. Because my parents lived in a different time zone, several hours ahead in fact, I concluded that they were probably sleeping. I gave up on them for the day and decided that I would try calling them early on Friday from my apartment, or on Saturday at the latest. I would not try reaching them on Thursday because I would be too busy celebrating the holiday with Ernest and Sylvia and, later, with Chan and Jocelyn.

I spent the remainder of the daylight hours in my room finishing the book on manic depression Claire had given me. Finishing that book was a victory in itself because it was the first book I had read from cover to cover in a very long time.

"So how was it anyway?" Claire asked at the same moment I closed the book and laid it on the nightstand nearest me. She was leaning in the doorway.

"Well, I know much more about my illness today than I did when I arrived here nearly three weeks ago," I told her.

"So you think that the book has been helpful then?"

"Yes."

"How?"

"Claire, I understand, more than ever before, that manic depression can only be treated with medications. I realize that the illness cannot be treated any other way."

"That's true, kiddo. I'm glad you are aware of that."

Jocelyn did not call once the entire night. I know this because the phone in my room did not ring a single goddamn time. I tried the number she had given me often, but I never once got an answer. Hours after midnight, I fell asleep. I did not stir again until it was time to have more blood drawn and take my Paxil early the following morning, Thanksgiving day.

Still needing sleep, but determined to stay awake, I shuffled into the study and looked out the window. The sun was beginning to break through the clouds and it was snowing very lightly. All at once, I got the feeling that Thanksgiving was actually going to turn into a very nice holiday as long as I could get a hold of Jocelyn. Unfortunately, that was proving to be a difficult task.

I tried calling her a few more times before it was time to eat, but to no avail. At dinner, I sat with Ernest and Sylvia. A few tables away, a tech named Bruce was eating by himself. Pauley and the little blinking man were nowhere to be seen. And neither was Claire for that matter. I did not bother asking where they were. Troubled by my inability to get Jocelyn on the phone and by a strong desire to mind my own business, I decided that I did not care enough to know anything about their whereabouts.

"Is it Jocelyn that's bothering you, Hunter?" Ernest asked me as he ladled more gravy onto his mashed potatoes.

"Yes," I admitted. "You know, Ernest, I keep telling myself that she is a big girl. I keep telling myself that she can take care of herself. That's when her fragile person flashes before my eyes and I know that I need to be the one to step forward and help her."

"Maybe she needs to help herself first, my friend."

"Maybe."

"Hunter, there's only so much you can do for her. You need to understand that."

I sat in the dining room by myself for a very long time after Ernest and Sylvia and Bruce had finished eating. I was trying to decide what my next move would be. I was trying to prepare a strategy. I still hadn't reached Jocelyn at the number she had given me and I was now contemplating making a return trip to her dad's house to see if he could provide me with another lead or two. That is when it occurred to me that I simply could not go it alone. I would need more help finding Jocelyn. I would need Ernest and Sylvia.

Before the three of us obtained the day passes we hoped would buy us the necessary freedom to find Jocelyn, we decided that we would stay together no matter what. Ernest had reminded Sylvia and I that a group effort would be much more productive than each of us conducting our own search. He reminded us that we would be able to "put our heads together" as needed. He made us remember that there is always a considerable amount of safety in numbers. As always, there seemed to be an ample measure of truth in the words Ernest spoke. There was also logic in the plan he devised.

Ernest's plan for finding Jocelyn was really very simple. First, I would try reaching her by phone one more time. Assuming that she would not answer, I would call Chan next and check to see if he had heard from her. If he had, we would take things from there. But in the case Chan had not heard from her, then I would cancel my plans to attend Thanksgiving at his parents' home and encourage him to do the same so that he could help us search for her. Whether Chan participated in our search or not, Ernest, Sylvia and I would stop by Jocelyn's dad's house to see if she was there, or to see if her dad could help us by telling us where Marcia lived, or by providing us with any other pertinent information. If we were still unable to find Jocelyn, we would stop by the all-night diner on the western edge of town. If she was not there, we would return to the hospital and, in all probability, call the police.

Jocelyn did not answer the phone. Chan, as always, answered on the first ring and told me that he had not seen her or heard a thing from her since the day the two of us had met her at the diner. Aware that I sounded very concerned about Jocelyn's safety, I asked Chan if he was willing to cancel his plans for Thanksgiving and, reluctantly, he said that he would. He also agreed to pick Ernest, Sylvia and I up at the hospital. Within a matter of minutes, he arrived to take us to Jocelyn's dad's house.

The three of us piled into Chan's truck. Chan turned quickly onto Lakeshore Boulevard and I glanced at the glass-like surface of the lake. The bay had frozen over already and the icy landscape was dotted with a plethora of skaters in colorful sweaters doing crazy eights and playing hockey. Scenes such as that one never ceased to remind me of my youth. Sitting in the cab of Chan's truck with Ernest and Sylvia, I remembered the time my dad and John and I had walked all the way across the frozen bay to the peninsula. I was a young boy then and I wasn't searching for a lost friend on Thanksgiving. I was just a young boy out on your typical lazy winter stroll with his brother and his dad. Years later, things would be much different. Years later, I would be riding in a friend's pickup truck with two manic-depressives searching for a mutual friend who was also mentally ill and, more likely than not, suicidal.

Chan shifted into low gear and drove cautiously onto the bridge and over the stream and turned left on Center street, leaving the hospital, Lakeshore Boulevard and the frozen bay behind us. We were now heading west, in the general direction of Jocelyn's dad's house. Ernest was the first to speak.

"Whatever you do, whatever you say, Hunter, remain calm when talking to this man. I sense that he is not a very patient or caring father. I sense that he wants nothing to do with his daughter anymore. I also sense that he does not like you."

"What should I say to him?"

"Tell him nothing. Act as if we are there to pick his daughter up for Thanksgiving dinner. And if she is not there, ask him where she went, when she'll be back. Whatever you do, play it cool."

"I hope she is there. God, I hope she is there."

"Same here," Sylvia said. "It sure would simplify things."

"Yeah, same here," Chan echoed. Minutes later, he parked the truck in front of the one house where I prayed Jocelyn was now staying once again.

"Remember, Hunter: remain calm." Ernest patted me on the shoulder and I stepped out of the truck and sank several inches into the snow. I pushed the door shut and made my way to the sidewalk that had yet to be shoveled. I studied the dark facade of the house as I climbed the front steps one at a time. The house appeared to be deserted.

He must have seen me coming because Jocelyn's dad opened the front door before I ever had a chance to ring the bell. I glanced back at the truck. I saw that Chan was staring straight ahead again. Ernest and Sylvia were staring directly at me.

"What is it this time? So did you find my daughter?" Instantly, I smelled alcohol on his breath. I noticed that his eyes were bloodshot. He moved away from the door, closed it and coasted to a stop less than a foot away from me. "I asked you a question, you idiot!" he shouted.

"I did not find her ... yet," I stammered.

"Then why are you here? What do you want?"

"Jocelyn was supposed to join me, I mean us, for Thanksgiving dinner," I lied.

"Fuck off! And take that bunch of nutcases with you!" He turned away from me, stumbled over the threshold, found his balance again and slammed the door behind him. I crawled back into the truck frustrated by the fact that I had come up empty again.

"Well, what now?" I asked.

"Did he tell you where Marcia lives? Or did you forget to ask?" Ernest was searching my face for an answer.

"I forgot to ask. He didn't give me time."

"We will call the number again from my place," Chan responded. He started the truck and steered it away from the snow that had been plowed high above the curb. The truck, as if it were being propelled by a sense of urgency all its own, shot forward and away from the house where Jocelyn's dad lived.

From Chan's apartment, I dialed the number Jocelyn had scribbled on the fifty dollar bill for what seemed like the one hundredth time. I was stunned when a woman finally answered with a simple "Happy Thanksgiving."

"Jocelyn?"

"No. This is not Jocelyn. It's Marcia. Who's this?"

"Marcia, it's Hunter." I was practically shouting now I was so excited. That quickly, my hope that we would find Jocelyn had been reborn.

"Well, give it up because she isn't here. She moved back in with her dad. Have not seen or talked to her since I last saw her at the diner." Now it was Marcia who was practically shouting.

I hung up the phone without speaking another word and told Chan, Ernest and Sylvia that Jocelyn was back at her dad's.

"Maybe she is," Sylvia stated. "But what can we do?"

"We can still check the diner." I was praying that she was not staying with her dad again.

That is when Chan came forward with a strategy of his own. Chan's plan, like Ernest's plan, was also rather simple. First, we would drive to the diner together. If she wasn't there, we would return to her dad's house and let Chan do the talking. If we were still unable to locate her, we would definitely call the police. Needless to say, we all agreed that it was the best plan.

I could have sworn that the temperature had dropped a full twenty degrees when we jumped back into the truck. Each of us was shivering violently when Chan turned the key and stepped on the gas pedal. We were still shivering when the engine failed to start a second, third and fourth time and it was obvious to each of us that the battery was dead.

It was Sylvia's idea to have Chan walk to the house where Marcia had claimed Jocelyn was staying so that he could try reasoning with her dad. It was also her idea that Ernest and I walk with her to the diner. If Jocelyn was at the diner, Sylvia would do the talking woman to woman. And then, after we had checked both places, whether we had found Jocelyn or not, we would meet back at Chan's apartment.

Why we did not bother calling the all-night diner before we set out on foot, I cannot say. Even today, after so much speculation, I cannot figure out why we opted to walk to the diner in the cold rather than place a single telephone call. After we had wished Chan luck and reminded him to be careful, we aimed our silhouettes toward the western edge of town, toward the little all-night diner where I had last seen Jocelyn. As we walked in and out of the lengthening winter shadows, I told Ernest and Sylvia about my last meeting with Jocelyn. I described how pale she had looked and how she had been unable to maintain eye contact with me for any length of time. I told them about how colorless her eyes were that day.

"It's going to be okay, Hunter," Sylvia whispered as soon as I had finished verbally sketching for the two of them the most recent mental picture of Jocelyn I owned, the picture of her sitting alone in an all-night diner staring at the ceiling and smoking a cigarette. "It's going to be okay," she repeated. "We'll find her. And she'll be okay."

I am not exaggerating when I tell you that Ernest, Sylvia and I were completely silent from the moment Sylvia had tried to reassure me that everything would be okay. I am telling you the truth. I am being honest with you when I say that the silence I was a part of that day was a different kind of silence, the kind of silence that forces a person to draw the worst kind of conclusions. The conclusion I drew while the three of us walked past houses with holiday wreaths hanging on their doors and strings of lights affixed to their gutters was indeed a strange one. For the first and last time since I had met Jocelyn, I envisioned her lying dead in a fetal position on top of her mother's grave in a faraway city. Yes, that is the conclusion I drew. That is what I envisioned while we made our way on foot to an out-of-the-way all-night diner that stood alone on the outskirts of town as another winter day slipped away.

A graying, frail-looking waitress whose oversized nametag read "Anna" was hanging a closed sign in the window when we finally arrived. We must have looked like an odd bunch to her, three underdressed adults out walking on a freezing cold Thanksgiving afternoon as evening approached. I also think that we must have startled her when Ernest tugged on the door that was locked.

The waitress named Anna pointed to the sign she had just hung and, shrugging as if to apologize, shouted that the diner would reopen the following morning at six. Anna reminded us that they always closed early on Thanksgiving and Christmas. Not to be turned away without first exhausting every facet of our plan, Ernest, stepping closer to the window and the closed sign, described Jocelyn and asked Anna if she had seen her lately. Anna hollered that she had not seen her in days and Ernest thanked her and we made our way back to Chan's house still wrapped in an awkward kind of silence.

It was apparent that the three of us felt defeated because not one of us spoke a single word even after we were back inside Chan's apartment. Once again, our plan had failed to produce a result and we were now facing the likelihood that we would end our search for the day without any more leads. Chan showed up a short time later and also appeared to be at a loss when he reported that Jocelyn's dad had not answered the door. Frustrated by our joint failure, and aware that we were almost out of time, Ernest and Sylvia and I decided that there was nothing left for us to do but return to the hospital empty-handed.

Chan loaned us extra jackets and reminded us that everything would work itself out in the morning, on Friday. Minutes later, we crossed the bridge and the darkening stream and reentered the hospital. Claire was already there, waiting in the lobby, with an uneasy smile.

"I'm not sure where the three of you have been. I'm fairly certain that I don't want to know but I have a message for you from Jocelyn. Hunter, she said that she is staying at her dad's and that she will meet you Saturday at his house. She said that she is looking forward to staying with you 'for a while' and getting 'back on track,' as she put it."

Ernest and Sylvia looked to be extremely relieved. I could see the smile of victory on their faces. I could see a sparkle in their eyes I had never seen before in anyone. I saw an improvement in their postures and I could tell that they were suddenly feeling warm inside and out again. Good news can do that to a person, you know. After all, I was suddenly feeling as warm as I had ever felt. The search for Jocelyn was officially over.

I called Chan to share with him the phone message Claire had relayed to Ernest, Sylvia and I but there was no answer. I got his answering machine and promptly hung up. I decided that I would tell him the good news soon enough, on Friday, after I was discharged and in person. I would tell him that everything was going to be better than "okay."

Because it was Thanksgiving night and there were so few patients on the ward, night group was cancelled. After I had taken my nightly dose of lithium, I took a shower and recorded what had transpired over the course of the last few days in my journal. As soon as Claire reminded me that it was lights out, I crawled into bed and fell into the deepest, most satisfying sleep I had experienced since I had been admitted onto Seven Southwest. I did not awaken a single time the entire night.

I had several dreams that night but only one has stayed with me to this day. I dreamt that particular night of all the things I would do once I was discharged. More than anything else, I dreamt of writing a novel, of completing a novel. For what seemed like hours, I dreamt that I had finally become a successful novelist. I awoke early that Friday morning with a renewed energy. I awoke feeling empowered and full of hope.

When I opened my eyes, I saw that a handful of people I had never seen before were standing at the foot of my bed. I was not sure who they were but I would learn much later that they were the team of doctors who had invested the most time in saving me. They were staring at me, waiting, I was certain, for an answer, for an explanation as to why I had done it. When one of them finally asked me what my reason had been, I knew that I would never be able to explain to them all of the reasons I had for attempting to kill myself. I understood that there simply would not be enough time for me to share with them an explanation, my explanation, and so I closed my eyes until I knew that they were gone. I never saw any of those doctors ever again.

CHAPTER 35

❀

I remember my final morning on Seven Southwest vividly. After my blood had been drawn and I had taken my morning Paxil, I returned to my room to pack and get cleaned up. I showered quickly and dressed in a pair of blue jeans and a faded gray sweatshirt. I was too excited about my pending release to eat breakfast but I went to the dining room anyway so that I could bid farewell to Sylvia. But Sylvia was not in the dining room, or in the community room for the matter. In fact, I could not locate her anywhere. Her room was empty. The study and the laundry room were vacant as well and, because of the early hour, the lobby was empty, too. When I asked Claire and Jane and the tech named Bruce where she might have gone, where she might be, not one of them seemed to have a decent answer. Claire and Jane each stated that she had either gone "visiting" for the day, or that she was with a psychiatrist. Bruce maintained that she was "wandering" around the hospital grounds on a day pass and that she would be back "soon enough."

I was double checking to see that I had not forgotten to pack my journal when Dr. Goodwin peeked his head inside the door to the one room I would soon be leaving forever.

"Good luck to you, Hunter," he said as he walked into the room and shook my hand.

"I'll be seeing you again, won't I?"

"Call me in a couple of weeks and we'll take it from there."

"Sounds good."

"Continue to take your medications as I have prescribed them."

"Don't worry, I will."

"And keep in mind that you are no longer a child; you are an adult and you need to face the responsibilities of being an adult the same way an adult would."

"I know that now, Dr. Goodwin. I understand that. I've changed, or grown, at least a little while I've been a patient here."

"And, Hunter, remember to laugh once in a while. And, in the words of Elbert Hubbard, 'Don't take life too seriously. You will never get out of it alive.' Those words makes some sense, wouldn't you agree?"

"Elbert Hubbard said that, huh?" Briefly, I thought back to the day from long ago when Emily Ryan had quoted Elbert Hubbard, the deceased American author and philosopher. That strange day seemed a million light years away. I was definitely a much different person now. There was no doubt about it.

"Yes, I'm certain that it was him. Regardless, it's advice to live by, don't you think?" Dr. Goodwin turned toward the door. "Smile and laugh when you can. 'A day is wasted without laughter' I believe."

"More Elbert Hubbard?"

"I don't think so. I saw those words written on a subway wall in Vienna years ago."

"Yeah, a day probably is wasted without laughter. I agree." I watched Dr. Goodwin make his way down the corridor, passed the nurses' station and into another patient's room. I was relieved to know that I would be seeing him again very, very soon.

A short time later, Jane and Claire were following closely behind me as I walked slowly in the fateful direction of the thick doors that stood ominously between the inner sanctum of Seven Southwest and freedom when Ernest stepped out of his room and tapped me lightly on the shoulder. I was instantly upset that I had almost forgotten to say goodbye to him, my friend and Seven Southwest's own resident American philosopher.

"You'll be okay out there, Hunter," he said, nodding.

"How do you know?" I asked him at the same moment I set my heavy duffle bag on the floor.

"Maybe I should tell you a story. It's a story I've never told anyone—not anyone. Do you have time?"

"Of course. I'd like to hear it." My interest was instantly piqued.

"When I was a boy, I had a kitten, a little white one, just your average kitten. He was nothing special, but cuter than hell. I loved that kitten."

"Okay."

"One morning, I was playing outside with him when my mom called me in to breakfast. I was in a hurry to eat, so I left him on the back porch. I'm not sure why I left him out there. Maybe I thought that he would be safer out there. I still do not know. I suppose it doesn't matter anymore. Anyway, after I had finished eating, I went out to the porch to get him. What I saw there, what I found next, scared the hell out of me."

"What did you find?"

"I found my kitten crawling across the concrete floor of the porch. You see, he was pulling himself along by his front paws. His hind legs were not moving. They were being dragged along behind him."

"What happened?"

"I can only speculate. I can't be sure. I can only speculate."

"Well, what do you think happened?"

"I think, or believe, that he tried to crawl up the screen door. I believe that he fell. Finally, I believe that he did not land on all four feet, as cats are supposed to do. He crash landed. And when he crashed onto the concrete floor of the porch, he broke his back. That's why he couldn't move his hind legs."

"That's too bad, Ernest. Really it is."

"I know."

"I have to ask you, though, what became of him? Did he ever get better? Did he ever recover? If I had to guess, I would guess that he did not."

"That's what I need to tell you ... Hunter, he never did recover."

"So what happened to him then?"

"I'm not sure. Again, I can only speculate."

"And?"

"I came home from school one day and he was gone. No one ever said what became of that poor, injured kitten, my kitten. At first, I asked about him all the time but no one would answer me, not even my parents. After a while, I stopped asking about him altogether. Then one night, a few days after he had disappeared, I was lying in bed missing my little kitten and thinking. That's when it occurred to me that I had seen my dad standing behind the barn one morning before I had left for school several days earlier, a short time after my kitten had broken his back. When I started walking in the direction of the barn, my dad hollered at me to stay away. He had never hollered at me like that before. Instantly, I stopped, turned and ran. I don't know why I sprinted all the way to the bus stop that day, but I did. I sprinted the entire distance without looking back. It's likely that I knew that my dad had been in the process of euthanizing my kitten and that I'd almost witnessed my cat's premature death by accident. Maybe that's why I was running. Maybe I was trying like hell to escape the present and return to the past, to a time when my kitten was able to walk." Ernest cleared his throat and rubbed his eyes. Then he looked at me and I knew that he was waiting for me to respond.

"It's a sad story."

"Do you understand what I am trying to convey to you, Hunter?"

"You are telling me that death touches us all."

"Yes, but even more important, I am telling you that not all cats land on their feet. Some cats do, some cats don't. But you will. You will land on your feet, Hunter Kraven. I'm sure of it."

"Thank you for the story, Ernest. I do understand what you are telling me. And thanks for believing in me. I know that I will land on my feet." I reached out to shake his hand, but Ernest stepped forward, past my outstretched hand and hugged me. I hugged him back. Over his shoulder, Jane and Clair were leaning against the thick doors, propping them open with their backs, waiting for me. I released my grip on Ernest and he released his grip on me.

"I'll see you sometime, okay, Hunter?"

"You bet, old buddy," I said. I threw my large duffel bag over my shoulder.

I moved away from Ernest and in the direction of Jane and Clair and toward the thick doors. Before I reached the threshold, I turned and took one last sweeping look at the ward, at Seven Southwest itself. A few nurses I had not seen before were walking from room to room. A couple of doctors were standing behind the nurses' station whispering. I saw Pauley walk into the community room and wondered if he had been the man who had screamed late the night before while the other patients had been trying to sleep. I had no way of knowing for sure. Today, I still do not know whether it was Pauley. All I do know is that I felt tremendous compassion for the man who was in so much pain he could only scream at the nighttime darkness that filled the corridors of Seven Southwest.

I glanced at Ernest's room. He was standing with his back to me now, folding clothes and stuffing them into a suitcase. I considered his unselfishness; I understood that he had not mentioned his own pending discharge because he was more concerned for me than he was for himself. Yes, Ernest, unselfish Ernest, was going home soon, too. And, like me, he would land on his feet.

"It's time, Hunter."

"I know it is, Jane." I took one last look at the collection of rooms that comprised Seven Southwest. From my vantage point near the thick doors, I glanced inside every one of them as best I could. That is when I realized, for the very first time, that every single one of those damn rooms was occupied. Every room was "home" to a man or a woman who was still in pain.

"It's time, Hunter," Jane stated a second time.

"Yes, it's time, Jane. It's time to go home."

Jane and Claire escorted me through the lobby, passed the gift shop, the information desk and walked beside me to the front doors of Lakeshore General. They took turns shaking my hand. Before I exited the hospital, I asked each of them if I would ever see either one of them again. Claire did not respond. She only smiled. But Jane told me, quite simply, that time would be the "deciding factor."

Chan was standing outside the main entrance. He had put a new battery in his truck and was waiting to drive me home, back to the apartment we had worked so diligently to restore.

"Chan, I think I can take it from here."

"What do you mean?"

"I want to walk."

"Really? Are you sure?"

"Yes, I'm sure."

"I'll see you when you get back then. You'll be okay?"

"Of course. I'm going to walk so that I can relax a little. Then I'll take a nap. And then I will pick up Jocelyn at her dad's house."

"Sounds as if you have a plan."

"Don't worry, Chan, I do have a plan. And this plan is going to work."

There wasn't a breeze that particular morning and no snow was falling. As for the sun, it was fighting to hold onto a position in front of a series of muddy-blue clouds. I was in no hurry to get back to my apartment because I was not scheduled to pick up Jocelyn until late that afternoon and so I decided that I would stop somewhere for a cup of coffee.

From inside a small restaurant on Main Street, I eavesdropped on a trio of elderly men who were seated at a little round table near the center of the room while I sipped decaf, the only kind of coffee I was now allowed to drink.

"More snow late today," one man said.

"Well, that's all we need," said another.

"So did you here about the Fisher kid?" asked the third man.

"Yeah, I did. It sure is sad what he did," the first man responded.

"What happened?" the second man asked.

"He committed suicide last night."

"He did?" I asked, forgetting that I did not belong in the conversation and remembering that I had known "the Fisher kid" for years. All three men looked at me as if I had just insulted them.

"Shot himself in the head," the first man finally responded. "I'm not sure why he did it, though. It was probably over a girl, or something like that. It usually is."

"I knew him. He was a friend of mine." I said, glancing at the clock on the wall. The hands on the clock that read half past ten seemed to be frozen in place. I dropped the fifty dollar bill on which Jocelyn had written Marcia's phone number onto the counter suddenly afraid for myself and for Jocelyn and for every other depressed person in the world. A waitress gave me a funny look and counted out my change. I handed her four dollars, a sizable tip for a cup of coffee, and started for the door. But before I opened the door, I turned to face the three elderly men. "You may not believe this, but his suicide wasn't caused by any one thing. A culmination of unfortunate events led him to think that suicide was the answer when, clearly, it was not. You should all think about that."

I was back at my apartment about one hour later. I was extremely distraught over Fisher's death and so I dialed my parents' number hoping that they would be able to console me. When they did not to answer, I collapsed onto the floor and cried tears I knew were not only for my dead friend Fisher but for all of the people who had ever committed suicide. I cried until I had fallen asleep on the floor in the middle of my apartment. I did not awaken until late that same day, long after the sun had given up its fight for position in front of the endless series of muddy-blue clouds.

It was now time to pick up Jocelyn. On my way downstairs, I stopped by Chan's apartment to let him know that I was leaving. Chan offered to drive, but I refused. He told me that more snow was on the way and that I could take his truck if I wanted but I declined. I'm not sure why but I was determined to walk to Jocelyn's dad's house whether it snowed again or not.

I will never understand what propelled me down the sidewalk that ran in front of Jocelyn's dad's house to the point where her footprints left the concrete. Perhaps my change in direction had something to do with the reality that no one answered the door when I rang the bell. Maybe it was simple intuition telling me to take an alternate route home or just a hunch I had that caused me to detour in that particular direction. Nevertheless, when I saw Jocelyn's footprints in the snow, I knew that she was sitting alone in the woods sipping coffee from the same metal thermos she had carried the day the two of us had sat sharing various details of our depressed lives.

I don't seem to remember much about my casual walk into the woods early that evening. I do seem to recall that I thought a lot about Fisher and how he had never shown a single sign that he was suicidal, at least not to me. I considered the likelihood that no one had seen his pain, the pain that ultimately led to his suicide. I also thought about Ayden and Ernest and Sylvia and all of the other suicide survivors I had ever met. I considered that they were survivors in every sense of the word and that their valor for having faced their illness was immeasurable. But mostly, I thought about Jocelyn. I asked myself if she would ever land on her feet. I told myself that she would. I told myself that she would only improve. I made up my mind that she had nowhere to go but up. Yes, she would get better. But then, for some reason I have never fathomed, I changed my mind. As quickly as I had decided that she would heal, I decided that she would never get better no matter what medications she was taking, no matter how much counseling she was receiving. Just like that, I concluded that Jocelyn would not land on her feet ever again.

My casual pace quickened as the sun fell behind the treetops and the snow began to fall. As I rushed up the trail, it occurred to me that I might have known from the beginning that I would eventually find her there, resting deep within the silent wilderness. It is certainly plausible that I had suspected from the very onset of the search that I would be the one man facing the difficult and unenviable task of locating her. That is probably why I had agreed to exhaust all other "options" before I hiked into the woods by myself to the very spot where the two of us had sat talking in secrecy days before.

That I had found her at the "scene of the crime" after it was already too late to save her one final time, after it was already too late to save her from herself, did not seem to upset me as much as it probably should have. Well, not at first anyway. The pain and anger I would eventually associate with her death, her suicide, would come much later, after I had accepted that she was never coming back. It is likely that my suffering had been "delayed" because the deep-seated and foreboding feelings that had been pulsating from somewhere inside of me for many days had been sequestered by my hope that I would soon find her alive and living.

She was lying in a disturbing and broken heap, a fallen soldier in the war against manic depression, on the bridge that spanned the stream beneath the tallest spires of sleeping pines. As soon as I spotted her "lying" there beneath the shadows, I knew that my world view would be forever altered. My outlook would never be the same. And as I approached the body of my dead friend, it crossed my mind that nothing—and I mean nothing—can ever prepare a person for a suicide. There is no precedent whatsoever when it comes to dealing with a suicide. There simply is no training for that type of thing.

I knelt next to her. Her lips were frosted a bloodless blue, having been kissed by the unforgiving chill of winter's breath. Her broken form was "blanketed" in the thinnest layer of snow, a veritable sign that her spirit had probably been gone for a very brief period. I noticed the color of her eyes. Her eyes were glazed a very bothersome gray, a gray so bothersome I knew I would never forget that color. They were "staring" into a different world, a new world, a world that only exists beyond that which is real and tangible.

Exactly when Jocelyn had reentered the suicidal dimension she described to me the first time we met, I cannot say. I can only guess that she had been trying to reenter that dimension since the last time she had been discharged. Kneeling over her lifeless body, I concluded that it takes a manic-depressive a long time to unlock the doors to that dimension. I also concluded that once those doors have been unlocked, there usually is no turning back.

I was suddenly running downhill with abandon, the ugly truth that Jocelyn was now dead chasing me, my body beginning to lose track of the trail completely. That is when I saw a kind of "tunnel" form, or open, directly in front of me. I was soon running inside that tunnel. The world around me was consumed by the ever-darkening internal walls of that goddamn tunnel. I coasted to a stop, almost slipped, and turned to face the direction from which I had come. I could not detect any light there. The trees and the sky had vanished. And I was lonelier than I had ever been.

I tried to run downhill again, but my legs would only move at an awkward and troubling pace, in a disturbing and painful kind of motion I really can't describe. A warm sensation soon crept through my skin, through my muscles and into my eyes. I stopped weaving downhill and stared straight ahead. I tried to see a light, but I only saw the darkened form of a man walking toward me instead. Not a muscle in my body twitched as I waited for the man to reach me. I was frozen in place and I remembered instantly a game I had played with other children when I was young, a game called freeze tag, a game in which no one moved, but only froze in place once they were tagged "it," once they were touched. Even though the last game had ended years earlier, I was the one frozen in place this time. I was the "it."

My lungs stopped aching as I waited for the man to meet me face to face in the tunnel. Slowly, I recaptured my breath and I was aware that I was confused, dazed by the premature death of Fisher and, especially, by the untimely death of Jocelyn.

"Hunter!" the man shouted at me.

"Who's there?"

"It's me, Chan!" the man called out. I saw that it truly was Chan moving ever closer to the spot where I had stopped so that I could breathe once again. "Hunter, it's me! It's Chan!"

I was running downhill again. I ran passed my old friend Chan without saying a thing to him, as my body steadily picked up speed, running, it seemed, on top of the snow. In what seemed like only seconds, but may have been hours, I had emerged from the tunnel. Instantly, I fell onto the snowy ground in front of Chan's truck.

"Is she, Hunter?" Chan asked as soon as he fell out of the woods and landed in the snow, gasping. He did not wait for my response. He threw me into the cab of his truck instead. He steered the truck away from the curb, away from our footprints, the footprints that had obliterated Jocelyn's own tracks in the snow, the same footprints that led downhill and out of the tunnel.

"How did you know?" I turned and studied Chan's ageing profile. "How?"

"When you did not return with Jocelyn as planned, I knew that you needed my help, so I stopped at her dad's house and banged on the door. I was not at all surprised when I did not get an answer. The house was still dark and lifeless. This time, though, I decided that I would make my way around the house to the back door. That's when I saw the footprints leading into the woods, the footprints I knew belonged to you. So I followed them."

Chan must have also known about the county road that paralleled the trail for quite some time because he navigated its snow-covered surface without incident. Minutes later, he parked his truck on the side of the road behind another pickup truck and disappeared into the woods. I jumped out of the truck and followed the tracks he had left behind. A minute or two later, I was standing at his side staring at the bridge. What I saw there, who I saw there, I will never forget. But there he was, on his knees, holding his dead daughter in his lap, rocking back and forth and sobbing softly.

CHAPTER 36

❀

I did not attend Jocelyn's funeral days later. I know now as I knew then that I was too angry, too bitter, too frustrated and hurting far too much to sit in front of her casket and pay my respects to a woman who had refused to face her depression and trust me the same way I had once trusted her. Furthermore, I did not want to listen to a stranger deliver a eulogy for someone he had never known, a manic-depressive he would never understand. Had I gone to Jocelyn's funeral, I am certain that my anger toward her would have only deepened. I could not see myself dealing with any more pain than the pain I was already facing.

I suppose you could say that I had my own "ceremony" the day after I found her dead in the woods. You see, I returned to the bridge where she had put herself to rest and dropped rose petals off the bridge and into the stream. I sat on the bench and yelled at her memory. I yelled incoherently into the trees until I was sure that her spirit had heard me, until my voice had become hoarse and my pained echo had died away. God, how I yelled at her that day. I screamed as loudly as I possibly could and yet I knew that my screaming would never match the unforgettable screams I had heard one day earlier, the wounded screams of Jocelyn's dad, the retired Army colonel, as he caressed his daughter's lifeless face for what would probably be the very last time.

Her thermos was barely visible but there it was, lying in the snow, near her frozen footprints, in front of the bench. I could have left it there but I picked it up instead. I turned its cold shape over in my gloveless hands to study what appeared at first to be a label on one side. I thought that her name might be inscribed there but when I saw that the "label" had been bound to the thermos by a single rubber band, I knew that I had found something, a handwritten letter, a letter I would carry with me in my mental scrapbook for the rest of my life. There was no way I would be able to ignore the contents of the letter. I knew that the words it contained were the product of a man's gentle touch; I knew that Colonel Layne had written the letter himself ...

> Dear Jocelyn,
>
> I remember my tour in Vietnam often. While there are those times when the war seems to be lost in the past and I am simply stranded in my own memory, there are also those times when I remember the war as clearly as if it happened only yesterday ...
>
> I was standing on the sands of Chu Lai when I received word from your mother that you had finally entered my life. I knew instantly that I loved you. More important, I knew that I would never stop loving you.
>
> Even though there have been some rough times between us, I hope that you will find a way to forgive me for things I have said, for things I have or have not done. Please understand that the past is the past and nothing more. I ask that you not judge me until you have walked in my footsteps and loved a child of your own.
>
> I realize, after so many years, that you are still keeping pace with your own drummer. There is nothing wrong with that. Just be sure that you don't fence out the people who love you most.
>
> Nothing will ever change or take away the love I have for you, Jocelyn. I pray that you never lose sight of that love.
>
> Dad

At first, I had every intention of returning Jocelyn's letter to Colonel Layne. But then I changed my conviction. That I have kept the letter in my possession after all these years may seem unjust to you but I had decided many days after I discovered it that I would never be able to return it to the man who had written it. To do so, would not be fair to him. Returning a letter such as that one would only inflict more pain on the author and give way to more guilt, a troubling entity, a dangerous monster.

Perhaps you are thinking that I should have destroyed the letter. But why? The part of Jocelyn that was still living just beyond the stream would surely have died with it and that is something I did not want. What I did want is for the letter to endure so that I could continue to learn from it, so that I could include it in my fiction someday. I have opened the note only two times since the day I originally found it. The first time was to remember Jocelyn and to try and interpret what had been going through her mind after she had read it and before her world had turned from gray to black. The second time was to include it in this text. I have now closed the note forever and hope to give it a "proper burial" inside the old thermos I still hold in my possession. I plan to bury that old thermos in the woods where there sits an old bench near a stream where I am certain Jocelyn's soft voice still resounds from time to time.

As for the evening I found her, I am positive that Colonel Layne never saw either Chan or myself standing on the very trail that led directly from where we had parked on the county road to the bridge. Truthfully, we had slipped away long before he ever had a chance to notice us. Only minutes after we had located the two of them, we were running as fast and as silently as we possibly could, as fast and as silently as the snow-covered trail would allow, in the direction of Chan's truck. I lead the way through a part of the woods that was foreign to me at the time and we raced against the falling darkness until we had located the two pickup trucks. With Chan at the wheel, we went for help and left Colonel Layne and his daughter alone together beneath the pines.

The newest plan called for me to stay at Chan's apartment that night. Chan's home was the one place I might feel safe. As I recall, I went upstairs to my own apartment to pick up some clothes and some bedding and my toothbrush, numbed by what had transpired the day of my release from Seven Southwest. I did not notice the note that was taped to my door. Chan, who had come looking for me, found it first. When he handed it to me without opening it first, I knew what Chan was thinking; I knew that it could only be from one person. I have included the note in its entirety:

> If I ever have the opportunity to speak to my friend again, I know what I will say to him. I will tell him that he was correct when he maintained that depression is the ultimate adversary, the ultimate antagonist. Even more important, I will remind him that the act of taking one's life is the culmination of many painful events. And finally, I will tell him to never stop fighting

the mental illness that is manic depression. That is what I will say to my friend—if I ever have the opportunity to speak to him again.

Goodbye for now,

Jocelyn

I was not at all surprised by Jocelyn's admission that I was correct when I had claimed that depression is in fact an adversary, the ultimate antagonist. I was, however, confused by the shortness of her note. Why hadn't she described her pain, what was going through her mind? I tried to think of a decent answer to that question but I couldn't. Then it occurred to me that her note had been brief for a reason: Jocelyn had heard her name being called. For Jocelyn, it was simply time to go. And no more words needed to be shared with me or with anyone else ever again.

I awoke late that night after having cried off and on for many long hours. Chan was sitting at my side drinking coffee. His face looked as if it were more than a century old and I asked him what was wrong, what had happened to him. When he reminded me that Jocelyn had ended her own life hours earlier, I asked that he call her. I told him that he had been dreaming and that he was mistaken. That is how truly disoriented I was the night I found Jocelyn's body lying on the bridge that spanned the stream deep inside the woods.

Chan must have sensed my confusion from the moment I awoke. When I told him a second time that he had dreamt of Jocelyn's suicide and insisted that he call her at her dad's house, he handed me a couple of small bone-white pills and a glass of water. Trusting Chan, I swallowed the water and the pills that were new to me. I soon fell asleep for the second time that night.

Memories awakened inside of my dreams, inside of me. They were peaceful memories, dreamy memories from my own life, a life that now seemed full of hope and fixable. I dreamt of my first encounter with a deer in the wild and of Christmas cookies made by a child's hands. I dreamt of birthday parties and of Saturday matinees and of grade school pranks that always produced a laugh. I dreamt that my parents had come to see me and that we had gone out for breakfast together.

I would learn sometime later that while I had spent the night sleeping, Chan had spent the night watching over me, prepared to give me more Ativan if needed. He had also been waiting to tell me that I had been beating the fucking odds for years and years. He had been waiting to tell me that life does in fact go on and, finally, that life is in fact worth living. My good friend Chan, the man who had saved my life, had intended to tell me all of those things. But when he started to relate his thoughts early the following morning, I shook my head and told him that he need not say more. I informed him that I already knew those things. I had been beating the odds. I knew that life does go on. I knew that life is worth living.

CHAPTER 37

❧

It is true that I had my reservations that I might never live to share with you this account of my having survived my flight to hell and back. It is also true that I should have died from acetaminophen poisoning, or of liver or kidney failure, or from a loss of blood. Perhaps I should have died from a deadly combination of all of the above. But somehow I had survived two sobering attempts to take my own life and had managed to crawl and then walk through the dark of night and back into the light of day.

I should tell you that many of the darkest days I have ever known were those very dark days I was lying in a bed on Seven Southwest. Those days were the grainy days that were as dark as the darkest nights. Those days were also the very dismal days I suspected that I would never ever be released from the shadowed confines of my depression, or from Lakeshore General to walk, or even write, ever again.

Then came that all-important moment when I accepted my diagnosis without any hesitancy whatsoever. It is possible that there does come a time in the life of some manic-depressives when they realize that something simply "is not right" and decide that some changes need to be made. Maybe they hit that place so often referred to as "rock bottom." That is how it was for me anyway. I had survived two very serious suicide attempts and had hit my very own rock bottom. And once I admitted that I was there, at rock bottom I mean, I came to understand that something just wasn't right within me and with the way I approached life, my life. And then I made a change.

While I was being treated on Seven Southwest during those three critical weeks in November of 1994, I had reached a vital crossroads and accepted—yes accepted—the fact that I was mentally ill, that I was bipolar, that

I was indeed a manic-depressive. Perhaps the "defining moment of acceptance" came when I acquiesced and swallowed the single Haldol pill Big Nurse had bribed me into taking. Perhaps that defining moment came when I took my first doses of Paxil and lithium. Regardless, I had, at long last, resigned myself to the verity of my situation. With that resignation came the realization that my mental illness had had a negative effect on my life in general. You might even say that that particular realization ushered in the belief that I truly needed to accomplish something in my contemporary life, my newest life, as Ayden had been able to do. Almost instantly, I understood that I needed to do something positive, something for the better, in order that I might "regain" the life I had lost and justify my own difficult and painful fall from grace.

You see, after so many days and so many weeks and so many months and so many years spent hurting and so many, many times spent wanting to die, my mind and my body were finally functioning as one and in unison and without all of the pain of yesteryear. Because I was now able to admit that I was not as perfect as I had once thought, I was no longer experiencing the strange pain I had lived with prior to being delivered to the hospital. Also, because that particular pain was now gone, I no longer felt beaten or cheated. I finally wanted to live. Yes, I wanted to live.

I can still remember how I seemed to step out of my injured person and how I seemed to float upwards into the calm November sky the night the paramedics strapped me to a stretcher and delivered me to Lakeshore General for the first and last time in my life. I can still remember how I stared down at my suffering body and how it occurred to me then that I did indeed have a driving force to accomplish something positive inside of me after all. I saw my dying self in the third person that night and on countless occasions during my hospitalization for a reason or, as my dad had shouted at me from the edge of the disturbing dream I have already told you about, the dream in which I could finally make some sense of his words, for "a purpose."

I did have strong suspicions that tender November night that writing this novel was my very own purpose and as I looked down upon my blood-covered physical whole lying on a stretcher, I realized that my aching self had become my voice and that my voice, in turn, would one day become my ticket to a "new and better place," a place where the truths about manic depression matter the most. But first, I would have to accept the fact that I needed both medication and counseling to make myself well, to enable me to put to use that newfound voice and ultimately find that coveted "better place" in life.

So now I knew that I had a bona fide driving force to do something worthwhile with my life breathing inside of me and a legitimate purpose for living, a purpose that was mine and only mine. Imagine that: me, Hunter Kraven, actually having a purpose, a reason to exist. I had trouble accepting the notion at first but as soon as it occurred to me that I could share my story with others, I felt that my newest life was definitely worth living. Just like that, I had stumbled upon a profound sense of self-worth.

After discovering that facet of my newest self, I reentered that place Jocelyn Layne had referred to time and again as "the real, tangible world" with my goal to write clearly in mind, with my goal to tell my story very much in hand. I stepped directly back into society with determination and not dread. What's more, I returned without any doubts whatsoever that I would be able to capture a brand new life, a life I knew I had never really experienced before.

Yes, I had been delivered from society onto a psychiatric ward at a local hospital without any say of my own and had persevered. More important, after I had arrived at Lakeshore General, I had learned to withstand for the first time the emotional and physical stressors manic depression creates, the same stressors that, in the end, had recreated me as a stronger, more secure manic-depressive. And once I felt that I was ready, that I was prepared, I embraced my diagnosis, my medications and Dr. Goodwin's cognitive approaches to living well and returned. Yes, I returned and reintegrated myself into the community and into civilization with my guts, my heart and my good intentions still very much in tact. I returned to my shattered life and picked up the pieces one at a time. Like so many people before me, I put the pieces back together again.

Even though I had successfully traveled so very far in order that I might walk with grace among the populace again, I had to face the certainty that life had moved on, progressed without me, just as Jane had often said it would. While I was serving time on Seven Southwest those three crucial weeks, waiting to see if my broken self might become repaired, waiting not only for my body to heal, but for my mind to do some healing as well, the earth had continued to rotate on its axis. There was simply no denying that basic fact.

And while the planet was steadily revolving around the sun, a crowd had gathered. The throng that seemed to want a closer look at a real, live manic-depressive suicide survivor was, more often than not, vicious. That insensitive mob degraded me almost constantly. Sure there were those people who walked on eggshells in an odd silence whenever they were in my presence but, even more upsetting to me, were the attitudes of those people who opted to stigmatize me by treating me as if I were a "whacko" for having attempted to take my own life, or for having logged time on a psychiatric ward, or for both. The majority of people in my life shunned me. Many more mistreated me by abusing me with names such as "psycho," or by referring to me as a "kook," or by calling me names I wish not to repeat right now—if ever.

The actions of those uncaring people definitely hurt me. I would be lying to you if I said that their actions did not mar my character to some degree. But, unlike those naïve people, I had been gradually changing on the inside, that place where it always counts the most. That change enabled me to "bounce back" and I told the people who were apparently clueless where my illness was concerned that I had been taken to the hospital for a "mental tune-up" of sorts. Perhaps that is putting it too mildly. But then again, maybe it is not putting it too mildly at all. Nevertheless, I had come out of the hospital feeling better than I had when I first entered it. I was taking my medications religiously now and I would soon be seeking counseling and so I told those clueless people that I had a diagnosis of what I was and that I was as repaired as I had ever been and deserving of another chance.

While some people have made it a point to mistreat me, others have opened their hearts and their minds and walked beside me. It is with those people, the patient and caring people, that I share the names of my medications, namely Paxil and lithium. I share with them exactly how Paxil and lithium are working to sequester the manic and depressive extremes of my illness. Furthermore, I reveal to the people who are patient enough to listen that I have a chemical imbalance that truly is not my fault, an imbalance that is related to conspiring forces that include both environment and biology, among other factors. Finally, I share with as many people as I can the fact that I am bipolar, that I am indeed a manic-depressive. After my release from Seven Southwest, I wanted more than anything to discuss my depression as candidly as I could with as many people as I could. And so I have endeavored to do just that.

I still talk openly with anyone who will make the time necessary to listen to me speak about my being a manic-depressive despite the many stigmas that are so often associated with people suffering from a mental illness. I tell the people who make the time to listen to me that I understand depression in ways they do not. I remind those people that I can help them realize what it is I am up against on a daily basis. I try my best to enlighten them, to teach them what they themselves do not know. I speak with whomever will listen whenever I can. I listen to whomever I can whenever I can. Yes, I listen to people irregardless of their stance on manic depression. I listen to their thoughts on my illness, an illness that affects millions of people, devoid of prejudice. The way I see myself and my illness and my life right now, right this minute, I know that I cannot afford to think or act otherwise.

Eventually, my physical wounds healed and so did my emotional abrasions. Sure there were the physical scars on my wrists that would never go away. I knew, however, that I could live with those scars if living with them meant that I might attain even a small amount of peace within myself. I was, as Jocelyn had once articulated, "branded." And so I knew that I had to accept those scars if I was to live with those scars. They were mine now, you know.

From the very moment I was released from Lakeshore General to try living again, to pursue my newest life, I thought that my manic trip, my manic journey, had officially come to a long-awaited end. I thought that being released from the confines of Seven Southwest was the final step down that road less traveled, the road that is rarely taken. But then it hit me that my journey to my very own real, tangible world was just getting underway. That is when I came to a simple understanding with myself, an understanding that I had to walk with caution if I was ever going to keep stride and eventually run alongside society again.

I suppose you could say that I am still cautiously moving forward, still progressing. Nothing appears to be slowing me down. Much like my illness itself, there are the pathetic people who try to ambush me, but I ignore them and continue to gain a steady momentum. Sometimes, I come close to obstructing my own path, the path I am always trying to forge to a land of normalcy because, sometimes, I feel so good about myself and my life that I am tempted to stop taking my medications. That is when I admit to myself that I might be feeling somewhat manic, just a little too "high," or just a little too complacent and summon the necessary fortitude to continue swallowing Paxil and lithium, the medications that have improved my quality of life, the same medications that are almost solely responsible for saving me from myself. That is when I remind myself that depression never ever goes away completely. Depression can improve and there are those instances when depression seems to be nonexistent, but depression is always lurking in the shadows of a manic depressive's life. Always.

My wife Sarah shares much credit with my medications for having saved me from myself. While my meds have served to lessen my depression and have stabilized my moods, Sarah has helped to guide me through the various awkward situations that are forever presenting themselves when one is both a suicide survivor and a manic-depressive and I am thankful that she is there. More than the light of day, or a lamp on the nightstand, or any number of imagined angels, she is now my best companion, my truest confidant. Sarah is, in a matter of speaking, my very best medicine. Sarah is also my best friend.

It is Sarah and not my mom or my dad, or Jane, or Jocelyn, or Ayden, or Dr. Goodwin, or Emily Ryan, or anyone else, who has taught me, through the most patient venturing, to highlight life's positives. Sarah is responsible for my having put trust in the kind words of encouragement those people who do happen to understand my illness unselfishly bestow upon me. Even more important, Sarah has taught me to trust the kind words I share with myself. And it is those words of encouragement a manic-depressive shares with himself that are the most important words spoken, the most important words of all.

So many years have slipped by me now. I am keenly aware that so many, many years have expired. With each passing year, people continue to enter and exit my life. Some of those people want information. They want to know more about my strange, manic life and, believe it or not, ask me quite often what is the best thing to ever happen to me since I crash-landed on Seven Southwest. Always, I want those inquisitive people to know the full story and not just a few miscellaneous details. And always, my answer is the same: Sarah. The fact that I am alive and living well while being "properly" medicated and counseled has an awful lot to do with Sarah's presence in my life and her never-ending patience. Sarah is, as I have already told you, my best medicine. The manner in which I have continued to stay medicated in order that I might better arm myself against depression so that I can live a life that is worthy of me is definitely another positive worth highlighting but Sarah continues to be the very best thing to have ever happened to me.

There are those times Sarah and I discuss my experiences on the Seven Southwest openly and, yes, even intimately. Quite often, we will reminisce about the people I met on Seven Southwest while being treated for manic depression in order that I might continue to learn from them. From time to time, I tell Sarah about Jocelyn, the woman she never had an opportunity to meet, the woman who was desperately trying to survive an illness that was destined to defeat her because she had refused, near the end of her life especially, to comply and take her meds as needed, as required. Sarah, in turn, reminds me that Jocelyn's "untimely death" is one of the many reasons I have continued to take my meds so faithfully. "Her sad, sad death, her inevitable suicide, has inspired you to stay medicated whether you realize it or not," Sarah has told me on more than one occasion but especially during those rare occasions when

I am feeling so good about myself and my life that I contemplate stopping my meds altogether.

I have also told Sarah about Jane and her gentle disposition, a disposition that once enabled me to find my way again. I have shared with Sarah examples of Jane's no-nonsense approach, such as the time she told me outright that I was not crazy when I was sure that I had lost every ounce of my manic mind. Sarah understands and appreciates Jane's soft-spoken side as well as the side that is a roughhewn drill sergeant. Sarah believes, as I do, that Jane did the right thing when she forced me to go to group therapy for the very first time, that time Ayden and Jocelyn and I were justifiably critical of Kris, the group facilitator who was, I vehemently believe, lost in outer space.

I still speak of Ayden often. While Sarah has never had the chance to meet the enigmatic writer face-to-face, on any ground, she feels as if she knows him anyway. You see, sometimes, on those rare occasions when sleep happens to escape us, Sarah and I take turns reading and rereading passages from his best-selling novel. The words he has pieced together seemingly with precision and deliberate care are never lost upon me or Sarah. The views expressed by a man as secure with his mental illness as Ayden is serve to inspire me to live a fuller, better life as well as to push myself as a writer despite my being a manic-depressive. Perhaps it is Ayden who has been my greatest influence when it comes to writing while taking medications. The writer who once experimented with disowning his own meds before concluding that he needed them to write well, has had a tremendous effect on my life as the fledgling writer I once was and, even more important, on my life as the successful novelist I am today. Ayden, my dear friend and mentor, if you are reading this, I want you to know that I am really very honored to know you.

While Sarah has never been fortunate enough to meet Ayden, she has met Dr. Goodwin many times. She likes him I think. And if she doesn't care for him as a person, she really does appear to respect him as a doctor. "You are both lucky that Paxil and lithium are improving your life because working with antidepressants and mood stabilizers is as much an art as it is a science," Dr. Goodwin once informed Sarah and I while we sat in his roomy office staring at framed prints, multi-colored abstracts, by the late Mark Rothko, a manic-depressive artist who died by his own hand long before his time was due. I agree with that particular assessment because, over the years, I have met many manic-depressives who, only after so much trial and error, after so much hit and miss, have finally found a combination of medications that is working for them. They too are some of the lucky ones.

Because Dr. Goodwin and I were fortunate to find my own meds early on, I am now attaining many of the goals I had originally outlined in group therapy: I am going to bed each and every night and waking up each and every morning. I am staying friends with myself. I am helping others understand manic depression. And I am writing.

After so much time gone by, I still find myself reflecting on that relatively brief period in my life, a time I suspect will be forever important to me, those crucial days and nights I spent on Seven Southwest doing my best to find my way, as well as myself. Remembering openly that critical period emphasizes the fact that I have not stopped defending myself from the mighty blows of the illness that is manic depression. You might even say that I am actually fighting back. You might say that I continue to "stay on course" and wage war on my illness at every turn—even when nothing seems to fit. I have not defeated manic depression just yet and I certainly have not outrun my mental illness, but I am now keeping pace with it. I am practicing good sleep hygiene, taking my medications religiously and seeing Dr. Goodwin on a regular basis. I am talking. I am listening. I am creating a balance. I am certain of that. I am also certain that I am putting forth my very best effort to live with a mental illness for which there currently is no cure. Sometimes I think that is the very best a manic-depressive can do.

And sometimes, when the world closest to me appears to be at peace with itself, I can hear the unmistakable sounds of a new life being born from a past life, anchored by distant tides of depression. And sometimes, when my mood is just right, I can hear the sounds of that new life resonating from beyond the corridors of a psychiatric ward, or from somewhere beyond a stream that flows through the very center of town, or through the very heart of my contented mind. I am speaking the truest of truths when I tell you that those soothing sounds reverberate from somewhere deep within me, from somewhere within the vastness of my rested soul, a soul that has long-since forgiven itself for the manic sins committed so many years ago.

The reverberating sounds that travel to my ears these days are not the pained screams of souls trapped in a manic-depressive's lonely universe that are audible to me, mind you, but the absolute voices of people who have always carried with them healing words of both love and support. Those words, words so vital to living a life of meaning, a life of significance, a life devoid of gray and ominous clouds hanging overhead, are emitted from the minds of people I now trust more than anyone. Those words of inspiration are the most gentle words spoken, the kind of words that are born not only from the most caring individuals, but from the most caring voices as well, the same voices that will undoubtedly live inside of me forever, the very same voices that are always resounding inside of me as if in a series of the most uplifting and encouraging of echoes, those voices beyond the stream.

Afterward

❦

I slipped into the cold outside air by design very late one winter night recently, having decided long before I donned my overcoat that I would walk along the path that leads downtown and to the doors of Lakeshore General Hospital for the first time in many, many years. While on my way to the hospital that had served as my address for three life-altering weeks, I made an intentional stop at the wooden bridge near the bench where Jocelyn and I had sat shoulder to shoulder telling secrets one snowy November day, the same bench where I would eventually find her defeated body devoid of a living spirit only a few days after the Thanksgiving Holiday of 1994.

From my vantage point just above the water, I studied the stream in the moonlight. Although spring was still several weeks away, the stream flowed steadily, propelled by sheer gravity and, seemingly, by its own will. Clutching the weathered railing in both hands, staring into the darkened waters at mental images from a lifetime spent battling manic depression, I listened to the stream's comforting melody, a song that spoke to me, bringing to mind the night I had tried to hear its distinct rhythm over the irregular din of my depressed heart and the humming and buzzing sounds that had ricocheted inside my head so many, many years before. Several minutes came and went, as did the visions of that crucial night. At last, I turned my back on the stream and on the single bloody vision of a mannequin-man doing his best to conjure up a life-force from within.

With the memory of that frightening night, the night my bloodied self struggled to cling to life, now officially filed away in a locked chamber of my mind, I vacated the bridge and navigated my silhouette in the general direction of Center Street, listening to the stream's tune until it finally changed direction in the distance, shards of moon glow lighting my way. Nearly two hours later, I found myself standing alone directly across the street from Lakeshore General. I surveyed the dark shapes on the snowy lawn. I searched the hospital's grand facade for signs of life, but the building was asleep. No lights shone in the windows of Seven Southwest and it was, I knew, a very quiet night on the psychiatric ward.

I crossed a deserted Center Street and followed the long sidewalk that wound its way between the hedges to the back of the building and to the emergency room entrance. There I froze, hands in pockets, neck arched as far as it would go, touched, all the while, by the building's immensity. Then, nearly blinded by memories of my deliverance, my arrival and my return, I found myself watching and waiting to see if the glass doors would open, imagining that I might actually recognize a face or two from my disrupted past. Eventually, those doors did slide open and a security guard with a linebacker's build and a serious disposition ushered me off of the property, a place I no longer belonged, without a single word spoken.

I decided then and there to put as much space between myself and the hospital as I possibly could. Without further deliberation, I turned right at the corner and ambled down East Avenue. In time, I arrived at the wrought iron gates of the public cemetery. I stared between the wrought iron fence posts and out into the blackness that always seems to shroud a graveyard at night. I could not see Jocelyn's resting place. I knew, though, that she could see me. Without a doubt, I knew that she could see me standing there by myself. And I knew that she was looking over my shoulder, watching my back, still intent on guiding me, as best she could.

I swear I heard her call out to me from somewhere beneath the tall trees that appeared to be embracing the sky in their twisted, leafless branches. As always, her voice was gentle and soothing and honest. In a calming tone, she made it clear that I did not belong in a cemetery yet. She reminded me to continue to face the future, to keep moving. I considered her kind message and concluded that the cemetery and my own grave were indeed places that could wait for another day, for another time. I still had so much to live for, so much to learn about my mental illness, so much to teach others.

I continued wandering in an easterly direction. Eventually, I came to the sleeping house where I'd once sat upon the roof until sunrise, seemingly lost in some kind of stupor, a manic stupor if you will. That particular house was the same house I had resided in when I had attempted suicide for the first time in my life. And as I sorted through cognitive pictures from that time so long ago, I realized once and for all that the aging residence was no longer mine but just a house, a place from an era best forgotten because someone else now paced the floors of my old attic bedroom on sleepless nights. Someone unknown to me slept late on Saturdays and read the morning paper in the sunlit kitchen that smelled of coffee. And someone else, someone who could not possibly know anything about the mania-ridden existence I had survived for decades, now lived some semblance of a normal life there, the kind of life I had never really lived myself.

Shortly thereafter, I was heading south, in the direction of the bridge that spanned the stream nearest the lake, to the one room apartment where I had attempted suicide for the second and final time in my life. As I walked along Lakeshore Boulevard, I remembered in a nutshell that scary night, the night I am always striving like hell to forget, the night Chan saved my life. I remembered how I should have died. I called to mind how Chan would not allow me to die.

I thought of Chan exclusively. I recalled my last visit to Chan's apartment in the early fall of 1996, nearly two full years after he had rescued me. A cognitive snapshot of Chan walking to the kitchen for another beer developed in the nocturnal sky. A second picture of the empty hallway leading from his modest living room to his tiny kitchen flashed before me. A collage of black and whites of me walking down that hallway to the kitchen many minutes later and finding my friend lying dead on the linoleum floor, the victim of a heart attack, stalked my thoughts until it occurred to me that it was time to go home.

By the iridescence of the only streetlight on the corner, I inserted my key into the lock. A simple turn to the right and I was inside. I shed my overcoat by the light of the fire and shook away the coldness. I kicked off my shoes and made my way to the bed where Sarah lie sleeping. I leaned over her and placed the softest kiss on her forehead. "I love you, Hunter," she whispered, stirring slightly, her eyes still closed against the night. "I love you, too," I whispered in return fully aware that I could not love anyone more and very aware of my desire to send my love, support and a very heartfelt goodnight to all of you who suffer from mental illness and feel lost and alone when stepping into the shadows of manic depression.

978-0-595-69926-1
0-595-69926-X

Printed in the United States
88010LV00009BA